The Impossible Fortune

The Thursday Murder Club Series

The Thursday Murder Club

The Man Who Died Twice

The Bullet That Missed

The Last Devil to Die

Also by Richard Osman

We Solve Murders

The Impossible Fortune

A Thursday Murder Club Mystery

RICHARD OSMAN

PAMELA DORMAN BOOKS / VIKING

VIKING
An imprint of Penguin Random House LLC
1745 Broadway, New York, NY 10019
penguinrandomhouse.com

Copyright © 2025 by Six Seven Entertainment Ltd.

Penguin Random House values and supports copyright. Copyright fuels creativity, encourages diverse voices, promotes free speech, and creates a vibrant culture. Thank you for buying an authorized edition of this book and for complying with copyright laws by not reproducing, scanning, or distributing any part of it in any form without permission. You are supporting writers and allowing Penguin Random House to continue to publish books for every reader. Please note that no part of this book may be used or reproduced in any manner for the purpose of training artificial intelligence technologies or systems.

A Pamela Dorman Book/Viking

The PGD colophon is a registered trademark of Penguin Random House LLC.

VIKING is a registered trademark of Penguin Random House LLC.

Set in Adobe Jenson Pro
Designed by Cassandra Garruzzo Mueller

ISBN 9780593653258 (hardcover)
ISBN 9780593653265 (ebook)

Simultaneously published in hardcover in Great Britain by Viking, an imprint of Penguin Random House Ltd., London, in 2025.

First United States edition published by Pamela Dorman Books, 2025

Printed in the United States of America
1st Printing

The authorized representative in the EU for product safety and compliance is Penguin Random House Ireland, Morrison Chambers, 32 Nassau Street, Dublin D02 YH68, Ireland, https://eu-contact.penguin.ie.

For Mat and Anissa

The Impossible Fortune

They show you how to make bombs on the internet. If you know where to look.

What to buy, where to buy it from. How to fit the whole thing together. There are even videos. Men in balaclavas with screwdrivers. Soldering wires on tidy workbenches in cinder-block garages.

They don't really tell you about the risks. But the risks stand to reason. Be careful with explosives, that doesn't need to be spelled out to anyone, surely? No one needs to say, "Don't try this at home," do they?

There are instructions for big bombs, small bombs, nail bombs, chemical bombs, all the bombs you could ever want to make.

Small to medium was the right choice here. Stable enough to carry around, powerful enough to kill.

In the end the easiest thing to do was go to one of the websites that does all the work for you. Custom-make the bomb to your specifications, deliver it, even help you to place the thing if that's what you need. This particular company had received very good reviews. They even offered a money-back guarantee if the bomb failed to go off. They're called Boom or Bust.

It's not cheap, when you add up the expertise, the manufacturing costs, the delivery and, most expensive of all, the secrecy of the whole thing. If you want to know the actual cost of a human life, it's somewhere around twenty-seven thousand pounds. But no tax or VAT. For the obvious reasons.

Worth the extra few quid though. When the bomb finally goes off, money is not going to be an issue, is it?

It's not all about money, of course. Quite the opposite in some ways.

Okay, then, no time to waste.

Time is ticking, and it's not the only thing.

1

Joyce

It's been a while since I wrote, I know that. I'm ever so sorry.

You must have been wondering where I'd got to? Run away to the Bahamas with a police dog handler perhaps? That is actually a dream I had the other night. Then I woke up because Alan was barking at a squirrel he'd seen out of the window.

It's just that I've been so busy with the wedding, I haven't had time to think. It's been a whirlwind.

There was the florist, there was the cake—how can a cake be that expensive? It's just eggs and sugar and a bit of marge, isn't it? I know it's decorated, but still. Then there was the dress, that was quite a fun bit, we all had a Buck's Fizz. I even went to a nail bar—I'd seen nail bars, of course, but I'd always been too shy to go in. They were very nice, and perhaps I'll go again if somebody else gets married.

Tomorrow is the day. A Thursday wedding? I know. What is it with us and Thursdays?

It's not every day your only child gets married, is it? Some people around here, they have grandchildren getting married, but not Joanna, she took her time, and I think that was probably for the best. Whatever I might have said to the contrary over the years. To think this time last year she was still with the football chairman?

Before Paul.

Joanna and Paul met online. People—well, Ron—often tell me I should do online dating, but I worry that everyone would just be after my credit card details. Ibrahim told me I must never tell people Alan's name in the park because they can use the information to steal your password. I said that I don't use Alan's name in any of my passwords, but he was insistent. So if people ask me Alan's name I say he's called Joyce. And if they then ask me my name, I bid them a polite goodbye.

I mentioned the florist and the cake and the dress and so on, but I didn't mention that Joanna and I have *rowed* about all of them, and plenty of other things besides. For example, there are to be no hymns, just "Backstreet Boys." It got to the point where I had to say, "If you don't want me to help, just tell me," and Joanna said, "I don't want you to help, Mum," and that set me off crying, and then that set Joanna off crying, and she said of course she wanted me to help, and I said I know I interfere, I know, and poor Ibrahim walked into the middle of this whole scene, and then backed slowly out of the room. I've said it before, Ibrahim is no fool, except when it comes to dogs and passwords.

Joanna and I have different ideas about weddings, that's to be expected. If we have different ideas about gluten, we're going to have different ideas about most things. There's my way of doing things (honed over a long and happy lifetime) and then there's Joanna's way of doing things. What Ron calls "the London way."

The very first row was about forty-five seconds after she and Paul told me they were getting married. I was thrilled. I mean, it was fairly soon after they'd met, and you hear all sorts of stories on Netflix, don't you, but I was thrilled nonetheless. Paul is lovely, not at all like the people Joanna usually dates, who seem to be, largely, millionaires or Americans. Now I have nothing against either millionaires or Americans, far from it, look at George Clooney, for example, but variety is the spice of life, and Paul is a professor at a university (only Middlesex, but even so). And being a professor is a job for life in the way that being a football chairman or a millionaire isn't.

So, the first row.

I'd given Joanna a hug, and I'd given Paul a hug, and I asked Joanna if it was going to be a big wedding, and she said absolutely not, no, she wanted a small, intimate wedding, and I said, I can't remember the words precisely, but something like, "Oh, that's a shame, but never mind," something very neutral, you know me, and she said, "What's a shame?" She said that very politely, because Paul was there, but I could tell that trouble was brewing, so I thought, well, I'll just defuse this, and I said, "Oh, don't listen to me, I just thought, as an older bride, there might be lots of people who would want to come," and she said, again, keeping her cool, "An older bride?" and I thought, you've done it now, Joyce, and I said, "No, not older, it's just a lot of people, if they get married at your time of life, it's a second wedding, after a divorce," and, again, I could tell that hadn't helped. Paul said something at this point, but neither of us was listening because we knew we were at a very delicate stage in our argument. Joanna smiled (not with her eyes though, that's how you can tell, isn't it?) and said a small wedding suited her, and it was her wedding, so that's what was going to happen. I saw her point, but you know me, my head was full of bridesmaids, and handsome ushers, and bouquets, and dancing. Something like *Bridgerton*, if you've seen it. I could see a big crowd of happy friends, all wiping away tears and complimenting my hat. I could see Elizabeth, Ron and Ibrahim with me. I'd be in the front row; they could sit behind. They could lean forward and tell me how beautiful I looked. This was all going around my head, when I said, "I'm sure you know best. You always do, don't you?" At this point Joanna asked Paul to go and make us all a cup of tea.

Written down like this, I do see I might have handled it differently.

Joanna came in very close and told me she wasn't going to lose her temper, because Paul had never seen her really lose her temper, and she thought it was probably best to get eighteen months or so into the actual marriage before he saw her in full flight. (It wasn't the time, but I wanted to say she was absolutely right about this. By the time Gerry first saw me really unleash, we were living in a three-bed in Haywards Heath, and I was pregnant, so it was far too late for him to get cold feet.) Then she said she was having a small wedding, with no fuss but a lot of love, and I said, and I'm aware I shouldn't have said anything at all, that a big wedding isn't a fuss, and that perhaps she wasn't thinking straight, and Paul walked back in and asked where the milk was, and we both said, "Fridge," without taking our eyes off each other.

I knew she was right, by the way, I really did. But I've been excited about her wedding since before she was born, and I've played it through in my head so many times, and that's why I was being unreasonable. I see all that now, but I didn't see it then. When Gerry and I were married, we couldn't afford a big wedding. It was a lovely day, but it was small. Just our parents, our neighbors from Number 17 (but not from Number 13, due to an incident with a hedge trimmer), Gerry's best man from work, a few of my nurse friends and two cousins who wouldn't take no for an answer. We had sandwiches in the pub (private room) afterward and we were both back at work the next day.

So, anyway, I told Joanna all this. I knew I was on the back foot, and thought that if I mentioned Gerry it might buy me some time. And then she leaned in and hugged me, and she said, "I keep imagining Dad walking me down the aisle," and, well, I didn't have to imagine that, because I've imagined it so many times it's become real to me, and I hugged her back, and I realized that life can't always be *Bridgerton*.

So Joanna was crying, thinking about her dad, and I was crying, thinking about him too, and Paul walked back in with two cups of tea and said, "I couldn't find the sugar either, but I was too scared to ask," which is just what Gerry would have said, and then I realized I didn't care about a big wedding or a small wedding, I only cared about my beautiful daughter and this lovely man. Though, small or not, Joanna couldn't stop me buying a new hat.

Paul gave us both our teas, and a tissue each, and I told Joanna I loved her, and she told me she loved me, and Paul said, "For future reference, where is the sugar?" and I said the cupboard above the microwave, and Joanna asked if there were any jewels or cocaine in my microwave, or a gun perhaps, and I said no. It's been a quiet year in that regard.

We still meet every Thursday, of course, Elizabeth, Ron, Ibrahim and I, and we're in and out of each other's flats on a daily basis (less so with Elizabeth—she still needs a bit of time), but we've managed to stay out of any real trouble for a while now.

I told Joanna that Elizabeth, Ron and Ibrahim would be so excited for her, and that they would understand it was a small wedding, so there wouldn't be invitations for them, and Joanna said that of course they were invited, and I said, "That's too much, a small wedding is a small wedding, and there must be other people who should be invited first," and then Joanna said, "Mum, when you say you want a 'big wedding,' how many people do you mean?" and I said, "Well, about two hundred, that's the number in my head," and she laughed. She said that her friend Jessica (Jacinta? Jemima?) had eight hundred people at her wedding, in Morocco.

And so I asked Joanna what she thought a *small* wedding was and she said, "About two hundred, Mum."

And so there we have it. Joanna is having the small wedding she has always wanted, and I am having the big wedding I have always wanted. Sometimes it pays to be different from your children.

I then asked if Bogdan and Donna could come, or perhaps Chris and

Patrice, and Joanna told me not to push my luck, and that they could come to the evening do, which would be four hundred-odd. That's some small wedding, Joanna.

Anyway, my wedding clothes are ironed and laid out on the spare bed. I keep going in and looking at them. My new hat is in a box. Mark from Robertsbridge Taxis has got hold of a minibus to take us all to the venue tomorrow. It's not a church, which, again, in my dreams it had been, but a lovely house in the Sussex countryside, which is actually much more beautiful than a church would have been, and has taught me you mustn't always trust your dreams. Or that you must allow others to have their dreams instead.

So next time you hear from me I will be a mother-in-law. Also, Paul's dad, Archie, is a widower, early eighties, with a mustache and the air of someone who needs to be looked after. I can see from the table plan that I am sat next to him at the top table.

Because if trouble has been in short supply, so has love.

So here's to tomorrow, and here's to love, and to no trouble.

Thursday

2

Elizabeth is starting to feel again. Precisely what she is starting to feel, she couldn't say. But there's something there, and it's not just the brandy. She's on alert, but, as yet, with no idea why.

To her left, Ron raises a pint to the Sussex sunset. "I've been to a lot of weddings, mainly my own, but that was the best yet. To Joanna."

"To Joanna," says Ibrahim, raising a whisky. During the ceremony he had cried even more than Joyce.

"And to Paul," says Joyce. "Don't forget Paul."

"Hell of a speech his best man made," says Ron.

The best man. Elizabeth has been thinking about him.

"He was nervous," says Joyce.

"Either way," says Ron, "you don't throw up. It's not your wedding, mate."

"He pulled focus," agrees Ibrahim.

Even before the unfortunate vomiting, there was something off about the man. Was that what Elizabeth has been feeling? She could have sworn he looked at her at one point. Just a glance but a deliberate one.

"What did you make of it all, Elizabeth?" Ibrahim asks.

Elizabeth thinks for a while, and musters a small smile. The smile is real, she knows that, and she knows that one day it will be bigger. "It was wonderful—they looked very happy. And Joyce looks very happy."

"She's half a bottle of champagne to the good," says Ron.

Joyce gives a slight hiccup. The four friends watch the sunset in silence, the stone terrace of the grand house all to themselves. From inside, the sound of music and laughing.

Elizabeth looks at her friends, and thinks about Stephen. Joyce spots it—Joyce spots everything—and puts her hand on Elizabeth's arm.

"Thank you for coming though, Elizabeth," says Joyce. "I know it's still hard."

"Nonsense," says Elizabeth, ready to launch into a lecture about self-reliance. But Joyce is right: it is still hard. Almost impossible, in fact. She takes another sip of brandy and looks down. "Nonsense."

Elizabeth turns as Joanna steps through a set of double doors onto the terrace. "Well, I wondered where you'd all crept off to. What are you doing? Shooting up?"

Ron stands and hugs her. "Just looking for five minutes' peace. How's the best man?"

"Nick?" says Joanna. "He's rehydrating."

Nick, that was the name. Nick Silver.

"And the tablecloth?" Ibrahim asks.

"Ruined," says Joanna. "That'll be coming out of the deposit. Now who's coming for a dance? Mum? Everyone wants to dance with you. They seem to find you charming."

"I am charming," says Joyce, then hiccups again. "That's where you get it from."

Ron helps Joyce to her feet. "Perhaps Paul's dad might like a dance, Joyce?"

"Not interested," says Joyce.

"I mean," says Ibrahim, "you did have your hand on his knee for the entire meal."

"I was welcoming him to the family," says Joyce.

"Never heard it called that before," says Ron, and downs his pint.

"And, Ibrahim," says Joanna, "I wonder if you would like to dance with me?"

"Well, that would be my pleasure," says Ibrahim, standing. "What will it be? A foxtrot? A quickstep?"

"Whatever you can manage to 'Like a Prayer' by Madonna," says Joanna. Ibrahim nods. "We shall improvise."

Everyone is standing now, and they begin to head to the doors. But Elizabeth stays where she is. Joyce puts her hand on her friend's shoulder.

"Are you coming?"

"Ten minutes," says Elizabeth. "You go and have fun."

Joyce gives her shoulder a squeeze. How gentle Joyce has been with her since Stephen died. No lectures, no homilies, no empty words. Presence when she sensed it was needed; absence when she knew Elizabeth needed some time. Ron has been there with hugs; Ibrahim, the great psychiatrist, would try to nudge her this way and that, thinking she wouldn't notice. But Joyce? Elizabeth had always known that Joyce possessed an emotional intelligence she lacked, but the sheer grace with which she had conducted herself this last year was extraordinary. The gang disappear through the doors, and Elizabeth is alone again.

Again? Elizabeth is always alone now. Always alone, and never alone: that was grief.

The sun has disappeared behind the South Downs. Always alone, but never alone. Elizabeth feels her senses awakening again. But what is it?

From an avenue of trees beneath the terrace to her left, Elizabeth hears a noise. A man steps out from behind a tall oak and begins to walk toward her.

So that was it: someone was out there in the half-light. That was the sense that was reawakening. As he starts walking up the stone steps onto the terrace, the now familiar figure of Nick Silver, the best man, comes into the light. He nods at the chair next to Elizabeth.

"D'you mind?"

"Of course," says Elizabeth. She hears whooping from inside the house. That will be Ibrahim dancing, no doubt. Nick sits.

"You're Elizabeth," says Nick. "I know you know that."

"Afraid so," says Elizabeth. She notices, with relief, that Nick has changed his shirt. "Do you have something on your mind, Mr. Silver?"

Nick nods. He looks up at the sky, and then back at Elizabeth. "Thing is, somebody tried to kill me this morning."

"I see," says Elizabeth. Something jump-starts inside her. For the last year her heartbeat has felt like a machine, a mechanical pump keeping her alive against her will, but now it feels flesh. "You're sure?"

"Certain," says Nick. "When you know, you know, right?"

"And you have proof?" Elizabeth asks. "A lot of your generation can be overdramatic."

Nick holds up his phone. "I've got proof."

Elizabeth feels a familiar gravity begin to pull her in. Should she leap clear while she still can?

"Does someone have a good reason to kill you?" asks Elizabeth. She is not leaping clear. Of course she is not leaping clear. Where on earth would she leap to? She is all out of solid ground.

Nick nods. "Yep. A very good reason. To be fair."

A path clears in Elizabeth's mind: it's an old track overgrown with weeds, but there it is. "And do you know who?"

"This is just between you and me?" says Nick. "I can trust you?"

"That's a question for you, Mr. Silver," says Elizabeth. "Not for me."

The man is shaking, on a warm evening. "I can give you some names, yep."

"More than one person wants to kill you?" says Elizabeth, eyebrow raised. "And yet you seem fairly harmless?"

"Thank you," says Nick.

"Why have you come to me?" Elizabeth asks. "And not, say, our good friends in the police force?"

"I just . . ." Nick starts. "I don't want to tell the police, for all sorts of reasons, and I'd heard about you from Paul. Your reputation."

"I'm sure he has exaggerated it," says Elizabeth. One can forget that one has a reputation.

"I just wondered," says Nick, looking at her with a fear she has seen so many times over the years. The fear of a man with a single foot over a cliff edge. "If I tell you everything, do you know someone who could help me?"

Elizabeth had been ready to say no to this wedding. To stay at home and read. To look over at Stephen's chair. To punish herself. But she'd said yes instead. Something told her it was time to start again. She thought perhaps it was the prospect of seeing love at first hand, but, no, it was far better than that. It was a best man with a death threat.

Trouble is much like love: when the time is ready, it will find you. And so here she was at the wedding.

Does she know someone who could help him? Elizabeth looks at Nick, nods and takes his hand.

"Mr. Silver, I do."

3

"And if there's security?" Connie Johnson asks, taking a bite from her pain au chocolat.

"Then you kill them?" asks Tia.

Connie nods, thoughtfully. I mean, that doesn't sound unreasonable. Not what *she* would do, but you can't accuse Tia of not thinking things through. She's trying to impress.

"Or hold their family hostage?" Tia adds, clearly hopeful she's got the answer right.

This whole thing had been Ibrahim's idea. Perhaps it hadn't worked out exactly as he'd planned, but Connie could hardly be blamed for that now, could she?

While she was still in Darwell Prison, before the "unfortunate" mistrial and her subsequent release, Ibrahim had made her a proposition. "You must give something back to society, Connie," he had said. There was then a brief argument, during which Ibrahim had had to clarify that he didn't mean giving back any actual money, or other property she might have come across in her long and fruitful career. He had meant helping someone less fortunate than herself—"Again, not with money, don't panic"—and explained why he believed that Connie would make an excellent mentor to some of the younger inmates at Darwell. "Pass on some wisdom," Ibrahim said, "some life lessons." He promised it would do her good.

She knew Tia Malone from art class, where the youngster had been caught stealing glue. She approached her one lunchtime, and soon they were chatting. Ibrahim had been delighted at this development and predicted that Connie would find the relationship very rewarding.

"Fifty grand for you," says Tia. "And fifty for me."

Connie sips on her flat white. All in all she had done seven months on remand at Darwell, after that unfortunate business on Fairhaven Pier with the cocaine and the dead guys whose names she has forgotten. It wasn't as bad as it might have been. As a result of her outside connections, she was the only woman in the whole prison with a Pilates machine and a Netflix subscription.

"I could make fifty grand with one phone call," says Connie. "I don't need to get involved in this."

"Please," says Tia, "I promise it'll be fun. And you told me I had to dream my dream."

True enough, she had told Tia that. In their very first session. She liked Tia very much, liked her ambition. Tia had started her life of crime stealing Rolexes from rich tourists in the West End. There would be four of them on bicycles, weaving in and out of traffic, picking off targets. Once threats had been made, and the Rolex stolen, they would disappear down side streets, and be back in the safety of Vauxhall before the first siren was heard. Tia was the only girl in the gang, and always kept her mouth shut during the robberies to hide that fact. Eventually the whole gang was caught after a Deliveroo driver, who must have been after a medal or something, followed them back to the estate and led the cops to their lock-up. Even then, they rounded up three boys, and gave up their search after the fourth boy was nowhere to be seen.

"A hundred grand though, Tia," says Connie. "What have I taught you? Surely you can dream bigger than that?"

Connie had to admit it, she was enjoying being a mentor. Tia continued the bike robberies for a while, three new boys in tow now, her human shield reassembled, but she soon had a revelation. The sort of revelation Connie admired.

That's why they still meet up once a week, usually in Fairhaven's newest vegan café, Mad About the Soy. There are now more vegan cafés in Fairhaven than there are non-vegan cafés, but, relentless though the gentrification of the town is, Connie is delighted that the demand for cocaine remains robust.

"Bigger than a hundred grand?" Tia asks. In front of her, a coconut flapjack.

"Tell me what you worked out," says Connie. "When you were doing the bike robberies?"

"You know what I worked out," says Tia.

"I know," says Connie. "But tell me."

This was a technique she had stolen from Ibrahim. Ibrahim would get Connie to listen to herself. He knew where he wanted her to go, but she had to find her own way there. If you find your own way somewhere, you can go back whenever you choose. That was Ibrahim's idea anyway, probably nonsense.

"Someone would buy a Rolex in a shop," says Tia. "A jeweler's in Knightsbridge that we kept an eye on. And then me and my friends would follow them, steal the watch and then sell it."

"And?" says Connie, looking for more. It was annoying when Ibrahim did this, but it wasn't annoying when she did it. Ibrahim is at a wedding today. He sent her a photo. Connie would love to get married. Perhaps she should do something about that? What she really needs is a Tinder for criminals. Everyone could use their most recent mugshot.

"And," says Tia, "we maybe did this fifteen, twenty times. Cycle up there, identify a target, rob them, take the risk, cycle back. Fifteen or twenty different robberies, fifteen or twenty different chances to get caught. Great cardio but high risk."

"So you thought?" Ibrahim's best mate, Ron, was in the photograph. Connie has promised not to kill him, despite his part in her arrest. We'll see about that. Connie doesn't let grudges go lightly. Sometimes she thinks that without the weight of all her grudges she might simply blow away.

Tia finishes off her coconut flapjack. "So I thought, well, they've all bought these watches from the same shop. So why don't we just rob the shop instead? Rob all fifteen watches at once. The same reward but only one opportunity to get caught."

Connie is nodding. There is a lot of rubbish talked about young people, but Tia is a clear and intelligent thinker. She is a doer, a grafter. She still has to make the final step though. Has to work it out for herself.

"And the downsides to that approach?" Honestly, sometimes she actually sounds like Ibrahim. She was in a meeting last Tuesday where a cocaine importer had been shot in the leg, and Connie had found herself saying, "The pain is temporary, but the lesson the pain teaches you is forever." She hasn't told Ibrahim this because, although he would be proud to be quoted, he still disapproves of her business affairs.

"More planning to do, better security to beat, a more thorough investigation after you've done it," says Tia. "But I like that. I like the planning. That's the bit I enjoy."

"And it worked? The new plan?"

"Like a dream," says Tia. "Until we got caught."

"But you would have got caught anyway?" says Connie. "For something. At some point. Occupational hazard. Might as well get caught for something big. So go on. What have you learned? What's your new plan?"

"I've learned my lesson," says Tia. "This time, when the alarm goes off, I've got two minutes. Not a second more. Doesn't matter if the crown jewels are in the next case, when the two minutes are up, I go."

Connie nods. "That's what you've learned?"

Tia looks at her, the same way that Connie has looked at Ibrahim countless times. Tia knows it's a trick question. She knows that she should have learned something else, and she is bright enough to try to work out what.

"So," says Tia, thinking on her feet. Or, actually thinking while sitting on an uncomfortable artisan stool. "I used to steal Rolexes one by one."

"Mmm hmm," says Connie.

"And then I realized that they were all bought from the same shop, so I could just go to the shop and steal fifteen in one go."

"And so?" A mother pushes a buggy past the window of the café and glances in. What does she see? Connie wonders. A blonde woman in an expensive tracksuit, sitting with a black teenager, both just shooting the breeze. She doesn't know that Connie is actually changing Tia's life, right here, right now.

"And so . . ." Tia plays for time.

"I told you, Tia," says Connie, "dream your dream. A hundred grand is nothing."

"And so . . ." says Tia again, her mind scrolling through answers, until, finally, it finds the right one. "Where do the shops get their Rolexes from?"

Bingo.

Tia is thinking this through. "The shop in Fairhaven I want to rob has fifteen Rolexes. But there'll be a shop in Lewes with another fifteen. And a shop in Brighton with another fifteen. And they all came from somewhere."

"I mean, you'd think so, wouldn't you?" says Connie. She sees why Ibrahim takes such joy in his work. The feeling you have when you make a breakthrough.

Tia is nodding vigorously now, enjoying the work her brain is doing. "A warehouse, somewhere near the port—I can find out, I can find out. And we won't make a hundred grand—we'll make a million. In one go."

"Tough to rob a warehouse though," says Connie.

"Tough to rob anything," says Tia. "So if you're going to rob something—"

"Make it something big," says Connie. "Okay, count me in."

Tia beams, and pulls a notepad from her backpack. Connie looks at the backpack. She bets Tia has had it since school. Had taken it to her GCSEs, had swung it casually while talking to boys at bus stops. And now look at her.

"First, we need a gang," Tia says, writing in her book. "People we can trust."

What a glow Connie feels. She has to hand it to Ibrahim. When he's right, he's right.

4

Ibrahim is dancing with Joanna. He feels a fluidity, a grace, that is missing from his everyday life. He aches when he walks up stairs; he aches even more when he walks down. And yet here, on the wooden floor, the music loud and the lights sparkling, he feels no pain.

There are others dancing, Chris and Patrice, Chris dancing as awkwardly as you'd imagine. Donna is attempting to manhandle Bogdan around the floor but with little success. Bogdan is many things—a lover, a fighter, a painter and decorator—but he is not a dancer.

Ibrahim is aware, however, that a circle has opened up around Joanna and him. That people are watching them dance—a rhythmic clap starts to accompany their moves.

"Do you think it's too soon?" Joanna asks in his ear.

"Too soon?"

"I only met Paul six months ago," says Joanna.

Ah, this is why they are dancing. Joanna needs advice. That's fine by Ibrahim: he loves to dance, and he loves to give advice.

"Well, when did you fall in love?" Ibrahim asks.

"Six months ago," says Joanna. "It was immediate. Did that ever happen to you?"

"It did," says Ibrahim.

Madonna keeps singing, Ibrahim feels the beat coursing through him. Joanna says something, and Ibrahim indicates that he doesn't quite catch it.

"Are you lonely?" Joanna repeats. This takes Ibrahim by surprise.

"People mean different things by lonely," he says. Which is true.

"That's true," says Joanna. "But it doesn't answer the question."

"I have Ron," says Ibrahim. "I have your mother. Even Elizabeth at times."

Joanna nods. The circle around them has grown wider, the clapping louder. Of course he's lonely.

"So," says Joanna, "am I making a mistake?"

Ibrahim smiles. This is an easy one.

"Have you asked Joyce if you're marrying too soon?"

Joanna shakes her head.

"Then there's your answer," says Ibrahim.

"But I haven't asked her?"

"Exactly," says Ibrahim. "The answer to every dilemma is in whom you ask for advice."

Joanna twirls, lights spinning around her as she goes. She returns to face him.

"Go on, Professor."

"You have a dilemma," says Ibrahim. "Is it too soon? Has love really struck like lightning? Woe is me, I must know the answer. I demand truth! Who can I ask? Who can aid me in this troubled hour?"

Joanna looks over Ibrahim's shoulder. "Your policeman friend Chris has just tripped over a wheelchair."

Ibrahim turns to look. Chris, who, it turns out, is currently on firearms training, is apologizing profusely. Ibrahim turns back to Joanna. "So you need sage advice. Your mother would be a good start, and yet you didn't ask her? Why would that be?"

"Well, you know Mum," says Joanna.

"I do," says Ibrahim. "Joyce's only motivation in life is your happiness. That's a lot of pressure. Heaven knows what she might advise, terrified of saying the wrong thing, giving the wrong advice. So you don't go to your mother. And, of course, you can't go to your father."

"No," agrees Joanna.

"Because he's dead," adds Ibrahim. "He died."

Joanna gives a genuine laugh. "I can't believe you do this for a living."

"But your father would have given you the best advice," says Ibrahim. "Your father would have seen the truth?"

Joanna nods, her head on Ibrahim's shoulder.

"And I'm the next best thing," says Ibrahim. "Older, universally recognized as wise—ask anyone, they'll tell you the same."

Joanna starts laughing again. People often laugh at the most unlikely times, Ibrahim has noticed over the years.

"So you have the question. Goodness, is it all too soon, is Paul the man for me? Do I ask my mother, who will panic, or do I ask my father, who will look into my eyes and see the truth? I ask my father, because I already know the truth, and I just need someone to say it out loud for me. Of course it is not too soon. You found love, and you knew it as surely as finding a diamond. Or finding a KitKat where one of the fingers is made entirely of chocolate, which actually happened to me once—"

"Focus, Ibrahim," says Joanna.

"When we have a dilemma"—his KitKat story is true, by the way, but is maybe for another time—"we ask the person who will give us the answer we already know. And that's why you asked me. Paul is wonderful, you are wonderful, today is wonderful."

Their dance is coming to an end, as all dances must.

"Who did you fall in love with?" Joanna asks.

"A boy called Marius," says Ibrahim. "He is dead too, like your dad."

Joanna holds him tighter. "So that's why you seem lonely. You're waiting to see him again."

"I see him right now," says Ibrahim, and "Like a Prayer" begins to fade out. "He sat with me at the wedding. I should go and see if Chris is badly injured."

Joanna nods toward the circle of onlookers. "I think you're going to be busy."

Ibrahim looks too. A lot of women seem to be heading his way.

Joanna kisses Ibrahim on the cheek. "Thank you."

Her place is immediately taken by Patrice. She extends her hands toward Ibrahim's.

"You really mustn't feel obliged," says Ibrahim.

"Obliged?" says Patrice. "I had to elbow a bridesmaid out of the way."

5

Elizabeth stares at the photographs on her phone. A silver car, outside a very nice house. And something that shouldn't be there. Then some close-ups. Some very convincing close-ups.

"You believe me?" Nick asks.

"I believe you," says Elizabeth. Attached to the bottom of the car is a black box—the close-ups of which reveal what appears to be, in Elizabeth's opinion, an alarmingly professional car bomb. "Might I ask how you even noticed it?"

"Security," says Nick. "It's my job. I was checking for trackers."

"So where is the bomb now?" Elizabeth asks.

"Now?" says Nick. "I left it just where it was. I couldn't stick it in the recycling."

"You left it where it was? There is a live bomb still attached to your car?"

"I had a wedding to go to," says Nick, motioning over his shoulder.

Elizabeth nods. "And if it should go off sometime today—bombs do, you know—you'll be fine with it killing one of your neighbors?"

"I live on Hampton Road," says Nick.

Elizabeth understands. Big houses, big grounds. If the bomb were to go off, the worst that would happen is that someone complained about the noise.

"And also," says Nick, "you don't know my neighbors."

"Tell me your story," says Elizabeth. "And then we'll worry about the unexploded bomb."

Nick starts to speak, but his brain stops him. He's nervous, which excites Elizabeth a little. Nervous of *whom?*

Elizabeth sits completely still, and waits. It can take a while, but, if you are still long enough, they come to you. Fitful babies, zooming kittens, men with secrets. With nothing to bounce off, their nervous energy eventually seems ridiculous to them, and across they trot.

"We told only two people," says Nick.

"Told only two people what?" Elizabeth asks.

Nick puffs out his cheeks and looks over both shoulders.

"Tell me everything," says Elizabeth. "But be quick: life is short. No offense intended."

"It started at uni," says Nick. "Paul and I had a—"

"No," says Elizabeth. "Don't start there. Start this week."

"To really understand—" says Nick.

"No," says Elizabeth, a little firmer this time. You sometimes have to be firm with amateurs. She had learned that with Joyce, though Joyce could pass for a professional these days. "Start with the headline and we can work backward if I'm interested. You have ten words, or I'm returning to the party. Eventually they will play a song I recognize."

"I'm out of my depth," says Nick.

"That's five words already," says Elizabeth, getting up.

Nick places a hand on her sleeve. "They want something we have."

"Well, that's better," says Elizabeth, sitting down again. It turns out she didn't die with Stephen. She lives. She closes her eyes in silent apology to her husband. I'm still here, darling. Still here, while you are gone. I suspect I should just make the best of it.

"What is it that you have? That you told only two people about?"

"A code," says Nick. "A six-digit code. I have one, and my business partner has one."

"Business partner's name?" Elizabeth asks.

"Holly," says Nick. "Holly Lewis."

"And people might want these codes that the two of you have?"

"They would be very valuable, yep," says Nick. "Like, *very* valuable."

"And where is your code?" Elizabeth asks.

"In my head," says Nick.

"Nowhere else?"

"Locked in a solicitor's office hundreds of miles away," says Nick. "If Holly or I die, the other one gets their code. But not even the solicitor knows what he's got. The only place anyone could find it is up here."

Nick indicates his head.

"So someone wants to kill you for a code that exists only in your head? And a code that exists only in Holly's head?"

"Yes," says Nick. "I don't know who else can help. I can't have police near The Compound."

"The Compound?" Elizabeth asks. The tale gets wilder. And yet.

"Oh, Christ," says Nick. "It sounds so stupid when I say it out loud. You really have to let me start from the beginning. I own a company. A security company."

"A security company, I see," says Elizabeth. Well, this is interesting. There is very little in this world as dangerous as security.

"We specialize in cold storage," says Nick. "Do you know what that is?"

Elizabeth does not, but she has to admit she likes the sound of it. "I'm guessing it's not fridge-freezers?"

"It's not," says Nick. "Holly and I have something very valuable there, and earlier this week we told two people about it."

"I see," says Elizabeth.

"And suddenly," says Nick, "there's a bomb under my Lexus."

"The names of these two people?" says Elizabeth.

"Have you heard of Davey Noakes?"

"I don't think I've ever heard of anyone called Davey," replies Elizabeth.

"Ravey Davey, they called him. If you'd bought Ecstasy in the nineties, you'd have heard of him."

"I'll ask Ron," says Elizabeth.

"Then that game got more dangerous," says Nick. "And Davey turned his hand to high-end tech stuff instead."

"Legal high-end tech stuff?" asks Elizabeth.

"No," says Nick.

Good, thinks Elizabeth. "And the other name?"

"Lord Townes," says Nick. "He's a banker; we told him too."

"So you think one of those men planted a bomb under your car this morning?"

"Has to be," says Nick. "They're the only people who know what we're hiding."

The doors onto the terrace open once more, a blast of music escaping the party. Paul, Joanna's new husband, steps out.

"Nico, we thought you must be lying drunk under a hedge! Come on, we're cutting the cake."

Nick looks at Elizabeth. Elizabeth tilts her head in the direction of the doors. "My friend Joyce ordered the cake. We'd best see it cut, or she'll kill me before someone kills you."

"Can you come and see me though?" Nick asks. "Tomorrow? Please. I'll tell you exactly why one of those two wants to kill me."

"One of those three," says Elizabeth.

"Three?" asks Nick Silver.

"Well, Davey Noakes knows what you've got hidden. Lord Townes knows what you've got hidden. But I assume your business partner, Holly Lewis, knows what you have hidden too? So I make that three."

Nick gives her a long look.

"Is she here with us today?" says Elizabeth.

"No," says Nick. "She didn't want—" He shakes his head. "No."

Elizabeth shrugs.

"Tomorrow, then," says Nick.

Tomorrow, then. That's the problem with going out. One thing leads to another, and you find yourself going out again. Before you know it, real life creeps back in. Elizabeth doesn't want real life to creep back in. Because the one thing Elizabeth knows about real life is that Stephen is not in it. Everything in her body is telling her to say no.

But then a code and a bomb and three suspects? That doesn't come along every day.

"Tomorrow?" says Nick.

"Can't wait," says Elizabeth. "Glad you're feeling a bit better. Don't you dare get killed by that bomb before I see you."

"I won't—we're all staying here tonight," says Nick, writing quickly on the back of a business card and handing it to her. "I know this sounds ridiculous, but could you memorize this and burn it?"

He certainly has read a lot of spy books, Elizabeth will give him that. She takes the card and watches Nick disappear back into the reception.

The front of the business card reads NICK SILVER—COLD STORAGE SOLUTIONS. ABSOLUTE DISCRETION GUARANTEED. Well, there's no such thing as "absolute" discretion, Nick. On the back is an address and "1 p.m. tomorrow."

Memorize it and burn it? Oh, she can do that all right.

Another star returns to her sky.

It's baby steps, she knows that. Dipping her toe in the water. Codes and cold storage: it will probably lead to nothing. Even so, Elizabeth looks up to the stars and speaks to Stephen.

"A drug dealer, a lord and a car bomb, dear? It seems that I'm needed again."

She peers backs inside, where the music plays. She stands, then looks back up at Stephen.

"Shall we dance?"

6

Joyce

Well, that was just the most wonderful day. The most wonderful.

Mark from Robertsbridge Taxis just dropped us back home. Alan was beside himself. Gordon Playfair's daughter, Karen, came and took him for a walk earlier, and she left him in front of ITV3, which is his favorite, but he'd still missed me. He wanted to go straight out for a walk, but there are baby foxes over by Tennyson Court, and they need a bit of peace and quiet to explore at night.

It's nice to be missed though, isn't it?

Joanna looked beautiful today. I mean, she always looks beautiful, except for a few years in her mid-twenties when she did something with her hair, but she lit up the room. And it was a very big room.

I have a piece of the wedding cake in front of me. It's a lemon and raspberry sponge. I had a slice at the wedding and it was delicious. Perhaps I should keep this slice as a memento of the day? That would be the right thing to do. If I eat it, that's a minute or so of happiness; if I keep it, the happiness lasts a lifetime.

There was a "celebrant," rather than a vicar, but she was very jolly, and I'm assured she has the same authority as an actual vicar. She was very good when I asked her about it at least, and she told me I could always Google the legalities of it if I was really worried. I did, of course, and it seems fine.

I'd been upset a few weeks ago, when Joanna talked about Gerry walking her down the aisle. I felt I'd let her down, and she told me that was nonsense, and surely it was Gerry's fault for dying. She was trying to make me laugh, but she could see it hadn't worked, so then she said that it was *her* fault for getting married "at her time in life," and actually that did make me feel a bit better, because she was right. If she'd been married when she was twenty-six, like, say, Barbara from work's daughter, then Gerry would have been there.

Though Barbara from work's daughter got divorced last year, so the tables have turned now, haven't they, Barbara?

Anyway, we still hadn't solved the issue of who would walk Joanna down the aisle. I suggested Paul's dad, because he is at least a dad, and he would be there at any rate, so no need for extra chairs. Joanna said that while he was certainly *a* dad, he was not *her* dad. Then I suggested Ibrahim, but she said I wouldn't hear the last of it from Ron, which is true. So I started racking my brains some more, until I saw that Joanna was staring at me. Then she started laughing and I didn't know what at, and I hate it when people are laughing and I don't know what at, so I joined in. And then she said, "Mum, *you're* walking me down the aisle," and, well, then I stopped laughing, because mums don't walk brides down the aisle; mums sit at the front, so everyone can look at them. I made this point.

Then Joanna asked if, whenever I look at her, I see Gerry, and I said that I did. And she said that, well, she also sees him every time she looks at me, so she wanted me walking down the aisle with her. So she could see her dad.

And then I started crying. It's always been a roller coaster with Joanna. To be fair, I suppose it's often a roller coaster with me too. When it's your own roller coaster, you don't notice so much.

I did worry that people would find me walking Joanna down the aisle non-traditional, but actually nobody seemed to mind, although I couldn't really see through my tears. And also we walked down the aisle to "Backstreet's Back," and everybody seemed to like that too. I was worried that they might not save me a seat at the front, but they did.

There were no hymns, as I said, and, do you know what, you don't miss them. One of Paul's friends read a poem, which I didn't know, but Ron and I both remarked that it rhymed, which is not a given these days, and before you knew it Paul was kissing the bride, and I was a mother-in-law.

Talking of in-laws, there was nothing doing with Paul's dad, try as I might. They had an item on *This Morning* the other day about "asexuality," people who really weren't at all interested in sex, you could see that Alison Hammond couldn't believe her ears. Anyway, I had started to write off Archie as asexual, until Elizabeth walked back into the reception as they were cutting the cake and he made a beeline for her. I've seen it before with her. Show a certain type of man a pair of bosoms like Elizabeth's and their compass goes haywire. You can't win them all. One of Paul's uncles did slip me his phone number, but Paul says this uncle is still very happily married to his auntie, who had just gone outside to vape, and there would be hell to pay if she found out. Clearly Paul's uncle won't be discussing asexuality on *This Morning* anytime soon.

A funny old family, then, but what a wonderful man Paul is. I realize I haven't really taken to many of Joanna's boyfriends over the years. There was a nice landscape gardener when she was twenty, but university put paid to that, and there was an unshaven archaeologist I'd seen on television, so that was exciting for a few months. But really Paul is the only man she's brought home where I just instantly knew. I tried to hide my enthusiasm when I first met him, because I know what Joanna is like, but the first time he popped to the loo I started crying, and Joanna just looked over and said, "I know, Mum, me too."

When Paul came back in, he could see my tears, and so Joanna and I both pretended I have glaucoma. The next time he came over he brought a leaflet on new glaucoma treatments with him, and talked it through with me so patiently that ever since Joanna and I have had to keep up the lie. I shall have to get a miracle cure one of these days.

He has a gentleness, Paul, which worried me at first, because Joanna has never really gone for that. She's always liked ambitious and ruthless, you know the type? Driven. Even the archaeologist eventually got the sack from Channel 5 because he stole an urn from a church. And also sent a picture of his genitals to a camerawoman.

But the more you get to know Paul, the more you see that he *is* ambitious, just not for money. He is ambitious for happiness. For himself and others. You could tell with some of Joanna's boyfriends that they resented her success, didn't like her working longer hours than them or earning more money. But you can see that Paul is proud of her. He has a bit of money invested in his friend Nick's company (something to do with fridge-freezers) but otherwise is very happy on a university salary.

So Paul may not be the chairman of a football club, and he may lack the killer instinct, and he may have very strange taste in best men. But at the wedding he was talking to Ron about darts (or snooker, something like that); he was talking to Ibrahim about a program they'd both heard on Radio 4; he sat quietly with Elizabeth for a bit, asking her to guess which members of his family had been to prison; and, when I was in full flow, which was most of the day, he was very good at just nodding a lot and saying "Ooh, I bet" or "And what happened then, Joyce?" or "Shall I top you up?" every now and then.

So he'll do, don't you think? Alan likes him very much. Then again I've had gunmen in the flat trying to kill me who Alan liked, so you can't always trust him.

The gang seemed to have had a fine old time today too. Ibrahim was the star of the show, dancing with all and sundry. At one point Patrice tried to have two dances in a row with him, until one of Paul's aunties got her in a headlock.

Joanna and Paul aren't going on a honeymoon as such—"People don't go on honeymoons anymore, Mum," says Joanna. I would have argued, but it was her wedding day, but really people *do* still go on honeymoon, I am certain of it. In fact, all around the world there are long queues of people doing things that Joanna tells me nobody does anymore. Having honeymoons, drinking normal milk, watching television. I once told her that more people live the way I do than live the way she does, and she just pointed at my sandwich toaster and said, "I don't think so."

Anyway, they're having a couple of days away at a hotel somewhere. There's a spa, and everyone gets driven around in golf carts. If I had her money, I'd be off to the Caribbean. Which I am certain that people do still go to, because the new woman who has moved into Wordsworth Court has just got back from there and isn't shy about telling everyone. She had us all around for piña coladas, and Ron woke up in a hedge at two in the morning. One of the fox cubs was curled up on his tummy.

Okay, I should be absolutely honest with you and tell you that I just ate that slice of wedding cake. I shouldn't have, but I did. To be fair, Alan had a bit of it too.

I'm looking forward to seeing Joanna and Paul when they're back, as I can't wait to go into lunch with them and say to someone, "And this is my son-in-law." I'm nearly eighty and I've never been able to say that before.

When you think about my past few years I've really managed a lot of firsts. I solved my first murder, I met Mike Waghorn, I've had diamonds in my microwave, and now I have a son-in-law. I even watched a French film recently (Ibrahim). It's never too late. That said, I didn't enjoy the film, even when Ibrahim explained why I should, and Mike Waghorn seems to have changed his email address.

Now I know today was all about the wedding, but, before I go to bed and dream about the day all over again, I do have to announce something else. Another reason I'm writing.

Elizabeth is being mysterious.

It's something of a relief, of course, because it has been some while since she's been mysterious. She tells me we are taking the minibus to Fairhaven tomorrow morning, and it's also been a while since we've done that. What are we to do there? Information has yet to be forthcoming. "A nice stroll along the front" is what Elizabeth said, and if you believe that you'll believe anything.

Love and trouble. You can't beat it.

And, on that note, Alan has just thrown up some royal icing.

7

Danny Lloyd has had guns pointed at him before, but never by a woman. It makes, he notes to himself now, very little difference. The gun is the thing. Well, the bullets inside the gun are the *actual* thing, aren't they? Keep the bullets inside the gun, that's the trick.

It's his gun, of course—where else on earth would Suzi have got a gun from? Her book club? There's a loose brick in the changing room of the pool house, and she had obviously found it. There are four or five others scattered around, but he recognizes this one. A Beretta.

Will Suzi kill him? You couldn't blame her if she did, but at the same time it would be overdramatic. Which would be just like her. It's a toss-up. Perhaps she'll kill him. Perhaps she'll look away for a split second, and he'll grab the gun and make her pay.

Either way Danny recognizes their marriage is probably over this time.

"I told you," Suzi says.

She had told him. Plenty of times. But women say a lot of things they don't mean. He can already see the swelling beginning to form around her left eye. That's going to be a nasty one. Most times she'd go and have a little cry, stay in the house for a couple of days, maybe put on a pair of sunglasses to take the boy to school. But not today. Who knows why?

"Put it down, Suze," Danny says. "Let's talk about it."

Suzi shakes her head. "I don't want to hear you're sorry. Not this time."

Fair enough. And anyway he's not sorry.

"And I don't want to hear you won't do it again, because you will."

She's right: he will do it again. He'd do it this very second if the gun wasn't pointed at him. The shock of the gun is subsiding, and now Danny feels his anger beginning to rise. Who does Suzi think she is? Whose house does she think she's in? Who paid for the pool? Who pays for the holidays? The school fees? What does she actually contribute? There's a thousand women who'd swap places with her. He knows, because plenty of them ask to. But here he is, and this is what he gets for his troubles.

"Babe," says Danny, "I lost my temper. You know the stress I'm under."

"You're under stress?" she says. "I've had fifteen years of being beaten black and blue. Of hiding what you do to me. From our son, from my friends, from my family."

The family. That's the only thing that's ever really worried Danny. The brother especially. Suzi's brother would kill him if he found out. Would kill him, and could kill him. But Suzi knows that too, which is why she's never told her brother.

"I hear ya, babe, I promise I hear ya. Put the gun down: let's get a takeaway and tone down the emotions."

She's not going to shoot him. Danny's fairly sure about that. The boy's asleep upstairs. He'd hear. If she'd found the gun in the loft, which has a silencer, he'd be more worried. A bullet from the Beretta would also make a hell of a mess. It'd be all well and good dragging his body to the car and burying him somewhere, but sooner or later the police would come calling, and you're not going to get every drop of blood out of their Habitat sofa. No chance. That's a crime scene she'd never clear up, and she's been around long enough to know that.

"You're not going to shoot me," says Danny. Suzi'll calm down. She always does. A few roses tomorrow, do a sad face at breakfast, maybe he could cry a little—that always seems to bring her round.

"No, I'm not going to shoot you," she says. "You're going to leave."

He nods. Okay, this is more like it. She's letting off steam. "Good idea, babe—give us both a chance to cool down."

"I don't need to cool down," says Suzi. "I'm cool. You're leaving right now, and you're never coming back."

Danny laughs at this. It's actually nice to relieve a bit of the tension. "Babe, it's my house."

"Whose name is it in, babe?" she asks.

"Your name," he says. "For tax purposes. And because I love you. But it's my house, and you're not about to shoot me. So why don't I go and stay with Eddie for the night, and you can calm down, and we can pretend this never happened?"

She smiles. "I've pretended for so long, Danny."

"This ain't like you, babe, come on."

"I know," she says. "I haven't been myself for years. I used to be strong, Dan."

"You're still strong."

"I used to smile, do you remember? And now I only smile in public or in photographs."

"Then smile more," says Danny. "Don't blame me if you're not smiling."

She smiles.

"There you go," says Danny.

Now she starts laughing. "Do you know what I did before I got your gun?"

Danny doesn't love her tone here. What if she's done something stupid like call the police? They wouldn't need to be asked twice to search this place. There's the guns, couple of bags of coke here and there, fifty grand or so in cash, twenty or thirty passports. Surely she wouldn't? The police? She's not from the sort of family who'd even know their number.

"I packed you a little suitcase," she says.

Now he smiles. He can play this game. "Okay, Suze, I get the message. But I'll be back in the morning, and we can have a proper talk. Kiss and make up."

She shakes her head. "You're going for good. Everyone's told me for years, and I made excuses, but I'm out. I'm a big girl, Danny, but I'm not bringing up my son in a house ruled by a bully. You've broken me, but I won't let you break him."

"You're tired," says Danny.

"Yeah," she says, "I am."

"Put the gun down. I'll get my case, get my head down somewhere, and everything'll be better in the morning." Arsenal are on telly tonight: he can go to the pub and watch the match. Teach her a lesson tomorrow. She's usually good as gold, apart from the waterworks, but he's not going to let this stand, is he? She'll pay for it in the morning. The two of them can take the kid off to school, play happy families, and then he can remind her who's in charge.

He hasn't noticed up to now that she has her phone in her left hand. I mean, he's been concentrating on the gun, hasn't he? He notices now, because she raises the phone to her swollen eye.

"Babe . . ."

He hears the click of a selfie being taken.

"What's that?" says Danny. "Evidence? The police'll love that."

She shakes her head and presses another button on her phone.

"How far are we from Fairhaven?" she asks.

"What?"

"From Fairhaven, Danny, what do you think? If someone was angry and driving fast. Twenty minutes?"

"What's in Fairhaven?" Danny asks.

"My brother," she says. "I just sent him the photo."

The brother. Jason Ritchie. She finally did it.

"Your case is by the front door. I'm only giving you the chance to disappear because I don't want Jason going to prison for ripping you to pieces. If I ever see you again, or if Kendrick ever sees you again—or if anything ever happens to either of us—you're a dead man."

Kendrick. Danny should take his son with him, shouldn't he? Really break her heart. But he doesn't like Kendrick. And Kendrick doesn't like him. He'd be cutting off his nose to spite his face. He'll get a plane over to Portugal; he knows people there. Bit of sunshine. The gun is still pointed at him.

She'll regret this: Danny will make sure of that. Give him a couple of days, and he can have someone do a number on Jason, and then do a number on her. Bury them both so deep you'd never know they existed. And Kendrick? He can go and live with his grandad. He can keep that dumb lefty Ron company when his two kids have been killed. Danny smiles.

There are footsteps on the stairs. Danny turns and sees Kendrick. Kendrick is looking at his mum, who has a gun in her hand.

"Is that a real gun?" Kendrick asks.

"It's just a toy," says his mum.

"So you're playing a game?" Kendrick asks.

"Just a game," says Suzi.

"It's real," says Danny. "Because your mum is a psycho. You're both psychos."

"It's not real," says Suzi. "None of this is real."

"I think I am neurodivergent though," says Kendrick, walking down the stairs. "One of the teachers said. Does your eye hurt?"

"It does, Kenny," says Suzi. "But the pain will go when Daddy goes."

"Is Daddy going?"

His mum nods.

"When is he coming back?"

"He's not coming back, Kenny," says his mum.

Kendrick looks at his dad, then back at his mum. "Do you promise?"

"I promise."

Kendrick nods.

Danny can actually see upsides here. A bit of freedom. He'll be a single man, officially single. He'll be back to claim the house, of course, and the rest of his assets, maybe even go to both funerals, Suzi's and Jason's, but a few months in Portugal will do him a world of good.

"Just go, Danny," says Suzi. "Before Jason gets here."

"Is Uncle Jason coming?" Kendrick asks.

"He'll be here any minute," says his mum.

"Can I stay up and see him? Pleeease?"

"Just this once," says his mum. "Special occasion."

She walks Danny into the hallway and gestures to his case with the gun.

"Is there a passport in there?" he asks.

"A couple," she says.

"I'll be back," says Danny. "And I'll kill you, and I'll kill Jason."

"We'll see," says Suzi.

Danny sees Suzi move to put her arm around Kendrick. But Kendrick puts his arm around his mum first. Always thick as thieves, those two; it makes him sick.

He picks up the case and opens the front door. His front door. I mean, you never know with life, do you? One minute you're sitting there looking at tanning machines online, the next you're being forced out of your own home at gunpoint. There are surprises around every corner.

As Suzi and Jason Ritchie will find out very soon.

Friday

8

Elizabeth climbs the three steps onto the minibus. It's been a while, but Carlito is still there in the driver's seat, now with added mustache.

"Welcome back," says Carlito.

"Thank you," says Elizabeth. She sees Joyce wave to her from the back of the bus.

"For goodness' sake, Joyce, there's no need to wave. There are only twelve seats on the whole bus—I think I would have found you. I did use to be a spy."

"Me too," says a small man in the front row. Elizabeth considers him and suspects he might be telling the truth. She makes her way to sit beside Joyce.

"Ready for action, Joyce?"

"I have a flask of tea, some dried apricots and a hangover," says Joyce. "I'm ready. Any news on what we're doing?"

"We're going to see Nick Silver," says Elizabeth.

"My son-in-law's best man?"

"Paul's best man," confirms Elizabeth. At some point Joyce is going to have to stop saying "my son-in-law."

"And why are we going to see him?" Joyce asks.

"This and that," says Elizabeth, as the bus pulls away.

Joyce nods. Elizabeth notes that her friend has got so much better at not asking unnecessary questions. The two friends sit in silence for a while, Elizabeth adapting to the world whizzing by and Joyce leaning a flushed cheek against the cool of the bus window. Joyce looks over at her.

"You're not hungover? You drank just as much as me."

"The moment I got in I drank two raw eggs with Tabasco sauce," says Elizabeth.

Joyce nods. "I ate some wedding cake, then had a Baileys."

Elizabeth wonders why she has taken Joyce with her today. Nick Silver had approached her in confidence, had asked her to come and see him. She could easily have done that alone. Probably should have, in all honesty. Have a chat with the man, see what was what and find out exactly what those codes are hiding. Let it all filter through her mind and come up with a plan.

Perhaps there's nothing in it? If that is the case, it's simply two old women enjoying a day trip to the seaside. But what if there is something? One hopes so, one really does. The pictures of the bomb *look* real enough. She knows someone who'll know for sure.

Should Elizabeth really be worrying Joyce about all this? Nick Silver is friends with her son-in-law after all. Is it fair to Joyce to involve her? If Elizabeth has finally chosen to dive back into trouble, that's her business, but why involve her friend when she doesn't need to?

Elizabeth looks over at Joyce, who is morosely chewing a dried apricot.

"How much do you know about Nick Silver, Joyce?"

Joyce removes her cheek from the window and swallows her apricot. She breathes out slowly in the manner of someone not entirely convinced they're not about to be sick.

"Paul met him at university. Paul did Sociology, but I think Nick did a proper degree. Maths or something."

"And they set up a business?"

"No, Nick has a business with another one of their friends; Paul just put some money in at the very beginning."

"Holly Lewis?"

"Holly something," says Joyce. "I've never met her. You're asking a lot of questions."

She is asking a lot of questions, Elizabeth has to admit that. And then, of course, she understands exactly why she has asked Joyce to join her today. Because, however much Elizabeth has missed trouble, she has missed Joyce more.

"Fairhaven," calls Carlito from the front of the bus. "I see you here at three. Don't die, no refunds."

As they file out, Carlito takes Elizabeth's hand.

"It really is nice to have you back," Carlito says. He tilts his head toward a photograph on his dashboard. Carlito and a woman, both smiling, the photo and the fashions a little faded. From ten years ago perhaps? "It never gets better, but it gets easier."

Elizabeth squeezes his hand and follows Joyce out of the minibus. Time for them to get the measure of Nick Silver.

9

Ron, eyes firmly shut, is taking a little trip down memory lane.

He is remembering a very specific afternoon in the early seventies, when he had been engaging in some choice words with a young probationary police officer on a picket line in the West Midlands.

What Ron was doing in the West Midlands, he forgets. What the picket line was for, who knows? What he does remember is that after having a frank exchange of views with the officer, during which Ron questioned the officer's parentage, and the officer had offered an alliterative take on his view of Ron as a cockney, Ron had goaded the officer into striking him with his truncheon.

There was a press photographer nearby, and Ron thought it would make a good picture. The officer had demurred for a moment, so Ron then made an allusion to a shared romantic past with his mother, and Ron was struck, hard and clean, on the left temple. Bingo. He heard the click of the camera shutter moments afterward.

Ron had a very solid head in those days, and was fêted for his ability to take a truncheon blow and continue his business with the minimum of fuss, so this wasn't uncommon. It made him look a hero and the police officers themselves enjoyed it, so everyone was happy. If Ron ever left a picket line unhit, he couldn't help but consider it a wasted trip.

In fact, if anyone were minded to write a university thesis on the transition from wooden to aluminum truncheons in British police forces, they could do a lot worse than speak to Ron Ritchie. He had taken a lot of hits to the head in the late sixties and early seventies. He still had the odd scar, which barbers had to work around, but, other than that, no lasting damage had been done.

On this particular occasion, however, the officer had not thought that one hit was enough, and rained down four or five more blows on Ron's head (aluminum truncheon, springier but more durable), and even Ron had felt the need to fall to the ground. You never fell to the ground unless you absolutely had to, as a point of both pride and self-preservation. As Ron curled into a ball and felt blood trickling from his temple into his eyes, he consoled himself that the press photos were going to be spectacular. But, when Ron raised his head in the absence of further blows, he saw the officer swinging his baton at the press photographer's camera, and then at the press photographer himself. Those were different times. Pluses and minuses.

Ron had picked a bad day to be a hero. The West Midlands Police were in no mood to let a large cockney with a West Ham tattoo lie about bleeding on their concrete. Ron found himself half hauled to his feet by two other officers and dragged to a blacked-out police van, truncheons whipping the backs of his knees all the way. Interestingly one of the truncheons had been wooden, and the other aluminum, making it a fascinating case study. Ron had been thrown headfirst into the van, coughing up blood, and with the knee injury he now blames for walking with a stick when no one is looking.

After a drive of no more than a few minutes the van stopped, and Ron was dragged out onto a quiet country lane by all three officers, who then proceeded to aim kicks at his stomach and testicles until they ran out of breath, at which point they rolled him into a muddy ditch and went off for their lunch.

Although Ron understood the three officers had simply been doing their job in the best way they knew how, he was now in the middle of nowhere, face down in a ditch, caked in mud and blood, and bemoaning, not for the first time, that his testicles were not quite so damage-proof as his skull. He had a date that evening, and, while a fresh scar would be useful, the state of his testicles would not.

Had he wept with pain? Ron thinks so. Could he breathe with three broken ribs? Well, yes, but not without feeling like he'd been knifed. Was the pain so excruciating that he'd begun to think that not breathing at all might be the lesser of two evils? He remembers that it was.

He doesn't think about that ditch often. About the physical pain a human being can endure. But he's thinking about it now, eyes tightly closed, curled up on his bathroom floor, with Ibrahim holding a cold flannel to the back of his neck. He is trying to gauge whether his hangover means he is currently in more pain now than he was in that ditch.

"It was a lovely wedding," Ron mumbles.

"Do you think perhaps you drank too much?" asks Ibrahim. "In retrospect?"

"Got to toast the happy couple," says Ron. Could he open his eyes? Should he? "Rude not to. How did we get home?"

"Mark drove us," says Ibrahim. "And I was helping Pauline put you to bed, but you insisted on sleeping on the bathroom floor."

"Bed of kings, the bathroom floor," says Ron. He decides he will open his eyes, but it is a mistake. The world tips over a cliff and keeps rolling. He closes his eyes, and vows to never open them again. "Is Pauline still here?"

"Making breakfast," says Ibrahim. "I'm assuming you won't be joining us."

"Just a couple of eggs," says Ron into the floor. Will he die? If so, please, God, make it quick. "With Worcester sauce. And a bit of bacon, and there are sausages in the freezer. And mushrooms if we've got them. And beans. You have a nice time at the wedding?"

"A lovely time," says Ibrahim.

"Why aren't you on the bathroom floor, then?"

"Mainly because when Paul's uncle suggested doing Jägerbombs at three a.m. I politely declined."

"Clever," says Ron. "That's why you and Pauline are okay."

"Oh, Pauline had the Jägerbombs too," says Ibrahim. "Some people can just take their drink, can't they?"

There is a ring on Ron's doorbell. Pauline calls from the kitchen, "I'll get it. Is he still alive?"

"He is," says Ibrahim. "So I lose the bet."

Ron hears Pauline talk into the entry phone and buzz someone up. The last thing Ron needs is company. Who is it? Joyce? Ron's memory clears enough to remember Joyce drinking Jägerbombs too. So it won't be her.

"Jason to see you," Pauline calls. Okay, that's not too bad. Jason's seen worse.

"Shall we tidy you up?" Ibrahim suggests.

"Jason won't mind," says Ron.

"I might just pull your trousers up though," says Ibrahim. "Sorry to be so formal."

Ron gives a mute nod and feels his trousers being hoisted. Probably for the best.

Ron knows that he's not going to be able to move anytime soon, or even open his eyes. How is he going to have breakfast? Cross that bridge when you come to it, Ronnie, old son. At this precise moment Ron is very aware that he is a lucky man to have Pauline and Ibrahim at his side. Comatose on a bathroom floor is not the sort of trick you can pull too often. Collapse on a bathroom floor after a wedding and that can be quirky and charming; collapse on a bathroom floor every Friday night, and you'd soon find there's no one around to cook you breakfast and pull up your trousers.

So they'll indulge him for this one day, and he'll make it up to them.

At some point Jason and Pauline can help him up and plonk him on the sofa, where he can eat bacon and eggs and watch daytime TV with the curtains drawn. Someone, probably Ibrahim, can cover him with a duvet and let him take a six- or seven-hour nap. Then they can all forget today ever happened.

As Ron lies there on the floor, he feels beached and harpooned, hopelessly waiting to be rolled back into the sea. But he has lived a life, and has been through worse.

Ron hears the front door to his flat open and waits for Jason to come in and mock him. What should Ron say? "Should've seen the other guy?" Yep, that'll do.

But instead he hears a squeal of surprised delight from Pauline, and then small footsteps racing toward the open bathroom door.

A small hand pushes the door fully open.

"Grandad!" says Kendrick. "It's me. What shall we do?"

Kendrick. The single greatest human being on the planet, sure. But a human being that requires a huge amount of energy at all times.

"Why are you on the floor? What are you looking for?"

There will be no duvet for Ron today. No gentle nursing back to health. Sometimes you simply have no choice but to drag yourself out of a muddy ditch and walk four miles on battered legs.

Ron summons every ounce of every pound of every stone of spirit in his body, sits up and smiles at his grandson.

"I told Ibrahim that if you put your ear on the bathroom floor you could hear trains. He didn't believe me."

"And could you?"

"Yeah," says Ron. "Uncle Ibrahim was wrong."

Kendrick looks at Ibrahim.

"Unlucky, Uncle Ibrahim. Okay, if you're finished in here, we should probably play Lego."

Ron gets to his feet. An act that takes so much force of will he doesn't even stop to wonder why on earth Jason and Kendrick might be visiting his flat on a Friday morning.

10

"I'm afraid I'm buying a flapjack," says Joyce to Elizabeth. "And there's nothing you can do to stop me."

It's funny how relationships change, Joyce thinks, as she walks into Anything with a Pulse, now Fairhaven's fifth-largest vegan café. Once she would have been full of questions. "What are we going to ask him, Elizabeth?" "Why do you have a gun in your bag, Elizabeth?" "Would you like a fruit pastille, Elizabeth?" But today she'd stayed quiet, knowing there was no use rushing her friend. It was something to do with Nick Silver, and Joyce would be told precisely what at the point when she needed to be told and not a moment before. And, to be honest, the silence suited her this morning: she was quite surprised at the ferocity of her hangover. You shouldn't still be allowed to get hangovers at eighty years old, there should be some sort of law. She wishes she had Ron's constitution; Joyce bets he's not suffering like she is this morning.

Once Joyce would also not have simply announced that she was buying a flapjack. Wouldn't have dreamed of it. She would have floated it as an idea, looking for Elizabeth's permission. When Elizabeth has a job to do, she doesn't like being distracted. There's a schedule in her head that you are not privy to, but that she won't allow you to tamper with. Elizabeth will not have factored a flapjack break into today's mission, Joyce is sure of it, but, nonetheless, a flapjack break is happening.

Joyce has come to realize that, just occasionally, you need to let Elizabeth know who's boss.

"An almond and date, and a cherry Bakewell," she says to the boy behind the counter. The almond and date is hers; the cherry Bakewell is for Elizabeth. Elizabeth hasn't asked for it: she would balk at the idea that she might get hungry later in the morning. Indeed, she would say something like "Do you think I got hungry walking dissidents across the Czechoslovakian border for nine hours in 1968, Joyce?" but Joyce now has the courage of her conviction that Elizabeth is not always right.

Joyce glances over her shoulder and sees Elizabeth in the shop doorway, looking at her watch. The annoyance on her face makes Joyce happy, because it's exactly the look of annoyance that Elizabeth would have given before Stephen died. Her friend is still there.

Joyce pays by tapping her mobile phone on a small handset. Somehow that takes money out of her bank account and gives it to Anything with a Pulse. Ron still refuses to pay with anything other than cash, and now the only places in Fairhaven where he can actually buy anything are the bookmakers and the pubs. Which is fine by Ron.

Elizabeth strides away with purpose the moment Joyce reaches her, as if to say, "We have two minutes of flapjack time to make up for now, Joyce." Joyce happily trots along behind her. You just have to understand each other's rhythms, don't you? Time to let Elizabeth take charge for a bit.

"Do you have an address?" Joyce asks.

"Templar Street, 8b," says Elizabeth, still not looking round. "It's just off the front."

"And that's where Nick Silver is?" Joyce notices Elizabeth's pace drop slightly, and she allows Joyce alongside. The flapjack break is forgotten, as she knew it would be.

"It is," says Elizabeth. "He asked me to meet him there."

"And did he ask me to meet him too?" Joyce asks.

"We come as a team," says Elizabeth.

"And is he in some sort of trouble?" asks Joyce, having to step around a seagull that is refusing to move.

"Someone wants to kill him," says Elizabeth.

"Someone wants to kill him?" Joyce asks. "When did you find that out?"

"Yesterday," says Elizabeth. "He came to see me on the terrace. They planted a bomb under his car."

"Oh, Elizabeth," says Joyce. "It was supposed to be a wedding."

Elizabeth shrugs. "An awful lot of murders start at weddings, Joyce."

"I did think you perked up a bit during the reception," says Joyce. "I should have known killing was involved."

They take a right turn onto Ontario Street, a row of lovely three-story cream stucco-fronted houses, with the sea a wide wall of gray-blue at the end of the road.

"He says he has information," says Elizabeth.

Joyce nods. "I know we all played Trivial Pursuit one night, and he was very good at that."

They take a left onto Templar Street, a narrow road flanked by the back walls of big houses and lined with recycling bins. The sort of street where a busy town keeps its mess and its secrets. Even the seagulls are keeping their distance.

They pass a lamppost to which two rusted bicycle frames are chained, and Elizabeth and Joyce look up at a shoddily built two-story office building. There are boards nailed over the upper windows. It has a bright blue door on which the number 8 is daubed in white paint.

"It's very urban, isn't it?" says Joyce. "Very gritty. Are you sure it's the right place?"

Elizabeth waves her hands in the air, and Joyce sees a camera tilt in response to the movement. "I suspect it might be."

Beside the door is an entry pad with two buzzers. The bottom one has been ripped out, and the top one has a sticker reading DO NOT PRESS.

Elizabeth presses it.

They wait, and Joyce strains to hear any sound from within. Nothing.

Elizabeth presses it again, and is met, again, with silence.

"Joyce," she says, "go down that side passage and see if there's any way we can break in."

Joyce holds the bottom of her coat tight to herself and inches down a narrow, musty alleyway running alongside the building. There are no doors, and just two windows on the upper floor, both covered by solid metal grilles. At the end of the alleyway is a high wall topped with barbed wire, so there is no access to the back. She does notice something interesting, however. She makes her way back to Elizabeth. Elizabeth is running a slim metal file around the edges of the front door.

"Locked up tight," Elizabeth says, removing the file. No wonder he called it The Compound.

"No way in down there either," says Joyce. "But there's a heating vent poking out of the wall."

"Are you suggesting one of us climbs through a heating vent?" Elizabeth asks.

"No," says Joyce. "You don't always have to be facetious with me. But there was steam coming out of it. So either someone is in there, or has been in there very recently."

"Very good, Joyce," says Elizabeth.

"And Nick Silver was expecting you at one on the dot?"

"He was," says Elizabeth.

"And someone really put a bomb under his car?"

"Fairly thrilling, isn't it," says Elizabeth, "in its own way?"

"Don't say that, Elizabeth," says Joyce. "He's family."

"Joyce, your son-in-law's best man is not family," says Elizabeth.

"You choose your family these days," says Joyce. "I saw that on Instagram. We should be cautious and come back another time, shouldn't we?"

"We should," agrees Elizabeth.

"But we won't?"

"We won't," says Elizabeth.

"Then how do we get in?" Joyce asks.

Elizabeth scans the upper floors of the building. Then takes out her phone.

11

Tia has drawn up a plan of the warehouse complex in the back of what Connie realizes is a school exercise book. She is explaining the layout.

"So the lorry goes through these gates; there are two security posts, ten yards apart. Once he's through there, he drives thirty yards or so, then goes down this ramp to a sort of concrete apron and on to the loading-bay doors. Ninety seconds or so from start to finish."

Connie is distracted. A man in a suit in his mid-twenties has sat down in the booth next to them and is watching a video on his phone. The whole café can hear it, but he seems oblivious. Connie holds up her finger to stop Tia for a moment. She turns to the man.

"Could you use headphones, do you think?"

The man looks at her uncomprehendingly. "Uh?"

"Headphones," repeats Connie, then points to her ears in case he needs further help. "It's just everyone else can hear what you're watching."

"Why don't you mind your business?" says the young man. "Or I'll mind it for you."

"You don't think it's rude?" Connie asks. She's genuinely interested. The man is watching a video of a man laughing at a video of another man playing a video game.

"I'm on lunch," says the young man, as if that's an end to the matter.

Connie looks at him for a second, then nods. "Okay, I have a bit of business to do, so I'll deal with you in a minute. If you want to keep listening without your headphones, go right ahead."

"I will," says the young man.

Connie turns back to Tia. One thing at a time. "Sorry, Tia, underground car park."

"Security grille will be open. Driver plus two security staff unload the watches—four or five minutes—the boxes are put on pallets and a fork lift takes them inside to a service corridor—that's two minutes tops—and at the end of that service corridor there's the vault."

Connie follows Tia's progress on the drawing. She's doing well. The man on the video is now shrieking with laughter.

"Once it's in the vault," says Tia, "we can't touch it."

"But it takes the same journey when it leaves the vault again?" says Connie. "When the watches go out to the shops?"

"In smaller batches though," says Tia. "If you want the maximum return, it's in the nine minutes between the lorry arriving at the security gates and the boxes reaching the vault."

The video at the next table is still breaking Connie's concentration, but she takes her role as a mentor very seriously, and Tia needs her full attention. Ibrahim will be here for her own session in a few minutes. He's already late, some sort of emergency, a sick friend.

"So what are we doing?" she asks. "Bribing the guards?"

Tia turns to another page in her school exercise book. There is a list of numbers.

"What am I looking at?" Connie asks.

"This is what everyone at the complex gets paid," says Tia. "I've got all of them. The managing director—she gets the most, fair enough; the guards inside the vault—they're on nice money; the driver gets nothing; the guards at the gate are on minimum wage."

"Got to pay guards well," says Connie. "Otherwise—"

"Then, right down to the bottom of the list, there's the fork-lift driver, and the cleaners who look after the car park and the service corridor. Not even minimum wage once the agencies have taken their cut. Works out at eight fifty an hour."

"How did you get these salaries?"

"The big ones you get from LinkedIn," says Tia.

A lot of cocaine dealers are now using LinkedIn, Connie has noticed; she keeps getting requests. "And the fork-lift driver and the cleaner?"

"Well, I got them because I'm now one of the cleaners, and my mate Hassan is one of the fork-lift drivers." Tia takes an envelope from her bag and slides it across to Connie. "My pay-slip."

"This is very good, Tia, very good. You started working there yesterday?" Connie asks.

"Yep," says Tia. "I'm already one of the longest-serving cleaners."

"Do they search you on your way in?"

"They did," says Tia. "But I hid a bit of coke in my pocket, for them to find. So now they just want to buy coke off me and no one's going to worry too much about searching me."

"Where did you get the coke from?" asks Connie. She always takes a professional interest.

"Some guy from the twenty-four-hour garage with one arm," says Tia.

"Ah, Dan Hatfield," says Connie. She remembers when Dan Hatfield had two arms. The money he'd wasted on tattoos on that other arm.

"So you've been scoping it out?"

"Yep," says Tia. "I'm quite enjoying it. I'm going to miss it. There's a shipment due on Tuesday, probably two hundred grand or so, if you can handle it?"

"I can handle it," says Connie. You have to smile with the youngsters sometimes. Connie remembers when she thought two hundred grand was a lot of money. Gentler days in some ways.

"Great," says Tia. "I'm going to smuggle in two guns and hide the—"

"Good day, Connie," says Ibrahim. Tia closes the exercise book. "Please excuse my lateness."

"Ibrahim Arif, this is Tia," says Connie.

"Ah, you are being mentored," says Ibrahim. "How are you finding it?"

"Rewarding," says Tia.

"She's already doing a job," says Connie.

"Oh, congratulations," says Ibrahim. "I knew Connie would be a good influence."

"Tia, I'll leave you to it," says Connie, standing. "Why don't I meet you at my lock-up next Tuesday if you can get out of work quickly enough?"

"Will do," says Tia. "Very nice to meet you, Mr. Arif."

"And you, Tia," says Ibrahim. "And very best of luck with the job."

Connie takes Ibrahim's elbow and starts to lead him out of the café. She stops at the next booth, where the young man is now watching an anime cartoon of two eggs screaming at each other. Connie motions for Ibrahim to go on without her for a second. She sits down in the booth, takes out a gun from her handbag and points it at the man's groin under the table. He looks up, slack-jawed.

"I swear to God I will shoot you if you don't switch your phone off. And when I'm in court I'll tell them why I did it, and the judge and all twelve members of the jury will cheer and carry me out of the courtroom on their shoulders."

With some panic the man switches off his video. Connie digs the gun into his groin.

"I know it's your lunch," says Connie. "But I need you to know that you are the worst man in the world, and I just wonder if, in future, you could wear headphones when an old woman tells you to?"

The young man nods, mutely. Connie notices a dark patch seep across his suit trousers.

"Good lad," says Connie, and slips the gun back into her bag and rejoins Ibrahim, who is looking at meringues.

Connie takes his arm again.

"What would you like to talk about this week, do you think?" Ibrahim asks. "Have I missed anything interesting?"

"You never miss anything," says Connie.

"That's very true," says Ibrahim. "I'm a hawk. Honestly, the size of these meringues."

12

Donna De Freitas is not happy. She should be enjoying a day off with Bogdan. They'd been at a wedding reception last night: Joyce's daughter was marrying a man who seemed very nice, but who had a very interesting family when you looked him up on the police computer, which Donna had, of course, done. Donna looks everyone up. Paul Brett is the name.

She should still be in bed with Bogdan, watching *Homes Under the Hammer*, listening to him shout, "There is asbestos in that bathroom ceiling, you idiot," to a first-time property developer from Swansea. Occasionally, very occasionally, Bogdan will nod his head slowly and say, "That is good plastering." It is usually when the house buyer is Polish, plastering being a skill that, in Bogdan's estimation, takes a wild dip about thirty miles west of Gdańsk.

Chris is not at the station this week. He's still on his firearms training, and Donna is being destroyed by jealousy. If there's one place she'd rather be than watching *Homes Under the Hammer* in bed with Bogdan, it's doing firearms training. He wouldn't stop talking about it at the wedding. They let him have a submachine gun the other day. A submachine gun? Chris! Sometimes life isn't fair.

To make it worse, instead of being given an easy ride as she waits for his return, Donna has been called in for "extra duties." She has been sent out onto the streets of Fairhaven on "security patrol." There is a royal visit next week, and every available body has been drafted into sweeping and scouring Fairhaven looking for security threats. Someone acting out of the ordinary, a car parked where it shouldn't be. Half the station is pounding the beat with resentful looks on their faces. No one is revealing which royal is visiting Fairhaven, but after ruining Donna's day off it had better be a good one, like the King, and not just Prince Edward or something.

Very little was coming through the radio as Donna walked down the high street, peering into rubbish bins. There was brief excitement earlier when a man in Mad About the Soy said he'd had a gun pointed at him. But by the time an officer had attended the call, the man had decided he'd been mistaken and apologized for wasting everyone's time.

She feels her phone buzz in her pocket and takes it out. Elizabeth.

Elizabeth had been at the wedding. She'd been quiet, but it was nice to see her out and about. Three or four times a week Bogdan pops in to see her, and once in a while Donna is summoned too. She'll tell Elizabeth about some new murder or other, and Elizabeth will let her know where she's going wrong. But she's not the Elizabeth of old. She's more polite now, on the defensive. Her pain is keeping her quiet. Donna longs to be patronized and dismissed by Elizabeth once more. Bogdan misses Stephen, but he won't talk about it. Boys. Donna answers.

"Hello, Elizabeth." Nice and gentle.

"Are you roaming the town for this royal visit?"

Well, that was short and to the point. Encouraging.

"How do you know about the royal visit?" Donna asks. "It's confidential."

"I'm grieving," says Elizabeth. "I'm not dead."

Donna chances her arm. "I don't suppose you know who it's going to be?"

"The Duke of Edinburgh," says Elizabeth.

Ooh, the Duke of Edinburgh, okay, that's a good one. Donna will happily write down the number plates of parked cars for half an hour if she gets to meet the Duke of Edinburgh. He's a proper character.

"Is this a social call, Elizabeth?" Donna asks. "Or did you need something and Bogdan's not answering his phone?"

"No, I thought you might be in the area," says Elizabeth, "and I wanted to report a break-in."

"A break-in in Fairhaven?"

"No, a break-in on the moon, Donna," says Elizabeth. "For goodness' sake."

Ah, that old dismissive tone is back. Also encouraging.

"I see," says Donna. "And what makes you think there's been a break-in?"

"We saw it," says Elizabeth. "A man climbing through a window. Templar Street, 8b. The criminal might still be in the building, so you'll need to get in there. We'll wait for you."

"You're there?"

"Of course we're there—we're concerned citizens," says Elizabeth. "And how could we wait for you otherwise?"

"Elizabeth, just ring the police."

"You are the police, dear," says Elizabeth.

"But I'm protecting the Duke of Edinburgh."

Hold on, thinks Donna, didn't the Duke of Edinburgh die a few years ago? Donna doesn't watch much news, but she's sure she remembers that.

"Actually, isn't he dead?" Donna asks.

"That was the old Duke of Edinburgh," says Elizabeth. "This is the new one."

"There's a new Duke of Edinburgh?" asks Donna.

"Of course there's a new Duke of Edinburgh," says Elizabeth. "He used to be Prince Edward."

Donna shakes her head. All this for Prince Edward. "Okay, I'll be right with you."

"Tremendous," says Elizabeth. "We shall see you anon."

"I don't suppose," says Donna, thrilled by the return of the old Elizabeth, and a thought occurring to her, "that you were in Mad About the Soy half an hour ago?"

But Elizabeth has hung up, and the familiar, business-like rudeness of that gesture brings a huge grin to Donna's face.

13

One by one the barns in the lower fields are collapsing. There was a time when Lord Townes would have a team who would head down and patch them up, or maybe they'd throw a few quid at the problem and knock up a whole new barn altogether. The team is long gone, though, as is most of the money. And so the barns were now headed the same way.

In his great-grandfather's day Headcorn Hall had sat at the heart of four thousand acres of Sussex countryside, stretching from the cliffs, across the Downs and into the low valleys of Kent. His grandfather had sold off the odd packet of land here and there, more as favors to friends than anything else. His father had split the estate in two, selling nearly two thousand acres and plowing the profits of the deal into the casinos of Mayfair. It would have been quicker simply to give the land to the casinos. In actuality he'd sold a lot of it to house builders, and entire new villages had sprung up, much to the horror of the old villages already there; some had gone to the Ministry of Defense, which, in true government style, had wildly overpaid. The latter was, very briefly, good news for his father, but, in the longer term, good news for the Grosvenor Casino.

So Lord Townes, Robert if you must, had inherited a tract of land and a mountain of debt, and had diligently set about managing both. Headcorn Hall now has just eighty acres to call its own. Lord Townes could have driven the estate quad bike around the perimeter in less than an hour, if he hadn't already had to sell the estate quad bike.

His years in the City had been well paid, but he had spent an awful lot of the proceeds patching this place up. He then did a bit of consulting for a while, but not many people in the new world of the City really want to consult a fifty-nine-year-old man who can't work a computer.

He used to hire out Headcorn Hall for film shoots, which was tremendous fun. They'd had Joanna Lumley filming something here at one point, and there was an advert for Snickers that they'd shot in the Grand Ballroom. In the end he'd stopped hiring it out when he discovered that one particular company was using it to shoot pornographic films, something he'd discovered only when a friend down from London sheepishly admitted that he recognized the damask curtains in one of the guest bedrooms.

It is possible, however, that things are looking up. Holly Lewis and Nick Silver's visit was unexpected. Could he give them advice? Well, of course he could. Giving advice to people with money has always been his job. While diverting a little to himself in the process.

In any deal there are angles, and your only job is to spot more of them than the other man. Robert Townes has never been the most ruthless of men; he would have achieved a great deal more if he had been. Some of the very worst people he'd ever worked with were now some of the very richest. Miserable, almost certainly, but their barns were not falling down.

When he'd started at the Culpepper Ward Bank in the mid-eighties, the mantra was "You can make friends, or you can make money," and, as Robert already had money, he chose to make friends. People really seemed to like him.

But now that he has no money left? Where have the friends all disappeared to?

Over two hundred years Headcorn Hall has got smaller and smaller, as each successive Lord Townes has shrunk the estate. So much power and wealth disappearing under the auctioneer's hammer long before Robert was born.

Lord Townes pours himself a whisky. The expensive stuff for once. Because who's to say the fortunes of the family aren't about to be reversed?

14

"Well," says Elizabeth, surveying the wreckage of Nick Silver's office at 8b Templar Street, "this isn't ideal at all."

"Do you think they've killed him?" Joyce asks. A desk has been upended in the middle of the room, its drawers pulled out and scattered. Two filing cabinets have been prized open, and papers are strewn across the floor. If Nick Silver had been in his office, waiting for Elizabeth, he was certainly not here now.

"Killed who?" asks Donna. Not unreasonably, in Elizabeth's estimation.

Donna had argued for a while against breaking in, and that was to be expected, applauded even: we all need our self-respect. "Did you really see someone breaking in, Elizabeth?" "Don't you think I have better things to do, Elizabeth?" "Is Elizabeth making you do this, Joyce? Blink twice for yes." But eventually the combination of Elizabeth's helplessness and Donna's resentment at Prince Edward costing her an easy week meant that she relented.

In the end, Donna had commandeered a local locksmith, who was only too happy to help—locksmiths not always being entirely above the law, and therefore eager for any opportunity to get on the good side of the police. The locksmith, however, had no luck: the door was made of tougher stuff than his tools and expertise combined. So Donna rang Bogdan, who was nearby helping to renovate the local Polish community center, and he rushed around. Within forty-five seconds or so they were inside.

"The question is," says Elizabeth, "was this a burglary or was this a kidnapping?"

Had the violence unleashed on the room also been unleashed on Nick Silver?

Elizabeth scans the room. "Look for signs of a struggle."

"There's a broken lamp," says Joyce.

Elizabeth considers the lamp. "That might have been disturbed by flying files and drawers."

Joyce tries again. "The rug? It's covered in glass?"

"That comes from the skylight," says Bogdan, looking up.

"Presumably where someone entered the room," says Elizabeth.

"Can I ask what's going on?" says Donna.

"Oh, goodness," says Elizabeth. "You're so impatient."

Donna looks at Bogdan.

"Don't speak to Donna like that," says Bogdan, apologetically.

"Stop simpering, Bogdan," says Elizabeth. "It doesn't suit you."

"This feels like something the police should be getting involved with," says Donna, looking around her.

"No police," says Elizabeth. "You're lucky you're here at all. If I'd thought about it, I would have just called Bogdan directly, so don't push it."

"Surely she can tell Chris?" Joyce says.

"Yes, Chris is fine," says Elizabeth. "Just not normal police—we've got too much thinking to do. Two possible scenarios present themselves. Either a simple burglary, perhaps looking for the code. Or someone was following Nick Silver, he led them here, and they took their shot, killing or kidnapping him? Annoyed that their bomb had somehow failed to go off?"

"You would be annoyed," nods Joyce. "I had to send my air fryer back because of the thermostat. They were very good about it."

Donna says, "May I just ask three questions?"

"You may ask one question, dear," says Elizabeth. "I don't need to hear endless bleating from police officers."

"Don't speak t—" starts Bogdan, before Donna lets him know it's okay to leave this one.

"Okay, well, I'm going to ask three but very quickly," says Donna.

"That's clever," says Bogdan.

"What code?" says Donna, counting the questions down on her fingers. "What bomb? And who's Nick Silver?"

"And also is he dead?" Bogdan asks.

"Codes are codes, and bombs are bombs," says Elizabeth.

"And Nick Silver was my son-in-law Paul's best man," says Joyce.

"The puker?" says Donna.

"And perhaps he is dead, Bogdan, yes," says Elizabeth. "Who's to say?"

"He did say he'd be here to meet you," says Joyce. "And he wasn't."

Precisely what Elizabeth is thinking.

"What does he do, this guy?" asks Donna.

"Cold storage," says Elizabeth.

"Like fridge-freezers?"

"Of course not like fridge-freezers," says Elizabeth.

"Then what?"

"Storage," says Elizabeth. "A storage system but an unusual one. Non-traditional."

"Ah, you don't know," says Donna. "You know it's okay just to admit you don't know sometimes?"

"Donna," says Elizabeth, "I do know—I just don't know *yet*."

"Oh, that's good," says Joyce.

Elizabeth regroups. "Joyce, we have to talk to Holly Lewis."

"As I say," says Joyce, "I haven't met her, but—"

"Where can we find her?" Elizabeth asks.

"I'll ask Paul," says Joyce, then turns to Donna. "My son-in-law."

"Can I go now?" Bogdan asks. "I left a Lithuanian to do the plastering."

Elizabeth waves this away and turns back to Joyce. "Ask Paul if Holly might like to visit us for dinner this evening. And tell him to let you know if Nick Silver contacts him. If he does, we'll know he's gone into hiding, and if he doesn't—"

"Then he's dead," says Joyce.

There is a beat.

"You know," says Donna, "this really *does* feel like a police matter."

"It does a bit," agrees Bogdan. "Even I think."

"Donna, we don't need you running around the county solving murders when you could be protecting Prince Edward," says Elizabeth. "And, Bogdan, you have a roof to fix, so we all have jobs to do, don't we? If someone has been murdered, I'll be sure to let you know. Until then, we have a minibus to catch."

Among the chaos of the room, Elizabeth sees a file tucked neatly behind a radiator. Lifting it out, she sees that it is not just a file: it is a file with her name written on the front of it. She slips it into her bag.

Elizabeth leads Joyce, Donna and Bogdan down the stairs. Is there any sign that someone has been dragged down here? Any blood on the banister? Handprints smeared on the wall? Nothing that Elizabeth can see at first glance.

Perhaps he was waiting in his office, heard noises on the roof and, spooked, ran for safety? That would explain his leaving the file. And, if so, surely he will contact Paul? Or perhaps even her?

Out of Donna's line of sight, Elizabeth takes the file from her bag. Inside is a single Post-it note.

Help me, Elizabeth. You'll work out how.

She flashes it to Joyce and places a finger to her lips.

Joyce whispers, "So he's alive?"

Elizabeth whispers back, "Joyce, this doesn't tell us he's alive. Just that he was alive when he wrote it."

"Of course, sorry," says Joyce.

Elizabeth leads them back out onto Templar Street, and realizes, to her shock, that she is hungry. When was the last time she was hungry? These days she has to force herself to eat, and yet here she is, suddenly ravenous.

The return of her appetite. Who would have seen that coming?

"Before we get on the bus," says Joyce, reaching into her bag, "I thought you might like your flapjack. It's cherry Bakewell."

Who would have seen that coming, indeed?

Elizabeth takes the flapjack from her friend.

Joyce stops. "Do we know who planted a bomb under his car?"

"We don't," says Elizabeth. "Though our current suspect list consists of an online fraudster named Davey Noakes, a banker called Lord Townes and Nick's partner, Holly Lewis."

"A lord wouldn't kill anybody," says Joyce. "Honestly, Elizabeth."

Elizabeth takes a bite of her flapjack.

"Tell me, Joyce," says Elizabeth, "have you ever seen a bomb before?"

"No," says Joyce. "I once saw someone with a Hoover attachment up his backside though."

Elizabeth nods. "Thank you for that, Joyce. Tell Ron to come and pick us up from Hampton Road. We have a car to look under."

15

Kendrick is building a Lego Death Star while Ron lies, flat out, on the sofa. Jason has made him a cup of tea. He'd offered his dad a beer, and Ron had been tempted, but one thing you truly learn with age is that you have to know your limitations. Pauline has left for work, seemingly as fresh as a daisy. Ron checks that Kendrick is out of earshot.

"What gives? Why's Kenny here?"

Jason speaks slowly and quietly. "Suzi rang, just said Danny's left her. Done a runner."

"Left her?" says Ron. That's not unwelcome news.

"So she says," continues Jason. "Said she had a few things she needed to arrange, and could I look after Kenny for a day or two? Nothing more than that."

"Is he gone for good?" Ron asks. "Danny?"

"Let's hope so," says Jason.

Ron hears a grunt of frustration from Kendrick at his dining-room table. He calls over, "Problem, Kenny?"

"Not a problem," says Kendrick. "Just thinking about Darth Vader. Why are people like that? Can I have a glass of water?"

"Course you can," says Ron. "I keep it in the tap."

Kendrick bounces off to the kitchen. Ron turns back to Jason.

"What about the house, then?"

"All hers, she reckons," says Jason. "He's letting her keep it."

"That doesn't sound like Danny," says Ron. Something's not right here. "You're telling me everything? No big row, anything like that? He just left?"

"Nothing, Pops," says Jason. "Marriages fail, don't they? You remember that."

Jason's lying to him, Ron can see that. Lying to protect him probably, but Ron doesn't need protection. There will have been something—a bust-up, an incident—it's all too quick otherwise. And if Jason's going to lie to him, maybe Kendrick won't. Kendrick comes back in from the kitchen.

"Day off school, then, Kenny," says Ron. "Lucky thing."

"So lucky," agrees Kendrick. "I do like school, but sometimes you have to have a break to recharge."

"Got that right," says Ron. "Was there a lot of noise at yours last night? Your mum and dad?"

Kendrick fixes a laser cannon to his model. "No noise."

Ron looks at Jason. Jason's face gives nothing away.

"So your dad's taking a little break too?"

"Yes," says Kendrick. "He took a case with him, and we waved from the front door."

Say what you like about Kendrick, the kid knows how to lie. Ron tries a different approach.

"Your dad can shout sometimes though, can't he? Was he shouting last night?"

Ron looks at Jason again. Jason is drinking his beer without a care in the world.

"Well, sometimes you shout too, Grandad," say Kendrick.

"I don't shout," says Ron.

"At the television," says Kendrick.

"Oh, at the television, yeah," says Ron. "You have to shout at the television or they won't hear you. But no shouting last night? At home?"

Kendrick shakes his head. "I didn't see anything or hear anything."

Ron nods. The Ritchies are a family who refuse to grass, whatever the problem. And Kendrick is a Ritchie. An unusual Ritchie, sure, but still a Ritchie. Okay, change course again, Ron. "You know, when I go into my bank, Kenny—"

"You have a bank?" Kendrick asks.

"Not the whole thing," says Ron. "Banks are a tool of the state."

"Okay," says Kendrick, nodding. "Like the newspapers and the water company?"

"Exactly, good lad," says Ron. "Anyway, when I go into the bank, and I want to take money out for something, they always ask me what it's for. Pay a builder, something like that."

Ron sees Jason looking at him, wondering where he's going with this.

"So I tell 'em what it's for, and then they say, 'Has anyone told you to lie to us, or coached you into giving that answer?' So they know it's not a scam, see?"

"That seems a good idea," says Kendrick. "I'm glad they do that."

"Better safe than sorry," agrees Jason.

"So can I ask you that question, Kenny? When you said, 'I didn't see anything or hear anything,' has someone, maybe in this room, told you to lie to me or coached you into giving that answer?"

"No, Grandad," says Kendrick.

"Even to protect me?" asks Ron. "Uncle Jason didn't tell you to say that?"

"If Uncle Jason had told me to say it, it would have been 'I didn't see nothing or hear nothing.'"

Jason laughs and raises his bottle of beer at his nephew.

Ron is now being lied to by both of them. Which makes him think three things.

Firstly, something very bad has happened. Danny Lloyd isn't a man to leave silently in the night, neat little case packed, thanks for fifteen years of marriage, here's a handshake and I'll see you around. Was there a row? How bad was it? Physical?

Secondly, he feels loved. He is being lied to for his own good, because Jason and Suzi, and now it seems even Kendrick, don't want him to be hurt.

But mainly it makes him feel old. Ron used to be the one doing the protecting. His job was to protect Suzi and Jason, and now their job is to protect him. When did that happen? And now even his grandson is in on the game. When had Ron turned from a lion back into a cub?

Ron doesn't know what happened last night, and what might happen next, but he knows one thing. He feels weak. Is this how it is from here on? Should he just accept it? To the family he looked after for so many years—as provider, protector, barbecue chef, turkey carver and chief rabble-rouser—he's now the old man on the comfy chair in the corner? That's where they are?

He looks at Jason and Kendrick, and he thinks about Suzi. Why is she not here? What is she having to "arrange"? Why is Kenny not at school?

Danny Lloyd is a very dangerous man, always has been, and Suzi was a fool to marry him. But Suzi's mum was a fool to marry Ron, so no one was in a position to judge. Ron already knows this story isn't over, and they haven't heard the last of Danny Lloyd. But whatever fight there is to come, Ron is scared that he might not have the heart for it.

"You want to stay here for a couple of days, Kenny?" Ron asks.

"Can I?"

"It's your home too," says Ron. "You stay here as long as you want."

"That might be nice, Dad," says Jason. "Just over the weekend."

Ron nods at his son. "Whatever you need. You're a good kid, Jason, don't think I don't know it."

"Learned from the best," says Jason.

"And I might still have a few tricks up my sleeve," says Ron. "If you need me."

Jason nods. "Another cuppa?"

"I'd kill for one," says Ron, and lays his head back down. Does he really still have tricks up his sleeve? He supposes he'll find out soon enough.

Ron's phone buzzes. A message from Joyce. Probably just waking up, the poor thing, needs someone to bring her soup and painkillers.

Ron, it's Joyce, but you know that, because my name will have come up, I find this thing so fiddly, don't you? Elizabeth and I have been in Fairhaven this morning and we just broke into an office and, anyway, someone might be dead. Nick Silver? The vomiter? Also Bogdan has had a haircut. I can tell you all this when I see you. Why does texting take so long? Can you come and meet us on Hampton Road in Fairhaven? You know, the one with all the houses.

Okay, so she hasn't just woken up. And the best man might be dead? And Elizabeth's been into Fairhaven? Jason comes back in with the tea.

"Can I get you anything else, Dad? Soup? Painkillers?"

Ron pushes himself up from the sofa. "Things to do, Jase, can't just lie on my arse all day. You boys can stay here if you like? Go see the llamas?"

"Grandad, you're the best," says Kendrick, springing up.

Ron smiles to himself. His head is splitting, his knees are aching, his constitution is clearly weaker than Pauline's and Joyce's, but he's still alive. He's alive, he's loved, and there may be trouble ahead on Hampton Road. Bring it on.

"The Death Star will still be here when you get back," says Kendrick.

"The Death Star's always here," says Ron. "The trick is learning to live with it."

"Where you off to, Dad?" says Jason.

"As always these days," says Ron, standing tall and proud, "exactly where I'm told."

16

Elizabeth appears, crawling on all fours, from undergrowth. She stands and steps back onto the pavement. "No," she says, "it's not that one."

Joyce has caught glimpses of Hampton Road from the minibus window, but it's fun to see it on foot. The houses are private, and all set back from the road. Every time you pass a security gate, you can peek over and see a thatched roof or a turret through the trees. When the security gates are too high, Elizabeth scurries off into the bushes to find a better view. They are looking for the house in the photographs Nick Silver sent to Elizabeth.

So far, no luck, but it is, nonetheless, a lot of fun.

Joanna has recently introduced Joyce to Rightmove. It's a website where you can see houses for sale. You click on them and they let you look inside! Thousands of strangers' houses! Twenty, thirty, sometimes forty pictures. You can see their sofas, their kitchen cabinets, where they've put their wooden LIVE, LAUGH, LOVE signs, what they've done with their gardens and so on. And this site is free! Joyce doesn't believe in all progress, self-service checkouts, for example, but she is certainly happy that somebody invented Rightmove.

Joyce can spend hours on it now. She was watching a detective drama set in Devon the other day, and she liked the look of the town that the grizzled, alcoholic detective lived in, and thought perhaps she might like to live there too. So she Googled the program and found out it was set in a place called Budleigh Salterton. Bingo, put Budleigh Salterton into the Rightmove search box, and you have a good hour's worth of entertainment—both imagining a new life for yourself and judging other people's interior design choices. A nice three-bed apartment on the front for £475,000. You could certainly imagine sitting on the balcony with a glass of wine, but, really, £475,000 with that lino on the bathroom floor?

In the old days, when she was a Rightmove rookie, Joyce looked only at the properties she could hypothetically afford, but Joanna had put her right, and now that Joyce has no upper price limit the whole world has opened up to her. They have houses on there for ten million if you look in the right place. Those houses are all either estates with fifty acres of land and enormous marble-and-gold entrance halls or they are four-bed flats in the middle of London. Rightmove teaches you an awful lot about the world, and also a lot about people's taste in curtains.

And so it is that she is looking up houses on Hampton Road as they walk up the hill to find Nick Silver's house.

"The one with the turrets at Number 16 last sold for £2.75 million," says Joyce. "And it has a fountain."

Up ahead of them a Daihatsu pulls up to the curb, and Ron steps out, looking very much the worse for wear.

He gives Joyce a hug. "You reek of booze, Joycey. That's just how I like my women."

Elizabeth has crossed the road and is on tiptoe next to a pair of wooden gates. She calls, "Found it! Nick Silver's house."

Joyce and Ron walk over to join her.

"How do we get in?" Joyce asks.

Elizabeth climbs the gates and opens them from the inside.

"Oh," says Joyce. "Like that."

"So you're saying Nick Silver's dead?" says Ron, as they start the walk down Nick's driveway.

"No," says Joyce. "Only *might* be dead. Someone put a bomb under his car."

"Okay," says Ron. "Bomb, is it? And where's his car?"

"It's at his house," says Joyce.

"But this is his house," says Ron.

"Yes," says Joyce.

"So what are we doing here?"

"Elizabeth just wants to take a look," says Joyce. "You know Elizabeth and bombs."

"Just want to borrow the thing and get it analyzed," says Elizabeth. "Find out who planted it."

"We're going to take the bomb with us?" Ron asks.

"That's why you're here, Ron," says Elizabeth. "We needed a car. An old friend of mine called Jasper has agreed to assess it, and it'll be quite safe at Coopers Chase."

"But—" says Ron.

"Bombs are fairly robust, Ron," says Elizabeth. "So long as you don't drive over any speed bumps, we'll be fine."

They round a bend, and the house from the photographs rises before them.

"Done all right for himself, Nicky Silver," says Ron. "Nice gaff."

In front of the house is Nick's car. Again, just like in the photograph.

Except.

Elizabeth takes a long look. She gets into a crouch, and then rolls herself under the car.

"Don't blow up," says Joyce.

Pushing herself up again, Elizabeth looks at Joyce and Ron and shakes her head.

"It's definitely the right house?" says Ron.

"Yes, Ron, it's the right house," says Elizabeth.

"And it's definitely the right car?" says Joyce.

"Yes, Joyce," says Elizabeth.

It is the right house, and it is the right car.

But the bomb is nowhere to be seen.

17

Joanna is halfway up a climbing wall, and not happy about it. Paul bounds up just above her, grabbing the Day-Glo hand-holds with graceful ease. Like a gazelle that all the lady gazelles fancy.

Joanna, however, is stuck.

It's her own fault. On their first date Paul had said he loved climbing, and Joanna had wanted to sleep with him so badly that she told him that she did too. It just came out. She also said, "No way? Mumford and Sons are my favorite band too!" It was that sort of evening. With apologies to Mumford & Sons.

White lies on one-night stands can be quickly forgotten, of course, but the next afternoon Paul had texted asking her for a second date. She had waited the requisite forty-eight hours and replied saying that would be very nice, and he'd suggested an "urban climbing" wall underneath the Westway.

In retrospect this would have been the time to come clean. But she still wasn't in a place where her head was doing the thinking and she said, yes, I'd love that, I might be a bit rusty but count me in.

Ordinarily a second date might be at a slightly nicer restaurant than the first date, but, in Joanna's view, each new relationship was a doorway to a new version of oneself. And perhaps new Joanna was a climber?

How hard could climbing a wall be? Also, maybe they'd have to shower off together afterward?

"You all right down there?" shouts Paul over his shoulder. He's about two holds from the top.

"You worry about yourself," says Joanna. "I'm trying something new."

Paul bounds up the final two holds and sits on the top of the wall.

The day before the date Joanna had booked an indoor climbing lesson and discovered exactly how hard climbing was, and had given up almost instantly. So what to do? She had nipped into Boots on her way back to the office, bought a bandage, strapped up her wrist, sent Paul a photo in which she was pointing to the wrist and grimacing, and offered to book a nice restaurant instead.

It worked a treat. There was absolutely no climbing, but they did still shower off together afterward.

Job done.

Since then Joanna has managed to avoid the subject altogether, until Paul discovered with glee that their hotel was a five-minute drive from the National Indoor Climbing Center. She couldn't pull the wrist stunt again, and so here she was, every muscle in her body aching and still only eight feet off the ground.

Joanna's climbing and Joyce's glaucoma. The things we do for love.

Paul will have his secrets too, Joanna is sure of that. Little white lies that will come out over the years. They're not even lies, are they? Little reinventions. Course corrections. One day she will tell Paul that she doesn't like Mumford & Sons, and one day Paul will tell her that he doesn't actually enjoy her reading *Financial Times* articles to him in bed.

Joanna sees that Paul is heading back down toward her. She lets go of her hand-holds and dangles in mid-air, waiting for him, the climbing cat very much out of the bag now. It's a relief, to be honest. No more lies.

She sees Paul's huge grin as he reaches her. "So you love climbing?"

"Love it," says Joanna. "Never done it but love it."

"Climb on my back," says Paul. "I'll take you down."

"I'm too heavy," says Joanna.

"Climb on," says Paul again, and so she does, and he takes her down the eight feet to the floor.

"I knew you didn't climb," says Paul. "It's the nails."

Of course he knew. He knew, she knew. The little lies are all part of the fun. The big lies are what you have to be careful of, and Joanna hasn't told Paul any big lies about herself. He knows who she is, what she believes in, what's important to her. That was the thing, wasn't it?

Has Paul told Joanna any big lies about himself? You never know, do you? Paul seems so simple, and passionate and kind, but who knew, really? She's as sure as she can be, and that's all you can do. She knew Ibrahim was right: that Paul was the man for her. Completed her in a way that finally made sense to herself.

"Champagne in a hot tub?" says Paul, unstrapping his harness.

"Yes, please," says Joanna.

"You're sure?" says Paul. "Perhaps you don't really like champagne?"

"I wanted to sleep with you," says Joanna. "You should be flattered."

"I was flattered," says Paul. "You really should learn how to bandage a wrist properly too. It was all over the place."

Joanna takes her phone from a locker.

A message from her mum. She takes a look.

"Mum wants Holly's number."

"Holly?" says Paul.

"They want to invite her for dinner," says Joanna. "Poor Holly."

Paul gives a non-committal grunt. Very unlike him. But he's just been climbing a wall, and he's probably knackered.

"Will you send it to her for me?" Joanna asks.

"Huh?" says Paul.

"Holly's number," says Joanna. "Will you send it to my mum?"

"Course," says Paul, but without enthusiasm.

Something is not quite right here.

If Joanna has found one of Paul's lies, she hopes it's a small one and not a big one.

18

Joyce loves a trip to London, even under such unusual circumstances. She likes the posh bits with the umbrella shops and the palaces, she likes the noisy bits with the Moroccan food and all the lovely fabric shops, and she likes the modern bits with the high-rise flats and the swimming pools up in mid-air. Which one would they be visiting today?

They might not have the bomb, heaven knows where that is right at this moment, but Elizabeth has the photographs, which she says are the next best thing. Joyce could imagine them being analyzed in any of those places. Perhaps a fake bookshelf in a centuries-old cigar shop pivots open to reveal a darkroom? Or, in the smoky back room of a Lebanese café, a man sits with a visor, a microscope and a scowl? Maybe, in a marbled boardroom on the thirty-fifth floor of a skyscraper, a hologram of data hovers over an enormous table.

It was somewhere in the middle of this final reverie that Elizabeth had woken Joyce to let her know they were getting off the train at Purley, three stops and a million miles away from the cosmopolitan buzz of London proper.

Still, even then, who knew? Perhaps sleepy Purley had hidden depths? An underground gambling den? A warehouse run by the Yakuza? Joyce had recently watched a Netflix series on the Yakuza, and they did turn up in the most surprising places. There was one of them in Spain, for example.

But instead they walked through suburban streets until they found a quiet crescent of bungalows that Joyce could honestly have found anywhere.

Her disappointment was not any sort of value judgment on the street itself, far from it: Purley seemed delightful, and bungalows were always at a premium. It was just she was expecting adventure, in one or other of its forms, and Birch Drive seemed unlikely to deliver.

Number 17 Birch Drive had seemed less promising still. A neatly trimmed front lawn, with orderly flowers, and the only sign of personality a large porcelain ginger cat guarding the pale beige front door.

Perhaps inside she might be shocked. That had been her final hope. The outside so ordinary, so everyday, the inside a lair, a laboratory, a gleaming hub of computers hidden away in plain sight.

Instead they had got an "old friend" of Elizabeth's called Jasper, who wore a shirt and bow tie, but also tracksuit trousers. In his front room were no piranha tanks, no flashing monitors and no lightly smoking test tubes. Instead there were more porcelain cats, maybe fifty or so. There were porcelain cats playing snooker, porcelain cats riding tandems, porcelain cats singing carols, and porcelain cats in sunglasses smoking what Joyce, after prolonged exposure to Pauline, recognizes as joints of marijuana. Joyce has yet to notice any real cats though.

But here they are, and, disappointed or not, you must always try to make the most of it.

"Do you have any actual cats?" Joyce asks.

"Cats?" asks Jasper. He looks at Elizabeth for guidance, then back at Joyce. "No? Why do you ask?"

Every time you met someone Elizabeth used to work with, there was something or other.

"Sorry for the mess," says Jasper, taking a seat at the dining-room table. "My wife was always the one for visitors, I've never quite got the hang of it. Where are these famous photos, then?"

Elizabeth sits next to him and shows him her phone. "It looks real to me, but I'm not the expert, am I, Jasper?"

"No, no," agrees Jasper, then looks at Joyce. "That's me. I'm the expert."

"I wish I was an expert in something," says Joyce. "Even if it's bombs. Do you have to keep up with all the new bombs?"

"Keep up?" says Jasper. "Umm, let me think. I do get a regular invitation to a little place on the south bank of a river; you just might have heard of it—it's called the Thames."

"That's nice," says Joyce. Jasper seems very jolly. "Yes, I have heard of it. Some lovely shops."

"Let's just say that this particular shop is of the secret variety," says Jasper. "And we shall say no more on the matter. Naughty Jasper, hush my mouth."

"Oh, I understand," says Joyce. She doesn't, but there's no need to offend anyone.

"He means they still let him go into MI6," says Elizabeth. "The building is on the South Bank of the Thames."

"I'm sorry," says Joyce to Jasper. "I didn't pick up on that."

Jasper waves two hands to let Joyce know it simply couldn't matter less. "I pop in from time to time, see what's what. Shouldn't really talk about it."

"I'm used to it from Elizabeth," says Joyce. "You'd think no one else ever worked for a living."

Jasper scrolls through the images.

"What do we think?" Elizabeth asks.

"Oh, it's real," says Jasper. "It's Russian. Or Russian-made at least, not that that signifies anything. Pretty solid bit of kit, stable. It didn't go off?"

"Our man spotted it," says Elizabeth. "Decided to take a taxi that morning."

"Very wise," says Jasper. "Very wise indeed, I would say. So where's the bomb now? May I see it? I'd love that. Have a tinker? Try not to wake the neighbors."

"It seems to have disappeared," says Elizabeth.

"Ah," says Jasper. "A disappearing bomb. Happens, doesn't it? Though they often make their presence known sooner or later. Ha, ha, ha. One shouldn't joke about bombs, of course. Bombs are very serious, Joyce."

"Understood," says Joyce.

"You're certain it's real?" Elizabeth asks.

"Who is ever certain of anything?" Jasper asks. "But if it's not real, someone has gone to a great deal of trouble to make it look real."

"And big enough to kill?" Elizabeth asks. "Or just send a message?"

"Big enough to kill," says Jasper. "And then some. Blow you straight through the roof still holding the steering wheel. Send you halfway to space. Ha, ha, ha. Again, one shouldn't joke, one shouldn't joke."

"The sort of thing a connected criminal might be able to get their hands on though?" Elizabeth asks.

"Oh, with ease," says Jasper. "You can pick these things up online these days."

Elizabeth's phone starts to ring. She walks over to a corner and answers. "Donna, about time. What do you have on The Compound?"

Jasper looks up at Joyce. "I know I shouldn't wear these trousers with this shirt, by the way. I do know that. A part of me wants to make the effort, but the other part of me . . . well, perhaps you know."

"I do know," says Joyce. Elizabeth still paces, listening to Donna. It occurs to Joyce that this whole thing could have been done over the phone, but Elizabeth had decided to come in person. Why was that? Is she rediscovering the thrill of the chase maybe? Good for her if she is.

Joyce looks around again. "What a lot of cats you have, Jasper? Which is your favorite?"

"Favorite?" asks Jasper. "I can't bear them."

"I see," says Joyce.

"I got one for Christmas once from an aunt," says Jasper. "And you know how over-enthusiastic one gets when one receives a disappointing present?"

Joyce nods. "Joanna bought me a water purifier and the grinning almost killed me."

"Every Christmas and every birthday since, they'd come," says Jasper. "Oh, he'll love this, old Jasper. This is just the thing for Jasper. My wife found the whole thing a hoot, started encouraging them. It was funny, I admit that."

"But why still have them all on display?" Joyce asks.

"You never know when people are going to come round, do you?" says Jasper. "And if they don't see their present on display, what would they think?"

Elizabeth finishes her call. "Come on, Joyce, work to do. Has Paul got back to us about Holly Lewis?"

Joyce looks at Jasper. He is trying to hide his disappointment that his visitors are leaving.

"I don't suppose you could make us a cup of tea, Jasper?"

"No time, Joyce," says Elizabeth.

"I'm afraid I don't have any tea," says Jasper.

"Not to worry," says Joyce.

"Or teacups."

"Perhaps you should buy a couple of mugs?" Joyce says. "And keep some PG Tips in the cupboard?"

Jasper nods. "Where would I buy mugs though?"

"I saw a lovely charity shop on the high street," says Joyce. "Near the station. A British Heart Foundation."

Jasper grimaces, as if this might be beyond him. Joyce hugs him, and feels his initial resistance soften as she does so.

"We'll see you soon, Jasper," says Joyce.

Jasper nods. "Maybe if you find the bomb, you could bring it with you? I'd really like to get my screwdriver in there and have a poke around."

Joyce looks at Jasper's tracksuit trousers, sagging and old. She looks at his eyes, pale and watery, glad of the company and sad to see it go.

Joyce knows then that she will be coming back to see Jasper again one day, and she will make sure Elizabeth will be coming too.

How many men like Jasper sit behind beige front doors in quiet bungalows, not knowing how to dress or what to eat or where to go? Wanting above all else not to be a nuisance? Joyce wishes she could save them all.

19

"And I can still do sit-ups," says Ibrahim, topping up his glass of wine at the contemporary upscale restaurant at Coopers Chase. "I still have both the muscle mass and the flexibility."

"I see," says Holly.

There is nothing Ibrahim likes better than somebody new to talk to, but Holly Lewis is not proving the easiest customer. But she has just been summoned to dinner by four pensioners, so perhaps that's understandable.

Elizabeth brought him up to speed before the dinner. Nick Silver had information. Somebody planted a bomb under his car and then Nick disappeared. The lady opposite them, Holly Lewis, is Nick's business partner, though even Elizabeth is currently hazy as to exactly what their business might be. Storage. A very profitable business all round. People always needed storage, didn't they? Ibrahim currently has some pots he's not sure what to do with, for example.

Also, if Elizabeth is to be believed, Holly Lewis is one of three main suspects in the attempted murder of Nick Silver, so it's possible he is making small talk with a psychopath.

Not for the first time.

"You are very kind to come and see us, Holly," says Joyce.

"I don't know if it's kindness," says Holly. "I want to find Nick. I thought perhaps you could help."

"Even so," says Joyce, "I baked you some brownies to say thank you."

Joyce hands over a Tupperware box. Ibrahim notes that the box looks quite heavy.

"They're a bit dense, I'm afraid," says Joyce. "But I didn't have a lot of warning you were coming, and I accidentally overdid it with the flour."

Holly nods a thank-you, and puts the brownies in her bag, Ibrahim noting the handle of the bag straining on the chair as they land.

"Are you Joyce?" Holly asks.

"For my sins," says Joyce.

"Joanna's mum?" Holly asks.

"Yes," says Joyce. "I mean, more than just Joanna's mum, a woman in my own right, but, yes. Are you friends?"

"No," says Holly. "I know her by reputation."

"All good I hope!" says Joyce.

Holly doesn't reply.

"Of course strength training is important too," says Ibrahim. "May I pour you a glass of white, Ron?"

"Not this evening, thanks," says Ron. "Wedding headache."

"It really was a terrific wedding, Holly," says Ibrahim. "I'm so sorry you couldn't come."

"Work," says Holly. "And once you've been to one wedding—"

"You're not married, Holly?" Joyce asks.

"Am I wearing a ring?" asks Holly.

"Well, no," says Joyce. "But Joanna says not everybody wears a ring, so I didn't want to assume."

"Is Joanna wearing a ring?" Holly asks.

"She is," says Joyce.

"I'll bet," says Holly. "Good for her."

Ibrahim is not sure he remembers the last time that Joyce met someone she was unable to charm.

"No kids, Holly?" Ron asks.

"They're not compulsory," says Holly.

"Don't blame you," says Ron.

"Haven't met the right man, perhaps?" says Ibrahim.

"Something like that," says Holly. She turns to Elizabeth. "They said you can help me find Nick?"

"Yes, if you can help us, I think we can help you," says Elizabeth. "Nick tells me you work in 'cold storage,' and I can't quite get to the bottom of it. In my line of work 'cold storage' was where you kept corpses until it was politically expedient to return them to their mother country, but I'm guessing that's not what you do?"

Holly stops eating her broccoli tart for a moment. "No, that's not what we do. We work for companies, individuals, and we look after the security of their computers or their files. Anything they want kept secret."

"Ah," says Ibrahim. "That's what I suspected. Online security, firewalls, the cloud. I have read around the issue."

"The exact opposite," says Holly.

"Yes, yes," says Ibrahim. "I thought as much, the exact opposite. Three hundred and sixty degrees."

"What do you mean, the exact opposite?" asks Elizabeth.

"We've all got so used to security being online," says Holly. "Financial details, corporate secrets, crypto trades, all hidden behind walls."

"Crypto is Bitcoin," says Joyce, tucking into her shepherd's pie. "You mustn't tell Joanna, but I lost fourteen thousand pounds."

"I don't really know Joanna," says Holly. "I told you."

"Oh, she's terrific," says Ibrahim.

Holly ignores him and continues her train of thought. "But at the very, very top level of security, because of hackers—"

"Computer hackers," says Ibrahim, nodding wisely.

"Companies and individuals turn to 'cold storage.' Whatever secrets they want to keep, they never go near any sort of connected computer. Instead they use companies like us, and they store their documents, more usually their hard drives, with us. We physically lock them up."

"What's the advantage in that?" Ron asks.

"It's easier to keep out robbers than it is to keep out hackers," says Holly. "However well protected you might think your information is behind whatever firewall you've installed, there's always someone in Russia, or Dubai, or Brazil, working out how to access it. Whereas if it's in a locked box, with an impossible combination in an unknown location, it's a lot easier to protect."

"So if you want to steal the secrets," says Ron, "you have to steal them physically?"

"You do," says Holly. "That's cold storage. And with the system we have in place, I would say stealing them physically is impossible."

"That's very useful, Holly, thank you," says Ibrahim. "Confirms a lot of my thoughts."

"It's been a tough day today, you understand that?" says Holly. "I discover my business partner has gone missing, could be dead as far as I know. Then I'm told Joanna's mum and her friends would be able to find Nick for me."

"We can certainly try," says Elizabeth. "Nick thought that either Davey Noakes or Lord Townes was trying to kill him. Does that sound reasonable?"

Holly looks away, looks back, then nods. "Very reasonable. They both knew."

"Knew what?" asks Elizabeth. "That's the piece of the puzzle we're missing."

Their desserts arrive. Along with another bottle of wine. Ibrahim does the honors.

"You're sure I can't tempt you, Holly?" he asks.

Holly hovers her hand over her glass. "Driving."

Ibrahim nods. Very wise.

"This whole thing is all about one single safe," says Holly. "The Compound is one room, a vault, and the walls are lined with safes. Each one about the size of a shoe box. Nick and I have one."

"What's in it?" asks Joyce, enjoying her Eton mess. "Jewels?"

"It's always jewels with you, Joyce," says Elizabeth.

"One of our first jobs," says Holly, "was for a company—"

"What company?" Elizabeth asks.

"We never ask," says Holly. "That's one of our selling points. We stored some bits and bobs for this company, and the yearly fee back then would have been twenty grand, something like that, and this company asked if we'd like to be paid in Bitcoin. And we talked about it, and I was interested in that sort of thing, and Nick was interested, so we said why not? We've got two hundred units in the vault, why not take a punt with one of them?"

"When was this?" Elizabeth asks.

"2011, something like that," says Holly. "And the twenty thousand price worked out at about five thousand Bitcoin, give or take, and occasionally you'd read something or other about it, but, really, we forgot about it. We stopped dealing with this company—"

"Went to prison, did they?" asks Elizabeth.

"Probably," says Holly. "Didn't need our services anymore, certainly. We had these five thousand Bitcoin, or a string of numbers that represented our ownership of the Bitcoin, literally written on a scrap of paper in one of our files."

"That's how it works," says Joyce. "It's a string of numbers, not a real coin. They call it a key."

"I know that," says Ibrahim.

"Sounds like a racket," says Ron. "Numbers on a bit of paper."

"All money is just numbers written on pieces of paper," says Holly. "A couple of years in, things started to get interesting. And these Bitcoin, which were worth about four pounds each when we first got paid, were suddenly worth forty each, and we had two hundred thousand pounds on our hands. We discussed selling them there and then, but we're both gamblers, so we said let's keep hold of them. But we decided to use one of our safes at The

Compound for the key. Lots of people store these keys online, but hackers steal Bitcoin, and, you know, that's the whole point of the company, so we locked it away. Anyway, there was lots of toing and froing, the price was very volatile, but a couple of years later it went up to five hundred and fifty, and that single piece of paper was worth two point seven five million."

Ron whistles through his teeth. "Still a racket though."

"I say at that point that we should sell," says Holly. "But Nick says we hold on. That's how it's always gone. One of us says sell, the other says hold on. As I said, it was very volatile, and sometimes it would lose half its value in a week, but the peaks were getting higher and higher. Knowing what we had locked away now, we agreed on two things. We'd sell only when both of us wanted to, and we'd figure out a way to stop one of us from ripping off the other. So, from around 2016, there was no way that safe could be opened without authorization from both of us. Nick can't open our unit without me, and I can't open it without Nick. That's what we agreed."

"The six-digit codes Elizabeth was telling us about?" says Ron.

"Sounds like Nick told you a lot," says Holly. "I hope he was right to trust you?"

"Might I ask," says Elizabeth, "what its value is today? If it was worth nearly three million then, what is it worth now?"

"Varies day to day," says Holly. "It had a big peak a few years ago, about seventy thousand a coin."

"That's when I bought," says Joyce.

"But within a year," says Holly, "it was back down at sixteen thousand."

"That's when I sold," says Joyce.

"But, again, whenever it collapsed, the peaks kept getting higher, and in 2024 it was up at around seventy-five thousand a coin. If we sold today, that key would be worth about three hundred and fifty million pounds."

That quietens everyone down.

"Why haven't you sold?" asks Ibrahim.

"Nick kept saying we didn't need to," says Holly. "He'd say the business is doing well, we have nice houses and nice cars. But he changed his mind earlier this week."

"Earlier this week?" says Elizabeth.

"We had a long lunch and Nick said, 'It's time,'" says Holly.

"So you sold?" asks Joyce.

"My shepherd's pie's on you," says Ron.

"No," says Holly. "Although we agreed to cash out, selling hundreds of millions of pounds of Bitcoin in one go isn't simple. So we started asking around, making it known we were looking to trade."

Elizabeth looks thoughtful. "Nick and Holly suddenly very popular."

"Holly and Nick," says Holly. "Always Holly and Nick. 'Nick and Holly' sound like a tiresome couple you meet on holiday."

"So," says Elizabeth, "the people you asked for advice were Davey Noakes and Lord Townes?"

"They were," says Holly. "Lord Townes was a banker and knows the traditional way of dealing with these things—"

"And Noakes knows the untraditional way?" says Ron.

Holly nods. "We thought that was a good combination."

But Ibrahim is sensing the issue. "Did you tell them how much it was?"

"We might have let it slip, yes," says Holly.

"So Nick agrees to unlock a couple of hundred million, and, before you know it, someone tries to kill him," says Ron.

"And then he disappears," says Holly.

Elizabeth has something on her mind. "Might I make an observation, Holly?"

"Can I stop you?" Holly asks.

"You seem very keen to find Nick?"

"Of course I'm keen to find him," says Holly.

Elizabeth continues, "But you don't seem particularly worried that someone might try to kill you too? That would be at the forefront of my mind if I was in your position. I'd be asking for our help to protect you."

"You don't know me," says Holly. "I don't frighten easily."

"If Lord Townes or Davey Noakes had put a bomb under Nick's car," says Elizabeth, "why wouldn't they put one under yours?"

"Perhaps they'd found out Nick's code?" says Holly. "They haven't found out mine, so they have no reason to kill me."

"Is your code not written down anywhere?" Joyce asks. "I always write mine down."

"Codes," says Ibrahim, trying to sound enigmatic.

"Our solicitor has them," says Holly. "In case of our deaths."

"Then your solicitor would be a suspect?" says Ibrahim.

"He doesn't know he has them," says Holly. "He just knows he has something to pass on if either of us were to die. He's a nobody."

"So if Nick is dead, you'd get his code?" Ron asks. Ibrahim is glad that Ron has said this. Holly was not at the wedding; Holly seems to be the only person who might profit from Nick's death; and, Elizabeth is right, she doesn't seem to be worried that whoever placed the bomb under Nick's car might do the same to hers. And might the reason for that be because she was the one who planted it?

"He's not dead," says Holly. "We'll find him together."

And then what, Holly Lewis? thinks Ibrahim.

"I don't wish to be morbid," says Joyce, "but who gets the codes if you both die? Who does this solicitor pass the codes to then?"

Holly turns on Joyce. "Why are you asking me that?"

Joyce has been taken by surprise. "I just . . . I'm ever so sorry, I didn't mean to offend. I just wondered."

"No," says Holly. "Why are *you* asking me that? And not one of your friends?"

"I just . . ." says Joyce, "I just thought I hadn't said anything for a while. I was trying to be useful."

"You were being useful, Joyce," says Ibrahim. "Holly is under a lot of stress. I'm sure she didn't mean to snap."

"So who would get the codes?" Elizabeth asks.

"I honestly don't know," says Holly, who seems to be regaining some composure. "No idea."

If you were to ask Ibrahim, who likes nothing better than cracking the codes of the mind, he would say she's lying. Quite why, though, he couldn't tell you.

"Well, if you really don't know," says Elizabeth, "the two of you should start to think about writing your codes down somewhere safe and sound, so someone you trust could find them if you do die."

"Might be too late for Nick," says Ron. "You could just tell me your code if you like though?"

"No one is going to die," says Holly. "And, if you'll excuse me, I might call it a night. I've told you everything I can. You've got my number if Nick gets in touch."

"Of course," says Ibrahim. "You've been very kind indeed to come to see us."

Holly stands and swings her bag over her shoulder. Ibrahim sees that Joyce feels guilty about the weight of the brownies. That's what happens when you bake hungover, Joyce.

Holly gives stiff handshakes to Elizabeth and Ibrahim, and then refuses hugs from Joyce and Ron. She walks toward the exit, listing under the weight of the bag. The gang watch her go, waiting for her to be out of earshot.

"I knew that's what cold storage was," says Ibrahim.

"Somebody is after that Bitcoin," says Elizabeth.

"And is willing to kill for it," says Ibrahim.

"But Holly was right," says Joyce.

"Right about what, Joyce?" Elizabeth doesn't like her train of thought being broken.

"Why try to kill Nick if you don't know his code? Why plant a bomb under his car? If it was me, I'd kidnap him and then torture him."

"You used to be such an innocent woman, Joyce," says Ibrahim.

"No, she didn't," says Ron, and raises his wine glass to her.

"If you wanted to steal the money," says Joyce, "you wouldn't try to kill him. You'd try to get his code."

"Unless killing him was a way to get his code," says Elizabeth.

Exactly what Ibrahim had been thinking. They are all on the same page.

"The solicitor," says Ron, taking his jacket from the back of his chair. "That's clever. It's always the solicitors, isn't it? I bet it's the same guy who did my first divorce."

Okay, so maybe Ron isn't on the same page.

"I'd better head home," says Ron. "Pauline's looking after Kendrick. I'll leave you to catch the solicitor."

"Ron, not all solicitors are evil," says Joyce. "If Holly kills Nick, Holly has Nick's code handed to her."

"Worth three hundred and fifty million pounds," says Ibrahim. "That's quite the motive."

"Wait, Holly planted the car bomb?" says Ron, struggling with his jacket, then realizing the sleeve is inside-out. "The morning of the wedding?"

"I did wonder why she wasn't there," says Joyce. "They're all supposed to be friends. But you wouldn't come to a wedding if you'd just planted a car bomb under the best man's Volvo?"

"Lexus, Joyce," says Ibrahim. "But precisely."

"And now," says Elizabeth, "having failed, Holly is asking our help in finding Nick Silver."

"Or delivering him to her," says Ibrahim.

"Surely, if Nick's code was secret," says Elizabeth, "it wouldn't make sense for Davey Noakes to plant the bomb. Or for Lord Townes to plant the bomb."

Joyce nods. "Holly Lewis planted the bomb."

Ron isn't buying it. "I bet it was the sol—"

They feel the explosion before they hear the noise. A rush of wind that knocks them from their seats. And then the noises, a huge thunderclap, followed by rolling booms. The night sky outside is lit by intense orange flames. Elizabeth is first to her feet, and moves as fast as she can to the door and into the heat now filling the evening air. Residents are peering out of windows, and they are all peering at the same thing. The remains of a car, blown apart in the overspill visitors' car park. And Elizabeth knows just which visitor it will be. Joyce and Ibrahim are close behind her, Ron lagging a little. The heat becomes unbearable as she reaches the remains of what was Holly's Volkswagen Beetle.

The pain as Elizabeth moves ever closer is becoming unbearable, but Elizabeth feels pain differently now. Unbearable is the norm.

"Get back!" shouts Ibrahim. "She's dead!"

I know she's dead, thinks Elizabeth. I can see she's dead. It would have been instant—that's something at least.

"You can't save her, Elizabeth," shouts Joyce.

I'm not trying to save her. I'm trying to solve a murder.

And then she spots it, already starting to melt into the frame of the car.

Holly's mobile phone. Wrapping her scarf around it, she throws the scalding hot phone clear. The phone is destroyed, but, if she got there in time, the SIM card will have survived. There's always something useful.

So they were trying to kill Holly Lewis too?

Elizabeth knows what Nick has told her and she knows what Holly has told her. Perhaps the phone will tell a different story? She needs information. About The Compound. About Davey Noakes. About Lord Townes.

Somebody is willing to kill for all that money. But who?

20

Paul Brett emerges from under the water, and Joanna smiles at her handsome husband.

Joanna and Paul are drinking the promised champagne in the promised hot tub, on the terrace of an "Executive Lodge" nestled in the woodland grounds of a grand country-house hotel. Those grounds are so big that, while the hot tub is in north Dorset, the breakfast buffet is in south Somerset.

"Are you worried though?" Joanna asks. "About Nick?"

"I don't know," says Paul. "Not really my world, all that."

Joyce had rung Joanna an hour or so ago and, after a lengthy diversion into porcelain cats, had told her about the bomb under Nick's car.

"He'll text me any minute," says Paul. "It'll be a training exercise or something. Testing for weaknesses in their system."

"In The Compound?" Joanna asks. "I'm not really sure I know what it is?"

"Cold storage," says Paul. "Instead of storing secrets on computers, where hackers can get to them, you stick them in a safe room underground that's impossible to rob. It's very popular."

"An underground bunker where you can bury your secrets?" says Joanna. "Popular with criminals presumably?"

"I suppose so," says Paul. "Or maybe hedge funds?"

Joanna sticks out her tongue.

"Everyone's got secrets, haven't they?" says Paul. "That's how they've stayed in business all these years. They're very thorough, Nick and Holly."

"And you've heard nothing from Holly this evening?" asks Joanna. "Dinner with those four can be an ordeal."

"Holly can handle anything," says Paul.

"Can she now?" asks Joanna. "Why haven't I met her? I've met most of your friends. And her being so wonderful and everything?"

"One of those things," says Paul. "Just hasn't worked out that way."

Joanna downs her champagne and reaches for another bottle.

"Is she beautiful, and very much in love with you?"

"No," says Paul.

Joanna pops the champagne cork.

"No, she's not beautiful or, no, she's not very much in love with you?"

"Neither," says Paul. "She's perfectly acceptable-looking as women go, and, impressive though she is, you'd have to be an entirely different magnitude of woman to consider falling in love with me. You'd have to be a maniac of some sort. Or a monster. That sort of a woman."

Joanna will spend a couple of hours online this evening being the judge of *that*.

She smiles. "Sorry to tease you. I'm looking forward to meeting her."

"Don't hold your breath," says Paul.

"I'll curtsy when we meet," says Joanna. "And say how delighted I am to meet my husband's most perfectly reasonable-looking friend."

She fills Paul's champagne glass.

"When did Nick ask you about Elizabeth?"

"Morning of the wedding," says Paul. "I've told him stories about your mum, about the gang. He wanted to know if they were true."

"I'm afraid they are," says Joanna. "They'll help if they can, I know that."

They slide a little further under the bubbles.

"This is the stuff," says Paul.

"You know hot tubs are an absolute soup of bacteria," says Joanna.

"Happy honeymoon, darling," says Paul, and they clink glasses.

Paul's phone buzzes on the side of the hot tub. Paul and Joanna look at each other. Paul reaches over, dries his hand on a towel and picks up his phone. He gives a broad grin.

"I told you," says Paul. "Didn't I tell you? It's Nick."

"Thank God for that," says Joanna. "What does he say? Why didn't he ring instead?"

> Paul it's me. I have to lay low for a while but don't worry, I'm safe.

"Jesus," says Joanna. "Where is he? Message him back."
Paul types.

> Can we help? Anything at all?

"I'll tell Mum he's got in touch," says Joanna.
Another message comes through.

> No need mate, just wanted you to know I'm alive.

"Ask him to ring," says Joanna. "Elizabeth will want details."

Paul sends another message to Nick. Joanna starts typing a message to her mum with the good news. Nick replies to Paul.

> Can't ring this evening Paul. Will explain all soon.

"In fact, I'll ring Mum," says Joanna. "They might still be with Holly. Everyone will want to know."

Paul holds a finger in the air. "One second."

Joanna waits.

"He never calls me Paul," says Paul. "You know that, he calls me Paolo. I call him Nico. We have done since university."

That's true. It's embarrassing, but the sort of thing you ignore at the beginning of a relationship, and hope will become cute eventually.

"Well, he's calling you Paul now," says Joanna. "I mean, it's a serious situation—perhaps he thinks Paolo is a bit flip?"

"Or perhaps it's not him," says Paul. "Is that crazy? Perhaps someone has got hold of his phone?"

Joanna thinks, champagne in one hand, mobile phone in the other.

"Ask him something only the two of you would know," says Joanna. "Anything. As silly as you like. Just something that would prove it. Put your mind at rest."

Paul nods and starts typing.

> Nico, just want to be cautious here, I know you'll understand.
> What was the name of your first car? The Vauxhall Nova?

"We called it the Babe Magnet," says Paul to Joanna, a little apologetically.

"And was it?"

"Not so much," says Paul. "Not so much."

There is another ping. Paul reads out the reply.

> Sorry mate, what is this? A test of our friendship? I'm letting you know I'm okay, and this is what I get?

"Well, I don't love that," say Joanna.

"I don't love it either," says Paul, typing again.

> Come on Nico, I just need to make certain it's you. Play the game.

"There's zero reason, if it's really him," says Joanna, "why he wouldn't just tell you."

"Agree," says Paul.

Another ping.

> Jesus Paul. When I need you most, you pull this? We both know the name of the car. Stop messing around and let people know I'm okay.

"It's not him," says Paul.

"It's not him," agrees Joanna.

"Which means someone has got his phone," says Paul.

"And whoever has got his phone has got him," agrees Joanna. "I'm ringing Elizabeth."

There is another ping. Another message from Nick.

> I'm sorry if I've offended you Paul. I thought we were friends, but I can't trust you. Signing off for good now.

Joanna and Paul look at each other. Joanna taps at her phone. "No answer from Elizabeth. I'll try Mum."

Paul sends another message while she does. It bounces straight back.

"Jesus Christ," says Paul. "Who sent those messages?"

"No answer from Mum either—where are they?"

"Screenshot the messages," says Joanna. "We have to find Nick."

"Screenshotting them," says Paul. "I'll send them straight to the police."

Joanna puts her hand on his.

"Honestly? God bless the police, but it'll be quicker all round if we just show them to Elizabeth."

21

The frame of the car is still glowing orange in the dark of the night as it cools, but the flames have gone, as have most of the onlookers. Mist from the fire hoses hangs suspended in arc lights trained on the driver's side door.

The four friends are standing behind police incident tape, watching the crouching figures of officers picking through the wreckage. Further beyond the vehicle is a small tent, lit from the inside, where, presumably, the body of Holly Lewis is being examined. Holly who had been drinking their wine and reluctantly indulging their questions less than two hours ago.

Ron has his arm around Joyce. She's cold but also shocked. He looks at Elizabeth, who he knows must be desperate to go under the tape and join in the investigation. But she's already done her investigating. Whatever the officers find in the car, Ron knows they won't find Holly's phone, because what's left of it is currently in Elizabeth's bag.

Two police officers approach the group. Ron is disappointed to see it is not Chris and Donna, just a ginger bloke and an Asian woman, and neither looks particularly interested in dealing with them. The Asian woman, who appears to have rank, is straight into her questions.

"DCI Varma. I'm told the victim was having dinner with the four of you this evening."

Elizabeth holds up a hand to stop the others from speaking.

"Well?" says DCI Varma.

"Well, what?" says Elizabeth. "You didn't ask us a question?"

"I did," says DCI Varma.

"No, you stated something you'd been told," says Elizabeth.

DCI Varma nods. "Can you confirm my statement?"

"We thought it might be Chris and Donna," says Joyce. "Often when there are murders, Chris and Donna investigate them. They know us."

"Lucky them," says DCI Varma.

"Chris is on firearms training," says Ibrahim. "But perhaps the two of you will do. Perhaps we shall all form a fine friendship."

DCI Varma looks at her ginger sidekick, then back at Ibrahim. "No, sir, we will not be doing that."

"That's what Chris and Donna said at first," says Joyce. "Would you like to come to mine for some cake? I made some brownies, but they're a bit dense—"

"We're the police," says DCI Varma. "Not your carers. I just need information, and I thought this would be the quickest place to get it. So I don't need you to be charming, I need you to be quick."

"Holly Lewis, forty-five years old, from Lewes," says Elizabeth. "She was at Coopers Chase to have dinner with some of the residents."

"The four of you?" This is the ginger sidekick.

"Oh, you speak," says Elizabeth. "Yes, the four of us."

"What did you talk about?" DCI Varma asks.

"Goodness, this and—" says Elizabeth.

"That," says Joyce.

"Nothing that could explain what just happened?" DCI Varma asks.

Ron approves very strongly of not talking to police officers. Though he does wonder, given the unusual events of this evening, whether they might need to chat to Chris and Donna at some point? And this makes him think about Chris Hudson with a gun, and he lets out an involuntary laugh.

"This is funny to you, sir?" the ginger sidekick asks. "You fancy a laugh in the back of the police van?"

"Oh, mate," says Ron, "I've been beaten up in police vans by better coppers than you."

DCI Varma turns to the ginger boy wonder, then gestures toward the four of them. "It's one in the morning: we've got to go straight back to the station and start the investigation. I'm tired, and a woman has just died, so I can't do all this, I'm sorry. What was she doing here, and what do you all know about her that I don't? In short sentences."

"DCI Varma," says Elizabeth, "I'm afraid we are clueless. It was a social visit."

Ron really should take Kendrick to the swings or something tomorrow, but he knows now that there will be a Thursday Murder Club meeting. Because, wherever that storage facility might be, Elizabeth will want to find it before DCI Varma and Ed Sheeran here. Somewhere in there is three hundred and fifty million quid on a bit of paper, and almost certainly the answer to who killed Holly, and where Nick Silver might be right now.

"I'm told you were very brave," says DCI Varma to Elizabeth. "You tried to pull Holly out of the car?"

"Far too late," says Elizabeth. "Adrenaline. Forgotten I had any."

"I don't suppose," says DCI Varma, "that you came across Holly's phone? Probably the most useful thing we could find right now. Given how little we know."

"They melt," says Elizabeth. "I'm sure everything you'll need will be on her home computers."

That'll take a while for this duo to wade through. Meanwhile, Elizabeth will be making merry with Holly's SIM card.

Ron sees Joyce take her phone out of her bag and give the smallest of starts. The ginger sidekick spots it too.

"Anything you want to share with us, madam?"

Joyce puts her phone back in her bag and shakes her head.

They have walked far enough away for the car to be out of sight, a few wisps of smoke above Ruskin Court, the low hum of a police generator and a metallic tang in the air the only remains of the night's horror. Ron sees Pauline walking toward him, with a sleepy-looking Kendrick holding her hand. He hugs them both.

"He couldn't sleep," says Pauline.

"After the noise," says Kendrick. "Hello, everyone, do you remember me?"

It is agreed that everyone remembers Kendrick, and that pleases him.

"What was the noise?" Kendrick asks. "Pauline didn't know."

"A bomb from the war," says Ron. He looks at the police officers, and at least they have the good grace to nod.

"Sometimes they go off years later," says DCI Varma.

"So the police had to come?"

"Just to make sure everyone's okay," says Joyce.

"And was everyone okay?" says Kendrick.

"Everyone was just fine," says Joyce. "But Alan didn't like the noise."

"Dogs don't like loud noises," Pauline tells Kendrick.

"Me either," Kendrick tells her.

"Shall we get you back home?" says Ron. "Maybe have a hot chocolate?"

"Umm, a hot chocolate at one o'clock in the morning?" says Kendrick. "Are we allowed to?"

DCI Varma realizes that this question has been directed at her, and nods her assent.

"We shall see you in the morning, Ron," says Elizabeth. "Bright and early."

Of course they will, thinks Ron. He holds Kendrick's other hand, and he and Pauline walk him back to the flat, away from the gang.

So Kendrick was scared by the loud noise? That's new. Suzi still hasn't resurfaced. Jason's going to take Kendrick back on Sunday. Why can't Suzi come and get him herself?

Kendrick tugs at his hand. "Have you ever been in a war, Grandad?"

"Miners' strike 1974," says Ron.

Kendrick nods. "Why did the miners strike though?"

Ron feels his chest fill. "Let me tell you a few things about late-stage capitalism, Kenny."

"Yessss!" says Kendrick.

Saturday

22

You'd be forgiven for thinking that all is well with the world.

The sun is shining and the birds are singing as Ron and Bogdan sit in floral garden chairs on the patio of one of the most prolific Ecstasy dealers in British criminal history.

"And are you single?" asks Davey Noakes as his butler brings out three bottles of beer on a tray. Ron can't help but notice that there is also a gun on the tray.

"Me?" asks Ron. "No, I'm sorry. And I'm straight."

"No one's really straight," says Davey. "Not deep down."

"I think I might be," says Ron, and gives an apologetic shrug.

"Probably best for you," says Davey. "Saves you a lot of trouble in the long run. I'd ask you out, you'd feel you had to say yes—"

"Or you'd kill me," says Ron, looking at the gun, taking a beer and nodding his thanks to the butler.

"Or I'd kill you," says Davey, handing a bottle to Bogdan.

"Cheers," says Bogdan.

"I'd play with you for a couple of weeks," says Davey. "Then I'd get bored, and I'd blame you, and I'd probably get someone to run you down in a car. Not kill you but give you something to remember me by. They say dating's changed, but some things stay the same."

"I'm not single either," says Bogdan.

"I know that, you big prince," says Davey, taking his bottle and the gun from the tray. The butler retreats. "You go out with that police officer, don't you? Opposites attract, eh? You told her who you're visiting today?"

"I said I had business with Ron," says Bogdan. "I don't have to tell her everything, I'm my own man."

Ron laughs at this.

"So when the two of you turn up in a canal with bullets in your skulls," says Davey, "she won't come knocking for Ravey Davey? Good to know."

Not many people scare Ron, but Davey Noakes does. He is glad to have Bogdan with him. Surely he wouldn't kill them both? Not in one go?

Davey nods to the bottles. "Everyone okay with beer for breakfast?"

They all raise their bottles. Yes, everyone is okay with beer for breakfast.

"How's your son, Ron?" Davey asks.

"He's well," says Ron. Ron is now used to every single criminal on the South Coast being personally acquainted with Jason. He doesn't like to think about it too much. Jason has signed up to do panto in Hastings this year. Surely he wouldn't have signed up to do panto if he was still making money with the killers and drug dealers? "He's doing panto this year."

"He used to be a lot of fun," says Davey. "But then didn't we all? You've got five minutes to catch my attention, boys. Forgive the gun, but you've both got a reputation in your own way."

"Holly Lewis," says Ron. "She came to see you."

"She did," agrees Davey. "She's a handful, that one."

"And last night she died," says Bogdan. "In a bombing."

"I heard that," says Davey. "The news, anyway, not the explosion."

"And we just wondered," says Ron, "if there might be a connection between those two events?"

"I don't kill *everyone*," says Davey. "Who'd have the time? She wanted a bit of advice, that's all. Came to Uncle Davey."

"About the Bitcoin?" Ron asks.

Davey sizes Ron up. Ron has been "sized up" before, but this time it feels like it might be for a coffin.

"That rather depends on how much you know," says Davey. "And how you know it."

"We know there's three hundred and fifty million pounds sitting on a scrap of paper in The Compound," says Ron. "We know that Holly and Nick were finally thinking of cashing out, and that they came to see you and one other person for advice."

"And now Holly dies," says Bogdan. "Big boom. Not many people that good with explosives. Me, for sure—I like explosives—but maybe you too?"

"I don't *hate* explosives, sure," says Davey.

"And Nick Silver has disappeared, could be dead," says Ron.

Davey takes a swig of his beer. "Who else did they go to see?"

"No idea," says Ron.

"I see," says Davey. "And what's my angle? Why have I killed her?"

"Three hundred and fifty million is your angle," says Ron.

"Big angle," says Bogdan.

"I'd definitely like three hundred and fifty mil," says Davey. "But how would I get it?"

"The safe is encrypted," says Bogdan. "Holly had half the code; Nick had the other half."

"You found out Holly's half," says Ron. "She had it written down somewhere, and you can hack into anything. So you just need Nick's half now. Perhaps you're in the process of getting it? Perhaps he's locked up here somewhere with a gun at his head."

"Then the money's all yours," says Bogdan.

Davey nods. "Got it all worked out, boys. You're not worried I'll kill you now though? Because you worked it all out?"

"A bit worried, yeah," says Ron, looking at the gun.

"If you kill Ron, I kill you," says Bogdan.

"With what?" says Davey.

"Bare hands," says Bogdan.

"Yes, please, what a way to go," says Davey. "And if I kill you?"

"Then Elizabeth will kill you," says Bogdan.

"Who's Elizabeth?"

"You don't want to find out," says Bogdan.

"Perhaps I'll kill her too?" says Davey.

"You can't," says Bogdan. "Only God can kill Elizabeth."

"And even he'd think twice," says Ron.

Davey looks between the two of them, weighing something up.

"I like you both," says Davey. "You're idiots, but I like you. Let's say I won't kill you for coming to my house and accusing me of murder. Usually I'd kill you for that alone."

"Davey," says Ron, "when did Holly and Nick come to see you?"

Davey thinks. "Tuesday. I'd just got back from aqua aerobics."

"So she tells you about the money on Tuesday, and then she dies last night. Come on. You'd be suspicious."

"That's your theory," says Davey. "I get it. Anything wrong with it that you can see?"

"Nothing," says Ron, but, inside, he's losing a bit of confidence. Perhaps there is something wrong with it? Ron isn't always the first to spot when something's wrong with a theory. Never show doubt though. If you show doubt, the other side has already won.

"Here's where your theory falls down," says Davey. Ron prepares to take notes. Elizabeth will want a full report. "Someone paid Nick and Holly twenty grand in Bitcoin more than ten years ago. And you're telling me I found out about this on Tuesday?"

"That's what we're telling you," says Ron. Don't back down. "They hadn't told a soul about it beforehand."

Davey nods and takes another swig of his beer.

"What sort of person might have paid them twenty grand in Bitcoin all those years ago?" asks Davey. "Would you think?"

"Uhh," starts Ron, but finds he has nowhere left to go. He looks at Bogdan, who shrugs.

"Sounds like the sort of thing a cyber-security expert might do," says Davey. "Perhaps with a criminal past, a few secrets that needed hiding. That sort of person? Don't you think?"

"So—"

"So that money came from me," says Davey. "All those years ago. I knew about it then, I've known about it for a decade. Every time I'd see Holly or Nick we'd talk about it. They'd do the sums, and I'd tell them to hold on to it. So I didn't find out about it on Tuesday, my brave lads. I've known about it for more than ten years. If I wanted to steal my Bitcoin back, I've had ten years to do it. No rush job."

"Ah," says Ron. Elizabeth's not going to like this.

"I paid them that money; they didn't have to take the risk of accepting it, but they did. I admired it then, and I admire it now. Holly and Nick knew how to take a risk. If I wanted to steal it, I'd have found a way a long time ago. But I didn't want to steal it. Not this week, not any week. Also, if I killed someone, no one would ever find a trace. Because that's how I kill people. I don't blow up their cars, and if you knew the first thing about me you'd know that."

"Apologies," says Ron.

Davey waves this away. "We're all square if you just let me know who else Holly and Nick went to see about the Bitcoin."

"I told you already," says Ron, "I don't know."

"I know," says Davey, picking up his gun and pointing it at Ron. "But you were lying, and friends don't lie to friends."

"Honestly, I d—"

Davey fires his gun into the air, then points it back at Ron. "Please, I've got Zumba at nine, I don't need this this morning."

Davey's butler emerges from the house.

"Sir?"

"Air shot," says Davey.

"I shall retrieve the casing," says the butler and disappears into the nearby undergrowth.

"Just tell me," says Davey. "I won't kill anyone."

"A lord," says Ron. "A banker, another client."

"Lord Townes?" asks Davey.

"Maybe, yeah," says Ron.

"Okay," says Davey. "Handsome little beggar. Have you been to see him?"

"Not yet," says Ron. "But we will."

That's probably one for Joyce. She'll enjoy that.

"Oh, I'd recommend it," says Davey. "Because someone must have killed her, and it's unfair to only suspect me, don't you think? Why not Lord Townes? Or don't lords kill people?"

"Everyone kills people," says Bogdan.

"Precisely." Davey considers Bogdan for a moment. "Are you ever looking for work, Bogdan?"

"No," says Bogdan.

"Shame," says Davey, as his butler appears out of the undergrowth with a bullet casing in his hand. "I'll let you get on your way, lads. What a mystery you have to solve."

"If it was you," says Ron, "we'll find proof."

"Oh, Ron, you lovely big bear," says Davey. "Look at my house. I get away with everything. Look under as many stones as you wish. You'll never find a thing."

"There're always more stones," says Ron.

Davey looks at his watch. "That's me off to Zumba. If you don't get there early they put you at the back."

Ron watches Davey walk toward the house. He pauses and turns.

"Talking of looking under stones," says Davey, "are you absolutely *sure* Nick Silver is dead?"

He raises a single eyebrow, and heads into his beautiful house.

23

"That must be the world's shortest honeymoon," says Joanna. "I feel like Liz Truss."

Paul gives a tight smile.

"Sorry, just trying to cheer you up," she says. The motorway has been empty almost the whole way, a benefit of driving at seven in the morning. The poor night porter at the hotel checking them out a day early had assumed the two of them had had an awful row. As they left, he'd mouthed, "Are you okay?" at her. She nodded and gave a reassuring smile. Easier than saying, "My new husband's best friend has gone missing, and his business partner has died in a targeted car bombing, so we're going to look at some text messages with my mum and an ex-spy."

"Mum and Elizabeth will know what to do about the messages," Joanna says. Joyce knows what to do about a lot of things these days. She's still uniquely annoying, but Joanna accepts that she's the only one who thinks so. Her friends at the wedding loved her. Her friends have always loved her. But then her friends say the most awful things about their own mums, some of whom are delightful. And Paul loves Joyce ("Because you don't know her yet," Joanna tells him). Only yesterday he said, "Your mum's glaucoma really seems to be clearing up."

"Do you think the car will still be there?" Paul asks. "Holly's car?"

Joanna puts her hand on his leg. "Mum says it's gone. They worked on it all last night."

What is Paul feeling about Holly? Joanna can't tell. He is very upset about Nick, she can see that. Perhaps he feels the whole thing is his fault somehow?

But how he feels about Holly is a closed book for now. Paul is a very straightforward man, and, the few times you can't see exactly how he feels on his face, he will tell you how he feels. Joanna likes to know where she is, and she always knows where she is with Paul. But a good friend has just died in an awful way, and Joanna can't get an easy grip on how it is making him feel.

"You can cry you know?" Joanna says. "Or shout? Not at me but out of the window. I know I never met Holly, but this must be horrific for you."

Paul looks out of the window. "I hadn't seen her for so long. I kept meaning to."

Joanna understands that. She's got friends she won't see for a year, but when they do meet up they just go back to the same conversation they were in the middle of when they'd last met. She remembered speaking to her mum about this one day, in that way she supposes someone does, speaking as if she's the only human being on the planet ever to experience a perfectly common phenomenon, and Joyce had said, "When old friends die, you're furious, because you've never quite finished what you were saying to them."

The whole gang are meeting this morning round at Mum's. Joanna has told Joyce about the text messages from Nick but hasn't forwarded them on. She thinks that she and Paul should present them. Nick was Paul's best man, he knows him, knows the language he uses, knows that the messages are not from him. It's important that Paul conveys that fact; quite what her mum's friends conclude from that is up to them. Joanna has asked everything she can about Nick and Holly's business, but Paul, investor or not, seems in the dark. Joanna doesn't think he's hiding anything from her, just that Holly and Nick had, over the years, hidden things from *him*.

"What if they're both dead?" Joanna asks.

"Don't say that, Jo," says Paul.

"But the business," says Joanna. "What happens to it?"

"I know you're just trying to distract yourself by thinking about money," says Paul.

That's true. Joanna doesn't want to think about burning corpses. Spreadsheets and cash balances are a great deal easier.

And, quite apart from anything, Paul owns five percent of the company, and has never thought to ask what that might be worth. It is unimportant in the grander scheme of things, but it's surely something to think about?

So a short honeymoon, that's for sure, but not everyone gets to visit their mum to talk about murder, do they? With a man they love by their side?

Would any of this have happened if her dad had still been alive? Mum and murder? You could never say, could you? Perhaps Mum and Dad might have moved to Coopers Chase together? Joyce might still have met Elizabeth. Elizabeth might still have introduced her to Ibrahim and Ron. Her mum's life might still have been filled with jewel thieves and spies and drug dealers and men waving guns. Her dad sitting in his gardening trousers doing the crossword as the madness played out around him? "Cup of tea, Dad?" "Only if you're making one." "Mum out, is she?" "Being shot at in a warehouse." "That's nice—need any help with the crossword?" "Seven-down, six letters, a fish beginning and ending in T."

The conversations you took for granted and will never have again. She looks over at Paul. He is deep in thought. He'd suit gardening trousers.

"What are you thinking?" Joanna asks. Not a question you should usually ask a man. By and large if a man is thinking anything halfway acceptable, he'll say it, and, if not, he'll just carry on thinking it instead.

"I'm thinking," says Paul, "if you don't mind my saying this. I'm thinking that all of this would be unbearable without you."

No, I don't mind your saying that. I don't mind your saying that at all.

Joanna takes a right turn over a familiar bridge. "Do you mind if I ask you a question? You might not know the answer."

"Ask me anything," says Paul. "Always ask me anything. No secrets."

They pass an old wooden bus stop. "What's a fish, six letters, begins and ends in T?"

"Easy," says Paul. "Turbot."

Joanna smiles and they pull into Coopers Chase. The two lovers clunk, clunk, clunk over the cattle grid.

24

Danny Lloyd steps out onto the balcony of his hotel, and the heat dances on his skin. He can hear church bells from the local village, and he can see an ex-pat foursome holing out their putts on the 15th green below. He'd flown out from Gatwick on Friday evening. He'd spent most of Friday working out what to do. First a chat with his lawyer. The house is in Suzi's name, and not a lot can be done about it. He'd asked about her will, and, as it stands, the whole thing would come back to him if she dies. Or, more accurately, when she dies, but that was another meeting.

But, while Suzi might be a psycho, she's no fool, so that will won't be in play for long. Long enough for him to get his hands on it maybe. If she changes it before she dies, so be it. If she doesn't, then win-win.

Finding someone to murder Suzi won't be easy. If she dies anytime soon, there's only one suspect, and that's Danny. He needs to put lots of layers between himself and the killer, money has to go through lots of different hands, and each of those hands gets to keep a bit of it on the way. But Danny trusts someone who trusts someone who trusts someone, and Suzi can meet with the sort of accident that might make the police suspicious, but will send them chasing their tails for a few weeks before they get dizzy and stop running.

Jason Ritchie is altogether easier. He's made so many enemies over the years, been in enough tricky situations, that when he turns up dead the poor police will have pages of suspects to deal with. Would Danny even be in the first fifty names? He doubts it. With Jason you can just shoot him from a speeding car, dump the motor at a friendly farm and be sitting down for a pint by lunchtime.

One of the faces on the 15th green looks up at the balcony. He shouts a greeting, and Danny waves back. Danny forgets his name, an amphetamine dealer from Billericay, enjoying his Portuguese retirement. You saw a lot of friendly faces out here.

Friendly, sure, but it still pays to be careful. Danny ducks back into his room and pulls the curtains. Don't want word getting out that he's here. Suzi and Jason Ritchie will be dead soon enough, but it's worth remembering that Jason Ritchie will probably kill him first if he finds out where he is.

What a business. There's nothing like it.

25

From the window of Joyce's flat, Ibrahim can see people heading toward the chapel for Saturday service. Some in couples but most alone. Some hunched or stooped, some with walkers, making slow progress toward hard seats and comforting words. There are people who have been to church every weekend for over ninety years. Today some of them walk past the site of the senseless murder of a young woman, yet still they walk. Ibrahim has never found answers in a church, but perhaps these people are asking different questions? We're all just trying to make sense of things, and you must take meaning wherever you can find it.

Alan takes a Polo from Ibrahim's hand and rolls on the floor in delight. We all have different needs.

They are enjoying tea and toast. Joanna had asked for coffee, but Joyce said she was making tea, and Joanna said surely it was all the same kettle for goodness' sake, and Joyce said it was too fiddly to do both, so Joanna said she would come and make one herself, but then Paul said shall we talk about these text messages first, and Joyce said six teas, then, and disappeared into the kitchen.

Joanna forwarded them to Joyce when she arrived, and Joyce has now forwarded them to everyone else. They start to read. It is shoddy stuff. Ibrahim doesn't like a job badly done, and this job is badly done.

> Sorry mate, what is this? A test of our friendship? I'm letting you know I'm okay, and this is what I get?

> Jesus Paul. When I need you most, you pull this? We both know the name of the car. Stop messing around and let people know I'm okay.
>
> I'm sorry if I've offended you Paul. I thought we were friends, but I can't trust you. Signing off for good now.

"Even Alan could see these were fake," he says.

Alan, upon hearing his name, wags his tail and nods.

"I got worried after the third message," says Paul. "It was Joanna's idea to ask the question about the car."

"That was quick thinking," says Elizabeth. If Joanna catches the compliment, she doesn't let it show. "It's his phone. But it's not him."

"So someone's pretending to be Nick Silver," says Ron. "Does that mean they've killed him? Sorry, Paul."

"If you want my view . . ." Joanna starts.

"We do," says Joyce, from the kitchen.

". . . if he was alive, they could have just asked him what the name of his car was. Instead of picking a fight and disappearing. That says to me they've killed him. Sorry, Paul."

Ibrahim sees Elizabeth nod. She had clearly been thinking that, but is glad that someone else has said it.

"So what now?" Paul asks.

"I have a question for you, Paul," says Elizabeth. "If you don't mind?"

"Please," says Paul. "I've never been questioned by an ex-spy before."

"No such thing as an ex-spy," says Elizabeth. "Did you know that Holly and Nick have a safe in The Compound containing three hundred and fifty million pounds in Bitcoin?"

Paul looks at Joanna. "Three hundred and fifty million? Is that why they killed Holly?"

"You had no idea?" Elizabeth asks him.

Paul shakes his head. "I knew they were doing well—Nick had money—but I didn't know about the Bitcoin."

"No idea they had hundreds of millions locked away?" Elizabeth is pressing him. Paul will be too polite to push back, Ibrahim knows that, but if she goes too far Joanna will have something to say about it. "Nick never even hinted? Holly never mentioned it? To their old friend?"

"Not a word," says Paul.

"I find that terrifically hard to believe," says Elizabeth.

Joanna has a look on her face that reminds Ibrahim of something. He can't quite place it, but he will.

She looks directly at Elizabeth. "Elizabeth, may I make an observation?"

"Can I stop you?" Elizabeth asks.

"No," says Joanna.

"Like mother like daughter," says Elizabeth.

That was the look. Joanna has the same look that Joyce has when another dog starts chasing Alan. A protective fury. A calm menace.

"Not everyone spends their life needing to know everyone else's business, Elizabeth." Joanna is very measured, as Joyce so often is.

"Murder changes that, dear," says Elizabeth.

Oh, goodness, Elizabeth, don't call her "dear."

"One of Paul's oldest friends has just been killed," says Joanna. "And another one has gone missing. We've driven three hours to get here on a Saturday morning to come and help, to show you the texts we received and to give you all the information we have."

Joyce walks back in with the teas, unaware of the heavyweight fight unfolding in front of her.

"Now," says Joanna, "you're in my mum's flat, and my mum adores you, but, and listen to this carefully, Elizabeth. Are you listening?"

Elizabeth says nothing.

"I'm sorry," says Joanna, sitting forward. "I asked if you were listening?"

"I'm listening," says Elizabeth.

"Good," says Joanna. "I am not my mum. I swear if you talk to my husband like that again, we're leaving. We should have taken these text messages to the police, but we're showing them to you instead. And we're showing them to you because we respect you. Please show us the same courtesy."

Elizabeth gives perhaps the smallest nod in recorded human history.

Joanna sits back. "Thank you, Elizabeth. I trust you understand me."

Ibrahim is so tempted to applaud that he has to start stroking Alan, to ensure he doesn't have both hands available.

Joyce offers a cup of tea to Joanna. "You know, I probably *could* find some instant coffee if you really fancy it?"

Joanna shakes her head and winks at her mum, who winks back.

"But you have money invested?" Ibrahim asks. While another fight between Joanna and Elizabeth would be glorious to see, for Joyce's sake he feels like he should start asking some of the questions too. "You never thought to get involved?"

Paul shrugs. "I gave them some money years ago, ten thousand I inherited from my grandad. Every now and again Nick would tell me things were going well. One day they'd sell and I'd do nicely out of it."

"How nicely?" Elizabeth asks. "If you don't mind my asking?"

"Not interested," says Paul. "I lent them the money because they were friends and they needed it. If I get some money back, that's okay; if I don't, that's okay too. I just liked seeing them do well. You can't let money be your master."

Joanna leans into Ibrahim. "When the hedge fund has social get-togethers, I don't let him speak."

"Let's control what we can," says Elizabeth. "We need to find The Compound, and I need to get Holly's SIM card analyzed. Find out if there's anything on there about Davey Noakes or Lord Townes. I can do that this afternoon if anyone fancies a trip up to London. Joyce?"

"Paul and Joanna have just arrived, so I might not—" Joyce's sentence is stopped by a look from Elizabeth. "But I'd love to, yes, London it is."

"We'll look after Alan while you're in London, Joycey," says Ron. "Kendrick's desperate to take him for a walk."

"He's staying today as well?" Ibrahim asks. It is always a delight to spend time with Ron's grandson, but something is amiss there.

"I asked if he could stay until Sunday," says Ron. "Going home to his mum in the morning."

Just his mum. Ibrahim tucks that observation away.

The meeting is at an end. Ibrahim flattens the creases on his trousers before getting up. Lots to think about.

What do they know? Holly Lewis is dead, and if Nick Silver isn't dead too something very peculiar is happening with his phone. A huge sum of money is buried somewhere nearby, and there are two six-digit codes needed to claim it.

That should be enough to be getting on with, shouldn't it? He'll enjoy thinking about the codes, that's for certain.

Still, Ibrahim feels at a slight loss. Elizabeth and Joyce are heading off together. He could probably join them if he really wanted to, but one doesn't like to ask. Ron has Pauline, Joanna has Paul, even Alan has Kendrick. Ibrahim feels a long day is stretching ahead of him, and wonders how he might fill the empty hours.

Murders are all well and good, but who does *he* have?

26

Joyce sits on a dining-room chair, stared at, once again, by the many, many porcelain cats.

They are back in Purley. Joyce bets that not many people go to Purley twice in two days. I mean, some people live there or work there, so they'll be back and forth all the time. But civilians like her? Twice? In two days? Joyce doubts it very much.

They'd walked past the British Heart Foundation shop on their way to Jasper's. They really did have some nice mugs in there. Joyce thought perhaps she should buy a few for him, but decided it was too presumptuous. Give him time.

Elizabeth sits next to Jasper. He still wears his shirt and bow tie, but today has switched to corduroys, which is a step up. Elizabeth hands him the SIM card. "A little charred."

"I've seen worse," says Jasper, taking a phone from his pocket and inserting the SIM card. The phone is about twice the size of a regular phone, even Ibrahim's new one, and is a sleek black with absolutely no markings.

"That's an unusual phone," says Joyce. "Joanna has a Samsung which she swears by."

"Can't get one of these in a shop," says Jasper. "If you know what I mean?"

"Jasper, of course she knows what you mean," says Elizabeth. "She knows you were a spy, stop showing off."

"You show off all you like, Jasper," says Joyce.

The screen of Jasper's phone lights up. He starts to scroll.

"Anything?" Elizabeth asks.

"It's not ideal," says Jasper. "It's not ideal. There's bits and bobs."

"I like your trousers, Jasper," says Joyce. "They really suit you."

"I found them in the back of a magazine," says Jasper. "Elasticated. And fifteen pounds."

"We're particularly interested in recent calls and texts," says Elizabeth. Joyce can see she is losing patience. Elizabeth has less interest in lonely men than Joyce does. "She died at around nine forty-five last night."

"Nine forty-five last night?" Jasper asks.

"Yes," says Joyce. "We'd been having dinner, I gave her some brownies, not my best."

Brownies! Joyce should have baked some brownies for Jasper. But when would she have had the time? Everything has been such a rush since the wedding. But still, Joyce curses her thoughtlessness.

"If she died at nine forty-five," says Jasper, "then I have a call you might be very interested in. Very interested indeed, I should say. On the interest scale, were it to be numbered one through ten, I might suggest a ten."

"Oh, for God's sake, Jasper," says Elizabeth.

"Your friend Holly Lewis," says Jasper, enjoying the theater, "who died at nine forty-five p.m., made her final phone call last night at nine forty-four p.m."

"Just after she left us?" says Joyce.

"Just after she left you," confirms Jasper. "And just before she met the bomb. Hello, Mr. Bomb. Or Mrs. Bomb. Are bombs men or women, do we think?"

Joyce thinks that perhaps bombs are women. Once they've exploded, that's an end to it. Men are more like guns: they're constantly reloading.

Jasper scrawls down a number on a piece of paper and slides it across to Elizabeth.

"How long was the call?" Elizabeth asks, looking at the number.

"Didn't get connected, but she tried it," says Jasper. "Perhaps she was rudely interrupted, ha, ha, ha. No, I know she died, that's very serious, I apologize." Elizabeth looks at Joyce. "So Holly Lewis was trying to call someone when the bomb went off."

Elizabeth is already calling somebody.

"I'll work on the rest of it this week," says Jasper. "See if I can find anything else useful for you. You came to see me at a good time: it's quite quiet."

There is a cat calendar hanging on the dining-room wall. Jasper's month is empty except for the word BINS written in painfully neat handwriting each Wednesday.

"A number for you," says Elizabeth into her phone. "Could you run it straight away? . . . Well, because I'm asking . . . I'm aware it's a Saturday, Clive . . . I don't even know what the Malaysian Grand Prix Qualifying is . . . Monday morning? For goodness' sake, Clive, you're not the Post Office, you're a spy . . . there's no such thing as an ex-spy . . . tell your wife to turn the potatoes down for a minute . . . Clive Baxter, I need to know who that number belongs to, which will take you a matter of moments; a young woman was killed last night, and your assistance would be greatly appreciated, as I suspect my assistance was greatly appreciated when you were being throttled half to death in Odessa in 1974 . . . Thank you, Clive, yes, I'll hold."

Elizabeth starts pacing. Joyce looks around once again at all the cats. The cats that Jasper hates. The cats that were still here on the off-chance that their absence might offend someone who had bought him one.

"Jasper," says Joyce, gently, "how many people who bought you these over the years are still alive?"

Jasper looks around the collection, assigning a name in his mind to each one. "Well, Cousin John is still knocking about, I suppose, but that would be it."

"And where is Cousin John?"

"New Zealand," says Jasper.

Joyce nods. "Why don't we pack some of them up?"

"Some of the cats?"

"Store them away somewhere," says Joyce. "Then you could really make the place your own, couldn't you?"

Jasper looks around as if seeing it for the first time ever. "A few bookshelves perhaps?"

"Make it a proper dining room," says Joyce. "Invite people over."

"Who would come?" Jasper asks.

"We'd come," says Joyce, indicating Elizabeth. At that moment Elizabeth begins nodding and writing something on a pad.

"That's wonderful work, Clive, wonderful," says Elizabeth. "Jill Usher. Wonderful, thank you. My love to Lady Helen."

"Got the name," says Elizabeth. "Jasper, you'll have to forgive us, we have to rush off."

"Yes, of course," says Jasper. "Of course you must."

"Give me one moment," says Joyce. "Please."

Joyce walks into Jasper's kitchen and finds what she is looking for. Empty cardboard boxes. She hears Jasper saying, "Not too many of the old gang left, are there? You heard Charlie died?"

As she leaves the kitchen, Joyce sees that there are three garish-looking mugs sitting on the worktop. One says I ♥ FISHING; another SOUTHERN ELECTRICITY BOARD CONFERENCE 1998; and the final one WORLD'S BEST GRANDSON. Each has a British Heart Foundation price sticker on it. Next to them, laid out in regimental order, are three tea bags. Joyce has to catch her breath.

Joyce walks back into the dining room with tears in her eyes and two empty cardboard boxes in her hands.

"What on earth are you doing, Joyce?" Elizabeth asks. "We have to head home."

Joyce shakes her head. It's not that she isn't excited by what Elizabeth has found. Holly left their dinner and was making a call when she died. It could open up the whole investigation. But it's not the only important thing in the world. She is not surprised that neither of them has noticed her tears.

"Elizabeth, Jasper has been a very good friend to you, so, until this room is clear, you and I will be putting porcelain cats into cardboard boxes."

"Joyce," says Elizabeth. "We have a job to do."

"We certainly do," says Joyce, handing Elizabeth one of the boxes. "And the sooner you start doing it, the sooner we'll get the train. Jasper, could you make us a cup of tea?"

"Yes, I could," says Jasper, with an excitement that breaks Joyce's heart. He bounds into the kitchen.

Joyce looks over at a scowling Elizabeth, then picks up a cat wearing a headband and holding a tennis racket. She places it carefully into the box. You have to start somewhere.

27

"Mr. Benson," says Davey Noakes.

"Mr. Noakes," says Bill Benson, pulling the cage door shut. "All aboard."

The Compound lift starts to descend. He's an old miner, Bill Benson. A John Grisham pokes out of the pocket of his heavy jacket. Nice enough guy, does twelve-hour shifts down in the deep. You can't get down here without his say-so.

How many times has Davey been down here since he first met Holly and Nick? As many times as Davey has secrets.

And Davey has a lot of secrets.

He looks at his notebook, and smiles. How can forty years ago feel like yesterday?

Davey had been unusual in the late eighties. Most drug dealers, if they kept records at all, kept them in notebooks just like the one Davey is holding right now. Writing down all the numbers, all the deals. Then they'd lock the notebooks away in a drawer, and go to prison for many years when the police found them.

Davey was ahead of the curve though. He kept all his records on a computer. An IBM PS/2. A museum piece these days. People laughed at him, called him all sorts of names, like "The Disco Nerd," but "Ravey Davey" was such a strong nickname it couldn't be toppled.

And Davey had been right. His little computer really was the safest way to keep a secret.

As the years went by, the other criminals caught on. That's the march of progress for you. You'd see armed robbers in East End boozers with copies of *What Computer?* Davey moved to Macs. By the turn of the century everyone was keeping everything on their computers. Log it all in, encrypt it, build a firewall around it, then build another firewall around that. All the way up to around the year 2000, if you knew what you were doing with a computer, the police couldn't touch you.

But then the computers all started talking to each other, and, before you knew it, your phone started talking to your computer, and your fridge started talking to your phone, and you willingly paid for a device that recorded everything you said and sent it to a server farm in the middle of the Nevada desert, just because it was easier than switching the radio on by yourself.

Davey realized before most people that the trusty iMac on his desk in Sussex might as well be in an internet café in Vladivostok. If Davey could break into bank computers in Adelaide and government computers in Kinshasa—and he had done both—he knew that armies of people just like himself anywhere in the world could get inside his computer whenever they chose. Computers were no longer safe.

And so it was that, around twenty years ago now, just when his competitors were buying bigger and fancier computers, confident in their forward-sightedness, Davey bought a stack of notebooks and started writing everything down instead.

The whole thing had gone full circle, and Davey had been ahead of the curve the whole way.

But where do you keep your notebooks?

And then he met Holly and Nick. The two of them were shiny and brand-new in those days, but, most importantly, they knew what he knew: that if you wanted to keep a secret, you didn't keep it on a computer.

Davey liked them, and liked what they were offering.

They'd bought a hole in the ground, and they'd turned it into a gold mine.

The Bitcoin, though, that really was ahead of its time. Davey needed a couple of different safes for a couple of different companies. Always keep everything separate. And for one of the safes the Bitcoin seemed like a neat idea, a cheap workaround, and a fun gamble for them all. When he'd pivoted from party drugs to online fraud, Davey had started getting paid in Bitcoin from time to time. It fascinated him. He wondered if it might fascinate Holly and Nick too. It did. They were canny, and they were happy to take a risk.

Twenty grand was it, at the time? And look at it now?

Holly and Nick must have thought their risk had paid off spectacularly. Their grins when they came to see him. Davey's had a few good paydays in his time, but nothing like three hundred and fifty million. He'd say they were lucky buggers, but they took the risk in the first place, didn't they? So that wasn't luck: that was backing yourself. Perhaps a bit of good fortune too, you always need that, but they had to take the credit.

Either way, that meeting had given Davey an awful lot to think about. How to play it? What move to make? And that's fine, that's part of the job; if being Davey Noakes was easy, anyone could do it, and it wouldn't be half as profitable, would it?

The cage reaches the bottom of the lift shaft, and Bill Benson opens the doors. He ushers Davey out.

"After you, Mr. Noakes."

"Much obliged, Mr. Benson."

They each press their thumbprints in turn on a pad, then scan their retinas, and the door to the vault opens. A small room, containing a couple hundred safes. God knows what was in them, but Davey bets a lot of them contain either a fortune or a prison sentence.

The meeting with Holly and Nick had been on Tuesday. He'd had a day or so to think things through, certainly. To work out his next move.

And then the phone call came. And that was a real stroke of luck for Davey Noakes.

28

Here they all are, then.

"Joanna," says Pauline, "you've always got the loveliest shoes."

"Thank you," says Joanna. "May I say the same about your earrings?"

"Yes," says Joyce, taking off her coat. "You always have the loveliest earrings, Pauline, I don't have the lobes for them. And my feet are too wide for shoes."

"Not all shoes, Mum," says Joanna. "You're wearing shoes."

"No, of course not all shoes," says Joyce. "The sort of shoes I would like. Of course not all shoes, Joanna."

"Why don't dogs wear shoes?" Kendrick asks.

"You took your bleedin' time," says Ron to Elizabeth, as she joins them at the table. Ron's flat is now fit to bursting. Just how he likes it.

"Joyce made me pack cats in boxes," says Elizabeth, and glares over at Joyce, also now taking her seat.

"Cats don't wear shoes," says Kendrick. "The only animals that wear shoes are horses."

Ibrahim leans over to Kendrick. "Though you might say 'shoo' to a cat!"

"That's a really terrific joke, Uncle Ibrahim," says Kendrick.

Ron looks around the table. This is the stuff, isn't it?

This morning, when Ron had said goodbye to Ibrahim and was heading back to his flat, something made him turn around. He couldn't have told you what it was. Why did Ron challenge the chairman of the National Coal

Board to an arm wrestle on live television in 1978? Sometimes you just follow your instincts, don't you?

What he saw when he turned was Ibrahim, standing exactly where he had left him. He was looking one way and then the other, deciding what to do next.

Ron walked back down the hill, as if he'd forgotten something. Ibrahim, lost in thought, didn't notice him until the last moment.

"Ib," Ron had said, "forgot to mention it but Pauline wanted you to come round for dinner this evening. I told her, late notice, he'll be busy, but if I don't ask you, I'll be for it."

"Well, I was . . ." Ibrahim started. "I had a thing, but I suppose nothing that can't be put off. If you think Pauline would be offended?"

"You know women," said Ron.

"Up to a point," said Ibrahim.

Pauline had understood, approved even, and suggested that Joanna and Paul might like to come over too. Elizabeth and Joyce have just returned, apparently with information about Holly's murder. Kendrick's back from a walk with Alan, which might make talking about Holly a bit tricky. But you never knew with Kendrick.

"Two names for you," says Elizabeth. "Donna has given me a number for a man named Bill Benson, aged seventy-seven and with an address in Fairhaven. Might be connected to The Compound. The limited biographical information we have suggests he is a former miner, so, Ron, might we leave him with you?"

"God's own people, miners," says Ron.

"Though if he knows what's locked up in The Compound, who's to say *he* didn't murder Holly?" Elizabeth reminds him.

"A miner?" says Ron. "I doubt it."

"Who got murdered?" Kendrick asks.

"No one, Kenny," says Ron.

"A lady called Holly who'd hidden three hundred and fifty million pounds," says Pauline. "Honestly, Ronnie, he's nine, not three."

"Where has she hidden it?" Kendrick asks.

"Ain't that the question," says Ron. "In a safe somewhere. They reckon there's codes."

"I like codes," says Kendrick.

"You surprise me, Kenny," says Ron.

"So, Ron," says Elizabeth, "Bill Benson will know where The Compound is. And I want him to tell you. Understand?"

"Yes, boss," says Ron. I mean, it's nice to see Elizabeth back at her fighting weight, but Ron had forgotten how rude she could be to him. He'd negotiated in some of Britain's largest ever industrial disputes. And while, if he really thinks about it, he had almost always been unsuccessful, he knows he can handle an interview with a miner about a murder. And, besides, maybe Ibrahim will come with him?

"And the other name?" Ibrahim asks. "Did you find out anything about Davey Noakes or Lord Townes?"

"Nothing," says Elizabeth. "The SIM card was almost a write-off, so nothing on either of them. But we may have found someone much more interesting."

"Holly made a phone call immediately after leaving us," says Joyce.

"Just before she died?" Ibrahim asks.

"Seconds before," says Elizabeth.

"To a woman called Jill Usher," says Joyce. "In Manchester. She's a teacher, like you, Paul . . ."

Joyce nods toward Paul. Ron knows she's keen to include him.

"I mean, I'm a professor of sociology, but, yes," agrees Paul.

"A nursery-school teacher, thirty-five years old, three children. She looks very nice on Facebook. She did a walk for Alzheimer's."

"So Joyce and I will be traveling to Manchester," says Elizabeth. "And in the meantime we need to redouble our efforts to find Nick Silver. I've had people looking into everything he does and everything he owns, and they can't find a trace of him. Paul, you really need to get your thinking cap on. Where might he go?"

"Ibiza?" Paul suggests.

Elizabeth shakes her head. "I've had all the ports and airports watched."

"Face it," says Pauline, "he's probably dead."

"Who's Nick Silver?" Kendrick asks. "And is he really dead?"

"Dead, God, no, he's . . ." Ron stops himself. "He's also hidden all that money, and, yeah, he might be dead too."

"If he's alive, he'll be heading for the money sooner rather than later," says Elizabeth. "Hopefully Bill Benson will take care of that for us. Paul, you're absolutely sure you don't know?"

"Not a clue," says Paul. "Somewhere secure, that's all I know. Nick said if he ever told me, he'd have to kill me. Which, at the time, you know, I thought was a joke."

"Maybe it's underground," says Kendrick. "That's where I'd hide something."

Everyone begins tucking into their food.

Ron looks around the table. It's been a strange year, all in all. They've been waiting for Elizabeth to come back to them. It's a funny old gang he finds himself surrounded by, and the force of Elizabeth's personality is the glue that binds that gang together.

Paul is sitting next to Joyce, and Ron overhears him saying, "I see, and what happened next?"

Kendrick is deep in conversation with Elizabeth, and Elizabeth is nodding seriously. Kendrick might be the only person Elizabeth has ever treated as an equal.

Ibrahim looks happy: he is explaining something to Joanna, and Joanna is saying, "Yes, I'm not sure it's exactly how that works, but you might be right."

Ron puts his hand on Pauline's and gives her a kiss on the cheek.

"This is nice," he says. "Sorry to spring it on you."

"Life is sprung on us, Ronnie," says Pauline. "I like surprises."

"You wanna come and meet this miner with me tomorrow?"

Pauline shakes her head. "I'm doing the lunchtime news. Makeup never sleeps. Maybe take Ibrahim?"

Ron nods now. He will. Bill Benson a miner, eh? And in his late seventies? Must have worked in one of the Kent pits; Ron wonders if they've ever come across each other.

On the other side of the table, Elizabeth is showing Kendrick a picture of Stephen in a locket around her neck, and now Kendrick is nodding seriously.

29

Joyce

Tomorrow we're off to Manchester. I have never been. I've seen it on television, of course, but you never get the full picture, do you? I also once had a colleague from Manchester, and she won the pools and marched into an operating theater and told a particularly unpleasant surgeon to go and eff himself, and then invited us all to join her in the pub after work. Again, it might not be the full picture, but it left an impression.

Elizabeth has told Jill Usher that we are genealogical researchers with exciting news about her family. She has asked me to invent something because she says I'm the one "with the imagination."

What a week it has been. Alan is shattered, and I don't blame him.

Who killed Holly? And have they killed Nick too? I do hope not, that's no start to married life for Paul, is it? It must count as bad luck, surely?

I do fear the worst though. Ibrahim has made us all printouts of the texts that "Nick" sent to Paul. The more you look at them, the more obvious it becomes they are not from him. Which leads to an unfortunate conclusion.

Joanna and Paul have headed back to London. Paul is going to be in touch if they hear from Nick again. He hadn't been as distraught as I imagined he might be over Holly's death. Perhaps they weren't as close as I'd thought. She didn't come to the wedding, so I suppose that tells a story. You can tell he's concerned about Nick though. He's desperate for us to find him. Holly was too, wasn't she?

When it came time for them to leave, I walked them back to Joanna's car, but by that time there was nobody around, so I didn't have the chance to introduce Paul to anyone as "my son-in-law, Paul, the professor," so that will have to wait. Joanna gave me a kiss goodbye and told me that she loves me, and in my head I thought I should say it back, but then I thought, it's so obvious that I love you, and so I just heard myself say, "Well, of course."

Joanna made Paul shine his torch under the car to look for bombs, which I thought was a bit much. He did it very gladly, I have to say. Let's see if he's still happy to check the car for bombs in seven or eight years' time. For example, I like grass to be neat, so Gerry would go out and cut the lawn every Sunday with a big smile on his face. Then, after about five years or so of the smiles, he said, "Do you mind if I skip a week?" He later said, "I've always hated it," and I thought, do you know what, that's fair enough. Well, actually what I did was to go out and cut it myself that first Sunday to prove a point, but discovered he was quite right: it is miserable work. So then he only cut it every three weeks, and I learned to love longer grass.

Anyway, there was no bomb, and they got home safely about half an hour ago. We're off on the early train to see Jill Usher tomorrow, and Ron is heading down to find Bill Benson. He asked Ibrahim to go with him, but Ibrahim said he has someone else to meet. Jason is coming to pick up Kendrick tomorrow morning, so we all said our goodbyes at the door. Poor Alan will be heartbroken when he realizes he's gone. When Joanna's friends used to come for tea, the first thing Joanna would do was to rush upstairs with them to show them her toys, and that's how Alan is with Kendrick, rushing in and out of the room, dropping toys at his feet.

I'm still not entirely sure why Kendrick has been here, and not at home. Perhaps I should ask if everything is okay? Or is that not my business?

In the end Elizabeth rather enjoyed packing away all the cats, I could tell. We helped with some other clutter too and left all the boxes in Jasper's garage. The two of them told war stories as we packed. The day Jasper blew up a bridge, that was one. I drank my tea from the Southern Electricity mug. He didn't have any milk, but one thing at a time, I think.

On the train home Elizabeth fell asleep, which is very unlike her. In the end she had her head on my shoulder, so I couldn't move. But I didn't want to either. My God, the older we all get, the more like children we are.

Sunday

30

"Well, bugger me sideways, it's Ron Ritchie."

Ron had thought that perhaps Bill Benson wouldn't know who he was, but it seems he needn't have worried.

"The very same," says Ron, and nods to an empty seat next to big, bald Bill Benson. "You Bill?"

"How did you know?" asks Bill.

"I can spot a miner a mile off," says Ron. "It's the hands."

Bill indicates that Ron should be his guest, and Ron lowers his frame slowly onto the wooden chair, and his pint onto the wooden table. Bill's neighbors had told him that Bill liked a Sunday drink in the Dove on the seafront.

"This is quite the honor," says Bill. "The next pint's on me."

"We've met, have we?" Ron asks. He loves all this. You get recognized less and less these days. That's understandable. But stick Ron in a proper old pub, with some proper old drinkers, and you'd think Harry Styles had walked in.

"Seventy-four," says Bill. "You wouldn't remember, I was on the picket line at Betteshanger, and you gave a speech that kept us all warm."

Give Ron a crate in those days and he'd stand on it. He can feel the adrenaline now. The crowds, the fists pumping, the flames leaping from oil drums, the sirens. God, Ron loved a picket line.

"I shook your hand," says Bill. "And then a copper hit you with a truncheon."

Ron raises his pint. "Happier times." Bill clinks and agrees.

There's football on the telly and a sea-view out the window. There's a waitress bringing out roast dinners with huge Yorkshire puddings. There's no music, and no one under fifty. It's bliss. Ron could happily pass the day here, five or six Sunday pints, a good natter with a good crowd. But he has a murder to investigate.

What's Bill's connection to The Compound? This solid slab of a man, his features broad and marked, like an open coal face.

"What brings you to the Dove?" Bill asks. "Your boy's in this neck of the woods, isn't he?"

Ron nods. "Jason, yeah. And I'm just up the road, near Robertsbridge."

"Oh yeah," says Bill. "Not in the big old people's home up there?"

"Nah," says Ron, not sure why he's denying it. Perhaps talk of 1974 is making his current age seem absurd. "Not me. And I think they call it a luxury retirement village. No, I came in to see you, Bill."

"Me?" says Bill, enjoying his pint. "The great Ron Ritchie's come to see me?"

Here we go. "To talk about Holly Lewis."

"Holly Lewis." Bill shakes his head. "You're talking to the wrong bloke. I know a Len Lewis, from bowls. Never heard of a Holly Lewis."

Ron looks at Bill Benson. He's a good liar, he'll give him that. But why is he lying?

"You trust me, Bill?"

Bill looks at him and puts his pint down. He takes the briefest of glances over his shoulder.

"Strictly, Ron, I'm not supposed to know Holly," says Bill, "let alone talk about her. You know what I mean?"

"Hush hush?" says Ron.

"Hush hush," agrees Bill.

Ron looks up at the football match on the big screen. Arsenal are playing Man City, and he hopes they both lose. "Tell me about her."

Bill picks his pint up again now. He looks at Ron with more suspicious eyes.

"How's it your business? Sorry, Ron."

In the far corner there's a table of six tucking into their roast dinners. Three couples, one of the women cooing over the gravy, one of the men letting his wife tuck a napkin into his shirt. You'd probably find a photo of the same six somewhere from thirty years ago, tanned and smiling, all raising glasses of sangria to the camera as a Spanish waiter took their photo. There'd be no napkin being tucked in, but the friendships would be the same, and the six of them would swear they hadn't aged until you showed them the photograph.

"First off," says Bill. He's trying to stay calm, Ron can tell. "No one knows I know Holly. And the fact you do know makes me suspicious. Even though it's you. You understand?"

Fair enough, thinks Ron, he'd be the same in the circumstances. How would Ibrahim navigate this conversation? Time to be honest but also to appeal to Bill's better instincts. "Just between us, Billy boy, I heard you might be connected to a place called The Compound?"

Bill shrugs.

"And since Nick Silver disappeared," says Ron, "we've been keen to find it."

"Disappeared?" says Bill, seemingly surprised.

"The day before Holly died," says Ron, looking up at the screen again, "someone put a bomb under his car too, and it's all something to do with The Compound, only we don't know h—"

Ron had a fair old way to go in this speech, but he stops, because he sees a look of profound horror on Bill's face.

"Bomb?" says Bill. He edges closer to Ron and grabs his arm. "Bomb?"

Bill hadn't known Holly was dead; he'd just found out from a blustering Ron. This is why it's always best to bring Ibrahim.

"Someone killed her?" Bill scans Ron's face for some evidence that it isn't true. He doesn't find it. "Holly's dead?"

"We need all the help we can get, Billy," Ron says.

At the big table, the man with the napkin is looking down into his lap, where he has dropped some of his food. His wife picks it off his lap with one hand, while stroking his hair with the other. The other friends continue their conversation around them.

Bill nods at Ron. "I can trust you?"

"I'm Ron Ritchie, of course you can trust me," says Ron.

"No police?" Bill asks.

"No police," says Ron. "Never."

"Okay," says Bill. "Let's go to The Compound."

31

It was your great-great-uncle," says Joyce. "Harry Ablett. He was a magician. He traveled round with circuses in Germany."

"I didn't know any of this," says Jill Usher, a sniffling baby on her lap and two toddlers zooming around her sitting room.

"People so often don't know the first thing about their families," says Joyce. "Elizabeth will tell you the same. We uncover all sorts, and we come and tell lovely people like you and they're amazed. Aren't they, Elizabeth? Aren't they amazed, some of them?"

Elizabeth nods. She has to accept that she'd been the one who had told Joyce to use her imagination. And use her imagination she had. Magicians, circuses. Normally the rule was to keep your cover story as simple as possible. But this was not a rule that Joyce chose to follow.

"He died in a hot-air ballooning accident," says Joyce. "In Sweden."

Jill shakes her head. "All news to me."

Jill Usher. The woman Holly Lewis rang before she died. But why? What was the connection? Today's job was to get as much information as possible.

"Do you have relatives in the south of England, Mrs. Usher?" Elizabeth asks.

Jill shakes her head. "Worked down there for a few years, Brighton, but Manchester born and bred."

Brighton. Possible connection there. Jill must be ten years younger than Holly Lewis, but that's not unusual in friends. Elizabeth would love just to say the name "Holly Lewis," but what if the two aren't, in fact, friends? What if they were quite the opposite, and Jill was involved in Holly's death? The key thing for now is not to spook her. Sometimes you have to unwrap the truth a layer at a time. Elizabeth will be patient.

"So I don't want you to get too excited," says Joyce. She really is loving this. "But he left no children, and his estate is unclaimed, so either it gets spread among his surviving relatives or it goes to the Crown."

Joyce assured Elizabeth that she'd seen a program about unclaimed estates and knows exactly what to say.

"So we'd rather find those relatives," says Joyce, "than let the bloomin' government get their hands on it."

An awful lot of what Joyce says in situations of pressure comes from television.

"And so," says Elizabeth, "the more details you can give us about yourself, the better. Family history and so on. Just helps us fill in the gaps, and makes sure the right money goes to the right people."

Jill nods. "Of course. I'll talk to Mum too—she'll enjoy that."

"It isn't much money," says Joyce. "Especially if we have to spread it around the different branches of the family, but, as I say, we'd rather the family had it than the government. Wasting it on . . . hospitals and what have you."

"Most of the family we've tracked so far are in Sussex," says Elizabeth. "So we might need you to head down at some point."

"That would be fun," says Jill. The baby is now asleep on her lap. A huge crash above their heads tells them the toddlers have gone upstairs.

"Perhaps you still have friends you could stay with from your Brighton days?" Elizabeth asks. Worth a shot.

"One or two," says Jill. That's encouraging. "Do you have any photos?"

"I'm sorry?" says Elizabeth.

"Of my great-great-uncle?"

"No, I'm sorry—"

"Of course we have photos," says Joyce, reaching into her bag. You never knew what was in Joyce's bag. She pulls out a manila folder, instantly recognizable as one of Ibrahim's, and opens it to reveal a series of photocopied pictures of a gentleman in a top hat and Victorian dress standing next to an assistant cut in half in two cabinets. Elizabeth can see Joyce and Ibrahim now, going through the internet to find pictures of Victorian magicians.

In the old days at MI6 you could walk down any given corridor and peek in through open doors and see people up to all sorts of things. A sudden image comes to Elizabeth's mind: Joyce and Ibrahim huddled over one of the old desks, sucking pencils and starting wars.

"How wonderful," says Jill, looking at the photos. "Harry Ablett" is on the same stage each time.

"May I keep these?" Jill asks.

"Of course," beams Joyce. Joyce will tell Ibrahim all about this when she gets home, Elizabeth knows that. "Job done," she'll say.

As Jill looks through the photographs again, a gentle smile on her lips, Elizabeth begins to fear the worst. She's seen criminals of pretty much every size, shape and color over the years, but nothing about Jill is suggesting anything other than quiet Manchester teacher. Which can only mean one thing. Jill Usher and Holly Lewis were good friends, and Elizabeth isn't desperate to be the one to break difficult news. But she has to. Because at least then she can ask a few useful questions, and come back from Manchester with a lead.

Had Jill been expecting a call from her friend?

Would Holly call Jill if she were in trouble?

It must be *something*.

Elizabeth hasn't heard from Ron yet, but hopes he's having more luck with Bill Benson.

As she prepares to mention Holly's name, they hear the front door of Jill's home open. The baby opens her eyes. Or his. Joyce had asked, but Elizabeth hadn't really been listening.

"That'll be Jamie," says Jill. Then she says, leaning into Joyce, "The better half."

A tall man in a faded rugby shirt appears in the room. He looks at Elizabeth and Joyce, and then at his wife.

"They're from the Heir Hunters company," says Jill. "I told you about them."

"Like you see on television," says Joyce.

Her husband nods. "Kids upstairs?"

"In their room," says Jill, then turns to Joyce. "This is Joyce."

You shouldn't give your real name, but Joyce really has a blind spot about remembering what she's supposed to be called, so Elizabeth usually keeps it simple for her.

Joyce smiles, but Jamie Usher does not smile back. "You got cards? Identification?"

"We freelance," says Elizabeth, and extends her hand. Jamie shakes it. She gives him a card. "Let's not disturb the Ushers' Sunday any more than we have already, Joyce."

"It was lovely to meet you," says Jill. "I look forward to hearing from you."

"I'll see you out," says Jamie, and steers Joyce and Elizabeth into the hallway.

Once out of earshot of his wife, he says, "If this is a scam, I'll find out about it, and you'll regret it."

Joyce is slipping on a summer jacket. "Does it look like a scam?"

Jamie looks from Joyce to Elizabeth and has to admit that it doesn't.

"Are you a teacher too, Mr. Usher?"

"I'm not," says Jamie, opening the front door.

Elizabeth pauses on the threshold. "May I ask what you do?"

"No," says Jamie. "You may not."

The door shuts behind them.

32

"Whoever killed her," says Bill Benson, leading Ron down into the cellar in pitch darkness, "this is why."

They are about five miles outside Fairhaven. Ron had worried they were in for a long walk, so was relieved when Bill came to a halt at the bus stop opposite the bookshop on the seafront. They hopped onto the 270, which took the steep coast road west out of Fairhaven. They jumped out by the Branscombe cliffs, busy with walkers and picnickers, turned away from the crowds and made their way across the coast road and into the trees, then down a long track toward a small two-story lodge. They stopped at a fence bearing a sign saying MINISTRY OF DEFENSE LAND—KEEP OUT. Bill keyed in a code on a metal keypad, and a door in the fence swung open. As they continued along the track, Bill pointed out a series of security cameras high in the trees. Eventually they reached the lodge, and Bill keyed in another code.

Walking down the cellar steps, Ron takes a moment to reflect that he is in an isolated house, with no mobile phone coverage, being led into a cellar by a man who, Kent miner or not, he has only just met.

"In for a penny, in for a pound," he says under his breath.

Bill flicks on the light.

Ron is disappointed that there is no great revelation. The cellar is stacked with everything cellars are supposed to be stacked with. There are leaning piles of dusty boxes, planks of wood resting against walls, paint tins crusted around the lids, an old sofa squashed into an alcove and a rusted washing machine in the corner. It is like any cellar anywhere in Britain.

Except, Ron notes, this cellar has extremely expensive video cameras in each corner.

"Sit," says Bill, pointing to the sofa. Ron does so gladly, even the half-mile walk from the bus stop had been enough for him. On the journey, with holidaymakers and locals sitting around them, they gossiped about the usual things: police brutality in the 1970s, whether Jarrod Bowen was a better goalscorer than Tony Cottee, friends with artificial hips. Anything but the murder of Holly Lewis in an instant fireball. Now Bill is ready to talk. He sits down beside Ron.

"We trust each other?"

"It's our best option," says Ron. "I'll tell you everything I know; you tell me everything you know."

"I worked for Holly Lewis," says Bill. "Running security in The Compound."

Ron looks around him. "And is this The Compound?"

Bill shakes his head, laughing. "No, this is a cellar. But this is how you get to The Compound. Takes about half an hour from here."

Ron looks at the ground for trapdoors.

"You won't find anything," says Bill. "Tell me what happened to Holly."

"You don't know anything?" Ron asks.

"I knew I hadn't heard from Holly or Nick for a couple of days," says Bill. "Nick's the other boss. But that's not unusual. Unless there's an appointment they usually leave us in peace."

"Us?" says Ron.

"Me and Frank," says Bill. "Frankie East. Also worked at Betteshanger. We do alternate shifts. He's going to lose it when I tell him I've met you."

"Any reason they employed two old miners to run security?"

Bill nods. "Same reason it'll take you about half an hour to reach The Compound from here. If you want to rob this place, you'd better not be afraid of the dark or tight spaces. Is Nick Silver okay?"

Ron sighs. "Definitely missing. Could be dead—we don't know. There were some texts from his phone, but someone else sent them."

"How do you know that?" Bill asks.

"A car called the Babe Magnet," says Ron. "Don't ask. Nick went missing very early on Friday, so Holly came to see us. Then she dies."

"Jesus Christ," says Bill. "What a mess. Who's in charge here, then?"

Ron shrugs. "You?"

"I don't want to be in charge of anything," says Bill.

"Holly told us there's a lot of valuable stuff in The Compound," says Ron. He sees Bill's eyes flick for the briefest moment to the rusty washing machine in the corner of the cellar. So that's the way in, is it? Leading to some sort of tunnel? Clever. Elizabeth will be impressed with his observation skills. Ron would love to be Columbo, he really would.

"I can't say," says Bill. "All that stuff I can't tell you."

"She also said that she and Nick have got something down there," says Ron. "And Nick Silver thought someone was after it."

Bill shakes his head. "No one could get anything from down there. Do you know when Holly's funeral will be?"

Ron will ask Paul. "I'll let you know."

"Thanks, Ron," says Bill. "They've got a unit down there, Holly and Nick. But I've been here ten years and I've never seen them open it."

"We know they had two codes to get in," says Ron. "Nick had six numbers and Holly had six numbers. What if someone got hold of those numbers somehow? What's stopping them coming down here and opening the box?"

"Well, they'd have to find the place," says Bill. "That's the first thing."

"But a client would already know where it is?"

"True," says Bill. "But if they get down there and I see them opening the wrong box, I lock the whole place down."

"You could just nick it yourself," says Ron.

"I can't get into the vault without a client," says Bill. "That's the only time me or Frank are allowed in. Retinal scans on the client, and one on me. Thumbprints from the client; thumbprints from me."

"A client could come down with a gun," suggests Ron. "And force you to help."

"Full body scanners," says Bill. "I can see the scans from downstairs, and, if I don't like what I see, I don't send the cage up."

"I bribe you, then," says Ron. "Or I bribe Frank? I'm a client, I know you. You let me in, turn a blind eye when I open the wrong box, you take me back up, I split the proceeds with you."

"Try it," says Bill. "See where it gets you."

Ron has always been good at thinking like a criminal. It's second nature. "So I'm an existing client, I've got my hands on Holly's code and Nick's code, I've bribed, let's say Frank and not you. What's stopping me coming in tomorrow night and stealing Nick and Holly's money?"

Bill thinks for a long while. "Nothing. Except that's a lot of ifs."

"Okay," says Ron. "Okay, at least we know. If a client makes an appointment in the next few days, you'd know? Would it usually be on your shift or Frank's?"

"Most appointments are on my watch," says Bill. "But some people are night birds. I've got one in a couple of days' time."

"Got a name?" Ron asks.

"Lord Townes," says Bill Benson. "Ain't seen him in yonks, but a nice enough fella."

Nice enough fella, thinks Ron. Elizabeth will have something to say about that. It's too much of a coincidence, surely?

"And you can't show me down there?" Ron asks.

"We'd need a client with us," says Bill. "The only way you could get down there is to persuade a client to bring you along, and persuade me to let you accompany them."

The two men go quiet for a moment.

"What have they got in their box?" Bill asks. "Holly and Nick?"

"Something worth stealing," says Ron. "Is there any way you can change their code? Something like that?"

Bill shakes his head. "Only Holly and Nick could change it."

"So it's just sitting there?" says Ron.

"I mean, behind about fifty doors, and retinal identifiers and fingerprint scans," says Bill. "But, apart from that, yeah, it's just sitting there."

"Thanks for trusting me," says Ron.

Bill nods. "Thanks for trusting me. Jesus, I can't believe she's dead. Who did it?"

Isn't that the question? Ron is thinking.

The two men are alone with their thoughts for a minute.

"We need to get that box open," says Ron. "Before someone else does."

"Well, best of luck, Ronnie," laughs Bill. "You need four things. Me, Holly's half of the code, Nick's half of the code and a client. And so far all you've got is me."

"Bill," says Ron, putting his hand on the big man's shoulder, "remember the strike in 1974? Everyone against us. The government, the coppers, the courts? Powerful people. Bullies. They threw everything at us, and we never buckled, we never raised the white flag, and we never gave in."

Bill nods, heartened, then has another thought. "I mean, we did lose though."

"Course we lost," says Ron. "We always lost. But we gave it a bloody good go, eh?"

33

Connie Johnson sits cross-legged on a coconut mat, eyes closed. One way or another it has been a stressful week, and she is enjoying the "Sounds of the Rainforest" playlist on Spotify. She has had to take out a premium subscription now, because you can't meditate when the sounds of the rainforest are interrupted every fifteen minutes by adverts for Burger King Whopper Meal Deals.

She breathes in slowly through her mouth and counts to three, then breathes out slowly through her nose for a count of six. A lot of people are resentful that she is back on the street. She'd been able to control her empire fairly well from her prison cell. The Wi-Fi could be patchy at times, due to the thickness of prison walls, but, all in all, deliveries arrived when they were supposed to, suppliers were paid on time and cash continued to be laundered in an orderly fashion. But the odd two or three dealers had got ideas above their station during her unfortunate absence, and she is having to deal with them one by one, which has been time-consuming, and stressful. More stressful for them, Connie admits that, but she has still earned a bit of down time in her yoga annex. Though she doesn't often have two guests with her.

"And find your center," Connie says. "Find your center, and let a flower bloom. Let the petals unfurl and catch the sun. Feel the warmth and feel the beauty. Let your mind drift on the breeze. Let your thoughts fade into nothing."

She hears Tia hum in contentment.

"I understand the principle," says Ibrahim, also cross-legged. "But I can't let my thoughts fade into nothing without thinking about my thoughts fading into nothing, so I now have a new thought in my head, the thought of thoughts fading to nothing, and what am I to do with that thought? It's cyclical."

Connie opens her eyes. "You don't love being 'in the moment,' do you, Ibrahim?"

"I don't," says Ibrahim. "The trouble with the moment is that there's always another moment on its way, and I find constantly being in them exhausting."

"Truth," says Tia.

"But you tell me all the time to relax," says Connie. "To find a new way of thinking and being."

"Yes, I think it's all well and good for other people," says Ibrahim. "I just can't manage it myself."

Connie is not entirely sure what Ibrahim is doing here today. Has she ever seen him on a Sunday before? She doesn't think so. But he asked to pop round, and she'd told him he'd be very welcome if he didn't mind joining her and Tia for a spot of yoga as they talked.

Connie pushes herself up. "How about a whisky?"

"I think that might be rather better at making my petals bloom, thank you, Connie."

Connie leads them out of the yoga annex, past the pool and solarium, skirts the snooker room, and takes a shortcut through the cinema and into the whisky bar.

"You have a lot of rooms," says Ibrahim.

"I've sold a lot of drugs," says Connie, stepping behind a bar and pouring them both a measure. "Tia?"

"Gotta go," says Tia. "Bit more prep for the job."

"That's very industrious," says Ibrahim. "Preparing for your job on a day off."

Tia shrugs.

"Fail to prepare," says Connie, "prepare to fail."

"I hope the job is going well so far?" says Ibrahim.

"It's coming on," says Tia.

Ibrahim smiles. "I'm sure you will be a great success."

Ibrahim is so excited about Tia's new job. He would be less excited if he knew the job was a warehouse heist, but what we don't know can't harm us.

Tia gives Connie a goodbye hug. "I'll see you on Tuesday."

"I'll be waiting," says Connie.

"See you, Mr. Arif," says Tia.

"Don't be afraid to ask if you don't know something," says Ibrahim.

"Thank you," says Tia. "I will."

They watch Tia leave, and the moment she is out of earshot Ibrahim says, "She'll make you proud, I know it."

She'll make me a couple of hundred grand is what she'll make me, thinks Connie.

"When she calls me Mr. Arif, I always mean to say, 'Call me Ibrahim,' but I've decided I quite like 'Mr. Arif.' Usually only doctors call me Mr. Arif. The last sentence in which somebody called me Mr. Arif was 'One has to expect some weakening of bladder control in one's eighties, Mr. Arif.'"

"What can I do for you today?" says Connie. "I'm not sure I've ever seen you on a Sunday, so I'm guessing it's a favor?"

"Well, life is about push and pull," says Ibrahim. "There might indeed be the smallest favor you could do for me."

"Shoot," says Connie. "Shoot" is a phrase she often has to be careful with. If you're ever in a room full of men with guns and someone wants to give you their number, it's better to say "Go ahead" than "Shoot."

Ibrahim looks over his shoulder. "Have you heard of a man named Davey Noakes?"

"Ravey Davey?" says Connie. "Of course I've heard of him, I don't live on the moon."

"Ah," says Ibrahim. "I hadn't."

Connie shakes her head. "Forty years in the business, Ravey had, and you've never heard of him?"

"I think you might be the only drug dealer I've ever heard of," admits Ibrahim. "We live such siloed lives, don't we? It's social media in my view, it atomizes our shared gr—"

Connie interrupts: "What about him?"

"You know him?"

"Met him a few times," says Connie. "Not your type, I'd say, but I can put in a word for you. Some guys like an older man."

"You are obsessed with romance," says Ibrahim. "He dealt Ecstasy, I understand?"

Connie Johnson shakes her head in amazement. "Dealt Ecstasy? Saying Davey Noakes dealt Ecstasy is like saying that Taylor Swift sells records."

"I see," says Ibrahim. "And does she?"

"He was a pioneer," says Connie. "Built the whole industry from scratch. Made his millions, never got nicked, got out before everybody started killing each other. Textbook drug dealer, textbook. You won't see another like him."

"And what did he turn his hand to afterward?" Ibrahim asks.

"Cyber stuff," says Connie. "Passwords, I don't know. But he's still making plenty of money."

"And how did your paths cross?" Ibrahim asks.

"I wrote him a fan letter once," says Connie, "and he wrote back, which, you know, he didn't have to. And I went to a charity ball at his house—there were police, criminals, everyone. Bradley Walsh was there, you know from the TV?"

Ibrahim nods. "Finally someone I *have* heard of."

"Why the interest?" Connie asks.

"Have you heard of a place called The Compound?"

"Of course I have," says Connie. The Compound, of all places. She wasn't expecting that today. What has Ibrahim got himself involved with?

"It was run by two friends of ours," says Ibrahim. "Holly Lewis and Nick Silver. I say 'friends'—Nick vomited at a wedding and Holly died shortly after meeting us."

"Sorry for your loss," says Connie.

"Anyway," says Ibrahim, "they met up with Davey Noakes not long before Holly Lewis's murder."

"Any idea what about?" Connie asks.

"I believe they had a security issue," says Ibrahim. "They called upon the counsel of two individuals and Davey was one."

"Well, that's Davey," says Connie. "He can cause your security issues or he can solve them, depending who he works for."

Ibrahim nods. "I wonder if I might ask two further questions?"

"Go right ahead," says Connie.

"Thank you," says Ibrahim. "Do you think that Davey Noakes is the sort of person who, under a certain set of circumstances, might murder someone?"

Connie laughs. "Of course."

Ibrahim nods. "And, secondly, are you a client of The Compound yourself?"

Connie tongs a couple of ice cubes into both drinks, and considers him. "Shall we retire to the cinema room? Anything you fancy watching?"

"Anything you recommend?"

"Do you watch *Below Deck*?" Connie asks.

"Jog my memory," says Ibrahim.

"It's a reality show following the crew of a super-yacht," says Connie.

"I have yet to catch it," says Ibrahim.

Connie leads Ibrahim into the darkness of the cinema room, two rows of four velvet armchairs all facing a huge screen. Ibrahim and Connie take seats in the front row, and she sees Ibrahim tilt his seat back.

"So are you?" says Ibrahim. "A client? You have things which require cold storage?"

"I'm a criminal," says Connie. "I use cold storage, hot storage, encasing-something-in-concrete-and-dumping-it-in-the-sea storage. My whole job is storage. Money, drugs, evidence, information."

"But The Compound specifically," says Ibrahim. "You use it? You could get into it?"

"Huh," says Connie. "Do you worry sometimes about our boundaries? As therapist and client?"

She has been reading about boundaries.

"I think you and I make our own rules," says Ibrahim. Connie loves that he makes stuff up as he goes along. Ibrahim's wisdom is artfully seasoned by self-interest. That's why they get along. "I, because I'm older, and have earned the right to make my own rules, and you, because you adhere to rules very badly. So our boundaries are porous."

Porous boundaries. Sure, thinks Connie. Whatever Ibrahim needs to tell himself. He speaks to a drug dealer every week, and he enjoys it. He disapproves of everything Connie does, and yet back he comes, like a dog to a favorite tree.

"The Compound's not really something I can speak to you about," says Connie. She really does need to shut this down if she can. "The less you know about it, the better."

"It's just two friends talking," says Ibrahim. "We are friends, I hope?"

For a clever man, Ibrahim can be very transparent. He wants Connie to talk about The Compound; Connie doesn't want to. He has approached her directly, and been rebuffed directly, and so she now has a whole afternoon of Ibrahim trying different tacks to get the information he wants. He has begun with flattery, but that's not where he will end. He will be insufferable. Connie doesn't want him getting tangled up with The Compound. Too many bad people, even for her. But if Ibrahim really wants to know something, there are very few places where she can hide from him.

"I'll make you a deal," says Connie. "If you can make it through an episode of *Below Deck* with me, I'll help you get into The Compound."

Ibrahim swishes his whisky around in its tumbler. "If I say yes, can we have more whisky?"

"We can," says Connie.

"Then it's a deal," says Ibrahim. "Let's get this *Below Deck* nonsense out of the way and then we can talk."

34

"She texted me a name," says Donna. "Jill Usher. Asked if I could look into her."

"But it's not your case, Donna," says Chris. "It's DCI Varma's case."

"She died at Coopers Chase," says Donna, as Patrice fills her wine glass. "Elizabeth was the first to reach the body. That makes it our case, morally, although, yeah, not actually. I should have a poke around at least."

"So you're going to do what Elizabeth tells you to do?" Chris asks.

"For now," says Donna. "Maybe when you're armed we'll be able to stand up to her."

"If you start investigating," says Patrice, dipping a carrot baton in some hummus, "who's going to look after Prince Edward?"

"That's the thing—Elizabeth knew I was bored," says Donna, sheepishly. "We broke into an office, and that was fun."

"Honestly," says Chris. "I leave you alone for one week."

It is a lovely, sleepy Sunday evening. Patrice has cooked a roast chicken, and Donna can smell it in the oven. Her mum has virtually been living with Chris over the summer holidays. Are her boss and her mum going to get married one of these days? Donna will cross that bridge when she comes to it. Chris has been regaling them both with tales of his firearms course.

At first he'd said he's been firing guns all week, but after a couple of glasses of wine he admitted that he's mainly been sitting in lectures being told how to avoid firing guns under any circumstances. But then they do have target practice.

"Be careful though," says Chris.

"You're jealous Elizabeth asked me to help, and not you."

"Not my case," says Chris. "Let someone else deal with the Thursday Murder Club for once. I've got guns to fire."

Donna raises an eyebrow.

"Okay, I've got lectures about firing guns to go to."

"I'll be careful, I promise," says Donna. "Won't tread on anyone's toes. If I find out something about Jill Usher, I'll pass it on, but that's it. She was squeaky clean at first glance though."

"And that's it?" Chris asks.

"That's it," says Donna.

"She's hasn't asked you to do anything else?"

"Not a thing," says Donna.

"Not even a tiny extra favor?"

"I mean," says Donna, shrugging, "she wondered if I could talk to Joanna's husband."

"She wants you to talk to Paul Brett?"

"Well, she can't," says Donna. "In case Joyce finds out."

"And you're going to do it?"

"You could come with if you fancied?" Donna says. "When your course is done?"

"I'm fine, thanks," says Chris.

"You must be a bit tempted to help?" says Patrice.

"Help the Thursday Murder Club?" says Chris.

"You love them," says Patrice. "You miss them. I think you once called out 'Joyce' in your sleep."

"Let me tell you a story," says Chris.

"Oh, fabulous, if you would," deadpans Patrice, and she and Donna laugh.

"A couple of months ago," says Chris, "Donna and I get a call. First thing in the morning. A garage owner in Rye has been found dead in his workshop. Nasty bang on the head, been hit by something a couple of hours before. Murder, no doubt about it."

"And you're saying Elizabeth did it?" Patrice suggests.

Chris ignores her. He's on a roll. "We visit the workshop, Donna and me. Scenes of crime are there, and they find nothing they can use, so we're probably dealing with a professional. Back we head to the office, and do our usual digging. Watkins, the guy was called: is he on our radar, who does he know, who might have a motive? And we draw another blank. Happens all the time."

"That chicken smells amazing, Mum," says Donna.

"The secret is to kill it yourself," says Patrice. "Go on, darling, you were saying?"

"So no forensics and no intelligence. Fine. A bit of old-fashioned police work, then. We go door-to-door—"

"Well, I went door-to-door," says Donna.

"That's true," says Chris. "Rank has certain privileges. Donna goes door-to-door with a little crew, but no one has heard anything, so everybody trudges back to the station. We're having our lunch and one of the junior PCs says he was harangued for twenty minutes by an elderly woman whose door he knocked on. She'd had her milk stolen that morning, and what was he going to do about it? The PC explains that he's investigating a murder and her milk isn't top of his priority list, and she whacks him with a walking stick and says, 'What about my Crunchy Nut Cornflakes?' which gets the laugh he was looking for."

"I can feel a lesson coming on," says Patrice.

Chris nods. "You're right. I'm listening to this PC, and I look at Donna. I want to get her attention, but she's already looking at me. The two of us get up from the table, drive back to Rye and pay another visit to the woman with the stolen milk. She's delighted we're taking it seriously and invites us in. We ask what time her milk is usually delivered, and she says five thirty in the morning. We ask her if she has CCTV and she says no, but the neighbor across the road does."

"She said, 'Because he's a pervert,'" adds Donna.

"Over we pop and take a look, and there's a man coming from the direction of Watkins's garage at about quarter to six in the morning, all in black, gloves, you know the drill. He spots the milk on the doorstep, trots up and pinches it. As he walks back down the driveway, we get a clear shot of his face. Surely that's our guy?"

"What has this got to do with the Thursday Murder Club?" Patrice asks.

"We circulate the screenshot from the CCTV," continues Chris. "And a DI in Worthing gets in touch and says, I know this guy, Johnny Jacks, record as long as your arm, muscle for hire, GBH, all sorts, so off we go and talk to Johnny Jacks. He's quiet, as they always are. Never heard of Watkins, never heard of Rye, only reluctantly admits he's heard of milk. We search his car, and there's a receipt for a petrol station just outside Rye, and there's a hammer covered in Watkins's DNA."

"There was even an empty milk bottle," says Donna.

"So we arrest him, we charge him, he's on remand, and when he comes to trial he's going to prison for a long time. And all because we figured that the sort of man who'd murder in cold blood is also the sort of man who'd steal a bottle of milk from a doorstep."

"Congratulations," says Patrice. "That's terrific work."

"Thank you," says Chris. "But I tell this story for one reason only. This year I've been involved in eight murder investigations. Solved five of them, know who did two of them but I'm still looking for evidence. A lot of hard work, a lot of wrong turns, a lot of late nights. But in that time, not once have I been visited by any pensioners demanding information from me, hiding evidence from me, intellectually undermining me, or in any other way interfering in any murder investigation. And, I'll be honest, I haven't missed it, and I haven't missed them."

Chris sits back. He looks exhausted. Point made.

Donna and Patrice look at each other.

"Yeah, you have," says Patrice.

"You have," agrees Donna.

"Donna," says Chris, "you do Elizabeth's bidding if you want. But I'm made of stronger stuff. I'm a good investigator—I don't need the Thursday Murder Club to help me."

"What if they need you to help them?" Donna asks.

"They never need me to help them," says Chris.

Matter closed.

"Anyway, he's too busy shooting guns with the boys," says Patrice.

"There's a woman there too," protests Chris.

"Let me guess," says Donna. "You all underestimated her and it turned out she's the best shot of the lot of you?"

"I don't want to be gendered about it," says Chris. "But she's actually coming joint twelfth out of fifteen."

"And where are you?" Donna asks.

"Also joint twelfth," says Chris. "I'd be eighth, but I shot a mum pushing a pram instead of a terrorist."

Monday

35

Bogdan has insisted on driving them and waiting outside.

Joyce honestly can't see the point. "We could have got a taxi, Bogdan. You don't need to give up your morning for us."

"I wait," says Bogdan. "In case he kills you."

"He's not going to kill us," says Joyce. "He's a lord."

"What about Lord Lucan?" says Bogdan. "He killed someone. I saw a documentary."

"I once met Lord Lucan," says Elizabeth.

"How long before the murder?" asks Bogdan.

"Oh, it was after the murder," says Elizabeth, at which point Bogdan turns into the driveway of Headcorn Hall.

The house squats before them at the end of the long driveway. The driveway itself is starting to lose the battle with the nature around it, weeds and wild flowers poking through the gravel. Joyce wonders why the gardeners haven't taken care of that. You wouldn't see a weed on *Downton Abbey*. The grasslands around the house have also seen better days, but perhaps Lord Townes is an environmentalist and goes for the "untamed" look. A lot of very rich people are environmentalists now. Ron says it's the ones who can't afford helicopters anymore. It was Ron who told them Lord Townes had booked in for a visit to The Compound on Wednesday morning. Elizabeth is keen to meet him before he goes.

Joyce is hoping that a butler might greet them outside. Not that she would say it out loud, but on the journey down, as Elizabeth and Bogdan were talking about the best things to do if you got kidnapped, Joyce imagined a butler with a deep voice who had served the Townes family for generations and been unable to find love, after a doomed, fleeting romance with a scullery maid forty years earlier made him close his heart. Many years later the man—Henderson perhaps, Phillips, Brabazon—meets a woman in a mauve cardigan, and is transported back in time. Nothing is said, but there is a glance, a stolen look, and, as she leaves, he bows his head and says, "Madam," and she bows her head and says, "Henderson." What happens after that is a mystery, as she'd fallen asleep, to be woken by Elizabeth saying, "The key thing if you're tied up in the boot is to kick out the brake lights."

As they crunch to a halt, Joyce sees there is no Henderson, so there goes that little dream. Lord Townes himself has come out to greet them. Of course there could be a fantasy in which Joyce marries a lord, but that is a lot less likely than a butler, and probably a lot less fun. Joyce resolves to make do. Meeting a lord is quite exciting in itself.

"You must be Elizabeth Best and Joyce Meadowcroft," says Lord Townes. "What an enormous pleasure."

"Lord Townes," says Elizabeth, and shakes his hand. Joyce curtsies.

"No need for any nonsense," says Lord Townes, grasping Joyce's hand. "Come on in the both of you. I'm Robert to friends, and I can tell we're going to be friends, so I'm Robert to you. Does your driver need anything?"

"Bogdan?" says Elizabeth, looking back at the car. "No, he's going to listen to a podcast about the fall of Carthage."

Lord Townes escorts them through an immense oak front door into a hallway lit with one small bulb. Joyce sees portraits and rugs and vases scattered around, but she also sees a lot of dust and peeling wallpaper, and, on this summer's day, feels an instant chill. Lord Townes—apologies, Robert—shows them into a drawing room, and Joyce sits in the cleanest chair she can find.

"I would offer you tea," says Lord Townes, "but the kitchen is a very long way away. You say this is about Nick Silver?"

"Yes," says Elizabeth.

"He was my son-in-law's best man," says Joyce. "My son-in-law, Paul, he's a professor."

"Well, I know Holly Lewis better than I know Nick Silver," says Lord Townes, "but do fire away."

Through an open double doorway to her right Joyce can see a snooker table with a stained cover on it, and a stag's head sticking out of an oak-paneled wall. The stag is missing an eye.

"They asked to see you," says Elizabeth. "Last week. May I ask what about?"

"May I ask why you want to know?" Lord Townes says. "It was a private conversation."

"Somebody killed Holly Lewis," says Elizabeth. "And Nick Silver has disappeared."

"Holly has been killed?" Lord Townes looks like the victim of a prank.

"I thought you might already know," says Elizabeth. "Car bomb."

"No," says Lord Townes. "Impossible, no."

Joyce doesn't believe him. Lord Townes already knew this information.

"What did you speak about?" Elizabeth asks.

"You are quite serious?" Lord Townes asks.

"Robert, you know who I am," says Elizabeth. "You know my background."

Lord Townes had rung someone "very high up" before agreeing to meet them. That person had immediately rung Elizabeth.

Lord Townes nods.

"We would very much like to find Nick Silver, and find the person who killed Holly," says Elizabeth.

Joyce keeps getting distracted by the stag with one eye. Poor thing.

"What do you know?" asks Lord Townes. "I will fill in whatever else I can."

"Holly and Nick run The Compound," says Elizabeth. "They came to you for advice about a financial matter, a very large sum of money in cryptocurrency, which they had been holding for many years, and had finally decided to cash out."

"That's the long and short of it," agrees Lord Townes.

"Why did they come and see you?" Joyce asks.

"My whole career," says Lord Townes, "such as it was, was banking. City banking, you know, the blue-chip stuff. I understand they also had advice from people who might know more about the modern side of things. Davey Noakes? He is on your radar, I hope?"

"He is," says Elizabeth.

"But I think they also wanted to talk to someone who could connect them with a few old hands they could trust. There is a lot of trickery in the world of cryptocurrency, and I think that, at some point, they wanted to talk to someone in a suit."

"And they told you how much was at stake?" Elizabeth asks.

"Somewhere north of quarter of a billion," says Lord Townes. "That was my understanding? To a banker, not an immense amount of money, but to two individuals, certainly enough to focus the mind."

Looking out of a huge bay window, Joyce sees that a light fog has settled across the garden.

"And what advice did you give them?" Elizabeth asks.

"I promised I would arrange some meetings for them, once the money had become liquid," says Lord Townes.

"And did you speak to anyone?" Elizabeth asks.

"I spoke to a few old friends in the City," says Lord Townes. "But I gave no names, no pack drill, just said a couple of friends have had an unexpected windfall, how do you fancy it?"

"So no mention of The Compound," says Elizabeth. "And no mention of Holly and Nick and the amount at stake?"

"I told them it would be worth their while," says Lord Townes. "But nothing else."

"And did you hear from Nick or Holly again after your meeting?"

"Only a note of thanks from Holly, and let's catch up next week," says Lord Townes. "I was preparing a document for her, a few runners and riders and what have you."

"You're very kind to help us, Robert," says Elizabeth. She will have noticed everything that Joyce has noticed. A man with a big house, and not enough money to keep it, suddenly informed of a large fortune. "What is your take on the thing?"

"Oh, we didn't discuss a fee," says Lord Townes. "But the usual—"

"No, sorry," says Elizabeth. "Your take on the matter at hand. On Holly's murder?"

"Well, it's a conundrum, isn't it?" says Lord Townes. "Games are being played."

"But the coincidence?" Elizabeth says.

"The coincidence?"

"That Holly and Nick decide to cash out after so many years, and a matter of days after first telling people of their decision one of them is killed and the other disappears?" Elizabeth gives him a terrifyingly neutral look. "That coincidence?"

Lord Townes sits back, and Joyce can see he is considering Elizabeth through new eyes. He smiles and looks down.

"Your supposition, I suppose," he says, motioning to his shabby surroundings, "is that a man running low on money and luck suddenly finds a mine full of the stuff right under his feet?"

"It's certainly one way of looking at it," says Elizabeth. "To a suspicious mind."

Lord Townes nods. "How do bankers make their money?"

Joyce has often wondered. Ron once told her, but he becomes quite hard to follow the angrier he gets.

"Money sloshes around," says Lord Townes. "Great globs of it haring here and there. Peter paying Paul, Paul paying Mary, Mary leveraging a buyout of Harry's company, Harry converting his debt into equity. Around it all swirls. And at the heart of it are bankers, shaking hands, introducing Peter to Paul, and Mary to Harry, and every time that money moves or transforms or grows, they take a tiny piece. A tiny piece from Paul, a tiny piece from Peter, all day, every day, until they can ski down their very own mountain of money."

This was different to how Ron explained it, Joyce is certain of that.

"So here's the way to look at the thing," says Lord Townes. "Holly Lewis and I had developed a relationship of trust over a number of years. Enough trust that when she had a big decision to make, she knew she could come to me. Did you meet Holly?"

"We did," says Elizabeth.

"Did you take her for a fool?"

"We did not," says Elizabeth.

"And Holly presents me with an opportunity. To broker a deal worth more than a quarter of a billion pounds. On which I would earn, and you can ask people familiar with deals such as this, a fee of around three percent. So you see"—Lord Townes sits forward now—"a deal which fell straight into my lap, in which all I would have to do is pick up a phone, put on a suit and get on a train to London, would net me somewhere around ten point five million. And that deal, it seems, might be about to go up in smoke. If you will pardon the expression."

Elizabeth nods. "Of course banking doesn't always work that way, Robert, as you well know. It doesn't always nibble around the edges of the cake, leaving everyone else enough to eat. Sometimes it sacks the baker and keeps the cake all for itself."

"Not my kind of banking," says Lord Townes. "I honestly think that Davey Noakes might be more fertile ground for you."

"Although of course you would say that," offers Elizabeth.

"And with good reason, Mrs. Best," says Lord Townes. "Because you are talking to a man who may just have lost a ten point five million pound deal."

Joyce looks out of the window again, and decides she has a question too.

"And you're also a client of The Compound?"

"Safest place in the country," says Lord Townes.

"And what do you keep in there?" Joyce asks.

"Well, forgive me," says Lord Townes, "but that's my business. Something valuable though, like everyone else."

Something valuable. That's interesting. When Joyce looked out of the bay window again, she had realized there was no fog on the lawn; it was simply that the bay window had not been cleaned in a long time.

"And are you planning to visit anytime soon?" Elizabeth asks.

"I am not," lies Lord Townes. Joyce and Elizabeth don't even share a glance. They know what they know. "You're assuming that someone is after the money? The whole lot?"

"It's a working hypothesis," says Elizabeth.

"If someone is trying to steal this money, it has to be someone who knows it exists," says Lord Townes. "It certainly isn't me, I'm a hopeless liar. Which leaves you with only two options. One, Davey Noakes. And two—"

"Nick Silver," says Elizabeth.

"Who, you tell me, has conveniently disappeared," says Lord Townes, standing. "So take your pick. One of two."

It seems the meeting is over. Lord Townes has been charm itself, but, as Joyce takes a final look at the stag with one eye, and the lord who has just lied about his visit to The Compound, she knows that he's their third option.

The only thing Joyce can be sure of is that the butler didn't do it. Because there is no butler.

36

When you're killing more than one person, the order matters.

There had once been an Albanian gang who operated in and around Gatwick Airport. Three brothers. One an accountant, one a cage fighter and one a certifiable lunatic. Classic set-up, all bases covered.

These three brothers had transgressed some code or other, skimming money off the top of a heroin shipment, something like that, Danny forgets the details. All he remembers was that a price had been put on their heads, and a guy Danny used to know from karate got the job. Callum was his name, God rest his soul.

Ideally you'd want to kill all three at once, but, for various logistical reasons—it was the school holidays, Danny remembers—they weren't all going to be in the same place anytime soon. So Callum kills the cage-fighter brother in his local gym, and the accountant brother in Center Parcs (the Longleat one, Danny thinks) and heads up to the Lake District to kill the certifiable maniac, who is on a walking holiday. While on the journey up, the maniac brother gets word that the cage-fighter brother has been killed. He doesn't love the news, but cage fighters get killed all the time, so he doesn't want it to spoil his holiday. He then gets the news that the accountant brother has also been killed, which can mean only one thing. Someone is coming for all three brothers.

He puts a status update on Facebook, showing the cottage he and his wife are staying in, and waits for Callum to arrive. When the dust had settled, Callum's head was in Lake Windermere, his torso was in Coniston

Water and his legs and arms had been sent by FedEx to his parents. The brother was back in Albania, and later died climbing Everest for charity.

There was some sympathy for Callum, of course—his ordeal, it later transpired, had lasted several days—but really he had to take some of the blame on himself. It was widely discussed, and agreed, that he should have killed the maniac brother first: nice, isolated cottage, kill the wife too, then tootle back down to Sussex and kill the cage fighter, and then a quick hop west to Longleat to pick off the accountant. Even if the accountant had got wind that his brothers had been killed, he simply would have flown back to Albania, without taking the trouble to kill and dismember Callum first.

All this goes to say that Danny is going to have Jason Ritchie killed before he has Suzi killed.

He has taken a Jet Ski along the coast and moored it at Playa de Bahínas. There's a restaurant on the beach that hauls seafood straight from the fishing boats and grills it over an open fire, with olive oil and lemon straight from the mountainous slopes overlooking the sand. It also serves burgers, though, and that's what Danny is having.

"When can you do him?" Danny asks, squirting ketchup into his bun.

The man looks at his watch and gives it some thought. "Tomorrow?"

Danny nods. "And where?"

"His house is tucked away," the man says. "I'll take round an Amazon delivery that needs signing for."

Amazon deliveries have been the single greatest boon for professional hitmen. Everyone is always expecting one.

"Then straight round to the next target?" Danny says.

The man nods. "She does the school run at three. I'll wait outside the house."

Danny hands the man an envelope. "Here's the first ten thousand."

The man tucks it into his jacket pocket.

"I'll see you here on Wednesday for the next twenty," says Danny. "Make it quick and make it clean."

The man nods. "Don't Callum it."

"Exactly."

Danny takes a bite of his burger. It's a bit cold in the middle, but it's still good. All being well, he'll get the call from the police—your wife's dead, come and identify the body, etc.—and he can fly home on Wednesday evening with the perfect alibi.

He can sell the house ("too many memories"), leave the boy with his grandad and see a bit of the world. Expand his horizons. Since he arrived here, he's already met a Moroccan counterfeiter and a German guy who sells fake vitamins on the internet. Travel broadens the mind.

The man stands, and they shake hands.

"Should have done this a long time ago," says Danny.

"See you Wednesday," says the man.

37

On Thursdays they still meet in the Jigsaw Room. But today is not a Thursday, so they are meeting in the hot tub. Ron's choice.

It's not often that Ron gets his way, but today he has. He supposes he's simply in everyone's good books because of the Lord Townes tip-off.

Ron is drinking a pint, Ibrahim has a mineral water and a plate of olives, Elizabeth has one of the protein shakes that Bogdan has got her addicted to, and Joyce is drinking a steaming-hot cup of tea.

"Here's how I see it," says Ron. "Yeah, maybe Ravey Davey's done it, he's got form. And maybe Townesy's done it—"

"Don't call him Townesy," says Joyce, blowing on her tea, and then on her own forehead. "He's a lord."

"They're the worst of the lot, Joycey," says Ron. "The worst of the lot. But this Nick Silver business seems too convenient."

"Mmm," agrees Ibrahim.

"Someone tries to kill him," says Ron. "And fails. A bomb goes missing. Someone smashes up his office, and he leaves you a Post-it note? Help me, help me? Does that all seem aboveboard to you, Lizzie?"

Elizabeth is having difficulty sucking her protein shake through a straw. "Hard to say. I don't love it, certainly."

"And off he pops, nowhere to be seen," says Ron. "Then whaddaya know, his partner in crime gets killed the next day."

"But he was my son-in-law Paul's best man, Ron," says Joyce. "I hardly think—"

"If Holly was a suspect for blowing up Nick," says Ron, "then, until we find him, Nick's a suspect for blowing up Holly."

"But the texts?" Joyce argues. "They clearly weren't from him."

"There'll be a reason for that," says Ron.

"And what is that reason?" Joyce asks.

Ron shrugs. There is a sudden gush from the jets of the hot tub, and everyone's feet float to the surface.

Officially the hot tub is a "massage therapy pool," but Ron and Pauline went in a hot tub in Tenerife and it was the same make and model as this one, so he knows it's a hot tub. And, if the rumors were to be believed, it got the same amount of action as the Tenerife hot tub. There's a group of newcomers in Wordsworth Court, younger guys in their seventies, and they've got badges saying I'VE JOINED THE HOT TUB CLUB, HAVE YOU? Flash little gang, they are, couple of them even play tennis. Ever since the badges started appearing, Ron only ever gets in the hot tub when it smells of bleach.

"I believe we should be focusing on the codes," says Ibrahim. "Ron knows Bill Benson, and Connie Johnson is a client of The Compound. Between them they can get us into the vault. All we'd need are the codes to Holly and Nick's safe."

"If Lord Townes hasn't got to it first," says Joyce. "He was wearing odd socks. A lord."

"That's all we need, is it, Ibby?" says Ron. "The codes? Anyway, I'm not working with Connie Johnson. End of discussion."

"I would love the two of you to get along," says Ibrahim.

"Mate," says Ron, raising his pint in the time-honored tradition of a man about to make an incontrovertible point, "she's a heavily armed drug dealer with revenge issues and I put her in prison."

His friend considers this for a moment.

"Sometimes it's best to focus on what we have in common," says Ibrahim, "rather than what separates us. How many people have threatened to kill you over the years? Yet here you are in a massage therapy pool with a pint of beer. And the extra bubbles you keep producing suggest you are very much alive."

What happens underwater stays underwater, that's Ron's credo. Besides, people have done worse in here.

"Connie or no Connie, we have no way of finding those codes, Ibrahim," says Elizabeth.

"There's always a way," says Ibrahim.

"Forget the codes and concentrate on the murder," says Elizabeth. "Ron is absolutely right about Nick Silver. The whole thing might be a smokescreen. But Davey Noakes and Lord Townes both have motives too."

"Though Davey's known about the Bitcoin for years," says Ibrahim.

"You could tell that Lord Townes needed money," says Joyce. "That poor stag."

"And we're still none the wiser about Jill Usher," says Elizabeth. "The Manchester connection."

"Davey Noakes," starts Ibrahim, "Lord Townes, Jill Usher, Nick Silver."

"One of them killed her," says Elizabeth, finishing the last of her protein shake with a grimly satisfied final gulp. "Any luck finding the mystery solicitor for us, Ibrahim?"

"I have sent an email about Holly and Nick to over four hundred solicitors' offices," says Ibrahim. "However, I made the mistake of sending the emails at ten minutes past four in the afternoon, so I received over three hundred 'out of office' auto-replies. But I shall keep searching."

Ron feels himself shutting down.

He knows his friends are having fun, and he enjoyed meeting Bill Benson, but Ron realizes he's finding it hard to get too excited about this Holly Lewis case. He should, he knows that. A young woman is dead, and there's money buried. But he's not feeling it. Why is that?

The four friends settle back. Ron could stay in here all day. He can see a woman in her eighties—Paula something—doing slow lengths in the pool, and a man in his nineties—Dennis—doing slow widths. Do what you can while you can. Their inevitable collision, when it happens, is very friendly, even flirtatious from Dennis's end. Again, do what you can while you can.

"It's been nice to see Kendrick," says Joyce.

Paula is now helping Dennis from the pool. He makes a "glass of wine" gesture, and she smiles and nods. Nice to see. Paula gives the briefest of glances toward the hot tub and, seeing it occupied, turns back. No badge for you today, Paula, Ron thinks.

"Yeah," says Ron. "He's a little miracle, that one."

"All that time with him was just lovely," says Ibrahim. "I notice Suzi didn't come to pick him up? It would be lovely to see her too."

"Suzi's got things on," says Ron.

Ron knows this is why his head isn't in the game. Something is happening with Suzi. He just needs Jason to tell him the truth. If Suzi and Danny are getting divorced, he can take it. Not just take it, he'd welcome it. And Jason knows that. So something *else* must be going on, and Ron doesn't like to think about what that might be.

"I do hope everything is well," says Joyce. As so often with Joyce, it's a mission statement rather than a question.

"My biggest worry is West Ham's defense," says Ron.

Mates are all well and good, but there are some things you have to face alone. Ron is momentarily distracted by the fact that he actually is also worried about West Ham's defense.

"Well, you know where I am," says Ibrahim. "If anything should be concerning you."

"Yeah," says Ron. "Hanging out with a woman who wants to kill me."

Where is Danny, and where is Suzi? Why is Jason taking Kendrick to school? He will talk to Jason, that's his only option. Ron refuses to be protected. He needs to get his family in order.

Then he can start concentrating on murders.

38

There are no appointments in his diary. No one is calling. No one needs help from an old man whose skills are blunt.

The last people to ask for his help were Holly Lewis and Nick Silver, and look how that's going.

He can sit and wait and feel sorry for himself, or he can get off his backside and actually do something. He looks up at the family crest, with its Latin motto beneath. Is Robert to be the last of his family in this house? On this land? Of all the fools who have gone before perhaps none had been as foolish as him.

Robert struggles to think of anything he has ever been good at. Mediocre at school, but still the place at Oxford awaited him. A degree in Classics about which he had little clue then, and less clue now. Then straight into the suit and into the bank. Was he any good at that? No better than the next man, he's sure of that. Robert had been born on a path with no obstacles, other than those he conjured up himself. A life of absolute ease, during which he cannot recall having proved himself even once.

There used to be people to keep this place clean, and money to keep it warm. The two ladies who came to visit him today, Elizabeth and Joyce. What must they have thought? What a sight he must be these days, in his old clothes, with his old hair and his old smell. Sometimes Robert goes into Fairhaven to the cinema. It's half price for seniors on a Wednesday. He sees people his age wearing all sorts. Jeans, hoodies, trainers. He can't imagine himself doing the same. And so he takes the same clothes from the same wardrobes, and polishes the same shoes every day, with nowhere to wear them to.

There are so many couples at the cinema too. Robert has never really got the hang of anything. Has never needed to get the hang of anything.

A life without worry or want, that's been Robert's downfall. How might he have coped under different circumstances? Had he been born into an ordinary house, in an ordinary town, with ordinary parents who didn't pack him off to school at the age of seven? Robert suspects he would have fared badly. Not bright enough, not funny enough, not handsome enough.

Not anything enough. Robert feels he has ended up exactly where he deserves. Cold and alone in a house that mocks him, surrounded by portraits that judge him. Not that they're in any position to. So many of those stern faces were fools; they were just fortunate not to still be around when the money finally ran out. Robert was not only mediocre; he was also unlucky.

No, not unlucky. He had simply outlived his luck.

So what to do? With no one to help him, no one to clear his path? There had always been teachers and bosses and wives and mechanics and travel agents and physicians to tell Robert exactly what was expected of him. But now?

Robert gazes up at the family crest. He remembers looking at it the day he left for school. His father had sent his mother from the room; they were to have a chat "man to man." Robert wasn't a man then and, looking up at the crest now, realizes he still isn't. Masculinity is forged in hardship, isn't it? No such luck for Robert.

His father had stood behind him and taken him by the shoulders. "The family motto, Robert, that's all you'll ever need to know. Stick to that and you won't stray too far from the path."

Aut neca aut necare.

Kill or be killed.

It had not helped Robert a single whit over these many years. If he thought of it at all, it was just as a memory of his father, and of his father's furious cruelty, hacking his way through life.

But what if his father was right? His father had died old and wealthy and unrepentant. And look at Robert. *Kill or be killed.* What if that was the trick he'd always failed to grasp?

Enough is enough. Robert Townes needs to take charge of his situation. It's all very well sitting and waiting if you're in a comfortable chair, with a good cigar, but what's the use in sitting and waiting if you're cold and lonely, and no one is coming to save you?

Which is why Robert Townes picked up the phone yesterday and rang The Compound.

There's still time to change his mind, of course, but Robert doesn't think he will. After a lifetime of stepping to the side, it's finally time to step forward.

Wednesday morning, then? Kill or be killed.

Let's see if his father was right all along.

For the first time since Holly Lewis and Nick Silver came to see him, Lord Townes feels in control.

39

Joyce

On a Monday evening on TV they have a lot of quizzes. They have *Mastermind*, which I can't do, then they have *Only Connect*, which I can't do, and then they have *University Challenge*, which I can't do. Ibrahim usually comes over and brings a bottle of wine while I heat something up.

He sits forward, hand on his chin, and happily shouts "Anne Boleyn" or "Argentina" or, if it's football, "Gary Lineker" at the screen all evening. Sometimes he gets things right and he looks at me as if to say, "Well, there we have it, Joyce," and, in fact, sometimes he actually says, "Well, there we have it, Joyce." When he gets things wrong, he makes a fuss and says the quiz has got the answer wrong, and then he goes on Google and we hear no more about it. He enjoys himself, and I enjoy myself because I get to potter in the kitchen and occasionally shout out "Marilyn Monroe" or something, and Alan enjoys it because there are two people to stroke him, and when he can tell you're getting bored, he swaps over.

On *Mastermind* this evening one of the specialist subjects was *Call the Midwife*, which infuriated Ibrahim because he doesn't think anything after 1950 should be allowed on *Mastermind*, but was fun for me. I didn't get any right, because it goes too quickly, but I enjoyed hearing words I recognized for once. The next contestant did *Middlemarch*, and Ibrahim was much happier. I didn't hear him get any right, but he nodded an awful lot.

Joanna left a long message while I was out with Elizabeth today, wanting to know if there were any developments. Paul has had no more messages from poor Nick Silver, which tells its own story.

We are having to work quickly on this investigation, which is quite fun. I went to a stately home today. I think it's the first time I have ever been to a stately home that didn't have a gift shop.

You can tell that Lord Townes—he says to call him Robert but can you imagine?—needs money, but he was very convincing otherwise. Though lords are convincing, aren't they? I suppose that's how they become lords.

Davey Noakes seems a far likelier candidate for the murder. I was saying this to Ibrahim earlier, but he hushed me because there was a question on earthquakes and Ibrahim is now interested in earthquakes because he listened to a podcast.

If you ever visit Ibrahim now, he is listening to a podcast. His favorite one is a scientist and a priest who argue about things but seem to get along. If you see him walking through Coopers Chase, he'll take his headphones out of his ears and say, "The History of Finland" or "Clouds" or something. Perhaps there is a podcast I might enjoy, but I don't know where to get podcasts from. I asked Joanna and she said something about "downloading" and I switched off. I think Radio Sussex suits me better than podcasts, because I know the people.

Perhaps I am being naive about Lord Townes. Perhaps because he's a lord and Davey Noakes was a drug dealer I have made assumptions. People tell you not to make assumptions, but they often save a lot of time. Clever people, by which I mean Ibrahim or Elizabeth, are happiest when something is unusual, or unexpected, or not at all what you think, but normal people, me and Ron, that sort of person, like it when a tree is a tree and a shoe is a shoe, and a drug dealer is a murderer.

The way I see it—again, I tried to say this to Ibrahim but there's no point—Holly and Nick visited Davey Noakes to ask his advice about the Bitcoin, Davey Noakes thought this might be his last chance to get his hands on the money and saw pound signs, or Bitcoin signs, took out the phone book and got someone to kill Holly Lewis. He must have found out Holly's code from somewhere, and is probably getting someone to torture Nick Silver's code out of him as we speak.

In the end I had to say all of this to Alan.

In *University Challenge* one of the students was originally from Egypt, and every time she got a question right Ibrahim would nod and say, "There we go," and "Quite right, quite right." At one point they had a round about flags and I said "Venezuela" for each one, because I always say "Venezuela" for questions about countries. It drives Ibrahim mad.

Anyway, this evening, the third flag they showed actually was Venezuela, and I said to Ibrahim, "I told you so," and he wasn't at all happy with me. I whooped and Alan barked and Ibrahim, who had said "Ecuador," said, "Venezuela and Ecuador have very similar flags," and I said, "Similar, but not the same," and he started stroking Alan so hard that Alan had to look to me for reassurance.

Sometimes I ask Ibrahim if he doesn't find our Monday-evening quiz night too stressful, and he says it's his favorite night of the week.

As Ibrahim was leaving, I finally had his full attention, and I told him that Davey Noakes is our man, I was sure of it, and he shook his head and said, "Joyce, don't rule out Lord Townes or Nick Silver. Surely we've learned to look beyond the obvious by now," and I said, "Well, I was right about Venezuela, wasn't I?" and he very slowly and very politely said, "Good evening, Joyce," and he walked out into the night, putting his headphones in his ears as he went.

I will say this. I am as confident about Davey Noakes as I was about Venezuela. I Googled it after Ibrahim left, and he's right, the Ecuadorian flag is very similar, but in life there is only one right answer, and you either get it right or you don't.

40

Joanna and Paul have been to the theater, and her verdict, as so often, is that David Tennant was very good, but the legroom was very bad.

They are having a post-show supper at a restaurant that throws a warm glow out onto a dark Soho alley. The noise of the diners manages to be both a murmur and a buzz. When she was a little girl this is what Joanna dreamed being a grown-up might be like. Paul is discussing the play.

"The broken chair was a metaphor for grief, I think," says Paul.

Joanna loves him, but this sort of thing she can do without.

"It was under the clock for a reason," he goes on. "The clock moves; the chair can't."

"And the Maltesers in the interval?" Joanna says. "What were they a metaphor for?"

Paul laughs. "You have to let me be pretentious, I'm afraid. I just need to get it out of my system every now and again. I can either do it here or at home."

Paul loves theater, loses himself in it entirely. Joanna envies him. Her concentration span is simply not up to the job. Joyce had once said to her that her favorite thing about the theater was the ice cream in the tiny tubs, and Joanna had, on reflex, rolled her eyes and called her a philistine. One day perhaps she will tell Joyce that it is her favorite thing about going to the theater too. On one of their first dates Paul had taken her to a play called *The Lehman Trilogy*. It was over three hours long, which might have ended their relationship before it began, but Paul explained that there were two intervals, and Joanna knew exactly what that meant. Two tiny tubs of ice cream. In fact, the moment Paul volunteered to join the ice-cream queue for the second time, without question or judgment, might have been the moment she truly fell in love with him.

There are many things she should probably tell her mum one day. But who can ever really tell their mum anything? Too much static builds up over the years.

"How's *your* grief?" Joanna asks. There is something very specific she has wanted to talk about since Friday. Paul and Holly Lewis. Now might be a good time.

"My grief?" Paul isn't sure what she's talking about. She sees he's not bluffing, and finds that interesting.

"One of your oldest friends died," says Joanna. "I don't think we've really talked about it. I know you're worried about Nick, but you can talk about Holly too, you know?"

Paul doesn't want to talk, Joanna can see that. But why? Is he hiding a small lie or a big lie?

"Why didn't she come to the wedding?" Joanna asks. Approach it from a different angle. "And don't say, 'She was working.' Come on."

Paul has been using his knife and fork to emphasize his opinions about the play, but now he puts them down. Real life, it seems, doesn't provoke the same emotions.

"We had an argument," says Paul. "Well, she had an argument; I just stood there."

A chef Joanna recognizes from TV has just sat at the table opposite them. She will tell her mum about that. "What was this one-sided argument about?"

"Our wedding being on a weekday," says Paul. "A workday. She accused me of scheduling it deliberately."

"But I scheduled it?" says Joanna.

"I know," says Paul. "But, as I say, it didn't feel like she needed me to contribute to the discussion."

So Holly was angry that the wedding was on a workday? She couldn't take a day off to see one of her oldest friends get married? There really is only one thing left to conclude. Joanna had concluded it anyway.

"How long did you date for?"

"Hmm?" Paul, bless him, is wondering if there is a way to avoid a collision. But there is not.

"You're not in trouble," says Joanna. "But it would be a very unusual thing for a platonic friend to object to."

"Yes," agrees Paul.

"And unusual that she might think it was deliberate too," Joanna adds. "So how long?"

"A couple of years," says Paul. "On and off. Awhile in our twenties, then again a few years ago."

"How many is a few?" says Joanna.

"Two," says Paul. "Slightly less than two."

"Should we settle on eighteen months?" says Joanna.

"That sounds about right," says Paul.

"Your last relationship before this, then?"

"I mean . . ." Paul is pretending to think. "It would, I suppose, yes, I suppose it would have been."

"So you rekindle a romance from your twenties with an attractive woman—"

"Don't," says Paul. Men can be so funny about previous relationships. There are three or four of her own previous relationships she has absolutely struck from the record, so she understands it. None of them had been murdered recently though. In one particular case she could but hope.

"Gave it another go in your forties," says Joanna. "Split up again, and then met the woman of your dreams, that's me, shortly afterward, extremely shortly afterward, and then got married within six months?"

Paul nods.

"I wouldn't have come to the wedding either," says Joanna. "I'd have been furious. You split up with her, I assume?"

"It was . . ." Paul is searching for words that are both truthful and also paint him in a good light. Which is the eternal struggle of all men who have ended relationships. "It had an inevitability by the end."

"So *she* split up with *you*?"

"No," admits Paul. "She's umm . . . She's a challenging human being. Was challenging. Nick would tell you the same. Often saw things in a different light to others. Her angles could take me by surprise at times."

He wants to say "nightmare" but refuses to. Another reason she loves him.

"And yet you still dated?" says Joanna, spearing some broccoli. A low blow but a fun one. She has dated a few nightmares in her time. Sometimes that's just where you are in life. That's the itch that needs scratching.

"I just . . ." Paul is not enjoying his turbot anymore. Joanna takes his hand.

"Paul, listen to me," says Joanna. "We found each other, I promise you never have to worry about anything like this. You dated Holly, I'm sure she had many good qualities, but perhaps it wasn't either of your finest hours. You moved on, perhaps she didn't, but you're here, with me, in a gorgeous restaurant and we both have rings on our fingers, and many, many notches on our bedposts—"

Paul cocks his head. "I wouldn't say 'many, many.' Would you say 'many, many'?"

Joanna hushes him. "I couldn't care less who you dated, when or why."

Paul nods. He still doesn't look delighted about his turbot, but some of the tension is leaving his shoulders.

A small lie, then, not a big lie. That's a relief.

"I will say this though." Joanna feels she should let him know, given the circumstances. "The police will be interested. They might want to talk to you at some point anyway."

"Oh, God," says Paul.

"Just be honest with them," says Joanna. "People date people. Those people don't usually get murdered not long afterward, but that's where we are. Just don't lie. There's no need."

The TV chef has just complained that his sparkling water is too fizzy. Joanna will definitely be telling her mum that.

"I don't know what to tell anyone about anything," says Paul. "I know nothing about the business, nothing about who might have killed Holly, nothing about where Nick might run to. I feel like people won't believe me. That they'll think I must know something about something."

"And do you?" Joanna asks. "While we're being honest? Is there anything else you're keeping to yourself? Because you feel guilty or embarrassed?"

"I feel guilty about one thing," says Paul. "To answer your original question, my grief is not as deep as it should be. I'm very sad about Holly, and it's awful, but am I grieving? I don't think I am. Perhaps it will kick in, but it doesn't feel like it will."

Joanna nods. "We're not in charge of who we miss. I had a dog I miss more than my grandmother, and, believe me, I loved my grandmother."

"A dog you had as a child?"

"Not even that: a neighbor's dog when I was in my thirties. We used to talk over the garden fence. He had wise eyes."

"Wow," says Paul. "Your poor grandmother."

Joanna nods. There really was something about that dog.

"You'd miss me though?" Paul says.

"It's a moot question," says Joanna. "Because you're never going to die. I won't allow it."

Paul smiles, and finally tucks into his turbot.

"Here's a question though," says Joanna. "Old friends, lovers, many years of emotional closeness. Any guesses on what her six-digit code might be? Anything she used for her bank cards or her phone?"

Paul shakes his head. The chef at the next table is now calling over the maître d' because of an issue with the butter. Something to do with either too much or not enough salt? The woman he's with, who could be his daughter or his wife—but Joanna knows where she would place her bet—looks long-suffering.

"What year was she born?" Joanna asks.

"Seventy-six," says Paul.

"Younger than me, then?" says Joanna.

"Looked older though," says Paul, which, even though Holly is dead, is the right thing to say.

Joanna lowers her voice. "Are you listening to this guy at the next table by the way?"

"Oh, God, yes," says Paul. "Your mum is going to love it."

Joanna will ring Joyce tomorrow and tell her all about it. Catch up about Holly Lewis too. Funny that murder is one of the few things they find it easy to talk about. Perhaps because it's something they didn't speak about growing up? There's no shared language to fracture them.

41

Jeremy Jenkins never takes his work home with him.

He knows some solicitors who drive home, passenger seat groaning with files, and work till all hours.

But if Jeremy Jenkins is to answer your correspondence, it will be between the hours of nine a.m. and five p.m. Four p.m., if he's honest—you don't want to start anything new too near to home time, do you? In case it spills over past five. The worst is house sales. You get an email at one minute past four from a buyer who needs to exchange before the end of play that day and you could be there till six. No, thank you: the office hours of Rochester, Clark, Hughes are on the website for everyone to see, and it takes just a modicum of common sense to understand one mustn't get in touch within an hour or so of home time.

If he's being entirely honest, he doesn't get an awful lot done between nine a.m. and ten a.m. either, because it's important to have a coffee and really think about the day ahead before you get stuck in.

But between ten and four, Jeremy likes to think he does a pretty good job. Are there better solicitors in Kettering? Possibly. Are there better solicitors in Kettering who still retain a healthy work-life balance? Jeremy doubts that very much.

There was a time when it was floated that Rochester, Clark, Hughes might become Rochester, Clark, Hughes, Jenkins, but in the end that was put on the back burner. And that was fair enough if you really took the time to think about it.

Today, however, he has a file with him. Belonging to a Ms. Holly Lewis. She deposited some documents with the company some years ago. Jeremy didn't deal with her personally, he's sure of that, but whoever did deal with her has obviously either left or died since then (in the past ten years, four solicitors have left the firm and two have died, including the original Rochester, who fell off a ladder in Mykonos), and Jeremy's name has found itself attached to the file.

It was placed on his desk at three p.m., well within the statute of limitations, so he took a look. The file contained two envelopes. One was marked IN THE EVENT OF THE DEATH OF HOLLY LEWIS and the other IN THE EVENT OF THE DEATH OF NICK SILVER.

His secretary, a man but actually not at all bad when you got used to it, had forwarded an email from Kent Hospital—this Holly Lewis had named the firm as her next of kin in an emergency—saying she had died. Which happens in the solicitor business. Would that it didn't.

Jeremy Jenkins's job, then, was to track down Mr. Nick Silver. To let him know that he, Jeremy Jenkins, had a package in his care with his, Nick Silver's, name on it.

They had a number for Nick Silver. His secretary had tried but received no answer. Jeremy then watched as his secretary tried the number again, because secretaries often dial numbers incorrectly if you don't watch them like a hawk. Nothing doing.

You often found these "Open in the event of the death" letters attached to people's estates, but this was a single file, containing only the two envelopes and three phone numbers. And that is unusual. No record of any correspondence other than the initial request to have the file stored.

It piqued Jeremy Jenkins's interest. He wasn't allowed to open the envelopes, naturally, but he would be interested to know what was in them. Engage this Nick Silver in a conversation, see what was what.

If Nick Silver is a working man, such as Jeremy himself, perhaps it is difficult for him to answer the phone during the day? Social calls are frowned upon at Rochester, Clark, Hughes too.

He has already rung the number twice, with no joy. He will try a final time just before nine, and then call it a night.

And, if all else fails, there is the third number in the file. He could ring that tomorrow.

Tuesday

42

What a day to be alive. Sure, she has to do the night shift this evening because Prince Edward has decided he wants to go to a Nando's, and she has to stand outside until he's finished his Lemon & Herb Chicken Pitta, but at least she is going to have some fun before that.

Jill Usher. The name Elizabeth gave her. Donna has done some digging and struck gold.

Donna isn't often in this position. Knowing that Elizabeth has made a mistake. It's intoxicating.

She is on her way to London to talk to Paul Brett, on Elizabeth's instructions. Donna doesn't have any qualms about that. If you've been invited to someone's wedding—the evening reception anyway—surely you're allowed to visit them and talk about a murder? That's not a police thing, that's a friendship thing.

Just don't tell Joyce. Elizabeth had been very clear about that.

Joyce's flat is a detour well worth taking, however. She really intends to make the most of it.

"You didn't notice anything out of the ordinary?" she asks Elizabeth and Joyce. "When you visited Jill Usher in Manchester?"

"If you have information," says Elizabeth, "kindly just tell us. I don't need you smirking, Donna. It's very unprofessional. Tell her, Bogdan."

"Is not my business," says Bogdan, wisely. He has tagged along because Elizabeth is having problems with her underfloor heating. This little gang certainly get their money's worth from Bogdan. He was off seeing Ron about something on Saturday too. It's nice to turn the tables on them a little.

"Just getting the full picture," says Donna. She sees Elizabeth calculating angles in her head and coming up with nothing.

Ever since she'd got the information from Manchester, Donna has been looking forward to this conversation. Elizabeth clearly decides to go on the attack. She usually does when she's rattled. Or when she's not rattled.

"Yes, we noticed something unusual," says Elizabeth. "We noticed a nursery-school teacher somehow tied up in a murder. Is that usual?"

"Is that usual?" Donna thinks out loud. "I'd say not, wouldn't you?"

"Ever so unusual," says Joyce.

"Ever so," agrees Bogdan.

Joyce thinks about it some more. "If I was worried about being killed, I wouldn't ring a nursery-school teacher? I would ring Joanna. Or, actually, Elizabeth, because I wouldn't want Joanna to worry."

"I swear to you, Donna," says Elizabeth, "if you string this out any further, I am cutting Bogdan out of my will, and it's a big will."

"I'm in your will?" Bogdan asks.

"You're clinging on by your fingernails," says Elizabeth. "Why did Holly Lewis ring Jill Usher?"

"Well, that's just it," says Donna. "I don't think she did ring Jill Usher."

"Ooh," says Joyce. "What has Elizabeth missed now?"

"You didn't meet anyone else?" Donna asks. "On your trip up north?"

She looks at them, and feels a rush of love for them both.

"The husband," says Joyce.

"Joyce gets it," says Donna. "The husband."

"The husband," says Elizabeth. Donna sees she is annoyed at herself for not spotting it.

"Always the husband," says Bogdan, nodding.

"Jamie Usher," says Donna, reading from her notebook. "The reason the Ushers left the South Coast in the first place. He has convictions for benefits fraud, insurance fraud and mortgage fraud. Moved up north, started again, and has been in no further trouble since."

"Hasn't been *caught* for anything since," says Elizabeth.

"Innit?" agrees Donna.

"So Holly wasn't ringing Jill Usher?" says Joyce. "She was ringing Jamie Usher?"

"It would make more sense," says Donna. "Perhaps Jill bought the phone, contract was in her name, she didn't trust him after everything he'd done, wanted to keep her eye on him? Who does Holly ring? A nursery-school teacher or a convicted fraudster?"

Elizabeth thinks. "But you haven't found any other connection between Holly Lewis and Jamie Usher?"

"Not yet," says Donna. "But Greater Manchester Police are visiting him today."

"His eyes were very close together," says Joyce. "I will say that."

"Like my friend Woyzeck," says Bogdan. "He can't even wear glasses."

"This is actually not bad," says Elizabeth to Donna. "Jamie Usher. You're really coming along. Chris being away really suits you."

"Thank you," says Donna. "Is Bogdan really in your will?"

"For now," says Elizabeth. "A bit of money, some weaponry."

There is a ring on Joyce's intercom, and she buzzes someone up.

"Will you stay for a cup of tea, Donna?" Joyce asks.

"Got to be somewhere," says Donna. Got to be in London, Joyce, to talk to your new son-in-law about a murder.

"Of course," says Joyce. "Can I pack you some cake for your journey? It's only fruitcake, but I saw it on *Saturday Kitchen* and thought of you."

"That would be lovely," says Donna.

"I walk you to your car," says Bogdan.

Donna takes the cake, and she and Bogdan head out and down the stairwell. Can she eat Joyce's cake before questioning Joyce's son-in-law? She'll give it a go. Besides, perhaps Jamie Usher is more of a suspect than Paul

Brett now? Donna certainly hopes so. Either way, she's enjoying her day off. As they leave the building, they practically barrel into Ron.

"My favorite police officer," says Ron, giving her a hug. "Mind you, that's like saying 'my favorite Millwall player.'"

Ron and Bogdan share a handshake.

Donna looks at them both. "Can I ask you a question, Ron?"

"If you arrest me," says Ron. "Sure."

"Where did you two go on Saturday? I never quite got to the bottom of it," Donna asks.

Bogdan looks at Ron. Ron puts his hand on Bogdan's arm, as if to take charge.

"Bowling," says Ron.

"Bowling?" says Donna. "Like ten-pin bowling?"

"Yes," says Ron.

"Bowling," repeats Bogdan. "Like ten-pin bowling."

"On a Saturday morning?"

"Half price for pensioners," says Ron.

"Where was this?" Donna asks.

"Fairhaven," says Ron.

"Fairhaven," agrees Bogdan.

"Who won?" Donna asks.

"I did," says Ron.

Bogdan looks at Ron but doesn't argue.

"Big win, poor lad," says Ron. "A lot of it is in the wrist. What you doing at Joyce's?"

"Just been telling Elizabeth about a new prime suspect," says Donna. "Jamie Usher."

"Jamie Usher?" asks Ron. "I thought it was Jill Usher?"

"Elizabeth got it wrong," says Donna.

Ron nods. "Well, she's had some time off."

"Do I need to worry about what you two are up to?" Donna asks.

"Course not," says Ron. "We were bowling."

"Bogdan?"

"Course not," agrees Bogdan.

Donna can tell he's not telling the truth, but she knows there will be a good reason. He's being bullied into something by Ron. It is very easy to bully Bogdan: you just tell him you need his help.

43

Tia keeps finding new bits of metal about her body, and apologizing each time. Coins, a Zippo cigarette lighter, earrings, a nose ring, a hair clasp.

"A lot of it is religious," says Tia. "A lot of the jewelry."

The security guard grunts. Tia knows that he can't put a tick on his computer until the machine stops beeping. Just her luck there's a new guy on today.

"Just turn the machine off," says Tia. "Or we'll be here all day—it's always playing up. I won't tell anyone."

"I'm not supposed to," says the guard.

"Jesus made us with free will," says Tia.

"I suppose so," says the guard, and flicks a switch. Tia walks through the metal detector again.

"No beep," says Tia, and continues on her way. The guard flicks his switch back on again. And that's why you should pay people properly.

Tia descends the ramp that takes her to the wide concrete apron surrounding the warehouse and walks over to the loading-bay doors. Is she excited? Tia guesses so. There's a bit of adrenaline, but not as much as she is used to. Something is troubling her.

The loading-bay doors are currently wedged open because Hassan has parked his fork-lift truck directly under the closing sensors. If a supervisor spots it, he'll shout at Hassan and move along. Tia walks into the warehouse and takes the two guns from her overalls. As she passes Hassan, she slips him one of the guns, and she then makes her way to the cleaning cupboard. She places her pass on the keypad, and the cupboard clicks open. Tia's pass is issued under the name "Tracey-Ann Corbett" and the photo on it is not hers. Nobody has, as yet, noticed. Mainly because no one has, as yet, looked. She wheels out her cleaning trolley and puts her gun into one of the compartments.

Any thrill yet? Not that she can make out. This should be the biggest score of her life? The start of even bigger and better things, the turning point? After this, school is out: she's a real-life, grown-up gangster now. Perhaps she's nervous, and that's taking the edge off the thrill? She once did a painting of a horse for a school competition, and she won and was called up on stage by the deputy head, who gave her a prize. She was so nervous standing up in front of everyone, she nearly threw up. And now look at her. Times change; you grow up.

The delivery should be with them in the next five minutes or so and, preparation all done, Tia decides she will kill some time by doing some actual cleaning. She enjoys it, enjoys making something dirty, clean. She wouldn't do it for the money they pay her, but it's good work. Perhaps not at a hotel, where there's time pressure, and people feel they can make a mess, but here, where people are neat and tidy, and no one's up in your business every five minutes, it's not so bad. Hassan enjoys driving the fork lift too. If they hadn't decided to rob the place, they might have found interesting careers here.

And perhaps that's just it? Wheeling a trolley with a gun inside it. Waiting to point it at a guy just doing his job. Can that be right?

Tia has been thinking about careers recently. She is good at a lot of things. She has a creative imagination, she is organized, people like her. But how does one go about getting a job? An actual job? Connie has been encouraging, obviously sees something in her, but perhaps one day it would be nice to do something that wasn't illegal.

Stealing stuff, selling drugs, protection rackets, it's all cheating really, and it would be nice to start something from the ground up, actually to back herself. Pay tax, employ people. Compete on a level playing field. Paint horses or something? But where are those jobs? They always seem to be taken.

Tia feels for her gun. If you have to point a gun at someone, you're not making a proper living. You're scaring people, and that's easy. "I will kill you if you don't give me your money" seems an over-the-top way of making money.

It's like the people who run this warehouse. If you can't afford to pay your staff proper wages, you're cheating. You're not making an honest living. You're stealing.

Look at the place. There must be companies paying good money to ship their stuff to and from this warehouse. Tia bets there are brochures with photos of the security systems. The brochures will show the metal detectors and the sensors and the security guards, all of which fall down when you don't pay proper money. You don't need a gun to do sales. Tia could do sales. It's just talking to people, isn't it? Tia likes doing that.

Outside the warehouse, she hears the delivery lorry clear the two security posts, drive down the ramp and make its way toward the warehouse. Make a bit of money, make Connie proud.

Make herself proud? As she sees the lorry driving under the security grille, it doesn't feel that way. The truck parks up, and the driver waits for two uniformed guards to come out of the secure unit at the heart of the warehouse. Benny and Bobby, they're called. Tia has tried to have as little as possible to do with both of them, and they've been quite happy with that arrangement. Bobby and Benny are uniformed but not armed. Worst of all worlds for poor Benny and Bobby.

Strictly speaking the driver should have stopped the second he saw the security grille was open. Anything out of the ordinary you stop. That's how Tia would run this place. Pay people properly, ask them to do their job properly. She knew the driver wouldn't stop though. He'll have too many deliveries to make today. No one can afford to stop these days. Every minute is precious when people won't pay you a living wage. It's why delivery drivers leave your parcels on the doorstep even though you're in. Going too fast and cutting corners is the only way to make your money on any given day. Miserable for everyone.

As Bobby and Benny approach the truck, they call Hassan over, and he drives the fork lift up to the back of the vehicle. The driver jumps down from his cab with an iPad, and there is some banter, presumably about football. Someone beat someone, and it has reflected poorly on Bobby's masculinity. He's taking it well though.

Benny, masculinity still intact by some quirk of the weekend's football results, checks through the paperwork on the iPad and signs his name with a fingernail. Hassan jumps down from the fork lift and makes his way around the blind side of the lorry. Here we go, then.

Tia pulls out her gun. She screams, "Everybody on the floor!"

Benny, Bobby and the driver whirl toward her. None of them gets on the floor. They just look at each other. Hassan is now in the cab of the lorry.

Tia fires a shot into the roof. "Everybody on the floor!"

Reluctantly the three men sink to their knees and then lie flat on the floor.

"A cleaner with a gun?" says Bobby.

"I don't think she's a cleaner," says Benny.

"We know you," says Bobby, looking up.

Tia points the gun straight at him. "What's my name, then?"

"We know your face," says Bobby.

"I doubt that very much," says Tia.

"Just steal the truck," says the driver. "I get the day off if you steal the truck."

Tia ties up the men one by one. She takes their phones as she does so. Hassan has got the lorry started, and she jumps up into the cab. There's not a great deal of point in tying the men up—by the time they've driven the truck through the security gates the alarm will be well and truly raised—but it's good practice to tie people up. Might come in handy for next time.

Next time? Tia puffs out her cheeks. Really? Do this again? Hassan drives the lorry over the apron and up the ramp. At the point he should slow down he speeds up, and the lorry plows through the security posts, then makes slightly tougher work of the outside security gates. Guards, including the man who let Tia smuggle her guns through not fifteen minutes ago, go through the motions of starting to chase the lorry, but, by this point, Hassan is gunning it toward the Coast Road.

It couldn't have gone a great deal better. Half a million-odd in the back. There's an old car park down on one of the estates by the power station, and Hassan has parked a van out of sight there. They'll transfer the watches across and head straight for Connie's.

There is a red light up ahead, and Hassan stops for it. Very wise. There won't be police looking for them for the next couple of minutes, but there will always be police on the lookout for people driving through red lights. The lorry stops, and the moment it does the cab is filled with a piercing alarm. Tia looks at Hassan. He puts his foot down on the accelerator, but the lorry won't move. A red smoke now begins to fill the cab, and they hear an electronic voice broadcasting:

> *This vehicle is being stolen, please contact the police.*
> *This vehicle is being stolen, please contact the police.*

At the junction of an industrial estate and the Coast Road, there is not much foot traffic. No "have-a-go heroes" to make a citizen's arrest. Hassan is trying to open the cab doors, but they have locked shut. The same with the windows; Tia and Hassan are trapped. Tia braces herself in her seat and swings both her legs with full force at the windscreen. Her legs bounce back, shooting pain through both. She takes out her gun.

"If that windscreen is bulletproof," says Hassan, "you'll kill us both."

"Yeah," says Tia. "But if it isn't, I won't."

She pulls the trigger and the windscreen shatters into a sea of diamonds. Tia and Hassan drop through the windscreen onto the road below. A little crowd is forming now, taking photos. Tia runs over to them and points her gun at the photographers.

"I'm so sorry," she says, taking the phones.

Hassan has run across the Coast Road and down into a pedestrian underpass that leads toward the power station. Plenty of places to get lost around there. Tia runs west along the Coast Road until she finds a turning into a residential road. She sees no cameras and, as sirens start to sound in the background, she hides in a small bus stop.

Tia can't go back to Connie's, she knows that. If she's spotted and followed, leading the police to Connie is a greater crime than stealing a few watches. And she can't get on a bus: they all have cameras. It wouldn't take long to track Tia's movements. Looking along the residential road, Tia sees the South Downs rising above her and decides the only thing to do is walk. No cameras on the South Downs.

Head down, Tia moves up the road toward the hills. What's on the other side? No idea. A stream of police cars has turned into the industrial estate. As Tia reaches the end of the road, she sees a stile leading onto one of the paths across the Downs. She is wearing cleaning overalls with bright pink Crocs, and has a loaded gun in her pocket. But people wear all sorts of things when they're out walking.

For the first time today, Tia feels a thrill. As she approaches the stile, however, a silver Tesla blocks her path. The passenger-side window opens, and she sees a familiar face.

"Connie!" says Tia.

Connie opens the door and beckons her in.

"Seat belt," says Connie, and throws the Tesla into a three-point turn. "When I was ten, my mum said I could walk to school by myself. I felt so grown up. She told me years later that for that whole first year she followed me to school. There was a whole group of them, the Mums. Just making sure we were safe."

"I messed up," says Tia.

"Ah, you tried your best," says Connie. "And you shot out the window of a security lorry. That's got to count for something."

Connie pulls out onto the Coast Road and drives them back past the abandoned lorry. The road onto the industrial estate is taped off already. Tia looks out of her window and sees that the area around the power station is also crawling with police. Hassan won't make it far. But he also won't tell the police anything.

"I don't know if this is for me," says Tia. "I didn't really enjoy it."

"I get it," says Connie. "If armed robbery was for everyone, there'd be chaos, wouldn't there?"

"I think I need to get a job," says Tia.

"I'm not the person to ask," says Connie. "But what I do know is that you need somewhere quiet to hide away for a few days."

"I can go back to South London," says Tia. "Someone will put me up."

"I've got a much better idea," says Connie, as she turns off the Coast Road and heads inland.

44

Jamie Usher does not like the look of this one bit.

A Manchester squad car right outside his house. Parked across his driveway, so there's no doubt which house they've come to visit. The curtains in the living-room window are closed, on a fine summer's evening. That means there will be officers inside, talking to Jill. She will have blocked the view of any curious neighbors. She has some experience of it. Poor Jill. He imagines her pulling the curtains closed, cursing him for bringing trouble to her house once again.

Guilt can wait though, Jamie has to think straight. What have the police come about? Could be a few things, but he knows where his money would be. And he's been so careful this time. Perhaps he hasn't. Sometimes, Jamie reflects, he's not good at all this. You can't keep kidding yourself, can you?

Jill will be furious, he knows that. He was supposed to have left all this behind him when they moved up here. That's *why* they moved up here, get him away from his old friends and his old haunts. But it's not so easy for him. Jill can just get a job in a nursery, meet new people, make new friends. But Jamie? Old habits die hard. You do what you're good at.

So far he's had no trouble from the Manchester police, hasn't raised a single flag as far as he knows. So why are they here on a Tuesday? Jill will have told them he's on his way home from work. She won't cover for him, won't defend him. Quite right too, Jamie absolutely gets it. You can only push someone so far, whatever it says in the marriage vows. Jill will want to know what the police have got to say. She'll want to know what he's been up to.

Watching from his car, Jamie tries to think about a mistake he might have made. The mistake that led to the police knocking on his door. Who even knows where he lives?

Jill will have made them a cup of tea, there will be small talk. She'll be all smiles for the police, but she won't be all smiles for him. This will be the end for them, Jamie is sure of that. He's done some bad things, but she's always forgiven him. But he'd promised her it was all in the past, and she won't forgive him breaking a promise. Flowers won't fix this one.

That's all long-term thinking though, and Jamie can't think about the long term right now, any more than a fox being chased by hounds can think about tomorrow's breakfast. What can he do *now*? That's the question to concentrate on.

He'll have to run, that's for sure. He has money on him, and he has access to more. Not much more, but enough to spend a few days away, and see if he can find out exactly what the police want with him? Perhaps it's a false alarm? Something minor? That would be a result. Perhaps it's routine? His name triggered on the police computer, "Sorry to bother you, sir," "Eliminating people from our inquiries, sir." It's only a squad car after all, not even real detectives. Not worth the risk until he knows for sure though.

Where can he stay tonight? Get out of Manchester, certainly. The whole point of Manchester was that the police didn't know him here. And now it seems they do, so it's goodbye Manchester. And goodbye Jill if it's something serious. But how to find out?

Who even knows where he lives?

Jamie thinks about the two old women who came to visit Jill. Researchers? Maybe. But a coincidence that they call out of the blue, and the police are here a couple of days later. What if that squad car, squatting outside his house for all the neighbors to see, has something to do with the women? The taller one had something about her, something that sent Jamie's radar haywire. Jamie reaches around into the back pocket of his jeans and pulls out the card she gave him.

ELIZABETH BEST, it says, followed by a phone number.

Jill will be expecting him any minute. If he's late, the police will be suspicious, and, if the police are suspicious, maybe they'll be on the lookout for his car. Best to get a few miles between himself and Manchester before that happens. Jamie starts the car and pulls away from the curb. He passes his own house. The house that was supposed to be a new beginning. But new Jamie soon fell back into the clutches of old Jamie, so here he is, running again. He reaches the main road. Left is north, and right is south. He looks at the ELIZABETH BEST card again. Where did they say they'd come from? Kent?

Jamie Usher turns right, and heads south. He switches on Radio 2. A bit of Sara Cox for the long drive ahead.

45

People make such a fuss. It is tiring. All Connie Johnson asks is to be allowed to live her own life. The police want to catch her—she understands that, it's what they get paid for. Competitors want to undercut her, to steal her market share, to kill her—again, no complaints, it's business.

It's just *this* sort of thing that Connie can't understand. You ask a simple favor, and this is the response you get.

"But why does she need to be hidden?" Ibrahim asks. "That's the only thing I can't quite compute."

"She just does," says Connie. "For once in your life don't ask questions."

Ibrahim turns to Tia. "Why do you need to be hidden?"

Tia looks at Connie, who shakes her head. It's the perfect place. Who would think to look for a teenage girl who held up a warehouse at gunpoint in the flat of an eighty-year-old psychiatrist? No one, that's who. Connie was proud of it as an idea, and thought Ibrahim would be glad to help. That it might make him feel useful.

"Ibrahim," says Connie, "have I ever asked anything of you?"

"Yes," says Ibrahim. "Many times."

"Okay, anything illegal?" says Connie.

"Again, yes," says Ibrahim. "So this is illegal?"

"It's quite illegal," says Connie. "But I'm sure it's fine."

"Connie," says Ibrahim, "I'm going to say to you what Captain Lee said to Eddie on *Below Deck*. 'We have a bond of trust. We trust each other to tell the truth.'"

Ibrahim WhatsApps her about *Below Deck* a lot now.

"The last time we spoke," says Ibrahim, "Tia was settling into a cleaning job, and you were giving her tips and advice. It was a very proud moment for me. Now you have arrived at Coopers Chase at some speed, and Tia has a number of small cuts to her face. I conclude that since I saw you both last, something untoward has happened, and, much as I would like to help, if you don't tell me exactly what that is, I shall have to ask you both to leave."

"We should leave," says Tia to Connie. "This isn't fair on Ibrahim."

"Ibrahim can look after himself," says Connie. Why is everyone ganging up on her? This should be so simple. Drop Tia off, pick her up again in a few days when one of her police contacts has let her know what's going on, and in the meantime Ibrahim and Tia can have a fine old time watching TV, or solving murders, or whatever Ibrahim does when she's not around. Connie is no great expert on what other people do when she's not around.

"Tia," says Ibrahim, "you are more than welcome to stay. But Connie has mentioned the word 'hidden' and I am simply doing my due diligence. Did you have a fight at work? With one of the other cleaners perhaps?"

"Oh, for God's sake," says Connie, "show Ibrahim your gun."

Tia flashes Connie an "Are you sure?" look.

"He's seen more guns than me in the last couple of years," says Connie.

Tia pulls the gun from her cleaning overalls and puts it on one of Ibrahim's coffee tables. Ibrahim slides a place mat underneath it.

"Tia robbed a warehouse today," says Connie. "That was her new job. She pointed a gun at the driver and two security guards, then tied them up and drove the vehicle out of an industrial estate with half a million pounds' worth of Rolexes in the back. A remote security protocol disabled the vehicle, and she had to shoot her way out and run, leaving the watches behind. Her accomplice was picked up by the police, whereas Tia, because she has a *responsible mentor*, was picked up by me and driven to a place of safety, which is here, to stay with someone I trust, which is you."

Ibrahim and Tia look at each other. Tia looks apologetic. Ibrahim gestures to a chair, and she sits. He turns to Connie.

"Excuse me?"

Connie senses she is in trouble, and doesn't much like it. She doesn't get in trouble very much these days, and can usually shoot or talk her way out of it. Sure, she's just been in prison for the best part of a year, but being in prison isn't the same as being in trouble. It's an admin issue. Ibrahim looks cross.

"It was her idea," says Connie. "I encouraged her, the way you told me to. I helped—I passed on the benefit of my wisdom."

"You let her plan an armed robbery?" says Ibrahim.

"When you say it like that, it sounds bad," says Connie. "But it was actually a good idea."

"So good you've brought her round to my home to escape the police?"

"Plans sometimes go wrong," says Connie. "I told Tia that too."

"She did tell me that," says Tia. At least someone is sticking up for Connie. Tia robs a warehouse, Ibrahim refuses to hide her, but it's Connie who's the bad girl? Everything's tied up in knots. It's like an upside-down world.

"Were you going to share in the proceeds?" Ibrahim asks her. She knows she's not supposed to say yes, but *of course* she was going to share in the proceeds. What sort of a question is that?

"It hadn't been discussed," says Connie.

"You let an eighteen-year-old girl, who still carries a school satchel, rob a warehouse with a gun?" says Ibrahim.

"You should have seen her in prison," says Connie. "She really fitted in."

"I imagine she was terrified," says Ibrahim. "After all the work we've done. After all the chaos of your own life? You chose to continue the cycle? To turn Tia into you?"

"I didn't know who else to turn her into," says Connie. "I'm the only example I've got."

Ibrahim shakes his head. "No, no. Not true. You're not stupid. You understand the world better than most. I think you just liked the power."

"Ibrahim," says Connie. But she doesn't know where to go next. He's not cross anymore; he's something else. But what? She tilts her head toward him, and really studies him.

"I'm sad, Connie," says Ibrahim. "You've made me sad. Feel free to shoot your way out of that particular problem if you wish."

"How do I . . ." Connie is at a loss. "I don't want to make you sad. With me. How do I make you not sad?"

"You could say sorry," says Ibrahim. "But not until you feel sorry."

"I'm sorry," says Connie. And she is. So this is what being sorry feels like. Ibrahim told her she would find out one day, and she hadn't believed him. She hopes it doesn't last long.

"Not to me," says Ibrahim. "To Tia. While you still can."

"No, it's okay," says Tia. "Honestly."

Connie turns to Tia. She didn't do a bad job, all in all. Smuggling two guns past security isn't easy. She should have known about the lorry, but she didn't panic. She'll get away with it too. And next time she'll know better. The first time Connie sold drugs to a stranger, the boy ran off without paying, and Connie took a beating from her boss. She never made the same mistake again. She made other mistakes, sure, that's how you learn, but you should never make the same mistake twice. A case in point is that that first boss tried to hand out another beating a few months later, and Connie left him in the hospital with bullets in both legs. The moral being, learn from your mistakes. Everything Connie had become could be traced back to that first mistake, how she responded. "What happened" is never what defines you in life; "What you did next" is what defines you. And what Tia does next will define her. If she can brush herself down, this one job will be the beginning of a long and lucrative career. A fine life of crime and everything that comes with it. It's all in Tia's grasp. That could be her future, and who wouldn't want that as a future? Connie looks at Tia, curling up on Ibrahim's armchair. She thinks of herself at the same age. Back when it all began.

Ibrahim puts his hand on Tia's arm. They could be grandad and granddaughter, the two of them. What does that make her?

"I'm sorry, Tia," says Connie.

Tia looks at her, then looks at Ibrahim. Tia looks scared for some reason. Ibrahim walks over and puts an arm around Connie's shoulders. He looks scared too. Why do they both look scared?

Connie hears an unfamiliar noise and realizes she is crying.

"We will hide her," says Ibrahim. "And then we will help her."

Connie would like that. Would like to do something good. It might stop her crying.

46

Jason Ritchie has made a few calls, and no one knows where Danny Lloyd is. He's out of the country certainly. Good riddance.

Kendrick is staying: Jason had insisted on it. He's in Jason's living room, doing his homework. Maths. Jason offered to help, but Kendrick said, "Probably best if I do this one myself, Uncle Jason." Suzi is staying with friends for a couple of days. Jason insisted on that too.

He needs to keep them both safe from Danny Lloyd.

Suzi's injuries are healing, the physical ones at least, but Jason must make sure that the story ends here. Danny will have to ride off into the sunset, and leave Suzi and Kendrick in peace. It'll be easier said than done, Jason knows that. Danny is not a rational man. He has what passes for pride in men who grew up with pride denied to them.

He didn't use to be that bad a guy, Danny. Always on the wrong side of the law, but Jason knows plenty of decent guys who've never done a decent day's work in their lives. Sometimes that's just where you grew up. Your dad's an accountant, you become an accountant; your dad robs banks, you rob banks. Danny's dad broke his back falling through the roof of the old Tesco building in Crawley years and years ago. Danny was never going to be an accountant. So he robbed shops and offices for a while. Wages, weekly takings, anywhere there was a lot of cash and not much effort needed to take it. Then, when he had a bit of money behind him, it was drugs. Even easier money. That's what he was up to when Suzi first met him. Walking around a nightclub with a wad of notes, big grin on his face. Jason liked him, Suzi fell in love with him, Ron always had his card marked.

But the cocaine had been what really did it for Danny. It was often the case. Turned him from a half-decent guy you could have a laugh with at Christmas into a violent thug. There are a few people who deal cocaine and who never touch the stuff—Connie Johnson, there was an example—but that path was not for Danny Lloyd. And the more and more he took, the more and more unpredictable he became, the less fun Danny Lloyd was, and the more dangerous.

Kendrick came along, and Danny chilled for a couple of years. Bought himself some nice suits, a few trips to Morocco and the Middle East every year, making bigger and bigger connections, but he fell back into it, like his old dad on that rotten roof in Crawley, and money was the only thing he had left to break his fall.

A rational man would walk away from Suzi and Kendrick and cut his losses. Let them have that nice house in Coulsdon, buy Kendrick presents for his birthday and Christmas, and get on with his life. But that's not Danny's style.

Jason smiles to himself, because it's not his style either. He's seen Suzi's injuries, and he knows he won't let them stand. Danny Lloyd needs to be taught a lesson. It's a question, Jason supposes, of who gets who first.

Kendrick wanders through to the kitchen. "Am I allowed orange squash?"

"Are you normally allowed orange squash?" Jason asks.

"At home, no," says Kendrick. "Because of the sugar, but at Grandad's, yes, because sugar never did him any harm."

Ron. What would Ron make of all this? Jason has to protect him for as long as he can. Sort it all out before he even finds out.

Jason's mind flashes back to his own childhood. Lying on the sofa with an orange squash and the telly. My God, what times. He wishes Kendrick nothing but what he had. A house full of noise and love and orange squash and TV.

"Then I say you can," says Jason.

"Do you have any?" Kendrick asks.

"No," says Jason. "I'm an adult, I don't drink orange squash."

"You should," says Kendrick. "It has calcium. And also it's good."

He's right, thinks Jason, he should drink orange squash, it's good. His Ring doorbell sounds, so he looks on his phone. Amazon delivery.

Is he expecting something? Did he order that book he saw on Graham Norton? Must have. Jason wouldn't mind going on Graham Norton, but Graham Norton wasn't around when Jason was at his most famous. Still, he wouldn't mind going on. Chatting to Margot Robbie and Mo Farah. The doorbell rings again.

"Can I get it?" Kendrick asks, and Jason starts to say yes before something stops him. Just an instinct.

"No, you get back to your homework," says Jason. He looks at his phone again. The guy's wearing an Amazon uniform and is carrying an Amazon package, but why not be safe? Jason presses the microphone on his screen.

"Just leave it on the doorstep, mate," he says.

The delivery driver doesn't miss a beat. "Needs signing for."

Jason looks at the package on the screen. Looks pretty small. Must be that book. They had a Formula One driver on. He was sitting next to Cher. "Forget it, mate. Just got out of the bath."

The man pauses for a moment. This is the point a real Amazon driver goes back to his car or van. But he doesn't. Instead he reaches into a bag.

Jason runs into the living room, scoops up Kendrick and is out of the back window before the first bullet thuds through his front door.

Danny Lloyd has made the first move.

47

Kendrick is not stupid.

If they know where Uncle Jason lives, who's to say they don't know where Grandad lives too?

That's why they have to go to Ibrahim's. They are rushing over now. Uncle Jason and his grandad are each holding one of his hands. His grandad's hand is shaking, but Kendrick has felt that before. Whenever it shakes too much, Kendrick squeezes it, because he never wants Grandad to worry that his hands shake.

He has never felt Uncle Jason's hand shake before though. That's new.

"All good, Kenny?" says Grandad, out of breath. "You all good?"

"I am," confirms Kendrick, because that's what you have to say sometimes.

Ever since he saw his mum with the gun and the bruises, life has been speeding up in a way that is making Kendrick feel uncomfortable. He keeps finding pieces of a jigsaw puzzle, but no one will show him the picture on the front of the box. Kendrick likes information, and at the moment he doesn't have enough of it.

"He was a diamond," says Uncle Jason. "A chip off the old block."

Where is his mum? That's the main thing he would like to know. Uncle Jason tells him that she is okay, and he trusts Uncle Jason, but he would like to see her. He would like to cuddle up on the sofa with her. They watch *Friends* together. His favorite is Phoebe, but Chandler is good too. He would like to be watching *Friends* now. Instead everyone is scared, and that makes Kendrick scared.

His grandad buzzes on the door of Ibrahim's building. Uncle Jason is pretending not to look over his shoulder, but Kendrick notices most things.

The man who had rung on the doorbell, the man who Kendrick now suspects was not an Amazon delivery driver, had kept firing shots at them as Uncle Jason had carried him across the back garden, over a fence and into woodland. They had hidden for a while, and that bit was okay. It is fun to hide, and Kendrick is very good at it. He has hidden from his dad many times. All you have to do is be small and quiet.

There is a buzz and his grandad pushes open the door. Jason ushers Kendrick in behind his grandad. He will be safe here, Kendrick feels it. But what about Grandad and Uncle Jason? What if they go back out? Will they be safe?

"Will we all be able to stay?" he asks.

"I'll stay this evening," says his grandad. "Get you settled."

Kendrick has always been aware of trouble—loud noises, late-night phone calls, raised voices—but he has always felt that the trouble was on the other side of a wall. On his side of the wall were his mum and his grandad, and school, and stickers, and lists you could learn, like all the countries of the world. If you concentrated on any of those things for long enough, the trouble on the other side of the wall went away, and everything was quiet again.

But now the wall is gone.

Uncle Ibrahim is there to meet them. Normally there is a smile and a hug, but he looks frightened too. He rushes the three of them in and closes the door behind them.

"I need to warn you, Ron," says Ibrahim. "I have guests."

They go into Ibrahim's sitting room and there is a lady with blonde hair who looks like maybe a model or a wrestler, it's hard to say, and another lady who is much younger, with her feet tucked up beneath her on a chair like his mum does sometimes.

"You know Connie, of course?" Ibrahim says to his grandad. It's the blonde lady. Maybe she looks like a racing driver or someone on *Britain's Got Talent?* Or maybe like a substitute teacher you never see again. Kendrick is usually very good at working out what people look like, but this "Connie" is proving elusive. What he *can* see is that she has been crying. A lot of adults are very upset at the moment, and Kendrick doesn't like it one bit.

"Connie," says his grandad. Kendrick senses that his grandad doesn't like Connie.

"Ron," says Connie. Kendrick senses that Connie doesn't like his grandad.

"Connie," says Uncle Jason. He doesn't like her either.

"Jason," says Connie. And now we have the full set. Kendrick needs some information.

"Everyone is being a bit rude to each other, Uncle Ibrahim," says Kendrick.

"Well, your grandad helped to put Connie in prison," says Ibrahim. "And then Connie threatened to kill him."

Okay. This is stuff Kendrick can work with, but there are still a few gaps. He looks at Connie. "Perhaps you deserved to be in prison? I'm Kendrick, by the way. This is my grandad."

"Nice to meet you, Kendrick," says Connie. "And, yes, you're right, I probably did."

"And you shouldn't say you'll kill someone—"

"It's okay, Kenny," says his grandad.

"No, he's right," says Connie. "I was probably angry, Kenny. I'm Connie. Can I call you Kenny?"

"Kendrick is better," says Kendrick. "It just flows better, doesn't it?"

"I was probably angry, Kendrick," she says. "I didn't like going to prison."

"No," says Kendrick. "I've seen pictures about it."

His grandad walks over to Ibrahim. "What's she doing here?"

"Meet Tia," says Ibrahim, and the other woman stands up. His grandad shakes her hand.

"Nice to meet you, Tia," he says. "You a friend of Connie?"

"More a student," says Tia. "I'm sorry someone shot at your grandson."

"I appreciate that, Tia," says Ron. "Nice sentiment."

Tia then holds her hand out to him, and Kendrick shakes it. She smiles. "I love your name."

Kendrick doesn't know what to say to this new woman with the soft voice. He always knows what to say, but his brain is currently a complete blank. It must be the shock. Diving through the window, running across the garden, hiding in the woods.

"Thank you too," says Kendrick. Thank you too? *Thank you too?* What does *that* mean?

"Can I make everyone a cup of tea?" says Ibrahim. Tia is back on her armchair. Her hair is so shiny. Kendrick is sure she uses conditioner. Sure of it. His mum does, so he knows.

"Depends if Connie still wants to kill me," says Ron.

"I'm prepared to let it go," says Connie.

"Connie is in disgrace," says Ibrahim. "Doctor-patient confidentiality stops me saying why."

"Something to do with Tia?" says his grandad. Isn't that a lovely name when you hear it out loud? Tia. Like the ringing of a bell.

"I can't tell you," says Ibrahim. "But, yes."

"Why don't we have a whisky?" says Connie. Kendrick still can't work out who or what she is. Someone who sells tickets at a circus?

"Connie," says Kendrick, "can I ask you a question?"

"Of course you can," says Connie. She really has been crying. She's tried to cover it up, but you can never completely cover it up. Sometimes his mum comes and sleeps in his room—"Thought you might like some company, Kendrick"—and every time she's been crying. She never cries when she's with him though, and Kendrick is very proud of that.

"What do you do?" Kendrick asks.

"All sorts of things," says Connie. "A bit of this on a Monday, a bit of that on a Tuesday."

Lots of things, he knew it. Ibrahim is pouring whisky from a decanter into some glasses.

"Not for me, thank you, Uncle Ibrahim," says Kendrick.

Ibrahim nods. "A squash perhaps? I think I have some Sprite too."

Kendrick looks over at Uncle Jason. "Uncle Jason, can I have a Sprite?"

"Your mum said no sugar," says Uncle Jason.

"She probably said don't let anyone shoot at him either," says his grandad. "Let the boy have a Sprite."

Uncle Jason nods at Ibrahim. This is all good. One, he gets a Sprite, and, two, his mum has given Uncle Jason instructions. Wherever she is, she's still in charge.

"Do you think I could get a Sprite too?" says Tia.

"Of course," says Ibrahim. "They're in the kitchen. Make yourself at home."

Well, well, well. Kendrick likes Sprite and Tia likes Sprite. What are the odds? Tia heads to the kitchen. Her hair is really swinging. It's conditioner for sure.

"Kendrick," says his grandad, "why don't you go and help Tia in the kitchen—there's going to be some boring grown-up talk in here for a while."

Kendrick nods. This is interesting. Normally Kendrick's favorite thing in the whole world is boring grown-up talk. He can sit for hours and listen to Joyce talk about a friend who's just had a hip replacement, but she went private and didn't she like to let people know about it, but they did it on the cheap and who's having to fix it? Only the good old NHS, that's who. He loves it.

But just at this moment he is being drawn to the kitchen.

The adults are all sitting down now. Uncle Jason, Grandad, Ibrahim and the mysterious Connie who does a bit of everything. Kendrick could see her renting out kayaks on a beach in the Caribbean.

He walks into the kitchen and Tia offers him a Sprite.

"Thank you," says Kendrick. "I am obliged to you."

Tia smiles again. "You have very good manners."

Kendrick nods. He has always prided himself on his manners. Not everybody notices, but Tia did.

"Are you staying here?" Tia asks.

"I think so," says Kendrick. "Are you?"

"I think so," says Tia.

Kendrick needs some conversation. If he was in the kitchen with Uncle Ibrahim, he could just say, "How long do you think an elephant can hold its breath?" and they'd be good for an hour or so. But he worries that won't work with Tia. He will try a different angle. Here goes.

"Do you like watching *Friends*?"

"I love it," says Tia. "Let's watch some."

"Ibrahim has Amazon Prime," says Kendrick. "So he can watch *Below Deck*. Who's your favorite *Friends* character?"

"Joey," says Tia. "Who's your favorite?"

Kendrick takes a sip of his Sprite. Joey, eh? Not Phoebe? Perhaps it's just the sugar talking, but something feels different here. Perhaps this is life on the other side of the wall? There are raised voices in the sitting room, but Kendrick couldn't tell you what they were saying.

He places his Sprite down on a coaster and says, "Tia, my favorite is Joey too."

48

Joanna is aware that Donna is not officially investigating the case. Joanna would place money that Elizabeth has sent her. Subtly rule Paul out of your inquiries, would you, Donna?

Nevertheless, Joanna is happy to see her. She needs a favor, and Donna might be able to help.

"Your house is amazing," says Donna, sinking back into a sofa. "I bet this didn't come from IKEA."

"Morocco," says Joanna. "But you get some lovely stuff from IKEA these days."

"You sound like your mum," says Donna, laughing. Joanna shoots her a look that suggests maybe she'd like her to stop laughing. She does.

"I didn't know it would be you, Donna," says Joanna. "I didn't think this was your case?"

"Making up numbers," says Donna. "The real coppers are out there chasing the real leads."

"And protecting Prince Edward," says Joanna.

"I don't really know what hedge funds do," says Donna. "Perhaps I should learn. I'd like a sofa like this."

"I mean, there's over a quarter of a billion quid hidden in a hole in Sussex," says Joanna. "I'd just steal that."

"There's what?" says Donna.

Joanna laughs. "Of course, of course. They didn't tell you. Holly and Nick have Bitcoin down there. Everyone's going mad trying to work out the codes to the safe."

"Jesus," says Donna. "Even when it's not my case, they don't tell me anything."

"How do you mean it's not your case?" Joanna asks.

There is a noise from the kitchen. Donna cranes her neck to make sure Paul is in there. "It's not my case. Elizabeth asked me to come."

"There," says Joanna. "The truth. I think we can still let Paul assume you're here on official business. He'd be a lot more frightened if he thought Elizabeth sent you."

"She just wants reassurance," says Donna.

"I get it," says Joanna.

"Is there really a quarter of a billion pounds buried somewhere?"

"Sort of," says Joanna. "Please don't tell Elizabeth I told you. I don't want her to bully my mum."

"I think it's usually the other way round," laughs Donna. "And I wish we were allowed to steal money anyway. They said so in our training."

Paul walks in with a tray of drinks. "Two flat whites . . ."

Joanna takes the two coffees, and Paul offers the tray to Donna. "And a builder's tea. Eight sugars."

Donna takes the builder's tea.

Paul sits down, and Joanna reaches for his hand. Elizabeth has to ask him a few questions, that's a given, but Joanna made sure she was at home when this happened. Donna can do a neat act of wide-eyed, hapless local copper, but this is a woman who has Bogdan, of all people, trailing in her wake. Woman to woman, Joanna has to respect that level of game.

Donna is no fool, and, while Paul is no fool either, it won't harm to even the sides up a little.

"This might be easier if I speak to Paul alone," says Donna.

"Easier for who?" asks Joanna, sipping her flat white.

"Simpler, I mean," says Donna.

"Sure," says Joanna. "If you can explain to me in five seconds why it would be easier and simpler for Paul if I left the room, I'll leave."

"I might raise certain things you don't want to hear," says Donna.

"About his family?" Joanna asks. "I think I probably know more than you."

"I'd rather Joanna stayed," says Paul.

"Even if you didn't," says Joanna to Paul, "I'm staying. I'm cheaper than a lawyer, I'm smarter than a lawyer, and I'm in love with you."

"Now you sound like a cross between your mum and Elizabeth," says Donna. She smiles as she says it. Joanna suspects that she and Donna might become firm friends, given the opportunity.

"That's better but still not great," says Joanna. "So who murdered Holly? Do your gang have any ideas? Or should I ask my mum and her gang? They usually work it out first, don't they? I mean, they knew about the Bitcoin and you didn't?"

"They'll know about it the second I get back to work," says Donna.

"Aren't you at work?" Paul asks.

"I meant back to the station," says Donna. "I am at work, yes. You see why you might be a suspect, Paul?"

Paul nods. "Of course. I suppose I control the business now. Probably worth a lot of money."

"And the Bitcoin," says Donna.

"He can't access the Bitcoin," says Joanna. "No one can access the Bitcoin."

Donna notes this down. "And not every member of your family has an unblemished past."

"We don't arrest people for that," says Joanna. "Not anymore."

"No," says Donna. "But we can talk like grown-ups about it."

"My family are interesting," says Paul. "I'll give you that. Absolutely nothing to do with who I am, but, if you want to take a shortcut that will lead you nowhere, I'm happy to chat."

"And how was your relationship with Holly Lewis?" Donna asks.

"Not as close as it once was," says Paul. "But old friends are always old friends, aren't they?"

"She wasn't at the wedding," says Donna. "That's quite unusual for old friends who live in the area?"

"We used to date," says Paul. "I think she felt a day at work might be preferable to my wedding."

Donna turns to Joanna. "Did you know they used to date?"

"I did," says Joanna. "Do you know everyone Bogdan has ever dated?"

"He's got tattoos of most of them," says Donna. "He's a people-pleaser."

"Donna," says Joanna, "Paul is many things—a wonderful professor, a kind friend, a surprisingly imaginative lover—but he is not a murderer. His uncle Neil sells illegal Ozempic online, his cousin Ben is a car thief—all of that is true. But he has no experience with explosives, and he wasn't out of my sight during the four days leading up to the wedding, as well as on the day of Holly's death. There is not a single shred of evidence you will ever find, because he was nowhere near this murder, and you know it. I understand you have to interview everyone, but let's all just admit that your suspicions rest entirely on a dodgy motive and an even dodgier uncle."

Donna weighs this up. "But he still stands to inherit a controlling stake in the company?"

"Only if Nick is dead too," says Paul. "What are your colleagues doing about that?"

"They're looking," says Donna.

"Tell them to look harder," says Joanna.

"I'll pass that on," says Donna. "They won't have thought of that."

Donna's phones buzzes. She reads the message, then reads it again. She punches the air in delight.

"Good news?" Paul asks.

"The best news," says Donna. "Prince Edward's got norovirus."

"Ahh," says Paul. "Well, I'm . . . very pleased for you."

Donna smiles. Her day has opened up in front of her. Ironically, she might actually go to Nando's. Bogdan gets very excited when he can keep refilling his drink. A good day is turning into a great day.

"While you're here," says Joanna, "a little favor the police might be able to do us."

"A favor from the police, is it?" Donna asks. "Like mother like daughter."

"They bully me too, you know," says Joanna. "Now, Paul is allowed access to The Compound CCTV. I wonder if you could make sure that he is granted that access? At the moment it's all been impounded by your IT team. We'd love to have a little scoot through it, see how the business runs."

"Would you be looking for something specific?" Donna asks.

"I shouldn't have thought so," says Joanna. "Would we be looking for something specific, Paul?"

"I shouldn't have thought so," says Paul.

"There you have it," says Joanna. "Neither of us should have thought so."

"Just access for Paul?" says Donna. "Not for your mum, not for Elizabeth?"

Joanna gives the slightest of shrugs. "Well, I suppose that's up to Paul, isn't it, Paul?"

"Just for me," says Paul. "Joyce can beg but I won't be broken."

Joanna and Donna share a look.

"In return for letting you know about the Bitcoin," says Joanna. "Only seems fair."

"I can't," says Donna. "I—"

"I'll tell you what, then," says Joanna. "Why don't I phone Fairhaven police station right now, let them know you're here. I mean they already know, of course, but I'll let them know we've been talking and—"

"Okay," says Donna. "Your wish is my etcetera."

"I thought it might be," says Joanna.

Donna's phone starts to ring and she looks at the number. She holds up her hand in apology and takes the call. After a few nods and a "yeah" and a "gotcha," she stands.

"Jesus," she says. "Someone just tried to shoot Jason Ritchie. I need to get to work."

"You're already at work," says Paul again, but Donna is halfway out of the door.

49

You shouldn't listen in on conversations, Kendrick knows that, but the flat is quite small. He supposes he could put his headphones on, but the wire is knotted together and would take ages to undo. So here he is.

The police arrived five minutes ago. Chris and Donna—he'd met them before. Uncle Jason told them he didn't want to speak to them, and they said that it would be in everybody's best interests if he did, and then Grandad said that, well, it wouldn't be in his best interests, and Donna asked if that was the butt of a marijuana joint in Grandad's ashtray, and Grandad said, "Heaven forbid you ever suffer from arthritis, Donna," and Donna said, "Heaven forbid we have to arrest you both for possession," and Grandad waved Kendrick in and said he and Tia should go to the spare bedroom. Kendrick said, "Good, I can do some homework," but he'd already finished his homework, so that's another reason he is listening to the conversation. It is always interesting listening to adults talking when they don't know you're listening.

"Somebody shot through your front door in broad daylight," says Chris. "And I know a thing or two about firearms these days."

"I certainly heard something," agrees Jason. "I'll take your word about what that was."

"Your neighbors reported you and Kendrick fleeing over your back fence and into woodland," says Donna.

Kendrick likes being mentioned.

Uncle Jason takes a moment before answering. "We go for a walk when Kendrick finishes his homework."

Not true, but Kendrick would like that. There are pine cones behind Uncle Jason's house.

"Why is Kendrick staying with you?" Chris asks.

"That sounds like family business," says Grandad. "Not police business."

That's true, Kendrick thinks. Kendrick knows that the police are important, and that they do a difficult job, but he trusts Grandad and Uncle Jason more than he trusts Chris and Donna. A policeman once came to their school and talked about the dangers of drugs, but Kendrick saw him having a cigarette afterward and had called out to him that he knew it wasn't his business, but nicotine was actually a drug too, and the policeman had looked at him and said, "I'm off the clock, son," and kept smoking.

"Jason," says Chris, "let us help you. Do you know who shot at you?"

"It was Amazon at the door," says Grandad. "Perhaps it was them."

Grandad is being cheeky here, Kendrick knows that.

"I'm not a Prime member," says Uncle Jason. "Perhaps that upset them."

"I heard Danny Lloyd has skipped town," says Chris. "What would you know about that?"

It's funny when you hear your dad's name read out in full.

"Is that why Kendrick's with you?" Donna asks. "A family falling-out?"

Kendrick thinks of his mum's eye, black and swollen. It will stay in his mind far longer than the image of his mum pointing a gun. "Falling-out" didn't seem the right way to describe it.

"Did he send someone to shoot you?" Chris asks.

Kendrick wonders if this is true. It probably is, isn't it? Dad sending someone to shoot at Uncle Jason. What if they'd shot Kendrick by mistake?

Kendrick hears his grandad standing up. "You know I like you both, you know that. But you know we can't talk to you."

"Just talk to us as friends, Ron," says Chris. "Give us a steer. There's someone out on the streets with a gun. Help us track him down."

His grandad sighs. "I can't, Chrissy boy, I just can't."

"We don't grass," says Uncle Jason. "I'd ask that you respect our culture."

"We don't grass." Kendrick has been brought up knowing that. Don't talk to the police. It's not something he's had to worry about until now. Surely Chris and Donna could help? Surely you can tell the police if someone's done something bad? It's a confusing one.

"Don't be so boring, Jason," says Donna. "It's the twenty-first century. You're not the Kray Twins."

Kendrick is sure he's heard of the Kray Twins. Are they those two blond YouTubers?

"You've helped us before," says Chris. "We've worked together."

"You're not dealing with the Thursday Murder Club anymore," says Grandad. "You're dealing with the Ritchie family."

Kendrick wonders if he will be a Ritchie now, and not a Lloyd. He'd like that.

"Don't do anything stupid, Ron," says Chris. "If somebody kills you, I'll have Elizabeth on the phone."

Chris is saying this with a little laugh, but Kendrick also hears that he's worried. Kendrick doesn't think that anyone will kill Grandad, but if a policeman is worried, perhaps he should be too? If his dad is gone forever, and Kendrick dearly hopes that he is, his family is quite small now. Mum, and Uncle Jason and Grandad. What if one of Kendrick's jobs is to keep everybody safe?

"Last chance, Ron," says Donna. "Please, let's all help each other."

"Sorry, Donna," Grandad says. "You know how we feel. Talking to the police is the worst crime of all."

Kendrick is proud that his grandad is so strong, but something is niggling at him. Because, while he knows that talking to the police is wrong, he also knows now that it's not the worst crime of all.

50

"Do you suppose you and Donna will get married?" says Elizabeth, as Bogdan takes down a light fitting in her kitchen.

"Maybe if she asks," says Bogdan.

"Perhaps she's waiting for you to ask," says Elizabeth.

"No," says Bogdan, taking the new fitting out of a John Lewis box. "She's in charge of that sort of thing."

"I see," says Elizabeth. "And what sort of thing are you in charge of?"

Bogdan shrugs. "The bins, I suppose. And being in love with her."

"Oh, yuck," says Elizabeth.

Bogdan clips the new light into place. "How much you pay for this?"

"I don't know," says Elizabeth. "It was on the website."

Bogdan, happy with his work, pushes himself down from the kitchen island.

"Does that look nice?" Elizabeth asks. "I'm not very good at knowing."

Bogdan looks up at it. "It's okay. Stephen would like it."

"That's the main thing," says Elizabeth.

"John Lewis though," says Bogdan, shaking his head at the box. "You should have asked me. I get you one half the price."

"Stephen bought everything from John Lewis," says Elizabeth. "I wouldn't know where else to buy things from. I just click and there they are."

"Always ask me," says Bogdan. "I get anything you need from builders' merchant. Anything I can't get, I make."

"Stephen bought everything from John Lewis," says Elizabeth. "And I like to keep him happy. So I'll spend the extra."

Bogdan sits on a kitchen stool. "You look happier. Not happy but happier."

"They don't tell you, Bogdan, no one tells you."

"About death?"

"About death," says Elizabeth. "Take every word anyone has ever written about grief. Every line every poet has ever written. Every word of every friend who breaks down in front of you, every tear you've ever seen shed. Take the whole lot of them and throw them down a well, and you wouldn't even hear them hit the bottom."

"You still must say them though," says Bogdan.

"I suppose so," says Elizabeth. "But here's the thing. Look at his chair."

Bogdan peers through to Stephen's armchair in the living room.

"Where is he, Bogdan?" says Elizabeth. "Where is Stephen?"

"Well," says Bogdan. "I think he's in a little pot, isn't he, remember?"

"Not his ashes," says Elizabeth. "I know where his ashes are. But where is Stephen? Where on earth did *he* get to?"

"Maybe you would like a cup of tea?" Bogdan suggests.

Elizabeth walks into the living room and runs her hand across the top of Stephen's chair. "The world is so full of people and moments."

Bogdan walks through to join her. "And trees. Lots of things."

Elizabeth looks up at him. "There's love everywhere, every day, and there's sadness everywhere every day. Imagine all of it together. All that sadness, and all that love. Every kiss, every heartbeat, every second waiting for a lover, and every second realizing your lover won't be coming. Can you imagine all of it?"

Bogdan looks up and to the left, really giving it a good go.

"It's impossible," says Elizabeth. "It's beyond comprehension."

Bogdan looks relieved.

"And yet," says Elizabeth, "it's all here in this chair. Every single bit of it, in a chair we bought in an antique shop in Stratford or somewhere or other."

And Stephen swore it would fit in the back of the car, but it wouldn't, so he lashed it to the roof. Cirencester, that was it, not Stratford. And we drove home at twenty miles an hour with Stephen's arm out of the window holding it steady, and when we got it home it wouldn't fit up the stairs, so someone had to come and saw the legs off—"

"Who did you get?" asks Bogdan.

"I don't remember," says Elizabeth. "Someone who'd done some work for Penny."

Bogdan takes a very close look at the front legs of the armchair. He shakes his head. "They haven't matched the grain properly. I wish I'd been here."

"And then we finally got it up here, and it didn't match the curtains."

"No," says Bogdan. "It still doesn't."

"But Stephen settled back into it and put his feet up," says Elizabeth. "Stephen and the chair. The chair and Stephen."

"And now just the chair," says Bogdan. "Because Stephen, you know."

Elizabeth can't stop a small smile. "You know, you don't always have to be so literal, Bogdan, I'm trying to be poetic."

Bogdan nods. "Okay."

"They *can't* tell you," says Elizabeth. "That's the thing about your own grief. No one can ever know it but you."

"I have some new batteries for your remote control," says Bogdan. "I noticed you need them."

"That's very kind of you, Bogdan," says Elizabeth.

"Batteries I can do," says Bogdan. "Words are difficult."

"They are," agrees Elizabeth. "You know, if you ever wanted to sit in Stephen's chair, you could? It seems a shame for it just to be sitting there."

"I can't sit in Stephen's chair," says Bogdan.

"Of course you can," says Elizabeth. "That's what Stephen would want."

"I can't," says Bogdan. "Stephen is still sitting there."

Elizabeth nods. "I'm glad you see him too. How ridiculous, Bogdan. A chair is just some pieces of wood covered in cloth, isn't it?"

Bogdan weighs up his next words, and thinks they are important.

"Well, it's often galvanized steel these days, but, yes, this one is wood."

Bogdan's phone buzzes. He glances at the name and ignores it.

"Who's that, Bogdan?" Elizabeth asks.

"Is no one," says Bogdan.

"It wouldn't make a noise if it was no one," says Elizabeth.

"A friend," says Bogdan.

"Which friend?" Elizabeth asks.

"Okay, it was Ron," says Bogdan.

"I see," says Elizabeth. "Read it."

"No, is okay."

"Read it."

Bogdan reads the message.

"And what does Ron want with you?"

"Just to see me," says Bogdan.

"Come on, then," says Elizabeth.

"He says, 'No Elizabeth.'"

Elizabeth places a hand on Bogdan's shoulder.

"And what do you imagine I'm going to say to that?"

51

Ron is back at his flat, with some thinking to do. Jason has come clean about the whole thing, and it is worse than Ron could possibly have imagined.

His daughter beaten by her husband. Suzi pulling a gun on Danny, and Danny running. And now Danny sending someone to shoot Jason. He feels powerless.

But Ron has felt powerless before in his life. It's a vacuum he has always filled with anger. If Danny Lloyd were in front of him now, Ron would kill him. Kill him, bury him and never look back.

And Ron knows that it might yet come to that.

"I'm going to need a new door," says Jason, sitting down. The two men sit across from each other. Father and son, of course, but in the emotion of the moment, two men above everything else.

What is to be done? And is it to be done with fists and guns, or with brains? Ron hopes it is with fists and guns.

To business. Kendrick is staying with Ibrahim and Tia. Ron felt guilty about asking, but Kendrick seemed quite happy. Ron has also made another call. Someone else who could help.

"But Suzi's safe?" Ron asks his son.

"Staying with friends," says Jason. "Knows she has to keep her head down."

"How long has it been going on?" Ron asks. He doesn't want to hear the answer, but the first rule of fighting back is that you don't run away.

"Couldn't tell you," said Jason. "She'd never told me. Ashamed."

"Not ashamed," says Ron. "Not Suzi. She just knew if she ever told you, you'd kill Danny Lloyd."

"Maybe," says Jason. "And she's right, I'm going to. He had one chance to get me, and he missed. Now it's my turn."

"We need to be smart about it, Jase," says Ron. "And we need him to know it's us. We need him to know it's for Suzi."

There is a buzz at the door, and both men freeze. Ron puts his finger to his lips and walks over to the entry phone. He sees exactly what he'd hoped. The huge, reassuring frame of Bogdan. He also sees something he hadn't hoped for. Elizabeth. Elizabeth will have a view on this, and it probably won't involve killing Danny Lloyd and burying him in a shallow grave. He buzzes them up and puts the door on the latch.

"He's brought Elizabeth with him," says Ron, sitting down again.

"Will you tell her?" Jason asks.

"Course," says Ron. "Course. She'll work it out anyway."

"How was it seeing Connie Johnson again?" Jason asks.

Ron shrugs. "The mood I'm in she can try and kill me and see where it gets her."

"Looked like she'd been crying to me," says Jason.

"I doubt it," says Ron.

Bogdan pushes the door open and walks in with Elizabeth behind him. He motions to her.

"Sorry," he says. "She wouldn't let me leave without her. I really tried everything."

"He really did," agrees Elizabeth. "It was very moving."

Ron waves this away. "It's Elizabeth. Nothing you can do about it."

"So the boys are having a little summit," says Elizabeth, taking a seat. "No doubt something that Joyce and I would be too delicate for?"

"It's Suzi," says Ron.

"Ah," says Elizabeth.

"So you can keep being flippant if you want. Or you can sit down and listen and not judge."

Elizabeth nods. "I can sit down and listen, certainly."

"Suzi's husband has been beating her," says Ron.

"I'm sorry, Ron," says Elizabeth. And she is. She doesn't need to say anything more.

Ron waves it away, however. Sympathy is too much for him to bear just now. "She pulled a gun on him. He's off on his heels somewhere, and just tried to have Jason killed."

Elizabeth nods. "And you, Jason and Bogdan are the cavalry? You're going to teach him a lesson?"

"That's the idea," says Ron.

"Get him before he gets me," says Jason.

"What do you need Bogdan for?"

"Driving," says Ron. "Nothing more."

"Should I?" Bogdan asks Elizabeth.

Ron knows full well that Elizabeth will say no.

"Of course," says Elizabeth. "You must help."

Elizabeth is not only sorry; she is angry. Ron can handle that more easily.

"Don't tell Donna about Bogdan," says Ron.

"Don't tell a police officer you're planning to kill someone?" says Elizabeth. "You boys have really thought everything through."

"We're not going to be dissuaded," says Ron. "Don't try."

"Wouldn't dream of it," says Elizabeth. "You go right ahead. Perhaps they'll put you all in the same prison? That would make it easier to visit."

"No one's going to prison," says Jason.

Elizabeth nods, reassured. "I wonder if anyone who ever said that before actually did end up in prison? Surely not."

"Elizabeth, you understand revenge as well as anyone."

"Can it wait until we've solved Holly's murder?"

"Somebody shot at me and Kendrick less than two hours ago," says Jason.

"So, no," says Ron. "The case can wait."

Elizabeth looks at the three men and takes to her feet again. "I shall leave you to it."

"Really?" says Ron. "You're going to leave it to us?"

"Really," says Elizabeth. "I trust the three of you to do the right thing, and I want to hear no more about it. Let me know when it's done. I would ask you to send my love to Suzi, but I suspect she would prefer that I never heard about the whole affair. I will ask one favor though."

Here we go, thinks Ron. This is where Elizabeth tells him what to do. Tells him he's being a fool, that he's letting his male pride and anger get the better of him. Report Danny to the police, let them deal with him.

"Ron, whatever you do, don't let Bogdan get shot or arrested," says Elizabeth. "And, Bogdan, whatever you do, don't let Ron get shot or arrested. That's all I ask."

"And me?" says Jason.

"You're your own man, Jason," says Elizabeth.

"So am I," says Bogdan.

Elizabeth pats him gently on the shoulder and walks to the door. As she opens it, she finds herself face-to-face with Connie Johnson.

"Goodness, they're out in force today," says Elizabeth.

Connie curtsies to Elizabeth, then looks around her to the three men in the flat.

"Ibrahim told me about your daughter, Ron," she says. "I wonder if you had room for one more in your little gang?"

"God help us all," says Elizabeth, and shuts the door on her way out.

"Okay," says Ron. "Jason, Bogdan, Connie. Let's talk."

52

"Up and coming area," says the estate agent. "Couldn't give these away a few years ago."

There must be a shop, Joanna thinks, where estate agents buy their suits.

"But there's the overspill now," says the estate agent. "People priced out of the Peckham Triangle, so they come here. Good buses, was near the primary school till that burned down, there're trees a couple of streets down."

Joanna and Paul had had a long discussion about whether to sell Paul's old flat or rent it out. Paul doesn't believe in the landlord economy and no amount of Joanna's spreadsheets about the financial benefits of letting it out could persuade him otherwise. The yield that man was willingly turning down took Joanna's breath away. So they're selling.

"I see it has a bathroom," says the estate agent. "That's a bonus."

Joanna hears a phone ring. Must be Paul's landline. She'd rung it a few times when they'd started dating. Paul and her mum were the only two people Joanna knew who still had a landline.

"Okay," says the estate agent, walking into the bedroom. "So this is where the magic happens."

Joanna decides to excuse herself and answer the call.

"Yes," she says. It'll be a cold caller, but anything to give her a couple of minutes' respite.

"Is that Mr. Paul Brett to whom I'm speaking?" a voice asks.

"This is his wife," says Joanna. Is that the first time she's ever uttered that sentence?

"Thank you for the clarification," says the voice. "My name is Jeremy Jenkins. Would you like me to spell that for you?"

"Spell 'Jeremy Jenkins'?" Joanna asks. "No, I think I'm okay."

"Very good," says Jeremy Jenkins. "I wonder, upon receipt of this call, if you might ask Mr. Brett to contact me at his soonest convenience. It's quite an unusual matter."

"May I ask what the matter is regarding?" It's certainly the first time she's ever uttered *that* sentence. There's something about talking to solicitors.

"I have a package for a Mr. Nicholas Silver," says Jeremy. "To be opened upon the death of a Holly Lewis, which, I regret to inform you, should you not already have prior knowledge of the matter, has recently occurred. Would that ring any bells?"

"Yes, both friends of Paul," says Joanna. "Friends of my husband."

"I have been trying to reach Mr. Silver by telephone," says Jeremy. "But with no success, despite best efforts. I thought Mr. Brett might be able to point me in the right direction."

"May I ask how you got this number?"

"Of course," says Jeremy. "I have Holly Lewis's number, which I was to ring in the event of Mr. Silver's death, and I have Mr. Silver's number, which I was to ring, as discussed, in the event of Ms. Lewis's death, which, as aforementioned, appears to have occurred. And I have a third number, this number, which I am to ring should both Ms. Lewis and Mr. Silver be indisposed. I am sorry to ring it, but, in the present absence of Nicholas Silver, I felt it was my only option."

"I see," says Joanna. "And, hypothetically, if Nick Silver were to be deceased, what action would you need to take?"

"Well, I very much hope that isn't the case," says Jeremy. "But, were it to be so, both envelopes would become the property of Paul Brett."

Joanna is silent.

"Your husband," says Jeremy, just to clarify.

Wednesday

53

The call came through about an hour ago. Elizabeth ate her breakfast—she eats breakfast again now—and called Bogdan. Wondered if he wouldn't mind popping over if he wasn't too busy helping Ron?

In the recent past, if Elizabeth had agreed to a meeting with someone she was worried might kill her, she wouldn't have that meeting in her own flat. Out of respect for Stephen—it was his home too—and also to make sure that he didn't get shot. It was one of the compromises of marriage, "for richer or poorer" and all of that.

But now she is free to meet potential killers wherever she chooses, and, when Jamie Usher rang her, she invited him straight over. Just the man she wanted to talk to, and it will save Joyce and her a trip.

She has asked Bogdan to come over, because she hadn't liked Jamie Usher's manner when they'd met in Manchester.

There are so many suspects that Elizabeth just doesn't buy in this case. Davey Noakes, Lord Townes, Joanna's husband—she can't see any of them as the culprit. Perhaps she's wrong?

The others are waiting to hear from her, and Elizabeth is aware they need something to go their way. As her doorbell rings, Elizabeth knows that everyone is hoping that Jamie Usher might be that something. If they can find out why Holly Lewis rang him that night, everything, the murder and the money, might unlock.

"You want me to be threatening or nice?" Bogdan asks.

"If I'm being nice, you be threatening," says Elizabeth. "But if I start being threatening, you be nice. Be the exact opposite of me."

"And if he tries to kill you?"

"Unleash hell," says Elizabeth. She walks to her front door, opens it and sees Jamie Usher looking at door numbers. "You found us, Mr. Usher, do come in."

Jamie looks nervous as he steps over the threshold. Signs of nervousness are always a red herring in negotiations, because guilty people are always nervous, but innocent people are always nervous too. It gets you nowhere.

"Do take a seat," says Elizabeth pleasantly. "This is my friend Bogdan."

Bogdan scowls at Jamie. If you tell Bogdan to play "good cop, bad cop," he will do it without question. On one level his look is chillingly threatening, but he looks so absurdly handsome when he does it that the impact gets a little lost.

"Thank you for seeing me," says Jamie. "I just . . . you're not a family history researcher, are you?"

"No," says Elizabeth.

"Okay," says Jamie. "Okay. The police were at my house."

"That's annoying," says Elizabeth.

"I don't like the police," says Jamie.

Bogdan leans forward and stabs a finger at Jamie. "My girlfriend is a policeman, you scumbag."

Elizabeth mouths "Bit much" to him, and he leans back and mumbles, "Police *officer*."

"What do you suppose they were doing there?" Elizabeth asks. "Could you hazard a guess?"

"I could hazard a few guesses," says Jamie.

"I bet you could," says Bogdan, coldly. That's a bit more like it. The quieter Bogdan is, the scarier he is.

"But it's funny they should turn up a couple of days after you did," says Jamie. "Is that a coincidence?"

"No," says Elizabeth. "Not a coincidence at all. I confess we came to see your wife, but you proved to be much more interesting. To me, and to the police as well."

"What do you know about me?" Jamie asks. "What is this?"

What is this? Well, that's very much the question of the day. Jamie is going to give them nothing until Elizabeth gives him something first. Sometimes it's best to jump straight in.

"Holly Lewis," says Elizabeth.

Jamie stares at her blankly. Elizabeth sees that Bogdan has balled his hands into fists. She has seen Bogdan punch people before and, though it's not something she would admit in polite company, she enjoyed the sight tremendously.

"Nothing?" Elizabeth asks.

"Holly Lewis?" repeats Jamie. "Nope, nothing. What is she saying I've done?"

"She's saying nothing," says Elizabeth. "She's dead."

"The dead don't speak," growls Bogdan. He'll have heard that somewhere. A film.

Jamie looks directly at Elizabeth. "Why did you come to see me? Or my wife? Have I upset you in some way?"

"If you planted a bomb under Holly Lewis's car, you've upset me," says Elizabeth.

"A bomb?" says Jamie. If he's lying, he's good. But a lot of criminals are good liars, and the ones that aren't don't last long. "That's why the police were at my house?"

"Does that surprise you, Mr. Usher?" says Elizabeth. "You're doing a very accurate impression of someone who is surprised. Why did you think they were there?"

"Of course I'm surprised," says Jamie. "I took out two mortgages. On flats in the city center. False names, my usual trick, but I thought I'd covered myself."

"That's why you thought the police were at your house?"

"Yeah, it's illegal," says Jamie. "This is the first I've heard of this woman and a bomb."

Bogdan leaps out of his chair and grabs Jamie. "Stop lying to us."

Jamie shrinks back as far as he can, and pleads, "I'm not lying. I con banks; I don't kill people."

Elizabeth drags Bogdan off Jamie but perfectly matches his level of threat.

"Then why," she whispers, like an executioner preparing a noose, "did she ring you on the night she died?"

"She didn't," cries Jamie. "I've never heard of her. She didn't ring me!"

"Stop lying to me," shouts Elizabeth, and Jamie curls up further into a ball as Elizabeth looms over him.

The room sits in silence for a moment, Elizabeth's anger hovering in the air.

"Would you like a cup of tea, Jamie?" asks Bogdan.

Jamie shakes his head and tries to avoid Elizabeth's eye.

"Let me know if you change your mind," says Bogdan. "It's no bother."

Jamie composes himself. "Understand this, I'm no one. I make my money with easy cons, nothing else. I'm not a criminal."

"You are a criminal," says Elizabeth.

"Well, yes, I am," says Jamie. "But not what you're talking about. Not planting bombs, not killing people. I'm a coward."

"Don't be so hard on yourself," says Bogdan. "We all have different strengths."

"But the question remains," says Elizabeth. "Why did she ring you on the night she died? Moments before she died."

Jamie looks around the room to see if an answer might magically appear, but nothing springs out. "I swear I don't know."

Elizabeth walks over to her desk and picks up a notepad. She turns to the page with the number that Holly rang, returns and shows it to Jamie. "This is your number?"

Jamie takes a look and nods. "Yeah, that's my number. That's what she rang?"

"Rang it," says Elizabeth, "got into her car and was killed instantly. That's why we came to see your wife, and, when we found out your record, our attention turned to you."

Jamie is shaking his head, trying to get rid of this reality. Criminals are good liars, but a criminal this good at lying would be a great deal richer than Jamie Usher. He doesn't have a clue what Elizabeth is talking about. Holly Lewis was not ringing him on the night she died, Elizabeth is sure of it.

"Your wife," says Elizabeth. "Sit up, Jamie, no one's going to hurt you. You have a criminal record—I wonder, does she?"

"Jill? Never been in trouble, hates the idea of it."

"Sometimes we don't truly know people," says Elizabeth. "Does she know everything about you?"

"No," says Jamie. "Of course not. I do bad things."

"Hmm," says Elizabeth. "Perhaps she does bad things and doesn't tell you about them. Why did you move up to Manchester?"

"Jill wanted a fresh start," says Jamie. He looks over to Bogdan and says, very meekly, "Actually, I wouldn't mind a cup of tea."

"Make it yourself," snarls Bogdan.

"We can drop it now, Bogdan," says Elizabeth.

Bogdan gives a happy nod. "Milk and sugar?"

"Uhh, just milk," says Jamie, and Bogdan heads to the kitchen.

"So it was her idea to go to Manchester?" says Elizabeth.

"Well . . ." begins Jamie, his brain making recalculations. "Yeah, it was, but because of me."

"And did she have any close friendships down here?" Elizabeth asks. Have they been blinded by Jamie's past? Have they been hoodwinked by the sweet little nursery-school teacher afraid of trouble? Too many people in this case have secrets. Does Jill Usher have a secret that explains the whole thing?

"A few," says Jamie. "Work friends and that."

"Did she ever mention a Holly Lewis?"

Jamie shakes his head, like he wants to help but can't. "Honestly, I've never heard the name before."

Bogdan walks back in with a tea for Jamie.

"Thank you," says Jamie, then looks at Elizabeth. "Who are you? Who was the woman you were with?"

"That was Joyce," says Elizabeth. "We're investigating the murder of Holly Lewis. And the whole investigation seems to hinge on why she rang your phone number."

"You have to believe me," says Jamie. "It can't be me, and it can't be Jill. It's not possible."

Elizabeth looks at Bogdan. He shrugs. "Perhaps it was a wrong number?"

Not Jamie and not Jill. But surely not a wrong number? Holly Lewis, in a panic, keying in the wrong digits?

Or was she keying in the right digits? Elizabeth almost laughs.

"I have Holly's code."

54

Bill Benson drags open the door of the cage and in steps Lord Townes. The Compound is high-tech in every way other than the cage. This cage and its mechanism were taken from Betteshanger Colliery after it had been decommissioned, and must be seventy years old. It had been in a working museum in Rye before Nick Silver purchased it. Bill and Frank had both told Nick Silver that they trusted it more than any modern lift and, by the time the museum custodians had discovered just how much money might outweigh a pristine example of Britain's industrial heritage, it had been more expensive than any modern lift too.

"Morning, Lord Townes," says Bill.

"Morning, Bill," says Lord Townes. Bill has always been waiting for the day when Lord Townes says, "For goodness' sake, don't call me Lord Townes, call me Robert," but that day has yet to come. You often found that. Back in the seventies the chairman of the Coal Board had been a "Sir" and would refuse to continue any negotiations until you addressed him as such. Nonsense. Frank would also refuse to answer if you didn't call him "Comrade." One of the many reasons negotiations went on for so long, Bill supposes. Bill is not a political man and will call you whatever makes you feel comfortable.

"How's the weather up there?" Bill asks.

"Clement," says Lord Townes. "Quite clement."

Bill nods. He has still never found anything Lord Townes likes to talk about. He's tried football, always his first port of call, but nothing doing.

He's tried boxing and horse racing, because the posh ones often go for that, but nothing again. Tennis hadn't worked, and golf hadn't moved the dial. Bill has now tried everything. The cage continues its slow descent.

"You a snooker man, Lord Townes?" Bill asks.

"Snooker? No," says Lord Townes. He looks nervous, which makes Bill nervous, but, really, what can go wrong here? Lord Townes just wants to collect something from his safe, none of Bill's business what. Bill has told Ron of his arrival, left him a message, but nothing back yet. Ron will be interested though, surely?

Yep, Lord Townes is nervous, but there's all sorts of reasons to be nervous in life. For example, Bill has a prostate exam tomorrow and is nervous about that.

Though he won't be sweating like Lord Townes is sweating right now.

The cage reaches the bottom of the shaft with the sort of reassuringly terrifying jolt a modern lift system just wouldn't be able to replicate. Bill yanks open the door and leads Lord Townes out.

At the door to the vault, Bill scans his retina and his thumbprint, and a red light turns green. Lord Townes does the same and a second red light also changes. Bill grabs the metal arm of the door and opens it. This time he lets Lord Townes lead the way.

The vault is a rectangular room, no more than twelve foot by eight, each wall covered floor to ceiling with individual safes, once silver and now a dull gray, each with a keypad set off to the left. Bill and Frank keep the place clean, but it is not a gleaming, sophisticated environment. It is a place of work.

Bill turns his back and lets Lord Townes go about his business. Safe 816, on the left wall. Bill hears a code being entered, a safe door flipping open and some sort of small box being taken out. He risks the quickest of glances—he knows he shouldn't, but what if this is connected with Holly Lewis? He sees Lord Townes place a small wooden box in his bag. Couldn't keep much in that.

The door shuts again, with a confident beep.

"Ready," says Lord Townes.

"Right you are," says Bill. Frank is always wondering what people keep in these safes—"All sorts in here, Billy, probably bring down governments"—but Bill never gave it a thought. Too many people thinking too much was the key problem with the modern world. Think about your garden, sure, think about what you're going to have for tea, think about some things you have some actual power over, but everybody spending all day thinking about things they couldn't influence, where did that lead? Who knows and who cares what's in those safes? No one has to know everything. Let people have their secrets.

Bill follows Lord Townes out of the vault and seals it shut once more. The cage is ready and waiting for them, and Bill escorts Lord Townes inside. This job was easier than hacking and hauling coal ten hours a day. Bill has had only two visitors all week. Lord Townes today, and Davey Noakes came on Saturday. He should probably have told Ron about Davey, shouldn't he? The rest of the time he has been working on his Fantasy Football team and listening to a podcast about Genghis Khan.

The cage starts to rise, with a whine that takes Bill all the way back to the seventies.

Lord Townes looks calmer now. Whatever he needed he has found. He'll have his secrets, no doubt, and good luck to him. You keep them locked away, my old mate, none of my business.

"I don't suppose," says Lord Townes, finally relaxing, "I don't suppose you watched the darts last night?"

Finally.

55

Joyce had got bored after breakfast, and decided to pop round to see Ibrahim. She's very glad she did. There's all sorts going on.

Kendrick is there. He has just been explaining how bombs work. He'd looked it up after Holly's death, and is now something of an expert. He is also, and this is a first, wearing a dab of Ibrahim's cologne.

Sitting opposite—and, Joyce suspects, the reason for the cologne—is a very charming young lady called Tia. Ibrahim is being fairly coy about what she is doing there, only that it is a favor. Perhaps the daughter of a client at the end of her tether. Either way Tia was full of questions about making bombs. In fact, most of her questions were about defusing bombs, which Joyce thought was very much to her credit. Some people spend their life planting bombs, and therefore everyone else has to spend their life defusing them. Elizabeth, she planted bombs. And Ron. And Joanna. Joyce defuses them. Cutting red wires and blue wires left, right and center.

"Joyce, you're talking to yourself," says Kendrick.

"Best way to get any sense," says Joyce. "Has Ibrahim got you searching for his code yet?"

"What code?" asks Kendrick, suddenly excited.

"A bit too complicated for you, this one," says Ibrahim.

"I like codes," says Tia. "Well, I like maths."

Who on earth is this girl? Joyce wonders. "There's a lot of money in a safe, and no one knows the code."

"Someone must know the code?" says Tia.

"Two people know half of it each," says Joyce. "But one of them is dead."

"And the other has disappeared," says Ibrahim.

"The dead one is called Holly," says Kendrick.

"Precisely," says Ibrahim. "I did tell your grandfather I wouldn't speak to you about this."

"It's okay," says Kendrick. "It was Joyce's fault, and Grandad won't be angry with Joyce."

"Who's Holly?" asks Tia.

"The co-owner of a very well-protected security compound," says Ibrahim.

"Her car blew up," says Kendrick. "That's why I was reading about bombs. If you're scared of something you should find out all about it."

"How much money is there?" Tia asks.

"A lot," says Ibrahim. "Certainly a lot more than the half a million pounds you were expecting from your robbery. But don't get ideas. No one can touch it until they have the codes."

For some reason Ibrahim seems to be saying this accusingly.

"Is there like a zillion pounds?" says Kendrick.

"Perhaps not quite that much," says Ibrahim. "Somewhere in the middle."

"And if you crack the code, you can steal the money?" Kendrick asks.

"Not exactly," says Ibrahim. "But it might help us catch whoever killed Holly."

"Or whoever killed Holly might steal it first," says Joyce.

The front door of Ibrahim's apartment opens and Elizabeth rushes in.

"But that door was locked," says Kendrick.

Elizabeth shrugs. "Hello, Kendrick, and you must be Tia. Ibrahim, I have Holly's code."

"Codes!" says Kendrick, excited.

"I do too, I think," says Ibrahim. "The year of her birth, that was the biggest clue. Seventy-six, or, if you flip it around, sixty-seven."

Kendrick nods.

"Holly Lewis wasn't ringing Jill Usher or Jamie Usher," says Elizabeth. "She was writing down her code."

"Nice one," says Tia.

"07941," says Elizabeth. "That's the same as Holly's own number. Then 416617. 416617. That's her code. It happened to connect to Jill and Jamie Usher, but the person the number belonged to was random and meaningless, which was why we couldn't find any connection. The number itself was the thing. Holly did exactly what I told her: she wrote it down for someone to find."

"That's very clever," says Joyce.

"I am very clever," says Elizabeth. "Don't you remember?"

"But you still need the other code?" says Tia.

"And perhaps you are wrong?" says Ibrahim.

"She had no reason to ring either Jill or Jamie," says Elizabeth. "She wasn't ringing a person; she was storing a number."

Ibrahim nods. "And I see it does have a seven in it. And two sixes."

56

Joyce

Well done, Elizabeth, don't you think?

We need four things to get to the Bitcoin.

We need Bill Benson's cooperation, and we have that thanks to Ron.

We need a client to go down there with us. And we have Connie Johnson, thanks to Ibrahim.

We need Holly's code, and now Elizabeth has cracked that.

So only one thing is missing: Nick Silver's code.

And only one person hasn't contributed.

And that's me.

That final six-digit code could be the secret to everything. But I don't think I can be much use.

Ibrahim came over yesterday with his pen and pad and was going through all sorts of combinations. He tried to let me join in, but all I really did was make tea. You have to play to your strengths.

I feel a bit of a spare wheel all round at the moment.

Why were Kendrick and Tia at Ibrahim's flat this morning? No one will tell me anything. Something is going on, and I shall wait to be told what it is. As far as I'm concerned, we're supposed to be concentrating on finding Holly's killer and finding the last code, but perhaps I'm missing something? I often do.

Let me think about Nick's code.

Ibrahim was explaining the Enigma Code to me. The code they used during the war. "Unbreakable, they thought," he said, but apparently someone broke it. I asked who, but you can always tell when Ibrahim has reached the end of his facts, because he changes the subject.

He was writing down names and numbers and all sorts. Birthdays, that's the usual one, isn't it?

When they ask for numbers, I just use the same code for everything. Because otherwise how do you remember? And I have my code written down in my wallet and in my diary. It makes everything so much easier. It's 6149.

With words it's more difficult. I wish you could always have the same password for everything, but sometimes they don't let you. I have used GerryMeadow for so many years, but sometimes you need numbers too, so I use GerryMeadow42, and sometimes you need special characters, and I use GerryMeadow42! When I had to use that one the other day, I got locked out, because I forgot that the exclamation mark was part of the password. I just thought I had been in a jolly mood when I wrote it down.

I had an email the other day that said that the password for my *Gardeners' World* subscription had been "involved in a data breach" and I should change it immediately. I don't know why anyone would try to hack into my *Gardeners' World Magazine* account—all I do is buy seeds and occasionally add a comment under one of Monty Don's articles—but I tried to do as I was told. I put in GerryMeadow and it told me "Password not recognized," so I asked to change my password, and tried to change it to GerryMeadow and it said, "Your new password cannot be the same as your previous password," which didn't make any sense at all, and so I have simply had to cancel my subscription.

Ibrahim sent Paul all sorts of questions about Holly and Nick, and wrote down the answers in a database. In the end he came up with a list of twenty possible codes that he thought might open the safe. "I can say with some confidence it is one of these numbers," he said. And, I'll give Ibrahim this, he *did* say it with some confidence.

In the end Elizabeth got the better of him, and you could see he was disappointed. Imagine how furious he would be if I cracked Nick Silver's code. It would be like Venezuela all over again.

How clever though. The phone number was the code. Jamie Usher was a fraudster, but he had absolutely no connection to Holly other than six random digits.

If I'd known when we met him that he was a fraudster, I would have asked him why someone was trying to hack into my *Gardeners' World* account. Or maybe ask him to look up my password for me.

It was nice to see Donna yesterday. She was coy about where she was heading next, and I do understand why. If she was dropping in on us, she was heading north. And a long enough journey for Donna to say yes to cake, but a short enough journey for her to skip using the loo before she left. So you'd guess London, wouldn't you? And I can think of only one person she might want to question in London, and that's Paul.

Of course somebody should question him, I'm not a fool. I've investigated enough murders now to know who's a suspect and who's not a suspect. But if he's involved, why were Nick's texts sent to him? And why did he show them to us? Also, I trust Joanna's judgment. I may not like the paint color in her new hallway (too dark—a hallway should be welcoming) and she is wrong about sushi, but she has her father's head on her shoulders, and if she doesn't suspect Paul, neither do I.

I note as well that Donna is not investigating this case, and so someone else must have asked her to speak to Paul. My guess is Elizabeth. It's not even a guess, I know it will have been Elizabeth.

This whole case is buzzing around me, and lots of other things seem to be too. I feel a bit useless. Perhaps the adrenaline from the wedding has finally left me?

Alan is wagging his tail at me, but heaven knows why. I haven't contributed a single thing to the case. Ibrahim has a house full of guests and no one is telling me why. My best friend doesn't trust me enough to tell me she's questioning my son-in-law. My brownies were too heavy. I forgot to tell Joanna I love her.

What use am I? I'm not going to discover Nick Silver's code. Some women make history, and some women make tea. I will never be Elizabeth.

I might go online and order a nice tea set for Jasper. That is something useful and practical I can actually do.

Life isn't all about solving murders, fun though it is. Sometimes you have to help people before they're dead.

I will never be Elizabeth. But, then, she will never be me. Perhaps I have my own job to do.

Let Alan wag his tail, and let Ibrahim crack the code instead.

57

Ibrahim brings in a tray with three mugs on it. Kendrick and Tia are lying on the floor, coloring in planets in Kendrick's book.

"I said it would be too babyish," says Kendrick, looking up. "But Tia said she didn't mind."

"They had coloring-in books in prison," says Tia. "They were very popular."

"I have made myself three hot chocolates," says Ibrahim. "But three is too many for one man. I suppose I could share them if one of you is thirsty?"

Kendrick and Tia both leap to their feet. Tia looks so much younger than she did when she arrived. Seeing her with Kendrick reminds Ibrahim that she is just a child. Whatever Connie wants to turn her into, Ibrahim is determined he won't allow it. What a life this girl might have.

Ibrahim sits down on the sofa, and Kendrick sits next to him. Tia sits in his armchair, tucks her legs underneath her and reaches for a mug.

"Elizabeth was very clever to work out Holly's code," says Kendrick.

"I like to think I helped," says Ibrahim.

"And Grandad," says Kendrick. "You all helped. The Thursday Murder Club."

"There was a murder club in prison too," says Tia. "They murdered people. What does your murder club do?"

"We investigate things," says Ibrahim. "And with some success."

"Like Holly's murder?" Tia asks.

"Mmm hmm," says Ibrahim. He doesn't really want to be talking to Tia about murders; it seems to rub against his plan of turning her away from that sort of life. But at the same time he does enjoy talking about them, and the cat is well and truly out of the bag now. She knows about the explosion, the money, the codes.

"So Holly had a code," says Tia. "And this guy Nick Silver has the other six digits."

"There you have it," says Ibrahim. "On the nose."

"So Nick Silver killed her," says Tia. "Case closed. This hot chocolate is amazing."

"Either that, or someone killed them both," says Ibrahim. "No one has heard from Nick Silver since the wedding, except for some texts that clearly weren't from him."

"She dies; he disappears," says Tia. "I bet he killed her."

"Yeah, I bet too," says Kendrick.

"Do you agree with everything Tia says now, Kendrick?" Ibrahim teases.

"Yes," says Kendrick, unteasable.

Ibrahim feels sleepy and happy. This feels like a family.

"How do you know the texts weren't from him?" Tia asks.

"I'll show you," says Ibrahim. "And you'll see."

He fetches one of his printouts of the text exchange and hands it to Tia. She starts to read.

"The language doesn't sound like him," says Ibrahim. "And he doesn't know simple information about his best friend."

As Tia is reading, Kendrick gets up from the sofa and slides onto the armchair beside her. It fits them both. Two children. One running from something Ibrahim has yet to discover, the other being protected from something Ibrahim knows only too well. Kendrick puts his head on Tia's shoulder as they read. How much longer does he have as a child, this clever boy? How much longer before life makes him an adult? Until his shoes have laces and his heart has scars? Until his shame deepens alongside his voice and he no longer wants to lie on the floor and color in the planets?

"No one talks like this," says Tia, rereading the messages, and Kendrick nods.

"I told you so," says Ibrahim. "Elizabeth and I have combed them this way and that. We can't say who sent them, but we can certainly say that it wasn't Nick Silver."

Tia nods and goes back to reading. Right at this moment Ibrahim wants to save these two from the world. To save them from Kendrick's dad, and from Tia's trouble. Tia is pointing something out to Kendrick. They could be brother and sister, the two of them. Ibrahim feels himself falling asleep. Ibrahim, Kendrick and Tia, three lost children. Of course you can't save people from the world, all you can do is—

"But you see it?" Kendrick says to him, and Ibrahim stops himself from dozing off.

"Mmm?"

"You see it?" Kendrick repeats. "You and Elizabeth? You see it?"

"See what?" Ibrahim asks.

Tia holds up the paper. "How many times have you looked at these messages?"

"Once or twice," says Ibrahim. Can he see *what*? "Five times perhaps, no more than that. Let's say twelve."

Tia tilts her head at him. "And you didn't spot it?"

Ibrahim reaches for an answer, but cannot, at present, find one.

"These are from Nick Silver," says Kendrick.

"That seems un—"

"You really don't see it?" says Tia.

"I think, umm," says Ibrahim. "I think I get the gist, but any input you have, you know, is gratefully received."

"Nick Silver's alive," says Tia. "And he's got a message for you."

58

Elizabeth has learned, in her long, long career, to accept help from any corner. Never be precious. Even so, she would very much like to work out what Tia and Kendrick have spotted before they tell her. She sees Ibrahim poring over the texts too.

"Is it invisible ink?" Joyce asks.

"Of course it's not invisible ink," Elizabeth snaps. Though she takes a quick glance down to double-check.

"If you take the first letters of each text," says Ibrahim, "it spells out PNCSJI. Now, if I can just—"

Kendrick holds up a finger. "I don't know if it's rude to interrupt, but could somebody read them out?"

"Ooh, me!" volunteers Joyce.

"You'd be so good at it, Joyce," says Kendrick.

"All of them?" she asks.

"One by one," says Tia. "If that's okay?"

Joyce looks down at the printout, then looks at Elizabeth, Ibrahim and Ron in turn. She really can't help building her part.

> Paul it's me. I have to lay low for a while but don't worry, I'm safe.

"Don't worry, I'm safe," repeats Tia, and Joyce reads on.

> No need mate, just wanted you to know I'm alive.

"No need mate," says Kendrick.

> Can't ring this evening Paul. Will explain all soon.

"Can't ring this evening," says Tia. "Do we see it yet?"

We don't, thinks Elizabeth, also noting that Tia is a very interesting proposition. Where has she sprung from? Joyce reads on.

> Sorry mate, what is this? A test of our friendship? I'm letting you know I'm okay, and this is what I get?

"A test of our friendship," says Kendrick. Elizabeth sees that Ibrahim has both his highlighter pen and his tongue out.

Kendrick gives Joyce a thumbs-up. "You're doing such good reading."

> Jesus Paul. When I need you most, you pull this? We both know the name of the car. Stop messing around and let people know I'm okay.

"When I need you most," says Tia.

> I'm sorry if I've offended you Paul. I thought we were friends, but I can't trust you. Signing off for good now.

"Sorry if I've offended you," says Kendrick.
"And there we have it," says Tia.
"Grandad," says Kendrick, "you've worked it out?"
"Course," says Ron. "Ages ago. Just waiting for the others to catch up."

Elizabeth has scribbled down all of these phrases but still doesn't see it. Perhaps it's slang? A young person thing. She hopes so. That would be a good excuse for not seeing it.

"Can I borrow your highlighter pen, Uncle Ibrahim?" asks Kendrick. "We're not allowed to use them at school, because Nathan Pearson was sniffing them and—"

"You can use it," says Ibrahim.

Kendrick lays his piece of paper on Ibrahim's table where they can all see it. He then highlights sections of each message.

Don'T WOrry, I'm safe

nO NEed mate

Can't ring thiS EVENing

A test oF OUR friendship

WheN I NEed you most

Sorry iF I'VE offended you

Well, Elizabeth has seen a few things in her time. There it was, all along. Would she have spotted that, even in her glory days? She suspects not.

"Two, one, seven, four, nine, five," says Ron. "I'll be damned."

"Six messages, you see," says Tia. "That's what started us thinking."

"So we started looking," says Kendrick. "Six numbers."

"He's still alive," says Elizabeth.

Ibrahim nods. "And we have both halves of the code."

The Following Thursday

59

You want a job done properly, you do it yourself.

Danny Lloyd should be fuming. Fuming that the guy he hired at great expense had failed to kill Jason Ritchie, and fuming that he's sitting in an Economy seat between two losers, on a flight back to Stansted. It was the only remaining ticket on the flight, and time is of the essence now.

It was a mistake to go to Portugal: you can't be in control of things when you're not in the same country. Danny is heading to the South Coast. He knows people, people know him, and there's other business he can be taking care of while he waits for someone to do a proper job on Jason Ritchie.

He clicks his fingers, but somehow the flight attendant fails to notice. No matter, no matter.

It's funny, isn't it, how your priorities change? How the thing that was so important yesterday can take a backseat today. Yesterday all he could think about was Jason Ritchie. Kill Jason, kill Suzi, see where the cards fell. Danny Lloyd is a disrupter. Rules are for losers. Rules are for the two guys sitting either side of him. Danny doesn't need them.

He'll still kill Jason; he'll have to now. Jason won't have taken kindly to being shot at, and, while Danny doesn't fear Jason, you do have to tread carefully in this game.

But something much more exciting has come up. The sort of thing that makes a two-hour Economy flight worthwhile. The geezer next to him moves his leg an inch. Danny turns to him.

"If your leg touches my leg again, the second we get to Stansted, I'm going to break it."

Danny turns away and shuts his eyes. He just tried to do a line of coke in the plane toilet, but all the surfaces are sloped.

He hopes he can get some sleep, because he's looking forward to his dreams.

60

The metal cage is just large enough for two, and Ron and Connie are nose to nose in a dim, artificial light. They have started their slow descent, and the cage whirrs and whines around them.

The question for the gang was who would go down into The Compound with Connie, but Ron would accept no argument. He was going.

No one had liked it. Elizabeth had said, "Your plan is to travel in a small cage with a woman who has threatened to kill you, to an underground vault, whereupon you'll retrieve a piece of paper worth a quarter of a billion pounds? That's your grand plan."

And, yep, that was his grand plan.

"What shall we talk about?" says Connie.

"Who's your favorite West Ham player?" Ron asks.

"Is this your small talk?" says Connie.

"Yep," says Ron. "Honed over many years."

"Maybe I will kill you," says Connie. "You have very fresh breath by the way."

Ron nods. "You too. My favorite West Ham player's Mark Noble. Who's your favorite James Bond?"

"That's a better question," says Connie. "Pierce Brosnan. I'd climb that man like a tree."

"Agreed," says Ron. "Except the bit about the tree."

The cage shudders. It would be a bad place to get trapped.

"Talking of men I'd bang till they passed out," says Connie, "is your Jason still with that woman?"

"He is," says Ron. "Might be serious."

"Shame," says Connie.

"You're not his type, Connie," says Ron, and Connie laughs.

"I'd have made a good daughter-in-law to you, Ron," says Connie. "I'd have paid for the wedding and everything. Bogdan still dating Donna?"

"Far as I know," says Ron.

"Why are all the handsome men with great arms taken?"

"Beats me," says Ron. "Can I ask you another question?"

"Is it about West Brom?"

"West Ham," says Ron.

"Is it about West Ham?"

"No," says Ron.

"Ask away, I'm not going anywhere," says Connie, looking around her, then returning nose to nose.

"What do you and Ibrahim talk about? You know, when you talk?"

The low light dims further, then flickers back to life. Connie thinks, then puffs her cheeks.

"I don't know," says Connie. "But I always feel better afterward."

"Same," says Ron. "How does he do that?"

"I think he likes people," says Connie. "That's his secret."

"Even us," says Ron.

"Even us," agrees Connie.

"You wouldn't really have killed me, would you?" Ron asks.

"Definitely," says Connie.

"I'm half dead anyway these days," says Ron. His nose is suddenly an inch lower than Connie's nose. "I can't even stand on tiptoes anymore."

"Who killed Holly, do you think?" Connie asks.

"Elizabeth thinks whoever did it will show themselves as soon as she's got that piece of paper."

"Well . . ." says Connie.

"Yeah, well . . ." says Ron.

Connie looks him in the eye. "You're sure you want to do this?"

Ron thinks for a moment.

"I'm sure," he says.

"You can still back out," says Connie. "Get the scrap of paper, give it to Elizabeth, be the hero?"

"Too late for all that," says Ron. "Much too late for all that."

The cage reaches its destination. Through the thick diamond grille they see the shape of Bill Benson. Ron looks up at Connie.

"Thank you. I know you don't have to do this. Especially for me."

"Don't mention it," says Connie. "I owe someone a good deed."

Bill opens the grille.

61

Joanna is buying a telecoms company in Brazil, while Paul marks essays. She is on a Zoom call with a series of lawyers, business analysts, accountants. It has, thus far, lasted for three and a half hours, because buying telecoms companies in Brazil is never as easy as you think it's going to be. She has muted herself, mainly because anything she has to say will make the meeting longer than it already is, but also so a room full of Brazilian lawyers can't hear Paul loudly complaining about AI as he reads identical essay after identical essay.

Joanna steals a glance at her husband. How well does she really know him? She should just tell him about the call from the solicitor, shouldn't she? Why won't she? Scared she'll see something in his eyes? A big lie, not a little lie?

The Brazilian woman, currently full screen, is saying, "The multiples don't work for us. You're applying European multiples to a much more elastic market, and the offer fails to take that into account . . ."

Joanna's current offer is three hundred million. The Brazilians want five hundred million; they will, Joanna knows, settle at somewhere around three hundred and seventy million, but she will have to sit through several more hours of this before they do.

As has become her habit on long Zoom calls, Joanna also has the CCTV from The Compound open on her screen. Any movement catches her eye, but, as with the telecoms negotiations, there is rarely anything moving, just leaves blowing in the wind.

But if you have two boring things to do, why not do them both at once? What is she looking for? At first it was just something, anything, that might help explain Holly's death. Now she feels a creeping terror that Paul's face will appear.

As a man in a beanie hat starts talking about synergy, and Paul mutters something about Émile Durkheim, Joanna gives the CCTV her full attention. It's a thankless task, even on fast-forward. She doesn't know what she's looking for, and, worse than that, she doesn't know when she should be looking for it.

Paul gently shakes an essay in her direction. "Best mark in the class, and she didn't even bother to show up to the lecture. What does that say about my lectures?"

Joanna laughs, and looks back at the CCTV. Didn't even bother to show up. That makes her think about Holly, and her annoyance that she couldn't even show up for an old friend's wedding. Petty jealousies are all well and good, welcome even, in Joanna's view, but come on. They dated, sure, but people move on and, besides, Nick Silver was there too. She should have shown her face.

Joanna keeps fast-forwarding, as, for a brief second, the face of a cat fills the Zoom screen. Might it be worth taking a look at the CCTV footage from the day of their wedding? Holly's excuse was that she was working that day. Perhaps she was working at The Compound?

It's a long shot, but it beats scrolling at random.

62

Ron shakes Bill Benson by the hand. "Nice place you've got down here," says Ron as they enter the vault.

Bill nods. "Decorated it myself. You want to open the safe?"

Ron nods in anticipation. "What happens if we've got the code wrong?"

Bill shrugs. "Mayhem. Whole place shuts down. Only happened once before. We had to sit tight until Nick and Holly both came down to override the system."

"Well, they're not going to do that this time," says Connie.

"No," agrees Bill. "So maybe don't get the code wrong."

Ron looks at the piece of paper in his hand. The code, written neatly by Ibrahim. Holly's numbers first—416617—and then Nick's—217495. The first one worked out by Elizabeth, the second by Kendrick and his new love interest.

Of course the next question is: in which order do you put the codes? Nick's code, then Holly's code? Or Holly's code, then Nick's code? A lot rested on that decision. It was Ibrahim—clever fella, that one—who remembered Holly at dinner saying, "Always Holly and Nick."

Holly and Nick. Always in that order. Well played, Ibrahim.

The digits on the safe have a slight greenish glow in the dim light.

Ron looks at the number 4 button. Holly, then Nick. Easy. He realizes he's singing to himself. The West Ham anthem, "I'm Forever Blowing Bubbles." It always calms him. He used to sing it to Jason in his cot. He reaches the line *Fortune's always hiding . . . I've looked everywhere*, stops, and shakes his head.

Ron's been having a little trouble lately. Nothing to worry about, he's sure, but Pauline's been on at him to see the doctor. It started with his shoelaces. He found he was fumbling at the knots, his fingers not quite doing what they were told. He'd laughed it off, but last time he went shoe shopping, he'd bought slip-ons, and now that's all he wears. No one's noticed. Or, worse, everyone's noticed and kept quiet. For Joanna's wedding he knew he wouldn't get away with slip-ons, and Pauline had tied his laces for him, like a child.

He was holding his pints in both hands now too, like you used to see the old boys do in the East End. His grip didn't seem to be there anymore.

It was probably nothing. But everything was nothing until it was something.

"Come on, Ron," says Connie. "You want me to do it?"

"I'm perfectly capable," says Ron.

He's not though. The numbers are close together. He can feel his fingers trembling in his pocket, and he knows it's neither nerves nor the cold. Ron needs this safe open. For once in his life, this is no time for bravado. He turns to Connie.

"Could you?" he asks.

Is this what it comes to? Every day a new indignity. Every day a man who has never asked for help suddenly relying on kindness. What must Pauline have thought, tying up his laces? Ron thinks back to the man in the pub, having his food cut up for him. Bit by bit you return to childhood.

"Bit nervous, fingers shaking."

Bill rests a hand on his elbow. "Same."

Ron looks down and sees that Bill is also wearing slip-ons.

Connie, in what appear to be jewel-encrusted stilettos, takes the piece of paper from Ron. "So this is the order?"

"Holly first, then Nick," says Ron. "It's always been that way round. Business cards, legal papers, all that. Ibrahim spotted it."

"Did he?" says Connie, looking at the numbers again. "It's definitely logical."

"Definitely logical," agrees Ron. "Stands to reason. You know Ibrahim."

"But . . ." starts Connie, shaking her head. "If you're going to go to all the trouble of having a code . . ."

Ron stops to think. "Why not add one little twist?"

Connie looks at him and nods. "Don't you think?"

"Ibrahim was sure though," says Ron.

"He's always sure," says Connie. She's right about that. "But what would you do, if you were Holly and Nick?"

"Me? I'd swap them round," says Ron.

"So would I," says Connie.

"Either way," says Bill, "I'd rather not get stuck down here. It'd be a hell of a job to get us out. Fire service, probably police, maybe even TV when the word got out we were trapped. Lot of questions about what we're doing."

"Is there food down here?" Ron asks.

"I've got a KitKat," says Bill. "I've had my lunch already."

Connie and Ron look at each other. Ron gives a little nod.

"Nick, then Holly," says Connie. "If we're right, we've got three hundred and fifty million. If we're wrong, we're those Chilean miners."

"Good lads, those Chilean miners," says Bill.

Connie steps up to the safe. She says each number out loud as she presses the buttons. "Two, one, seven, four, nine, five . . ."

"In fact, I think I ate the KitKat too," says Bill.

"Four, one, six, six, one, seven."

For a moment nothing happens. Deep, deep underground, in a place where no outside sound or light has ever reached, the ex-miner, the drug dealer and the man with the shaking fingers hold their breath. Ron looks at Bill; Connie looks at Ron. They all look at the safe door.

Ron shakes his head. "I think we're—"

There are three quick beeps, and the safe springs open. Ron puts his hands on his knees in relief, as Connie reaches in and takes out a piece of paper. Ron rights himself, and she hands it to him.

"That's it?" he asks.

Connie runs her finger along the paper. "See all those numbers and letters? That's the key, it's a sort of account number. Proves the Bitcoin's yours."

"Seen it all now," says Bill. "Your pals are going to think you're a hero, Ron, old son."

"I doubt that," says Ron.

"You want me to send you back up?"

Ron looks at Connie. "You ready?"

Connie nods. "You?"

Ron lets out a deep, deep breath. "Not really, Connie. But here we are."

63

Joyce

I'm watching *Flog It!*—it's about antiques before you get any ideas—but I'm not really concentrating. Something very strange has happened, and none of us is quite sure what to do about it.

Ron and Connie had gone down into the mine to open the safe. We have the codes, at least we think we do, and we have the order of the codes, at least Ibrahim thinks we do, and we all felt he was due a win.

The rest of us stayed on the clifftop. Tia and Kendrick and I had an ice cream from the van in the car park. We sat on a bench overlooking the English Channel. Tia had never had a chocolate flake in her ice cream before, which I found very hard to believe. I asked if they didn't have ice-cream vans where she grew up, and she said that they did have one, but the ice-cream man also used it to sell crack, and one day somebody shot him and set fire to the van, so I can see why her mother might not have been keen. The ice-cream man who lived in my village when I was little ended up in prison, but not for selling crack.

Different times.

Seagulls were circling in the sunshine. I do love their salty cries carrying on the breeze. It always lets me know I'm home.

There's a lady on *Flog It!* who thinks her vase is an original Troika, but I'm certain I saw the same thing in IKEA in Croydon. Coopers

Chase laid on a day trip there in the minibus. I had heard a lot about IKEA, but had never visited one, because you don't without a car, do you? Anyway, it was everything I imagined and more. I lay on all the beds and sat in all the armchairs, and then in the end I bought a candle, and some meatballs in the café. It was a thoroughly good day out and I would recommend it.

Ah, it turns out the lady on television was right, and her vase was worth fourteen thousand pounds. That will teach me.

But I'm getting away from the point. Tia, Kendrick and I were on the bench. Elizabeth and Ibrahim were strolling up the coastal path, plotting something or other, and Jason and Bogdan were taking it in turns doing press-ups, and then discussing their press-ups with each other.

I was glad to have a bit of time alone with Kendrick and Tia, because I'm still not quite sure what they are both doing here, and I'm beginning to feel left out. Ever since the explosion it feels like something else is going on.

Something is happening with Kendrick, that much is certain. Jason has been looking rattled, which he never does. Even on *Celebrity Watercolour Challenge* you could tell he'd held his nerve. Thirty minutes to paint Corfe Castle? Rather you than me, Jason. Tia appeared with Connie Johnson, which can't be a good sign, but seems a delight. Kendrick has clearly taken a shine to her, and I have too. The two of them both need somewhere to stay for a few days, and, if you can say one thing about Coopers Chase, it's that it *is* a nice place to stay for a few days. If you ever feel in need of being looked after, come and pay us a visit. Tell them Joyce sent you.

The official line is that Ron's daughter, Suzi, is away at a friend's, and that Tia is the daughter of one of Connie's old schoolmates, and needs a place to stay while her accommodation in Brighton has some building work done.

The woman on TV has just said she won't sell the vase, and I believe her about as much as I believe those two stories.

I asked Kendrick if he was worried about his grandad being in the mine with a murderer. I should have phrased it a little better than that, but, you know Kendrick, he takes these things in his stride, and said that no one would dare kill his grandad, and I said Elizabeth would dare, and Kendrick said that his grandad versus Elizabeth would be like Iron Man versus the Black Widow, and I didn't get the reference, but I got the gist and we had a good laugh about it.

But all the time I was thinking that Ron really had been gone for some while. I trust my friends, of course I do, but, you know, it's *Ron*, isn't it?

I saw Elizabeth and Ibrahim wandering back toward us, Elizabeth looking at her watch. She had said this was a bad idea from the start, and you could see her face was a combination of worry and annoyance, along with some happiness that she might be proved right. Elizabeth is capable of holding many emotions at once, while I prefer to concentrate on one at a time. Right at that moment my primary emotion was protectiveness toward the two children eating ice creams with me.

Tia said she thought whoever killed Holly would try to kill all of us, because it really is an awful lot of money, and they'd proved they were happy to kill people before. I saw that she had a point. Then Kendrick said, "Do you know in Italy, ice cream is called gelato?" and I said I'd never been to Italy, but I'd seen it on television, and that I had been to France, if that was of interest, and Kendrick said it was of interest and what was the best thing about France, and I said I once found a shop that sold English food and bought some digestives, and he nodded as if that was a perfectly good answer because he's very polite. Someone brought him up well, and I suspect it wasn't his father.

I have to tell you what happened next, but on *Flog It!* somebody just brought in some Victorian pornography. I'll let you know how that goes.

I have said that I don't know where Tia has sprung from, but that I warm to her, and that she reminds me a little of Elizabeth. A little. Without looking at Kendrick, she said, "It's only me and Joyce here—does your dad hit your mum?"

The arm around the shoulder is something that I would do, and Elizabeth wouldn't.

Asking that question is something that Elizabeth would do, and I wouldn't.

Kendrick nodded that he did, and Tia nodded too, both still not looking at each other, and Tia asked if that made him sad or angry, and he said a mixture of both, and she asked where his mother was, and he said he didn't know, and she asked if he was frightened for her, and he said he was.

She did the whole thing with such gentleness, and allowed him such dignity. I put my arm around him too, and we watched a container ship on the horizon, and then I thought I should take a leaf from Tia's book. Because I had known, hadn't I? Known that must be what was behind Kendrick's sudden appearance, but a sort of embarrassment had stopped me from asking. Stopped me from helping this kind, clever and scared little boy. That's a fault in me: sometimes I don't want to know the truth, because it's too painful. I didn't want that to be the story.

And so I asked him if he really *was* scared about his grandad being in the mine, and he looked at me, shook his head and said, "Grandad? No. Grandad can do anything."

And I thought about Ron, with his knees and his ears and his eyes, and I wanted to tell Kendrick that maybe there was a time when his grandad *could* have done anything, but that time was gone, and that, right now, he was an old man in a deep hole, and that with every minute that passed I was more and more scared for him.

But honesty only goes so far and so I gave him a squeeze and agreed that his grandad could do anything.

And then I realized that Ron must have known for the last two weeks what had happened to his daughter, and had kept it tightly locked up inside him. I needed to give him a squeeze too, but he was nowhere to be seen.

Right on cue, Elizabeth and Ibrahim joined us. Ibrahim looked at his watch, and then at the ice cream, and then said that ice creams are around sixty percent air, so we were eating air that we had paid for, and I asked him if he wanted an ice cream too, and he thought for a moment and said that he did, and headed over to the van.

Elizabeth asked us what we had been talking about, and Kendrick said "dinosaurs," and Tia said "ice-cream men who sell crack," and I said "nothing really," and I asked Elizabeth what she had been talking about and she said "nothing really" too.

And then she added that Ron really had been gone a very long time indeed, and it was at that point that Ibrahim returned from the ice-cream truck and said he'd received a message from Ron.

The codes had been correct, the key was in their hands, the mission had been successful.

Which begged the question where on earth was Ron? Because he hadn't returned.

And, writing this some six hours later, he still hasn't returned.

It was Elizabeth who asked another question that hadn't occurred to me but should have.

She asked, "What does he mean it's in *our* hands?" Because if Ron hadn't returned, that meant that Connie Johnson hadn't returned either.

So that's where we stand. Either Ron has the key, or Connie has the key, or they both do. And we have no idea where either of them is . . .

Forgive me, Joanna is calling, and I have a lot to tell her.

I'll just finish by letting you know that the expert on *Flog It!* has said that there are a lot of "avid collectors" of Victorian pornography out there. "Avid collectors"? That's what we call them now, is it?

64

Joanna types "24 July," her wedding day, into the CCTV, and begins to fast-forward through the darkness of the early hours of the morning. At six a.m. she sees Bill Benson arrive through the avenue of trees and disappear into the lodge. Around twenty minutes later she sees Frank East walk in the opposite direction.

What would Joanna have been doing at six a.m. on her wedding day? She was awake, certainly; in fact, she's not sure she slept at all. Her mum had messaged her at five a.m. and five thirty a.m. to say that she couldn't sleep, but Joanna had pretended not to see the messages. Why? Well, Joanna supposes she wanted to show her mum that she was a grown-up, and not some sort of excited toddler who couldn't sleep the night before Christmas.

But that's exactly what she was that night. An excited child who wanted it to be tomorrow.

She should have replied, shouldn't she? Should have told her mum she couldn't sleep either. Then Joyce could have come up to Joanna's room and they could have lain on the bed drinking hot chocolates and talked about Dad and Paul and love.

Why didn't she? That's a very good question. Why does she always push her mum away? There's something about that relationship, something about being a child, and the need of a child to be an individual, to be something more than the things she's been taught and the way she's been raised. The need to somehow teach a lesson to the person who has taught her so many lessons? Joyce's love for her is unconditional, Joanna knows that, but, really, unconditional love has a huge flaw. If you love me no matter what, who I actually am doesn't matter. If someone loves your essence, your very being, what can you do to make them love you more or love you less? Nothing: there is no space. So the only option left to you is to continually prod at that unconditional love, to test it and stretch it, to mock it even.

And it's not just that. There is a further problem with unconditional love, isn't there? Because what if you don't love yourself? What if, like Joanna, you obsess over your flaws and weaknesses, you constantly update the balance sheet of your own personality and find it wanting? Well, then the unconditional love of a parent is a sign that they simply don't know you. If they truly knew you, their love would be peppered with caveats. "I love you, but . . ."

Since meeting Paul, Joanna has come to understand that all of these things are on her, however, not on Joyce. Joanna should love herself the way Joyce loves her: that is what Joyce has been trying to show her. Joyce is well aware of Joanna's faults; she doesn't hide them. But Joyce loves her regardless. Loves her more, in fact, for her flaws.

That's the love that Paul showed her, and she accepted it, because Paul had chosen her, and she had chosen him. She learned to accept it, and she should now learn to accept it from Joyce. To accept that love, and to show her own in return. To stop constantly striving to prove that she was different to the little girl her mother held in her arms.

She should try, at least. She should try, because how nice would it have been to lie on the bed with her mum and talk about love?

There is movement on the CCTV, and Joanna slows it to normal speed.

And so it is that, just as an American business analyst wearing sunglasses indoors is saying, "Without an earnings cap the purchase is untenable . . ." and Paul is asking, "What does 'Karl Marx had mad riz' mean?" Joanna sees Holly Lewis walking down the avenue of trees.

And beside her walks a man in his sixties. What was that name Joyce had mentioned to her?

Joanna has a quick flick through Instagram and immediately finds her answer. A man in his sixties, raising a glass of champagne to the camera in a tux and tattoos. Well, well, well.

So Holly couldn't come to the wedding because she had to work. The previous week she and Nick Silver had spoken, together, to a man named Davey Noakes. But on this day, July 24th when she knew that Nick was out of circulation, Holly Lewis had met Davey Noakes alone, at The Compound.

Joanna can see from the CCTV that the two figures are talking. But what are they talking about?

Joanna decides she has to call Elizabeth. She takes a large piece of black card that she bought especially for Zoom calls and lowers it inch by inch over her screen to make it look like the Zoom has malfunctioned, then switches off the computer and reaches for her phone.

Elizabeth will want to know exactly why Holly Lewis and Davey Noakes were having a private meeting.

But, as she's about to call, Joanna changes her mind.

And she calls her mum instead.

It rings the customary seven or eight times. Joanna knows that her mum likes to make herself look presentable before she answers the phone.

"Hello, Joyce Meadowcroft here, whom is calling, please?" Her mum also has a phone voice.

"It's me, Mum," says Joyce.

"Ooh," says Joyce. She always sounds so excited when Joanna rings that it breaks her heart for all the times she hasn't rung over the years. "I'll just turn the volume down on *Flog It!*"

"You can pause it, Mum," says Joanna.

"My television doesn't have pause," says Joyce.

"It does, Mum," says Joanna. "I showed you last time we were down."

"Yes," says Joyce. "But the button you pressed doesn't pause anymore."

"It does, Mum," says Joanna. "You must be pressing the wrong button."

"I'm not pressing the wrong button," says Joyce. "I'm pressing the one you showed me."

"Mum, you are not pressing the one I showed you. If you were pressing the one I showed you . . ." Unconditional love, Joanna, unconditional love. "Perhaps, perhaps it has stopped working. I'll get Paul to take a look when I see you next."

"Oh, thank you," says Joyce. "He's very good at that sort of thing. Your dad was too."

"I'm also pretty good at . . ." Let it go, Joanna, let it go. "How much do you know about Davey Noakes?"

"Not a great deal," says Joyce. "I know we ruled him out of Holly's murder, because he's always known about the money."

"Did he tell you that he and Holly had their own private meeting on the day of our wedding?"

"No," says Joyce. "He did not."

Joanna has also got Paul's attention, and he puts down his essays and comes to look at the screen. Joanna puts her mum on speaker.

"I was scrolling through the CCTV and saw them together," says Joanna. "That has to make him a suspect, surely?"

"I'd say so," says Joyce. "Have you told Elizabeth?"

"Why would I tell Elizabeth?" Joanna asks. "You're the brains of the operation."

"Me?" laughs Joyce. "You might as well have called Alan. He's cowering in the bedroom, by the way, because he got frightened by a banana skin."

"I'm like that with mushrooms," says Paul.

"Hello, Paul!" says Joyce.

"Hello, Mum-in-law," says Paul, and Joanna can hear Joyce suppress a squeal.

"I bet Alan can work the remote control though," says Joanna, because politeness is all well and good, but you can't completely give up the fight.

"Do you have the CCTV from today?" Joyce asks.

"Today? Sure," says Joanna. "What are you looking for?"

"The strangest thing," says Joyce. "Ron went to open the safe today with Connie Johnson . . ."

"Connie Johnson?" Joanna raises an eyebrow to Paul, and he raises both of his at her.

"Long story," says Joyce. "He insisted. But they've both gone missing. I don't suppose the cameras caught them leaving? We're worried about Ron."

Joanna types in today's date. "What sort of time?"

"They went in at two-ish," says Joyce. "So anytime after half two."

Paul starts scrolling through, and Joanna senses an opportunity. "While we're doing this, Mum, could you do me a favor? See the button on your big remote control, not the small remote control, the big one? Find the button with two parallel lines on it, and press it for me?"

"Oh, that's worked," says Joyce. "It wasn't working earlier."

"That was the button you were pressing?"

"I could swear," says Joyce.

"Glad we could fix it without a big, strong man having to step in," says Joanna.

And, as she does so, she sees Ron and Connie Johnson walk out of the lodge. They disappear around the side of the building, and Paul switches cameras. They embrace—Ron Ritchie and Connie Johnson of all people—and then the two of them set off in different directions.

"They left at three, Mum, I've just seen them," says Joanna.

"Then where on earth is Ron?" says Joyce. "Did it look like he was being kidnapped?"

"It did not," says Paul. "It looked like they were in cahoots."

"Oh, that's a lovely word," says Joyce. "That's a very Paul word. Where were they both off to?"

"Let's find out, shall we?" says Joanna. "We're coming down to see you."

"Oh, goodie," says Joyce. "I've got shopping tomorrow morning, but I'll be around from lunchtime."

"We're coming down now, Mum," says Joanna.

"But I go to bed at nine thirty," says Joyce.

"Not tonight you don't," says Joanna. "We'll see you in an hour."

"Goodness," says Joyce. This was worth missing the price of Victorian pornography. "What should I tell Elizabeth?"

"Tell her that Joyce and Joanna Meadowcroft are in town," says Joanna.

"Ooh," says Joyce.

"And Paul," says Paul.

"And Paul," agrees Joanna. "And tell her we're all going to see Davey Noakes."

65

Has she been at her absolute best? She worked out the Jamie Usher angle eventually, but other than that? No, Elizabeth has to concede that she has not.

Is that understandable? Yes. She is old, she is rusty, she is grief-stricken. Does that make her useless? No.

Nick Silver reached out to her in the first place because of who she was. What she had done. And she may never be that woman again—the mind a razor, the body a spring, the soul a granite cliff face—but she doesn't need to be.

Because she is now part of a team. An odd team, she accepts that, as she sits on Davey Noakes's sofa between Joyce and Paul, with Ibrahim perching on a footstool because it helps with his posture. But a team nonetheless.

Elizabeth's grand plan had not gone as hoped. Find the key, then sit and wait. Because they had found the key, but it had immediately gone missing, straight into the hands of either Ron or Connie Johnson. She could understand Connie's angle for taking the key, but that razor-mind of hers could still not fathom Ron's angle.

Where were they both? Elizabeth is delighted that she saw them part company on the CCTV. That Connie hadn't immediately killed him. Which is not to say she didn't follow him and kill him later.

Joanna has the armchair, the alpha seat, which, historically, would be Elizabeth's. But she's earned it. She had found the footage of Holly and Davey, meeting at a time neither had mentioned. That has to be significant.

If Elizabeth does not have the key, Joanna's discovery is the next best thing. Davey Noakes knows something he isn't telling. Whether that makes him Holly's killer or not has yet to be established, but it is certainly why they are all here at close to midnight.

There are so many questions still unanswered: who killed Holly, where is Nick Silver, why did Davey Noakes and Lord Townes both pay visits to The Compound the previous week? Perhaps it is time that she stepped up and answered a few.

Elizabeth feels her phone buzz and sees she has a message from Donna. Sorry, Donna, you'll have to wait, we're cracking a case here. It's been strange. A whole case without Donna or Chris involved.

"Well, this is jolly," says Davey Noakes. "Shall we start with some idle gossip?"

Joyce takes him at his word. "I was just watching *Flog I*—"

But Joanna clearly wants to take the responsibility of the alpha chair seriously. "Why did you and Holly Lewis meet at The Compound that Thursday morning?"

That's certainly not where Elizabeth would have started things; you need to dance around a little first. That's where Joyce was so useful: she has a capacity for small talk that Elizabeth has always lacked. But Joanna has been very successful in her field, and perhaps in the world of hedge funds one simply came straight out and said things.

"Straight in, then," says Davey.

"It's an easy question," replies Joanna.

There's a time and a place for this sort of approach, certainly. Elizabeth remembers that a passenger had once slipped through Heathrow with a case full of enriched uranium and delivered it to a London hotel. Once they had tracked down this courier, directness was a necessity, what with the prospect of nuclear capability falling into the hands of a criminal gang, and so his interview had been fairly direct. Direct and robust. But Elizabeth's not sure if the same principles apply here.

Davey gives Joanna a curious look. "This doesn't, automatically, feel like it's any of your business."

Davey, it seems, agrees with Elizabeth.

"I've invited you into my house," says Davey. "It's late, and there are rather a lot of you. I'd be even more annoyed if you hadn't brought the eye candy."

He cocks a thumb at Ibrahim, and Ibrahim says, "I moisturize."

"I'll say you do," says Davey.

Okay, Elizabeth, put your brain into gear and see how it runs.

"Quite right," says Elizabeth. "Joanna has questions for you, which we all want the answers to, but perhaps, in the circumstances, you might have questions for us first? Forgive me, Joanna."

Elizabeth gives a slight bow of the head to Joanna, in deference to the alpha armchair. You have to be careful with people. But Elizabeth sees no defensiveness, and no pushback, just an understanding nod in return. Joanna is smart enough to read a situation in an instant and to let somebody else take a different approach. Behind the directness and toughness, Joanna has her mother's lightning-rod empathy. No wonder she's so rich.

"Thank you," says Davey to Elizabeth, and, just like that, the alpha seat is in the middle of the sofa, between a sleepy ex-nurse and a university professor wearing odd socks. Elizabeth sees Ibrahim give her a little wink.

"I don't suppose you have the Bitcoin?" Davey asks.

"We do," says Elizabeth.

"You cracked both codes?"

"We did," Elizabeth confirms.

"How did you manage that?"

"A number of different techniques," says Ibrahim. "Bit of creative imagination, bit of brute force. Was there luck involved? Well, I daresay you need luck in this business. But I find sometimes that the harder you work, the luckier you get."

He looks very pleased with his contribution, and that makes Elizabeth happy.

"And where is it now?" Davey asks. "Do you have plans to sell it?"

"Would you be in the market to buy it if we did?" This is Joanna again—not a bad question.

"Me? No," says Davey. "But I'd be keen to know that it's safe?"

Wouldn't we all, thinks Elizabeth.

"It's quite safe," says Elizabeth.

Davey turns to Joyce. "You were saying something about *Flog It!*"

"Only that someone brought in Victorian pornography," says Joyce. "I missed what it went for, but even so."

Elizabeth's phone buzzes. Donna again.

"Five grand," says Davey. "I was watching the end because I didn't want to miss *South East Tonight*."

"I've put *South East Tonight* on pause, because these two arrived in the middle of it," says Joyce, putting her hand on Paul's arm. "This is my son-in-law."

"Lovely," says Davey. "And does he have a name?"

"Paul," says Paul.

"It's the button with two parallel lines," says Joyce.

Elizabeth sees Joanna start to fidget. It is important not to be too direct sometimes, but it's also possible to swing too far the other way.

"Any other questions?" Joanna asks.

"So if you're not selling it," says Davey, "what's the big plan?"

Elizabeth takes this. "We simply want to use it to find Holly's killer, and perhaps discover what on earth has happened to Nick Silver."

"Well, I can help you with both of those," says Davey.

There is safety in numbers, certainly, but if Davey Noakes chooses to kill them all he would be well able.

"Let me make us all a cup of tea," says Davey. "Joyce, you can come through to the kitchen and we can have a natter about *South East Tonight*? I have such a crush on Mike Waghorn."

Joyce doesn't need asking twice and pushes herself up, leaning on Elizabeth's arm. How pathetically delicate the two of them feel, how their bones show themselves these days.

There is a third message from Donna.

"And when we come back," says Davey, "I'll tell you exactly who killed Holly Lewis."

"And where Nick Silver is?" Elizabeth asks.

"I can't tell you for sure," says Davey, taking Joyce's arm. "But I suspect the two are very much connected."

66

Ron sits in the darkness and waits. The lights are off, the curtains drawn. A casual observer would think there was nobody home, but Ron knows he was followed. He's frightened, because what if? What if?

But Ron is tired of being frightened.

"You're sure I can't make you a cup of tea?" Pauline asks.

"Shh!" says Ron. He told Pauline she shouldn't be here, with what's about to happen. But it's her flat, and she's Pauline, so she's staying put. Ron has also told her that's she's not allowed to play bingo on her phone while he's hiding, and, because of the prospect of gunfire, she has agreed.

They hear footsteps in the hallway. Ron motions to the bedroom.

"Good luck, lover," says Pauline, and kisses him on the top of the head before slipping away to leave him there alone.

Ron wonders where the others are. They'll be worried, he knows that. Ron's phone is off, but Joyce has been ringing Pauline. Pauline has had to lie to her and tell her she doesn't know where Ron is.

Ron didn't like asking Pauline to lie, but Pauline said not to worry, and that she enjoyed it. He's found a good one there.

The whole gang would be straight round if they knew where he was. And Elizabeth would blow her top if she knew what he was about to do.

They'd all blow their tops.

So much of what he's about to do would upset them. But that's okay. They weren't just the Thursday Murder Club, were they? They were four people, with their own stories, and, right now, Ron has his own story to tell.

The story of an old man who still wants to prove he can protect his family. Even if it kills him.

He hears what he has been waiting for, somebody picking the lock on Pauline's front door. Ron closes his hand around a small piece of paper worth a quarter of a billion pounds. He slips it into the right-hand pocket of his jeans, before remembering himself, and transferring it to the left-hand pocket.

Somebody is now slowly pushing open the front door, and there are soft footsteps in the hallway. He thinks of the gang again. They'll forgive him, he knows that. They might give him a hard time, but the four of them will work out who killed Holly, and everyone will be friends again. That's if he makes it through.

Ron is blinded by the lights being switched on and finds himself staring down the barrel of a gun.

"Surprise, surprise," says Danny Lloyd.

Well, you got that right, thinks Ron.

67

Davey and Joyce bring in a tray each, and people take their teas and their coffees. Ibrahim is worried that if he drinks caffeine this late he will never sleep, and has asked for a nip of whisky in his, which should counterbalance it nicely.

"Shall we begin?" suggests Davey.

"Please," says Elizabeth, now fully in charge. "What did you want to see Holly about? You see it looks suspicious? A meeting we didn't know about, the day before she was murdered."

"I do see," says Davey. "But are you asking the right question?"

"Usually, yes," says Elizabeth.

Paul—normally quite quiet, but then most people are normally quite quiet when in the company of the Thursday Murder Club—starts to raise his hand.

"Paul," says Elizabeth, "you have something to say?"

"It's, mmm, it's more of an observation," says Paul.

"Paul is very observant," says Joyce. "You found my lost oven glove, didn't you, Paul?"

"I found it, Mum," says Joanna.

"Well, Paul was there when it was found," says Joyce. "You don't have to turn it into *CSI: Miami*."

Paul waits to see if they have finished, and it appears that for now they have, and so he continues. "Holly was many things, but she was never a pushover. And, Davey, I know you less well, but you seem fairly relaxed with who and what you are."

"Doesn't he talk nice?" says Davey.

Ibrahim agrees. With the sentiment, if not the grammar.

"When Joanna found the footage of you, Davey, meeting Holly, there was an obvious question, the question Elizabeth asked. What did you, Davey, want to see Holly about?"

"Apologies that my questions are so obvious," says Elizabeth. Ibrahim can see that she can't really unleash on Paul, much as she would like to, because she knows he is under Joyce's staunch protection.

"Not obvious," says Paul. "Apologies, I phrased that very badly. A better word would be 'necessary.' You asked the necessary question."

Ibrahim nods. This guy is pretty good.

"But think of what we know," says Paul. "Not much, granted, but we do know a few things. We know that Davey has known about the money for many years and done nothing about it. Hasn't shown an interest. Equally we know that Holly and Nick had only just agreed to cash out, so was Holly perhaps the more motivated in that moment?"

"Very good," says Joyce. "Very good."

"What's very good?" Joanna asks her.

"Just that Paul has a lovely deep voice," replies Joyce.

Ibrahim sees where Paul is headed. If he's the man Ibrahim judges him to be, he'll let Elizabeth ask the actual question. Let's see.

"So, perhaps a different take on the question might be . . ." Paul motions to Elizabeth, as if he's interested to hear what she might have to say. Textbook stuff.

"It might be," says Elizabeth, "why did Holly ask to see you?"

"Bingo," says Davey. "She asked to see me."

"Well done, Elizabeth," says Ibrahim. Might as well get a few brownie points of his own.

"And what did she want?" Elizabeth asks.

"My approval," says Davey. "For a plan."

"Do go on," says Elizabeth.

"Holly and Nick had been partners for many years," says Davey. "But perhaps not friends for all of that time?"

"Agreed," says Paul. "The business worked; the friendship not so much."

"Holly was a nightmare," says Davey.

"I wouldn't say that," says Paul.

"No one knew their codes," says Davey. "And there's no way anyone could discover them—"

"Au contraire," says Ibrahim.

"But then Holly tells me that, as a fail-safe, they've each lodged their code with a solicitor. A random one, miles away, no idea where."

"Kettering," says Joanna.

"Sounds like the sort of place," says Davey. "So Holly comes to me and tells me she's killed Nick Silver, and, honestly, I think she thought I'd be impressed."

"Holly?" says Joyce. "I can't believe it."

"I can," says Paul.

"Put a bomb under his car," says Davey. "Got it from the internet."

"My God, you can get anything," says Joyce. "The woman in the flat above me got a pizza oven."

"On his death," says Davey, "Holly would get his code, and she wanted me to broker the whole lot. The whole three hundred and fifty million. Pleased as punch, she was."

"Did you ask her why?" Elizabeth asks.

"I did," says Davey. "And she said that three hundred and fifty million is a bigger number than one hundred and seventy-five million."

"What did you do?" Joanna asks.

"I asked her if the bomb had gone off, and she said she didn't know; we checked the news and there was nothing, so I told her to lie low for a few hours and I would investigate. I didn't know what to do with her, I couldn't call the police—"

"Why couldn't you call the police?" Joanna asks.

"No grassing," says Joyce.

"No grassing," agrees Paul.

"I sent Holly home," says Davey. "And I was straight around to Nick's house with one of my men, and we found the bomb, pretty solid piece of kit, and we took it off. She wasn't killing Nick Silver on my watch. Didn't seem fair to me."

"You saved Nick Silver's life?" Paul asks.

"I hope so," says Davey. "We'll have to see, won't we?"

"Is it still here?" Elizabeth asks. "I'd very much like to see it?"

"It's not," says Davey. "I thought I'd just keep it safe until I could help Nick. They're pretty stable now, bombs, not like the old days."

"Amen," says Elizabeth.

"I tried to find Nick," says Davey. "Let him know what was up, but he'd gone."

"Why did you smash up his office?" says Elizabeth.

"Not me," says Davey. "So Nick's missing but presumably alive, and I have to deal with the fallout. I have to deal with Holly."

"And you dealt with Holly by killing her?" says Ibrahim.

"Christ, no," says Davey. "What's the motive, except I didn't approve of her trying to kill Nick? If I killed everyone I disapproved of, I'd be a busy boy."

"Me too," says Joyce. "People who don't take their money out until they've packed all their shopping away. They'd be first."

"I just wanted to warn her," says Davey. "To make her think twice. Let her know it wasn't acceptable."

"And how, I wonder," says Elizabeth, "did you warn her?"

Davey lowers his head and nods, in acceptance of some private guilt. "Well, this is where I have to take some responsibility. I got my guy to deliver the bomb back to her. Just to let her know she'd been sussed. A little note on it that just said *Play fair*."

"Delivered where?" Elizabeth asks, though they all know the answer already.

"He followed her on the Friday night," says Davey. "And you know where she went. And while she was having dinner he placed the bomb, nice and secure, on her passenger seat. Note on top. Somewhere she couldn't miss it."

"Unless she left her glasses behind," says Elizabeth.

"Even then," says Davey, "she'd have had to dump something pretty heavy on it to set it off."

Ibrahim looks at Joyce. Those brownies really had been dense. Joyce gives him an apologetic look.

"So Holly was killed with her own bomb?" Joanna asks.

"She was," says Davey. "That bomb was made to ensure that only one of them could get the money, and it certainly did that."

"And where's Nick now?" Paul asks.

"My guess," says Davey, "is that he thought I was trying to kill him. So he's put himself in cold storage."

"He's in The Compound?" asks Joyce.

"Nope," says Davey. "Just somewhere I can't find him. He's cut himself off completely. No phone, no cards, no car, no computer, no CCTV. He'll be locked away. Little faceless hotel where you pay with cash and eat out of a vending machine. I've been looking, believe me. No trace of him."

"That's why he came to me," says Elizabeth.

"That'd be my guess too," says Davey. "Thought you might be able to find him when the coast was clear. I imagine you have techniques? Perhaps if I can't find him, you can?"

"Jasper will have a few ideas," says Elizabeth to Joyce, and Joyce claps her hands together.

"You *really* can't find Nick?" says Joanna.

"He is very, very good at his job," says Davey. "He'll stay missing for as long as he thinks I'm trying to kill him."

"Do you think that's why Lord Townes visited The Compound too?" Joyce asks.

"Lord Townes?" says Davey. "I wouldn't know. He'll have had a reason."

Elizabeth sits back. So Holly died at her own hand? Killed by her own greed? There was a poetic justice to it that Elizabeth could appreciate.

The whole thing seems neat enough. Nick staging the break-in to make her feel involved. Nick sending Paul his codes as some sort of protection against Davey Noakes. But is it *too* neat? Like the scene at Nick's office? Is this staged as well?

"How would you defend yourself against a suggestion that you and Nick Silver are in this together?" asks Elizabeth. "You say the whole thing was Holly's plan. We have only your word for that. Perhaps Nick hired you, and when he finally resurfaces, he cashes out the Bitcoin, and you ask for double your fee? It really is a fortune."

"There would be one problem with that plan," says Davey. "And no one's going to like it."

68

DCI Varma is eating a sandwich at her desk, and failing to solve a murder.

There are no forensics of any use. They haven't found Holly's phone, and her personal emails are so heavily encrypted as to be unusable. She thought there had been a breakthrough when a partial fingerprint had been found on a fragment of the bomb, and it had been fast-tracked through the lab. To everyone's great disappointment it had turned out to be Holly's own fingerprint. She must have touched the bomb before she died. Perhaps that was even what set the thing off?

Records from Companies House show that Holly Lewis runs some form of storage facility, but, despite a week of investigations, this facility has yet to be located. Her partner in this endeavor is a man named Nicholas James Silver, but he seems not to be at home. An obvious suspect but currently proving impossible to track down. Varma should probably be doing more about this, but, well, you know?

Then there was the lead from what's her name, De Freitas, about the Bitcoin. Three hundred and fifty million. Actually proved useful in the end.

The Financial Intelligence Unit had got in touch after she'd emailed them about the Bitcoin lead. A man called Lord Townes had been talking to everyone in town about a huge Bitcoin deal he was involved in. It raised a few flags, not known to be his style. She'd looked into it, and, well, what do you know, he was local, so that was a possible connection.

A couple of uniforms had popped round, but he wasn't in, so they'll go again tomorrow. Again, maybe she could be doing more.

They say you always want to solve your final case, but Varma doesn't see it happening.

She scrolls her way down her computer screen. If she's going to do her pottery full time, she's going to need a pretty good kiln. You can rent them or you can share them, but Varma wants to buy one, really. To really commit.

Varma has a photo of Lord Townes, so maybe she'll go round to Coopers Chase again to see if anyone noticed him around on the night of the murder. You never know. While she's still a detective, perhaps she should do some actual detecting.

She won't miss the job, and she knows the job won't miss her. It'd be nice to solve it though, of course it would. Nice to tie up all the loose ends. Maybe Lord Townes is—

Ooh, someone in Horsham has got a secondhand kiln for sale!

69

"Mr. Noakes," says Ibrahim, "what aren't we going to like?"

"Again," says Davey Noakes, "I don't come out of this wonderfully, but there we are. It was my idea to pay Holly and Nick in Bitcoin. I'd been paid some for some amphetamine in Amsterdam and accepted it as a novelty. I'd just started reading about it and thought, 'Why not?' Holly and Nick agreed to the deal, for much the same reason as I did. Why not chance your arm? It was only twenty grand, and everyone could afford to lose it, if it came to that."

"But now it's worth three hundred and fifty million," says Joanna. "And very few people could afford to lose that?"

Davey nods. "You're quite right. It has become a bigger and bigger deal as the years have gone by."

"Enough to kill for, in fact," says Elizabeth. "Which is where we came in."

"Three hundred and fifty million is more than enough to kill for," agrees Davey. "But I'm afraid that Holly and Nick's Bitcoin is not worth quite as much as that."

"How do you mean?" asks Paul.

Davey gives a big sigh. "The Bitcoin I got paid in, all those years ago—"

"The amphetamine Bitcoin?" prompts Joyce.

"The amphetamine Bitcoin," confirms Davey. "After I agreed to the deal with Holly and Nick, and I realized that all I actually had in my possession was a piece of paper with a string of numbers and letters on it—"

"And so?" says Ibrahim.

"So I got to thinking that Holly and Nick wouldn't really know any different," says Davey. "And so I took another piece of paper. And I just wrote some numbers and letters on that instead."

Elizabeth is shaking her head. "And that's what was in Holly and Nick's safe? Not Bitcoin at all?"

"Afraid so," says Davey. "Just an old piece of paper with random letters and numbers on it. It looked the real deal, I made sure of that, but if they'd ever tried to cash it out, it'd be worth the square root of bugger all."

"Oh, Davey," says Joyce.

"I know," says Davey. "I know. I thought there was no risk. Thought the whole thing would be a fad. I cashed out the real Bitcoin over the years, at various price peaks, and did very nicely thank you out of it, but I was aware that my little twenty-grand con was growing and growing into a bigger and bigger con as the years went by.

"When it reached two hundred grand, I thought perhaps I should come clean, you know? Tell Holly and Nick there had been a mistake, slip them the two hundred grand? But I like a gamble, I can't deny it."

"I like a gamble too," says Ibrahim.

"I kept thinking it'll go down again, it'll go down again, but it didn't, and by the time the value had passed into the millions, I thought, all right, it's not a fad, but I'm damned if I'm going to fork out millions to compensate Holly and Nick for a perfectly innocent scam."

"So what was the plan?" Joanna asks.

"No plan," says Davey. "None of it mattered, as long as Holly and Nick decided not to cash out. I'd done sterling work over the years persuading one or the other of them that the time wasn't right. They trusted me, you see?"

"And then less than two weeks ago," says Elizabeth, "in walk Holly and Nick, finally agreeing that the time was right."

Davey nods. "The money was too much to ignore, I suppose. It was always going to happen. My only hope of getting out of trouble had been to die before it did. After the two of them had left, I called my accountant in for a stocktake. My money's scattered here, there and everywhere, and I just wanted to check what it amounted to."

"I did that with my pension," says Joyce. "There was an advert and you can put it all in one place. It does add up."

Davey nods. "My money amounted to around thirty-one million pounds."

"Okay," says Joyce. "That's . . . okay."

"Nothing like enough to compensate Holly and Nick. Holly rang me, told me she wanted to meet, and I thought, here we go."

"You were going to tell her?" asks Paul.

Davey nods. "I was all ready to come clean, and then she tells me about the car bomb—"

"And events overtook you," says Ibrahim.

"That's a nice way of putting it," agrees Davey.

"So the piece of paper we took from the safe this afternoon?" says Elizabeth.

"Completely worthless," says Davey. "I'm ever so sorry."

70

Ron puts his hand in his pocket and closes his fingers around a piece of paper worth three hundred and fifty million quid.

Danny Lloyd is sweating. Mainly because he has clearly taken an awful lot of cocaine.

A man who hates you, high on cocaine, pointing a gun at your face. Even for a West Ham fan this is uncomfortable territory.

"Come to pick on a man for once, have you, Danny?" Ron asks.

"Shut up, Ron," says Danny. "And give me the Bitcoin."

"The Bitcoin?" Ron asks.

"The Bitcoin," repeats Danny. "You're about to learn the oldest rule in the criminal's book, Ron. Never trust Connie Johnson. She was on the phone to me as soon as you hatched your plan. You really thought she was going to share the money with you?"

Ron shrugs. "No, I knew she wasn't."

"We were having a good laugh about you this afternoon," says Danny.

"Well, it's good to laugh, isn't it?" says Ron. "That's important."

"Give me the piece of paper, Ron," says Danny.

"If I give you the piece of paper, you'll kill me," says Ron.

"Maybe I won't," says Danny. "It's a lot of money."

"What's she paying you?" says Ron.

"A lot," says Danny.

"I'm flattered," says Ron. "But she's not paying you to nick the Bitcoin off me; she could have just taken it off me this afternoon. She's paying you to kill me."

"Same difference to me," says Danny. "Business and pleasure, to be honest. You've never liked me, eh, Ron?"

"Has anyone?" Ron asks. "You got any friends who don't work for you? What a weak, angry little man you are. I've had a lifetime of people like you."

"The Bitcoin," says Danny.

"What's in it for me?" says Ron.

"Nothing," says Danny.

"Jesus, Danny, you're stupid as well as weak. If you're going to kill me, I've got no incentive to tell you where the Bitcoin is, do I? That's basic stuff, old son."

Ron looks at his son-in-law. This handsome, pathetic man. This muscled weakling his daughter fell in love with. My God, kids are nothing but trouble.

"So," says Ron, "we negotiate. You give me what I want; I tell you where the Bitcoin is. Then you can kill me."

Danny is sniffing and sweating. The gun is shaking slightly, but Ron knows that Danny has used guns before. When he pulls the trigger, he won't miss.

Danny nods. "What do you want?"

"Couple of things," says Ron. "You never see Suzi again. And no lawyer's letters, anything like that either. You leave her be."

"Done," says Danny. "Pleasure, in fact."

Ron had once pulled a cracker with this man at Christmas.

"Next," says Ron, "you never see Kendrick again. Even when you're an old man in prison somewhere, you let him grow into a real man."

"Done," says Danny. "But I'm never going to prison again. Too smart for all that."

"And last of all," says Ron, "you call off the hit on Suzi, Kendrick, Jason. All rid of you for good."

"Sure," says Danny. "For the Bitcoin."

"And I can trust you?" says Ron.

Ron sees that even Danny's palms are sweaty. One slip on that trigger and he's dead.

"You can trust me," says Danny.

Ron nods. "Prove it."

"Uh?" says Danny.

Ron remembers the two of them lying on the floor, helping Kendrick build a Lego fire station. "Firemen are all right," Danny had said to his young son. "They might look like cops, but they're not."

"Who did you hire to kill Jason?" Ron asks.

"Ron, we don't grass," says Danny.

Grassing. The greatest crime of all.

"Then ring him for me," says Ron. "Ring him now, tell him the hit's off. You give me Jason's life back, and you can take mine."

"I could be ringing anyone," says Danny.

Ron thinks about this for a few moments. Long enough to come up with the plan at least.

"Stick it on speaker," says Ron. "Let me listen. If I'm convinced it's the man you hired to kill Jason, you've got the Bitcoin."

Danny likes this trade-off. Ron wonders what Elizabeth would make of all this. He saw exactly what she did for Stephen. Exactly how far she would go for her own loved ones. She of all people would understand.

Danny is scrolling through his phone but coming up blank. He takes a different phone from his pocket and starts scrolling through that instead.

Joyce? What would Joyce think? Ron remembers the time a swan had chased after Alan. Poor little dog was terrified. To this day, whenever Joyce goes to feed the swans, she makes absolutely certain the swan who chased Alan gets nothing. Ron asked her how she could tell the swans apart and Joyce said it was easy, just look for the evil one.

So, yeah, Joyce would get it too.

Danny has found the number, and his phone is now on speaker. One hand is on the phone, the other still pointing the gun at Ron. Ron hears a metallic ring through the speaker.

Ibrahim? If they found Ron dead, what would Ibrahim think? Ron can't find an easy way through that one. No Stephen, no swan. Just his best mate, lonely. Would Ibrahim forgive him? It doesn't really matter, because Ron is not sure he could ever forgive himself. If he gets through this, he's going to tell Ibrahim exactly what he means to him. Neither of them will enjoy it, but he'll do it anyway.

If he gets through this. Danny's call is answered.

"Bobby."

"Bobby, it's Alpha 4."

"I'm working on it. It'll be done."

"Mission off. Release target."

At this the voice on the other end starts to drop the forced military tone.

"What about my twenty grand, Danny? You said ten up front and twenty when Ritchie was dead?"

Danny looks at Ron. Ron gives him a firm nod.

"You'll get your twenty grand."

"And your wife? We're not going to kill her either?"

This time Danny doesn't look at Ron.

"That's off too."

"But do I still get twenty grand for her too? I've done a lot of planning."

"Sure, sure. You'll get the full fifty, but don't kill either of them."

Easy day's work. "Thanks, Danny. Alpha 4, thanks, Alpha 4."

Danny now risks a glance at Ron. Ron nods again, letting him know the conversation was acceptable. So he was going to kill Suzi too? Of course he was. Ron will never be able to lose the image of Suzi, with her bruised eye, her nose and cheek starting to swell and shine. That's what this animal standing in front of him had done. Of course he would kill her. That's what animals do.

With his steroid-built muscles and cocaine-funded suits, Danny had always looked to Ron like a child's drawing of a man. He recognizes now that Danny himself was the child who had done the drawing. He had turned himself into someone that would never have to face his own weakness and vulnerability, who ran from all the things that turn real little boys into real men. In front of Ron was a wholly fake man, an absence of anything real or true. But a man whose actions had real-life consequences. That bruised eye was real, even if the fist behind it had been constructed from bravado and thin air.

"Happy?" Danny asks.

"You were going to kill Suzi too?" Ron asks.

"That's how it works," Danny says. "Law of the jungle."

"You grew up in Kent," says Ron. "You chose your own law. You hired someone to kill my son, and you hired the same man to kill my daughter?"

"And now I'm swapping them both for killing you," says Danny. "The Bitcoin, please."

Ron pushes himself up from the armchair and heads for the bedroom. At first Jason hadn't even told him about Suzi. Hadn't wanted to upset an old man. Didn't think Ron could protect her. But Ron is an old lion, and old lions will always protect their young. Whatever it might take. Jason took him and Kendrick to see Suzi first thing this morning. They talked, the whole Ritchie family. They talked; they cried.

From the moment Ron had seen the photograph of Suzi, he knew he would sacrifice anything to save his daughter. And that's exactly what he is about to do. The greatest sacrifice of all.

Ron pushes open the bedroom door, and three armed police officers in bulletproof vests and helmets run, screaming, into the room.

"*Armed police, armed police, drop your weapon, drop your weapon!*"

He hears the commotion continue as Pauline gives him a hug.

"You did great," says Pauline. "I'm proud of you."

Ron looks back through the open doorway.

Danny Lloyd, after his full and frank confession, is lying on the ground being handcuffed. Connie Johnson had delivered him, just as she had promised. What happens next to the money, God only knows, and who killed Holly Lewis remains a mystery, but, just for now, Ron's job is done.

One of the armed officers removes his helmet and gives Ron a thumbs-up. DCI Chris Hudson. Ron has missed the big lunk.

"Thanks, Chrissy boy," says Ron. "Nice gun."

It's important to have principles, it really is, but, Ron reflects, as he sees Danny being led away, face contorted in anger, he knows he did the right thing. He, Suzi and Jason had talked about it and talked about it. He and Connie had talked about it and talked about it. How to stop this man who had hit his wife.

In the end it was Kendrick. He'd overheard a conversation Ron and Jason had with Chris and Donna, and he, as so often with Kendrick, had an opinion on it, and in the end Ron had picked up the phone to DCI Chris Hudson, because they had all reached the same conclusion.

There *are* worse crimes than grassing.

The Next Six Weeks and Four Days

71

Even on a mild August evening the English Channel is choppy. The little cruiser meets each new crest with dread, and each new fall with relief. Lord Townes is glad he isn't going far.

He's not bad with boats; once had one of his own down at the marina in Brighton. Eighty-footer, couple of sleeping cabins, hot tub on the aft deck. He'd taken it as far as Santander once, but at the last minute his proposed companion, a woman he'd got talking to at golf, had come down with the flu and he'd made the crossing alone.

His boat was called *Bonus 98*, because that's what paid for it.

This current craft belongs to an old pal, Leonard, who made several tens of millions in zinc derivatives and is currently in prison due to a misunderstanding over the tax that was subsequently due. Leonard is learning Mandarin to pass the time in prison, because China's the future.

Gosh, the future, there's a funny thought. How important the future is, until the day it isn't.

Fate, luck, accident, whatever it is that tosses your life around like the Channel is tossing around the little cruiser. They say you can't control it, but Robert must politely disagree. He knows a way.

The box Robert took from The Compound is safely stowed in the cabin of this little cruiser. His insurance has always been there.

The night is cloudless, which is a nice touch. The sky is a blue granite, and the sea a blood black. It is streaked with moonlight, twisting like a ribbon on the waves.

It was just the latest in a long line of fortune, the Bitcoin. When Holly and Nick had taken him into their confidence, Robert had kept a straight face and a professional air, but he felt saved. He could have screamed for joy. Something always turned up.

Just the commission on a deal of that size would have kept the hall running for years to come. Would have repopulated the place with cooks and gardeners and drivers. Would have seen Robert nicely through the next twenty years, and he could have popped his clogs in peace and everyone would have agreed what a jolly good chap he was. The portraits would have nodded to him as he walked through the warm house. "Skin of your teeth, old boy!" they'd have said. "The Townes magic strikes again!"

He was born into an impossible fortune; all he had had to do was not waste it.

Something has always cropped up when Robert needed it most; he has grown used to it. The Bitcoin bonanza was simply the last cab on the rank. A place opening up at Oxford at the last minute, despite his appalling A-level results. The bank that wasn't recruiting suddenly needing an extra pair of hands. His father dying young. A string of good fortune, upon which Holly and Nick's visit was just the latest pearl to be threaded.

He became reacquainted with his old friend, optimism, read up all he could on Bitcoin, just to ensure he wouldn't come across as a complete buffoon. Then he'd paid a visit to some old chums of his up in town, and they all seemed jolly pleased to see him, as well they might, with three hundred and fifty million under his watchful command. All seemed well with the world again. Lunch at someone's club, little snooze on the train home and a taxi from the station, because why not?

And of course he checked the prices, checked and rechecked what his three percent transaction fee might be worth. When he had last checked, it had been worth, and he had written this down, ten point five million. He went to bed smiling, and woke up to the news of Holly Lewis's murder. He then rang Nick Silver, but to no avail. The man had gone missing, and so, it seemed, had the opportunity.

Robert goes into the cabin and switches off the engine. This is as good a place as any. He is far from shore, but Robert has been far from shore for a long time now. He takes the wooden box from the cabin and brings it out onto the deck. He sits on the bare boards and, with his feet dangling from the side of the boat, opens it. He thinks back again to the events of the last few weeks.

When all had seemed lost, Robert did what he was best at: he crossed his fingers and hoped for the best. Perhaps Nick Silver would reappear and all would be well? Perhaps Nick Silver wouldn't reappear, and Robert might be the only person with the knowledge of what was in that cold storage unit? Perhaps the whole lot might be his if the cards fell in the right way, which they had done so often for Robert before. What would the family portraits say about *that*? Robert sauntering around with almost a cool half a billion?

But Nick Silver never reappeared.

Even now, bobbing alone, far out to sea, Robert looks around to see if salvation might be at hand. A stately white galleon welcoming him aboard with fine news from home. There was a galleon in Robert's favorite book as a child. His mother read it to him before he had to leave. It was laden with treasure from the East Indies, and Robert would dream about it at night. You can't help the habit of a lifetime, can you? Was that the last time he was happy? No, that's not right, there had been plenty of happiness over the years, trips and friends and golf, but perhaps sitting on his mother's knee at the age of seven was the last time he was truly himself.

He has led a charmed life, but he can't say that he has enjoyed it. Who loved him? Robert can't think of a soul. His mother perhaps, but wasn't that a very long time ago? Life for Robert was just an endless succession of seeing what might happen next. He was incapable of making anything actually happen. You have to be real to make things happen, and Robert has known for a very long time that he is not real.

He never made anything but money. And then he lost that too.

He thinks again what life might have been like in an ordinary house in an ordinary town with ordinary parents. He will never know, but he wishes he could have found out.

Aut neca aut necare. Kill or be killed. Take a bit of initiative was probably the basic point, wasn't it? Don't always let life happen to you.

Robert opens the box and takes out the gun. It was his father's; Robert had never been allowed to touch it. "I wouldn't trust you with a gun," his father had said. "You'd probably blow your own head off."

His father, who had bent the world to his will his whole life, had died of a heart attack in a sauna in Marrakesh. They had found him fat and naked, and it had taken four paramedics to move him. The sauna closed a few weeks later. Even in death he demanded attention.

Robert pushes himself to his feet and perches on the top railing of the deck. If he shoots himself from this angle, his body will topple backward into the sea. No one will have to clear anything up and he won't be any trouble.

He can just float away, and it will be like he was never here at all.

Or he could just ride the waves to France? Start a new life. Leave the house and the debts behind and trust in his luck? Luck? He's probably had quite enough of that for one lifetime.

Robert raises the gun. His tongue finds a little crack in one of his upper teeth. It's been there awhile and he really should have gone to the dentist. He won't need to now. No more cracks in his teeth, no more holes in the roof, no more bills on the mat.

He angles the gun toward his head and looks down the barrel. He smiles—his father would be furious.

As his finger puts pressure on the trigger, Robert's eye catches something in the distance. He has to check again to make sure, but he sees it.

And what he sees are the broad white sails of a galleon. It is returning from the East Indies, laden with treasure.

72

"Timothy Dalton?" says Ron. "*Timothy Dalton?*"

"Of course," says Ibrahim. "Isn't he everyone's favorite Bond?"

"How are we even friends?" Ron asks.

"We both have a masculine energy," says Ibrahim. "We are like kings of the jungle. How is your rosehip tea?"

"Delicious," says Ron, taking another sip from a china cup. "You've forgiven me for lying to everyone, then?"

"Of course," says Ibrahim. "You used a worthless piece of paper to jail a violent man."

"Didn't know it was worthless though," says Ron. "What if he'd killed me and ended up with three hundred and fifty mil?"

"Then Connie would have killed him," says Ibrahim. "Though I'm glad it didn't come to that. That would have been very difficult for me professionally."

"Would have been difficult for me too," says Ron. "Being shot dead."

Ibrahim nods. "And Suzi is okay?"

"Physically," says Ron. "Who knows apart from that? She's made of tougher stuff than me. And she's glad to have Kendrick back."

"I was proud of Connie," says Ibrahim. "I think Tia finally got through to her. Finally made her do something good. You weren't ever worried that she was simply going to steal the money?"

"Not for a second," says Ron. "I knew she wouldn't."

"How could you possibly know that?" asks Ibrahim.

"Because she told me why she wanted to help me," says Ron. "And I believed her."

"And why did she want to help?" Ibrahim asks.

"She wanted you to be proud of her," says Ron. "She wanted to show the great Ibrahim that she wasn't worthless."

"For me?" Ibrahim asks.

"Uh huh," says Ron. "She said we could call in Chris and his gun pals. She even agreed to grass to make you happy."

"It did make me happy," says Ibrahim. "What a nice thing for her to do."

"There's something I think you don't realize, old son," says Ron. "And it upsets me, as your mate, that you don't realize it."

"There is very little that I don't realize, Ron," says Ibrahim. "I have a very clear and precise vision of myself and my world."

"Oh, you're a bright lad, I'll give you that." Ron takes another sip. "But I don't think you realize that you're loved."

Neither man looks at the other.

"Well, I . . ." Ibrahim takes another sip too. "Love is a word that can be used to cover a great deal of ground. It can mean many, many things."

"Connie loves you," says Ron. "I love you, God help me. Joyce and Elizabeth love you. Kendrick does. I know it's not the love you might have had in the past, your business that, but it's love. You're a very special man, Ibsy, and I'm proud I know you. And you're loved."

"I would, I suppose, agree in part," begins Ibrahim. "I sense, at least, that at times people are glad to have me around. I can fuss, I do know that—don't interrupt me, Ron, I know I do—"

"No one's interrupting you," says Ron.

Ibrahim continues, "But I can ring on Joyce's doorbell and she'll be happy to see me. Though I'm still fuming about Venezuela—it was a *pure guess*. And I know that you and I can sit and chat, and I haven't really had that for so many years. Friendship, I would call it. A deep friendship allied to a deep care."

"I've only said I love you to three men in my life," says Ron. "Jason, Billy Bonds after West Ham won the cup final in 1980 and I saw him down Broadway Market, and now you. When Kendrick turns eighteen, he'll be number four."

"And I can be helpful, I suppose," says Ibrahim. "I was helpful with the code. The right order, Holly, and then Nick."

"Couldn't have done it without you," says Ron. "You got that bang on."

Ron raises his delicate china cup, and Ibrahim raises his in return. Both men concentrate on sipping, neither wanting to speak next. Eventually the silence is broken.

"Do you need me to say it in return?" Ibrahim asks. "That I love you?"

"Not now," says Ron. "One day though. God knows how long we've got left, Ib, the four of us. Might as well let people know how we feel."

Ibrahim nods. "What you did was very dangerous, Ron. Very foolhardy. But I think you had no choice. You had to protect your family."

"Had to show I still could," says Ron.

"Had to show you still could," says Ibrahim. "And a few years ago I wouldn't have understood. Not particularly. But if anyone were ever to threaten Joyce, or Elizabeth, or . . . you, I would move heaven and earth to protect you. I want you to know that."

"Sounds like you love us," says Ron.

"I care about what happens to you," says Ibrahim.

"Sounds like you care a *lot*," says Ron.

"I care a great deal," says Ibrahim. "But I choose not to put a label on it."

"Has Tia left?" asks Ron. "I thought the police were still looking for her?"

"Elizabeth took her out for lunch," says Ibrahim.

"Poor Tia," says Ron. "From Connie's clutches to Elizabeth's."

Ibrahim looks down. "Okay, Ron, there's something I'd like to say."

Ron sits forward.

Ibrahim takes a deep breath, looks at the ceiling and then looks at Ron.

"The reason that Timothy Dalton is the best James Bond is his mixture of elegance and his training in the Shakespearean tradition."

Ron throws a cushion at his best friend.

73

"When you say prison?" the man asks.

"Just regular prison," says Tia. "Metal toilets, punishment beatings, art classes."

"Sounds like my school," says the man. "Except we didn't have art classes. And have you kept out of trouble since you left prison?"

"Yes," says Tia.

"She robbed a warehouse at gunpoint," says Elizabeth.

The man nods. "But other than that?"

Tia looks at Elizabeth.

"Other than that," says Elizabeth, "she has been a model citizen."

"And how did she come to your attention?" the man asks.

"She solved something," says Elizabeth, "which I had missed."

"Goodness," says the man.

"More to the point," says Elizabeth, "if Tia had gone to school where you went to school, I suspect she would have had a very different start in life. So why don't we give her that start now?"

"Eighteen is a bit young," says the man.

"Not too young for a little training though," says Elizabeth. "Send her off somewhere, give her a gun?"

"I could bring my own?" suggests Tia.

The man is thinking. "It would have to be off the books. The prison sentence rules out anything official."

"I think that would be altogether more fun," says Elizabeth.

"Can I ask a question?" says Tia.

The man indicates that indeed she may.

"What actually is the job?"

"A question I still ask myself," says the man. "After forty years in it."

"But is it legal?" Tia asks.

"A lot of the time, yes," says the man. "A good eighty percent or so."

"What do you say?" Elizabeth asks the man.

"It's irregular," says the man.

"Just like us," says Elizabeth. "And that's why you're at the very top."

"The top of what?" Tia asks.

"Oh, the whole shooting match," says the man. "The whole thing. Tia, if I were to send you to Belize for three months, what would you say?"

"I'd say, where's Belize? And when do you want me to go?" Tia replies.

74

Joyce

The photos from the wedding have just arrived. At first they were just on a memory stick for a computer and I told Joanna that I had no idea what use that was, and when would the actual photos I could hold in my hand arrive?

She said I could take the memory stick into Snappy Snaps and they would print them for me, but I doubted that very much. So Joanna said she would get them printed out for me, and that's what's arrived.

She told me to choose my favorites, and I said I wanted all of them, and she said, Mum, there's over a thousand and some of them are practically identical, and I said I didn't care and I wanted all of them. Seeing them now, in a big stack, I realize she was quite right. I was flicking through earlier, and there were ten photos of one of Paul's aunties raising a drink to the camera. While I liked this particular auntie, I'm afraid those went straight in the bin. Please don't tell Paul.

There was also another guest, an older colleague of Paul's from the university, and she was wearing the same hat as me. I'm afraid those went in the bin too. It was bad enough she was waltzing around in it all day, I don't need a permanent reminder.

Joanna looks so beautiful, and so happy. Which are often the same thing, aren't they? I look very old in them, I can see that, but I look happy too. And if you can be that happy when you get to my age, you must have done something right.

There are lots of shots of Nick Silver pre-vomiting, fewer afterward. They still haven't found him. Davey Noakes has a plan to find him that involves drones, and Elizabeth has a plan that involves a new machine to do with DNA that she's not allowed to tell me about but did.

Paul and Joanna came round for a cup of tea yesterday. I keep getting in trouble with Joanna for saying "Paul and Joanna." She says I should say "Joanna and Paul" once in a while, but I told her it didn't sound right, something was wrong with it, and she said, yes, you're the something that's wrong with it, and so I will try to remember every now and again, if only for a quiet life.

Paul also has a plan to find Nick, but Davey and Elizabeth seem to have more resources.

If they do find Nick, he's in for a shock, isn't he? Holly dead, the money worthless. I'm very glad Holly wasn't at the wedding. There would be so many more photos to throw away.

The police seem to have their own theory about Holly's murder. DCI Varma came round the other day with a few further questions. She agreed, after quite a lot of badgering, to join us for a cup of tea, and told us that a man named Lord Robert Townes had been boasting to some of his London friends about coming into some Bitcoin money, and she had wanted to question him. A few days afterward he took a boat from the harbor in Newhaven and hasn't been seen since. So, in the absence of any firmer leads, she's leaning toward him as a suspect. We "oohed" and "ahhed" at the appropriate moments. She asked if we recognized him at all, and I said he did look familiar, and she asked if perhaps he might have been at Coopers Chase on the night of Holly's murder, and I said I couldn't rule it out, which seemed to make her happy.

It makes you wonder where he has gone though? My worry, having met him, is that he might have done himself in. Apparently they haven't found the boat though, so who knows?

But the last few weeks haven't really been about the murder of Holly Lewis, have they? I thought they were, of course: her car blew up in the overspill visitors' car park, and that was bound to catch our attention. By the way, despite the appalling mess and the police investigation, the overspill parking area was back up and running the following afternoon. The Coopers Chase Parking Committee do not take weeks to fix things. They remind me a lot of China in that regard.

When a bomb goes off in life, it tends to grab your attention, doesn't it? But when I think back to that evening now, all I remember is Kendrick, in his pajamas, holding Ron's hand. That was where the story was all along, wasn't it? A frightened young boy, his frightened mum trying to protect him, and his grandad trying to protect them both.

We were all looking at the bomb. All that heat and all that noise. So we missed what was important. When things are noisy, and everyone is asking you to look at something right this instant, we mustn't forget all the things still going on in quiet corners. There's the news, and then there's life.

In the end there was no money, and in the end no one really killed Holly. She was killed by her own greed. I mean, there's an argument that Davey shouldn't have put the bomb in her car, but it's not an argument you'll hear me make, and certainly not something we've passed on to the police. "I'm not grassing twice" was Ron's take on the thing.

But there was Ron's bravery, and Kendrick's bravery, and, most of all, Suzi's bravery. Ron must have felt very low, mustn't he? I can't imagine it. And I know a thing or two about sons-in-law now.

Danny Lloyd is in custody, and that's down to Suzi and Kendrick, and to Ron.

He might not be able to kick and punch anymore, but he still knows how to fight.

I do hope they find Nick Silver, but, despite the excitement, this is not his story either. And I know I have all these photos spread out in front of me, of a wonderful day with my wonderful daughter, but it also doesn't feel like my story. It's the story of those quiet corners, I suppose? The stories that don't get told, because no one is there to hear them, or people are too distracted by louder noises.

It wasn't a story about codes and secrets and gunmen and money, and a young woman blown up in her car.

It was a story about a strong woman stuck with an abusive husband, and a story about one lonely man with too many cat ornaments, and another lonely man in a cold house at the height of summer.

I am traveling up to Purley tomorrow to see Jasper. I am bringing him a nice teapot they had at the Sue Ryder charity shop in Fairhaven. And also some milk.

It's not much I know, but perhaps it's a start?

75

I was clearing a few things out of the flat yesterday," says Paul, getting into bed. "And I had a call I thought you might be interested in?"

"Mmm?" says Joanna. She is reading about Uruguay in *The Economist*.

"Mmm," confirms Paul. "I spoke to a man named Jeremy Jenkins."

Joanna stops reading about Uruguay in *The Economist*. "Oh."

"Eager to talk to me, it seems," Paul says.

"I see," says Joanna. "How's the flat look—"

"Funny though," says Paul. "He asked if my wife had passed on his message about the envelopes?"

Joanna nods. "Mmm hmm. Huh, okay. Did you like someone referring to me as your 'wife,' by the way? It's nice, isn't it?"

"Oh, it's lovely," agrees Paul. "Warmed my heart. He said he spoke to you on the phone?"

"Do you know what?" Joanna says. "Yes, now I think about it. Jeremy Jenkins. A solicitor maybe?"

"A solicitor," confirms Paul. "He told me what he told you. About the two envelopes. The envelopes that we know contain the codes."

"That was it," says Joanna. "Yes, it's coming back to me. The codes. Sorry, mind like an absolute sieve sometimes."

"You forgot to pass it on?"

"Must have," says Joanna. "You know how busy I've been. That Brazil deal. And I got married recently."

"Uh huh," says Paul. "You forgot. It happens. Just to make absolutely sure. You didn't keep it quiet because a bit of you suspected me at that point?"

"Suspected you?" says Joanna. "No. God, no. I never doubted you for a second."

"But still," says Paul, "you didn't tell me?"

"I don't tell you about every phone call I take," says Joanna. "Where would we be?"

Paul smiles and reaches out his hand to hers. "Did you ever think it was too soon? You and me? Getting married?"

"Too soon?" says Joanna. "No, I knew. Instantly."

"Didn't think, perhaps you didn't know everything about me?" asks Paul. "Perhaps you were rushing into it all?"

"Never thought about it for a second," says Joanna.

"You *never* worried?"

"I did *worry*," says Joanna. "I mean, I knew you were the one, but who knows with life?"

"Who knows with life," agrees Paul. "On the surface I look like a professor of sociology, but what if I were a double-murderer?"

"Yup," says Joanna. "A bit of me thought that would be just my luck. There's always a catch, isn't there?"

"So," says Paul, "you took the call from Jeremy Jenkins?"

"Yes," says Joanna.

"And a bit of you, even if it was only a tiny bit, thought maybe I'd killed Holly?"

"Yes," says Joanna. "And Nick too to be fair. I didn't think you had, but a tiny bit of me thought 'What if?' I mean, I've met your uncles."

Paul nods. "I think that's fair enough."

"You do?"

"Of course," says Paul. "I told Jeremy Jenkins to hold on to the envelopes, that Nick would be in touch as soon as he could."

"If Elizabeth and Davey manage to find him," says Joanna. The two of them have teamed up but to little effect.

"Someone will think of a smart way to track him down sooner or later," says Paul. "Thank you for telling me the truth."

"I'll always tell you the truth," says Joanna. "From now on. Can I ask *you* a question though?"

"Of course," says Paul. "Have I committed previous murders?"

Joanna laughs. "Did you ever have doubts? That it was too soon? That we didn't know each other well enough?"

Paul hesitates. "We're telling the truth?"

"No more lies," says Joanna. "Big or small. Always the truth, except for surprise parties or presents; or, if there's a TV show you've seen that I want to watch, you have to pretend you haven't seen it before and you have to watch it again with me. Those are the only exceptions."

"Deal," says Paul. "I had a wobble. Not a wobble, an amount of self-doubt. Like, I never doubted you, I doubted myself. Does that make sense?"

Joanna thinks back to her chat with Ibrahim. His certainty echoing the certainty already in her heart. "It does. When was this?"

"Morning of the wedding, believe it or not," says Paul.

"You kept that quiet," smiles Joanna. "What did you do? Talk to Nick?"

Paul shakes his head. "I waited for the guests to arrive, and I talked to Ibrahim."

"That sounds like a good person to talk to," says Joanna. "That's what I would have done. He reassured you?"

"He did," says Paul.

"Let me guess," says Joanna. "He told you that you already knew the answer? That you had come to him specifically because you knew he'd say yes?"

"No," says Paul. "Is that what he told you?"

"I didn't speak to h—"

"No lies," says Paul. "Big or small."

"Yes," says Joanna. "That's what he told me. What did he tell you?"

"He told me not to be such an idiot," says Paul. "And then he told me I was punching a very long way above my weight."

"Ibrahim's got range," says Joanna. "I'll give him that."

"And then he said there was a key thing to understand about you," says Paul.

"Oh, God," says Joanna. "What's the key thing to understand about me?"

"That you have good genes," says Paul.

Joanna laughs, and finds that she can't stop. The love she has let into her life overcomes her. Paul. Her mum. The safety, the honesty, the sheer bliss of truth. No more lies. Big or small.

"On a more exciting note," says Paul, looking pleased with himself, "and talking of surprises, guess who bought us two tickets to see Mumford and Sons on the 17th?"

"The 17th?" lies Joanna. "You're kidding me? I can't go."

"Your PA said it was free," says Paul.

"My work diary is free," says Joanna, thinking fast. "But that's the day of Mum's glaucoma operation."

And that's not lying, that's just good genes.

76

Nick Silver is aware that he must have broken the previous record by some distance. Surely no one had stayed in this roadside Travelodge for more than two or three days before, let alone eight and a half weeks. But what was he to do?

Surely Nick had chosen wisely when he chose Elizabeth Best? Made his appointment and smashed up his own office before she arrived. She wouldn't be able to resist trying to find him and find who planted the bomb. Although it was fairly obvious it must have been Davey Noakes. If not him, then who? Lord Townes? Nick doubts that very much.

He is sure that the messages he sent to Paul will have their intended effect. Elizabeth will read them and know he's alive, and will track him down before Davey can.

So why hasn't Elizabeth found him? With her skill set? It must be because the coast is not yet clear. That stands to reason. So here he stays.

Although what if Davey has killed Elizabeth too? What if that's why Elizabeth hasn't come to find him? He unwraps yet another KitKat and switches on the hotel radio. Friday night is Pete Tong's *Club Classics* night. That's something to cheer him up at least.

He takes a sip of the Lucozade, which was the only drink left in the vending machine. The first thing he'll do when he is found is to eat some broccoli. Unless Davey Noakes finds him first and kills him.

Death or broccoli. Those seem to be his options.

He knows, however tempting it is, that he must not log back on to any of his devices, must not show his face on any surveillance cameras, must not give Davey the slightest lead as to where he is. Every night he watches the local news on his tiny hotel television; you never know what they might report. "Local woman slain, ex-spy found dead in retirement village," "Sussex entrepreneur Davey Noakes buys Brighton and Hove Albion Football Club," anything to give him a clue as to what's happening. But there has been nothing.

Of course there's always the possibility that he has hidden too well. But Elizabeth knows every trick in the book, and a few more that aren't in the book. The moment it's safe, she will find him.

Nick wishes the money had never existed; it has been nothing but a curse, buried away like the tell-tale heart, beating louder and louder as the years went by. If he's honest with himself, it had begun to destroy his friendship with Holly—both knowing it was there waiting for them, and neither able to access it without the other's agreement.

Nick had wanted to cash out almost straight away. The day it reached one hundred thousand pounds he'd tried to persuade Holly, but Holly had bigger ideas. He understood that: different people had different needs. A hundred thousand wasn't enough for her, even a million wasn't enough. Ten million came and went, and still Holly held out. It was greed, nothing more, nothing less, not that she would ever admit that to anyone, even herself. The friendship broke down entirely after Holly and Paul split up that second time, Holly accusing Nick of taking sides, the wedding the final straw. She'd finally said yes, because what was the alternative? He and Holly were surely going their separate ways? Cashing out the Bitcoin is just marking the end of their time together.

So three hundred and fifty million pounds. Nick's amazed by how little he wants it.

Nick could imagine spending a hundred thousand pounds—who couldn't? Ask anybody and they'd tell you. Pay your debts, new car, the deposit on a flat, a bit to charity, a bit to Mum and Dad to say thank you. It was the dream.

Nick could imagine spending a million pounds too. Buy a bigger house, buy

Mum and Dad a house, get a box at the football. Quietly slip the food bank a couple grand every week.

But a hundred million? How do you spend that? A bigger house, with gates and a long drive and security? A garage for your cars? A safety deposit box at the bottom of a deep mine for all your secrets? Being very rich seemed to drive people mad. Seemed to make them leave normality behind. As if the only possible reason for their vast amount of money was that they were born with powers above mortal beings.

Nick wants what his friend Paul has. A job he likes, a wife, a purpose. If he ever gets out of this room, that's the goal. Broccoli, then normality. He has money; he doesn't need more.

So, if the money is still there in The Compound, and he ends up with it, what will he do? Charity, Nick supposes.

No, keep a hundred thousand, and then charity. He'll enjoy spending that hundred thousand. Holly will disappear somewhere, no doubt. What a sad end to a long friendship.

Pete Tong has just been playing "Insomnia." It takes Nick way back. They'd seen Pete Tong DJ when they were at uni, Nick, Holly and Paul. Has there ever been a better decade than the nineties? Nick doubts it very much. When they'd got a bit more money, he and Paul had flown out to Ibiza to see Pete Tong too. Back when dreams were young and every twenty-pound note a marvel.

If ever Nick and Paul were in on a Friday night, they'd be listening to Club Classics: dancing in the living room if they were together; texting and reminiscing if they weren't. It was their own personal time machine.

What's next, Pete? Where are you taking me back to now?

This one's from Paul in London. Paul wants us to play "The Key: The Secret" by Urban Cookie Collective for his old mate Nick Silver, that's a great name, Nick Silver, that's a pirate's name. Paul says, "Nico, we've missed you, looking forward to seeing you tomorrow. Hope you're listening." Of course he's listening, Paul . . .

Of course he's listening. Nick takes his SIM card from a wallet lined with metal and slides it into a burner phone. He rings Paul. There is an instant answer.

"Of course he's listening," says Paul.

"Is it safe?" says Nick.

"It's safe," says Paul. "Where have you been? They've been looking everywhere."

Nick gazes out of the window and sees the back wall of a 24-hour garage, three overflowing recycling bins and rain falling through arc lights onto the motorway.

"Right now it feels like I'm back in Ibiza."

"Holly's dead, mate," says Paul.

"Christ," says Nick. "Who killed her?"

"Difficult to say," says Paul.

"And the money? You haven't found it?"

"Well, about that," says Paul.

The two old friends, many miles apart, tap their feet in time to a song they both love. A song that reminds them of what's truly important. Friendship, joy, dancing.

"I've got good news and I've got bad news."

ACKNOWLEDGMENTS

How lovely to have Joyce, Elizabeth, Ibrahim and Ron back together again, and in (slightly) happier times. I hope you enjoyed getting reacquainted. I can't tell you how many different ways I have just attempted to spell the word "reacquainted." The relief when the spellcheck finally waved it through was palpable. If you ever want to spend a long time writing a short paragraph, just put the words "acknowledgments" and "reacquainted" in it. That will be your morning gone.

I have many people to thank. My wonderful agent Juliet Mushens and her team, Alba Arnau Prado, Catriona Fida and Emma Dawson. My amazing editor Harriet Bourton, and the whole gang at Viking in the UK: Rose Poole, Rosie Safaty, Rosey Battle (I insist that all the many Rosies on the team spell their names differently to help with admin), the incomparable Olivia Mead, Kayla Fuller, Yazmeen Akhtar and new kid on the block, Joe Cooper.

Thanks to the sales teams: Autumn Evans, Lucy Keeler, Caitlin Knight, Emily Cornell, Chris Wyatt, Grace Dellar, Jessica Sacco, Carrie Anderson, Jessica Adams, Nadia Patel and Charlotte Owens. And special thanks, as always, to Samantha Fanaken.

Thank you so much to the amazing audio team: Meredith Benson, Helena Sheffield and Carmen Byers.

I am indebted once more to the forensic brilliance of Donna Poppy, Natalie Wall, Annie Underwood and Leah Boulton, and the continued creative mastery of Richard Bravery and Alisha Kruse.

In the US my undying thanks go to Pamela Dorman, Jeramie Orton and the team at Pamela Dorman Books. I think I have met all of them now, and I can confirm they are lovely. Thank you to Brian Tart, Natalie Grant, Andrea Schulz, Patrick Nolan, Kristina Fazzalaro and the only Fulham fan on the team, Kate Stark. Further thanks to Tricia Conley, Tess Espinoza, Diandra Abernethy (great name for a character), Mike Brown, Jason Ramirez, Claire Vaccaro, Mary Stone, Anna Brill, Rebecca Marsh, Magdalena Deniz, Andy Dudley and Rachel Obenschain.

I've been very lucky to spend time with so many of my foreign publishers this year, and I can't wait to see many more of you this year!

Heartfelt thanks to the booksellers and librarians of the world. You continue to make the world a better place by choosing love and empathy and imagination and understanding.

Particular thanks for *The Impossible Fortune* go to my brilliant brother-in-law Matt Bessey, for guiding me through the world of cold storage. Matt is a cybersecurity expert if you ever need one, but also a stone-cold dude who just three days ago managed to rig up a television signal so we could all watch the Eurovision Song Contest halfway up an Italian mountain. That's the type of family you're glad you married into.

Thank you to Dan Hatfield for donating to Action for Children to have a character named after him in the book. Sorry I cut your arm off, Dan. Thank you too to Luna and family for useful advice, and good luck in whatever you do next.

To you, the reader, I can't express my thanks enough. It's my greatest pleasure to enjoy these worlds with you—long may we all continue. I've just started the new We Solve Murders adventure, and then there will be more Thursday Murder Club after that. It's a lot of murder, I know, but it's a lot of love and laughs too.

As ever, I could do none of this without my family and friends. Thank you for everything. I will just single out my mum, Brenda, the beating heart of these books, my children, Ruby and Sonny, and the love of my life, now and forever, my wife, Ingrid.

I know Ingrid won't want her name to be the last in these acknowledgments, however, because, alongside our longtime awesome cat Liesl, we now have a new cat, Lottie, who, by sheer force of personality, demands star billing. Lottie is very much the chaotic Ron to Liesl's calm and thoughtful Ibrahim.

Here's to chaos and love, and to life and books. Until next time!